Presumed Dead

by

Jearl Rugh

Dedication

To Dick

My father, my teacher, my counselor, my friend.
To him I owe everything I am and hope to be.
Although his life's labors have ended, his spirit lives
on in my heart and inspires me to do good.

The weak can never forgive. Forgiveness is the
attribute of the strong.
—Mahatma Gandhi —

Chapter One

SUZANNE LOWEN TURNED the key in the front door lock of the Georgetown condo she shared with her partner and stepped inside. Trisha, visiting her sister in Colorado, with the exception of the cat, had left Suzanne to herself for the weekend. She swung the door closed and threw the bolt. As she passed through the cramped living room, her leg brushed against the extended foot rest of one of the matching fuchsia recliners facing the flat-screen television. Hmm, why's that out? she wondered.

In the kitchen, she dropped her purse and keys on the countertop. She had never cared for the taupe linoleum—too blasé—but with the condo a rental, the landlord was not about to change it, even if she was a cop. She took an opened bottle of Oregon pinot gris from the refrigerator. Closed up all day, the cool air rolling out caressed her chubby face and brought passing relief from the stuffy house. She lingered a moment.

"Freda," she said. It wasn't unusual for the cat not to greet her at the front door. Most days when she had been left alone for hours, Freda made her need for companionship known in any number of indifferent ways. By now, though, she should have been underfoot, pawing at something in the fridge.

The rumble of Amtrak's Coast Starlight a couple hours late on its final approach to Seattle's King Street Station shook the floor. As the clack of steel wheels and the shrill whistle faded in the distance, her grandfather's Swiss mantel-clock chimed a quarter before midnight—always five minutes fast. She dismissed the sounds, retrieved a wine glass from the cupboard, and favored herself with a generous pour. With both the glass and the rest of the bottle in her hands, she stepped in the hallway.

"Freda?" she called again as her Vans padded against the carpeted floor. Freda still didn't appear. "Where you hiding, girl?"

Because the crime lab had been slow, her Sunday night shift had dragged and she had left early. With nearly a third of her life dedicated to the department, what were a few minutes? And besides, a hot salted bath beckoned. When Suzanne reached the bathroom door, she flipped the light switch. The harsh glare over the white vanity, which seemed to ricochet off the eggshell-colored walls and mirror, blinded her tired eyes for a few seconds. She squinted to reduce the burn. *I think I'm due some candlelight tonight.*

She placed the glass and bottle on the edge of the tub. The box of scented bath salts waited in the cupboard below the sink. Once she fetched them and stood, she faced the mirror. *Ugh,* she thought as she tousled her short burgundy hair, already in disarray. She twisted away to the bathtub again, and, after turning the tap, sprinkled the minerals where the water splashed onto the tub's floor.

With both the temperature set and the water drumming a rhythm of renewal, she walked to the bedroom she shared with Trisha. Since she had entered the house, her body had broken into a prickly sweat, and she had to peel her pink scrubs and underwear off to drop them into the hamper. She covered herself and tightened the belt on a lightweight lavender bathrobe, and then flipped the light switch off as she left the room.

"Freda?" she called as she entered the hallway again. A bit of panic tensed her voice. Freda never hid long even if she was trying to make a point. "Where are you, girl? You're starting to worry me."

Across the hall from the bath, the door to Freda's room—the second bedroom—stood open. Freda had used up most of her nine lives and over the last few months she had lost the normal vitality in her step. Her veterinarian had said it was old age gaining a foothold. Suzanne knew it wouldn't be long before Freda either died in her sleep or had to be put down—but not tonight. She peered around the doorjamb to see if the cat was napping, or worse, dead.

In the darkness, her eyes pulled to the computer. Positive she had turned the system off after checking email earlier this afternoon, now the monitor was lit and Microsoft Word open. Trisha used the word processing application regularly, but she had been gone for days and Suzanne hadn't touched it in weeks.

"Sweetie, you in here?"

Still no lonely feline brushed against her bare leg. Suzanne walked across the room. The ambient light from the hall and the monitor penetrated the darkness enough to scan the shadowed edges of the room for the cat. There was no sign of her.

Above the smell of the litter box, a familiar scent wafted through the air. It lingered only for a second but she recognized it as the same cologne her father wore. Not since her divorce decree was handed down, and she came out with Trisha, had she seen him.

"Daddy?" She knew he couldn't be there, — wouldn't be there. An involuntary shudder rippled down her back as she realized that no men had been in her home for several weeks. She sniffed again. The odor was gone. It couldn't have been him. Just my imagination. It's nothing. Yet the desperate sense that she wasn't alone crept through the gloom and seeped into her pores.

Her eyes drew back to the words floating on the monitor. On instinct, her knees bent and she twisted into the seat of the desk chair. An unfamiliar four-line poem cast its shadow on the backlit screen. She read.

First the one who owes so much

Final payment by my touch
Breath of life fails to draw in
Pillow talk, my lethal sin

She recognized that the verse was a message meant for her—but what does it mean? And who ...? As if she was in her lab analyzing a crime clue, she read the lines a second time and the implication broke over her as powerful as the crash of stormy waves on the shore.

She tried to call Freda's name again, but the two syllables lodged in her throat and only a squeak rolled out. Her bowels cinched tight as a braided rope. A sudden reflex drew her hands to her face. They slipped over a halting breath, but her eyes stayed fixed on the lyrics. She couldn't tear away from the simple rhyme which she knew prophesied a future she couldn't accept. Then a dark dread, icy and resolute, slithered into her mind. My God, he's here!

She sprang from the chair and turned to face the hall door. No one waited there. In two steps she was at the doorway. With the urgency that the consequence of the two couplets meant that she was intended to be the next victim under the medical examiner's knife, her senses peaked. She listened for any sound that didn't belong—the low hum of the refrigerator, water flowing into the tub, the computer's fan whirring. Nothing unusual.

She peered around the jamb and searched the hall in both directions. No one. Suzanne hurried toward the master bedroom and the nightstand.

When she reached the table, she fumbled with the lamp until she located the elusive switch. She pulled the top drawer open, withdrew her Browning nine-millimeter from beneath her cotton panties, and picked up the phone. She sat on the edge of the queen-sized bed next to her, placed the telephone in her lap, and hazarded one last glance into the hallway before she dialed.

Halfway between the bathroom door and the bedroom, Freda sauntered toward her. At Suzanne's feet, she jumped onto the bed and crawled into Suzanne's lap. She wrapped one arm around the midnight black cat and whispered into Freda's ear, "Where you been, girl?"

Suzanne dialed 9-1-1. As the phone rang, she took deep breaths. Her pulse raged against her temples but she felt control begin to return. The police would be here in minutes. They'd make a thorough search of her home and, once they finished, she'd initiate a forensic investigation into the computer. Until then, she had the Browning. Freda purred, and Suzanne blew the fear from her lungs.

"9-1-1, what is your emergency?"

The sonorous voice in her ear jarred her. Suzanne looked up and pointed the gun toward the hallway. In her haste, she hadn't noticed before but now. The pistol felt light—too light. She released the ten-round magazine and found it empty. It slipped from her hand and thumped to the floor.

The acid in her stomach began to reflux. Her mouth turned to ash and she couldn't swallow the acrid taste. It seared her throat. She fought the terror with a jerk, and twisted her eyes toward the hall. Still no one lurked there.

"Suzanne, do you have an emergency?" the voice erupted again.

The last question confirmed her dread. The unseen voice speaking through the phone pressed to her ear also spewed out into the hall.

The sound of the water's surge into the bathtub stopped.

Her lips quivered to find an answer but words took no form. Suzanne jumped to her feet. The phone tumbled to the floor and Freda shot away. You traitor. You were cuddling with him. She swung behind her and toppled the lamp off the bedside table so he couldn't see her silhouette.

Alone in the darkness, she continued her frantic stare in the direction of the voice. He had steered her into a trap. The only escape from her condo was through the narrow corridor the monster now controlled.

Chapter Two

"HEAR THE WAIL from the cage
    Lifting its clamor in a rage—"
    "All units, all units."
    The dispatcher's voice grating through the radio
speaker in her cruiser drew Officer Kel Nyte's eyes
away from the new text message on her phone. The
disturbance less than a mile from her location on
Seattle's Elliott Bay waterfront, she triggered the
microphone.
    "Unit three-zero-four responding."
    The full text was still unread but, with a more
pressing priority, she stowed the phone back in its
belt holster. As she flipped the emergency strobe
lights and siren into action, her eyes drew a quick
glance right and left. Then, despite the red traffic
signal's caution, Kel pressed the accelerator to the
floor.
    A half block later, she changed lanes with a
quick jerk of the wheel to veer around a slow moving
container truck and a new 2010 Audi SUV stretch.
Kel turned her eyes to the time. Her onboard
computer's steady white display read 11:54, just

minutes before her shift would have ended at midnight.

She tapped the Bluetooth wireless device in her ear. While she waited for an answer, she slipped a lukewarm vanilla hazelnut latte from the cup holder and took a long pull.

In her ear, a halting voice answered and yawned with a sleepy groan. "'ello?"

"It's Mom, sweetie." Kel returned her drink to the console. "I'm sorry I woke you."

"Hey,   ... Mom. It's okay." With the grunts Chrissie uttered, Kel pictured her daughter stretching the sleep from body. "Saul and I fell asleep on the couch waiting for you. ... Uh... is that your siren?"

"That's why I called." Kel had raised her fourteen-year-old daughter off and on over the last eight years as a single parent. She hated to leave Chrissie alone for too many hours, but duty wasn't always convenient, and when it called, it demanded respect. "I just got called out and it may be a long one. Sweetheart, I probably won't see you 'til morning."

"Oh... uh... alright."

"You okay alone? I can get Aunt Shelia to pick you up."

"Mom," Chrissie said with a sing-song whine, "I sat for the Freeman kid over a weekend before. Just me and a six-year-old for two days. I think me and

Saul can handle one night. We'll be fine. Huh, Saul? Sure we will. That's a good boy."

Saul, Chrissie's Rottweiler, had been a good companion for her. Even more than the Neighborhood Watch Kel had helped start, she trusted Saul to protect her daughter while she served the city. "You two best get to bed, then. We'll have breakfast together. Okay?"

"Yeah... 'kay."

As Kel reached the intersection at South Washington and made a hard right, she said, "Love you."

"Love you more."

"Love you mo—"

Chrissie's click ending the call cut Kel off. "—most," she said out loud to herself. Chrissie, it seemed overnight, had started to mature into a young woman. Sadness, like a threatening thunderhead, rose in Kel's heart at the thought that another ritual— evenings with Candy Land, or dressing and redressing one of Chrissie's many dolls—might disappear forever.

The tears were still wedged in her throat as she approached First Avenue South. There, two homeless men, caught in her headlight beams, stumbled in the crosswalk. She slammed the brakes and tugged the steering wheel to the left. The light blue police cruiser went into a skid. The squeal of rubber biting asphalt sobered the men enough to shoot her a panic-filled glare while they lurched to the safety of the sidewalk beyond. The distraction cleared Kel's mind for what lay ahead.

Seconds later, she parked diagonally between the tree-lined median and the cars along the curb. The police sedan blocked the northbound traffic. She slipped her SPD ball cap over her head, pulled her shoulder-length brunette ponytail through the back strap and then jumped out into the warm July air. With her baton in its belt harness, she stepped onto the sidewalk near a bike racked at the curb. Her petite frame carried not an extra ounce of fat, but her size-seven boots still hammered with authority against the concrete as she made her way to the street-level bar.

The Pioneer Square watering hole had been a fixture in the community for more than twenty years and thrived during the summer baseball season. It stood at the foot of a four-story terracotta structure originally built at the end of the nineteenth century as a supply depot for prospectors on their way to the Alaska Gold Rush.

Kel pushed the door to the Wishing Well open to a raucous crowd. She knew it required an officer-needs-assistance call, but with the sound of sirens on approach, she didn't trigger her radio's shoulder mic. She took a single step inside and, as the door closed behind her, in the gloom she caught the whistle of air kissing a bottle's mouth. An instinctive duck to her right avoided the intended collision with her face.

The glass shattered against the door behind her and showered the back of her light blue uniform shirt with icy beer. She couldn't control the sudden shiver or the surprised gasp that poured the stench of flat beer—both leaching from the old paneled walls and spilled on the hardwood floor—through her nostrils. The suggestion of something else caught her by surprise. It was burned and stale, but even the whiff of coffee brought a craving for that latte she had had to abandon in her cruiser.

She shook it off, focused her eyes in the direction the bottle had come, and dared the pitcher to meet her glare. When no one turned her way, she pulled her nightstick and scanned the room. Except for the missing piano player hammering a lively tune on a tinny upright, the overturned tables and fists launching into faces reminded her of the classic Western saloon fights she and her dad used to watch on TV. At least no one's toting a six shooter—my God, I hope not, she thought.

"SPD," she shouted over Pino Palladino's lyric base line driving Melissa Etheridge's "I'm the Only One." "Everyone hit the floor!"

No one noticed.

Kel pivoted to a man with a Grizzly Adams' beard standing behind the dark oak bar. He stared back at Kel, shook his head, and threw his hands into the air. Frustration and rage converged on his face.

"Shut that music down!" Kel shouted to him with over-articulated lips in case he, too, couldn't hear her.

When the music went silent, many of the patrons turned her way. She addressed the spectators and cheerleaders on the periphery. "Leave your drinks on the table, and wait outside."

Most seemed to honor the uniform, and stood. Their heads shaking, they started a slow trudge toward the door. But two men at a ringside table held their seats. One glared back at Kel and, without balk, lifted his glass to take a defiant swallow.

The color and the way his auburn hair rested limp on his shoulders wrenched a familiar yet disturbed memory to the surface. "Lance," it whispered. The ethereal presence always showed up without warning and, most often, at an inconvenient time. She needed to close her eyes to banish the manifestation, but with the wreckage still falling around her, she couldn't take the luxury.

She shifted her five-foot-five, muscular frame toward him and fixed her eyes on the insolent man. With a sharp snap, she slapped the nightstick on the palm of her hand.

"Up. Out. Now," she bawled and held his gaze.

After a deliberate pause, he slammed the glass on the table top and beer splashed over the lip. As he came to his feet, his chair toppled over behind him.

"Free drinks," he bellowed and skirted behind the table to join his buddy already near the exit.

With the bystanders cleared, Kel glanced toward the fray. On the far right to the rear of the scuffle, one man gripped another's shirt. The razor-wire tattoo wrapped around his right forearm snapped back and forth like a Slinky while he punched the face of someone she recognized.

The white grease paint smeared across his visage and the bicycle she had noticed as she entered the Wishing Well indicated that Marcel was on the receiving end. No one knew his true identity, but over the last year or two he had imprinted his eccentricity in the downtown culture with his bike and red-tipped cane for the blind. With the mime face, and since he never spoke, he had been dubbed "Marcel Marceau."

With the brawl between them, Kel couldn't get to him—yet.

"Everyone hit the floor, now!" Kel shouted and slapped the nearest table with her nightstick.

Two women in their twenties scrapped five feet away. They pulled hair and ripped at each other's clothes. The other brawlers turned toward Kel's voice and began to take the position, but the two women didn't go down. Their disregard irritated Kel like itching powder sprinkled on a weeping rash. She stepped forward and grabbed the shoulder of the closest one, ready to slap the knees out from under her with her stick. The woman spun toward Kel and her right breast fell out from her torn shirt. Braless, she raised her fists.

"Really?" Kel couldn't resist a smirk. "Best think about your next move before you take on the SPD."

Braless paused and shot Kel an odious scowl. After several seconds, she dropped her hands and went to her knees. The second woman followed. Kel's eyes drew downward as the pair lay to their bellies and passed hateful glares between them. She glanced at the other bodies on the wooden floor. A dozen panting and wheezing drunks were sprawled at her feet.

But Razor-Wire still stood statuesque. He had dropped Marcel to the floor like a duffel bag of baseball bats. With the sweat glistening off his face and arms, he looked ready for the next contender. He connected a menacing glower, eye to eye with Kel.

She stepped around the two women toward him and shouted, "What part of 'hit the floor' didn't you get?"

Razor-Wire bolted toward the door. The pathway cluttered with prone bodies and toppled chairs, he jumped and staggered around them, but Kel stood in his way. She hardly had to stretch to plunge her nightstick into his belly. The sudden impact lifted him off the floor and he fell on top of Braless.

"Get the hell off me, you son of a bitch," she screamed, and sprung to her hands and knees. She bucked him to the floor. Razor-Wire landed face-up at Kel's feet.

Kel looked at the man. He seemed small now and anything but threatening. His eyes darted back and forth as if they were trying to find something solid on which to focus.

She placed the business end of her stick on his chest and barked, "On your face. Now!"

He turned his head as a gag reflex washed over him.

"No, you don't—" Kel shouted, but before she could move her foot, he retched again and coated her right boot with vomit.

"Ooow, you piece o—" She stopped short. He no longer listened as his eyes turned to glass and rolled back in their sockets.

With a shake of her head, Kel jammed the toe of her boot under Razor-Wire, wiped most of the fetid bile on his shirt, and forced him to his stomach. She drove her knee into his back and wrested his arms free. From her belt, she pulled out her handcuffs and secured his hands behind his back.

"Hands behind your heads," she shouted to the others on the floor.

She glanced over the crowd to make sure they complied and then looked back to the bar. Behind Grizzly, two female servers peered out onto the scene through the twin portholes in the swinging doors which lead to the kitchen. They stepped from their hiding place and joined the barkeep.

"What set this off?" Kel asked.

"The guy you're kneeling on," said the dirty blonde with a nod, "asked Marcel what he thought about the Mariners losing four of their last six home games. When Marcel shrugged, that guy grabbed him and started throwing punches. Then the whole place just went to Hell."

As she finished, the barmaid's eyes darted toward the door. Behind Kel, the sound of the shards from the shattered bottle scraped the plank floor and drew her glance back over her shoulder. Two officers entered.

"Looks like everything's under control here," Scott Nillson said, and gave Kel a wink.

"Hey, Scot-tay," Kel said with a warm lilt to her voice. A dimple on each cheek gave her smile life.

Scott had been her mentor when she was a rookie cop. They had ridden together as partners for her first two years on the force while she learned her way around the streets. She hadn't seen much of him the last few years as, while she had continued to be assigned to West Precinct, he'd been sent to South. Those years had added a few pounds around his middle, and the gray strands of hair poking out from under his cap replaced the black hair she remembered.

Kel flicked her eyes to the young female cop to Scott's right. "Say, who's your new partner?"

"Valarie," the woman said. "I'm just a rookie. Don't mind me."

"That's where we start, Valarie," Kel said, "and look where it takes you. Give it a few years and you too could be kneeling in some drunk's puke. Well," Kel continued, looking back at the scene, "you guys might want to start hooking people up." She stood, and nodded toward Braless and her sparring partner, who now hugged the floor. "And start with them."

With two officers to clear the rioters, Kel turned her attention to the motionless heap known as Marcel. She kneeled again and reached to his neck.

Chapter Three

KEL SLAMMED THE back door on the paramedic's rig and pounded on the side. After the clash, she'd been happy to find Marcel's carotid still throbbing. Unconscious when she got to him, if God was merciful, he didn't feel much of the beating. She knew that would change when he awoke, but hoped that a couple days of medical observation might prove him fit to carry on being Marcel.

"Quite a shift-ender," Scott Nillson said as he walked up behind her, having loaded the last of the rioters onto the police bus. He threw his arm around her shoulder and pulled her close with a gentle big-brother hug. "I was so sorry to hear about Lance."

"Thanks, Scott." It was so raw—still unbelievable—and she didn't want to give rein to her sentiments now. Those feelings were reserved for her and her alone. Show no weakness.

"Say, how's Marie and Mike?"

"Marie's in her element since Mike produced our first grandson. Named him after me."

"So there's a new Scot-tay in the house?"

"Absolutely." He reached for his phone. "Want to see pictures?"

"Try 'n stop me." When Scott found the digital album, she was glad for the emotional break and watched him scroll through the photos. "What a cutie, Grandpa. Look, he's got your ears."

"Actually, I thought little Scottie's Buddha belly was more the point of resemblance."

Kel looked up and saw that Valarie had stepped next to Scott.

"You've got a good eye." Kel patted Scott's stomach and smiled. "You'll make a good cop, Valarie. I just have this feeling."

The police bus rumbled past them a few feet away and one of its tires clattered through a pothole. Kel glanced at her watch. Under the street lamp she made the time as 12:58 a.m.

"Well, Gramps, congratulations are definitely in order, and I owe you a drink. But before you break out the cigars, I'm afraid this party isn't over yet. Paperwork, booking..." A breeze off the Puget Sound pressed against the back of her shirt, still damp from the beer spattered on it. She added, "And maybe a fresh uni before that. I'll be half the night."

"First responders have all the fun," he said with a chuckle. "But we'll be there."

"Right." Her sarcasm bit the word off. "What say we get this done?"

Kel turned away from them and walked back to her cruiser, still parked with lights flashing in the middle of First Avenue South. After she dropped into the front seat, a sharp rap on the driver's side window jerked her head to the left. She expected to find a citizen frustrated with her cruiser cordoning off the street. Instead, the blue flame of a lighter ignited the tip of a cigar. It illuminated a resolute face. His presence alone indicated that this meeting was not an accident.

"Good evening, Officer Nyte."

Kel powered the window open and looked into the face of the man she hoped to work for soon. Even in the dim light, she recognized the familiar circles of gray flesh sagging beneath Nathaniel Ballesteros's sixty-plus-year-old eyes. She felt they gave witness to firsthand knowledge of the base brutality that only human beings could inflict upon their own kind. Above them, his eyebrows looked like a pair of black woolly bear caterpillars had set up housekeeping. As he peered through the open window, they narrowed, as if they conspired with his will to constrain some darkness from finding the light.

She opened the car door. While she got out, he stood aside and pulled the cigar from his lips.

Short in stature, she tipped her head to look up into the full face that towered above her by at least eight inches. "Chief Ballesteros," she said, surprised to see the head of detectives on the scene of a bar disturbance. "Not much detective work here. Kind of a slam dunk."

"Heard it on the police scanner as I was leaving Benaroya Hall," he said, the tension in his brow on retreat for a moment. "The Summer Festival—Schumann, Mendelssohn, and Brahms chamber music. Always centers me. You responded to the call, and since I was close by, I wanted to see you in action." He lifted the cigar to his mouth again, and gnawed at the tip while he filled his lungs. "What happened in there?"

"Just a fight over a ballgame. Left one guy unconscious and a baker's dozen packed up to dry out."

He relaxed his thin lips from the Dutch Master and exhaled a cloud of blue smoke. It hid his face. "You were first on scene?"

"Yes, sir." Kel had never cared for the aroma of cigar smoke. This one, to her senses, however, wasn't as harsh as some.

"And you went in without backup?"

"The situation warranted immediate action, sir. I heard the sirens approaching, so I knew I didn't need to call the cavalry. The important thing was to gain control of the situation and stop the fight before someone got hurt bad or maybe even worse."

"And you accomplished that by yourself?"

"In less than five minutes, sir."

"Well, then," he said, his voice relaxing, "good work, officer. I like your initiative and I'll look forward to your after-action report."

"It'll be in the system by morning. I must say, though, it seems odd, Chief."

"How's that?"

"That you'd have interest in a report of a barroom scuffle."

"I have interests in many things," he said, and hooked his right index finger around the smoke. He drew it from his mouth. "You might just be surprised. Reports on routine brawls are not necessarily on my must-read list, but seeing your reports are. How else can I judge your fitness for my department?"

Kel had taken the detective's exam several months earlier. Even though she had not only passed it, but received the highest marks in her class, where others had moved forward, there had been no promotion for her.

"I didn't realize you were watching," she said. Kel allowed a smile but controlled the chortle that threatened.

"Oh, I've been watching, and I know you face odds."

Nepotism and politics had both played a significant role in her nine-year SPD career. As the kid of the Chief of Police, advancement had proven difficult. She had known this was a risk when she joined the department, but believed in the ideal that her dad had modeled: work hard, perform well, and progression in rank will be the natural outcome. But her commander, Lieutenant Louis Martinez, stood in the way. Promotion required a referral from her boss, and he was adamant not to give it. Her dad, with his rank, could have overruled him, but he didn't offer and she didn't ask.

But it was more than being the offspring of the top cop, Kel happened to be his daughter. Although it was never said out loud, Kel felt that a prevalent "boy's club" attitude reigned within the SPD. In the early 1990's the federal government had seen fit to lift the more than two-hundred-year-old ban allowing women to serve in combat situations. But here at home, gender seemed to Kel as much a part of the job qualifications as analytical and multitasking skills. After all, how could a woman hope to "bust her balls" to get the job done?

"You may not realize it," he continued, "but your dad taking retirement last month puts a new dynamic in place. I wouldn't be surprised to see a change in your near future."

"Sir, I appreciate your interest in me," she said, and realized this might be the opening she had been looking for. "Believe me, it's unexpected. But if you think I might have potential as a detective, then there's one thing I'd like to ask."

"Please." He nodded.

"I realize this may seem like it's coming out of left field, but Willie Jenkins' death is still unsolved."

Chief Ballesteros's biggest career embarrassment had been the SPD detective's unsolved murder.

Willie and his partner had been assisting the Port of Seattle Police to infiltrate a smuggling ring at the docks. He hadn't returned home after his shift one night. Then, a month later, his body turned up in a shipping container in Kuala Lumpur. Despite the Chief's vow to find and punish the killer, sixteen months later there were no suspects and the trail had grown cold.

"His wife and I were classmates at the UDub," she said. "It's been a real source of angst for my dad, and frustrating for me."

"What's your point, Kel?"

"I don't mean to pick at a sore, sir," she replied, and sensed a sudden seriousness in his tone, "but I wouldn't mind spending some of my off-duty hours digging around. Could you use an extra hand?"

"Look, your intentions are good, I'm sure, but my people are investigating every lead. We haven't given up. We'll find his killer." He paused. "I'll be watching for that brawl report, and don't leave anything out."

"With the scrupulous detail I'll provide," she said, and masked her disappointment with a grin, "you'll think you're reading a Greg Isles novel, sir."

He switched the cigar to his left hand. "That's what I want to hear."

"Well, Chief, if there's nothing else. I've got a busload of perps to book, a mountain of paperwork, and a daughter whose mom's already late getting home from work. I better get to it."

"Carry on then." Before he turned to walk away, he took her hand in his and shook it. "Again, good work tonight."

Kel watched him for a few seconds until he reached the intersection and disappeared around the corner. As she stepped back into the driver's seat of her cruiser, she remembered the unread text message she had received just before she was called out to the Wishing Well riot. She withdrew her phone from her belt and read it.

"DK: Hear the wail from the cage
Lifting its clamor in a rage
From the grave forever sealed
Secret things will be revealed
Witnesses their stories tell
Mine to teach the lesson well
Recompense is yours to pay
Mine to reap for Hell each day"

The message screamed troubled, but since she knew no one with the initials DK, she reasoned it might just as well be a joke. She touched the reply key.

"Wrong number?" She typed the question, pressed "send," and only then, realized it was from an out-of-state area code. Has to be mis-sent, she reasoned.

Kel dropped the phone next to her, slipped the cruiser into drive, and eased north a couple of blocks toward Cherry Street. With hope that a promotion might be coming, she gave her thoughts to the report she had promised Chief Ballesteros. Since his eyes were on her, it needed to be lucid and precise.

As she pulled up the hill, the traffic signal at Fourth Avenue showed red. While she waited, the phone vibrated against her leg. She picked up the device. The backlit text read, "DK: Right Nyte, Kel."

Chapter Four

KEL MADE THE final edit to the incident report at Central Booking and consulted the watch strapped to her wrist. Minnie Mouse had never lied to her—3:07 a.m. As she predicted, it had taken half the night at the King County Jail to book the tavern brawlers, even with Scott and Valarie's help.

She slid the computer's mouse over the "submit" button on the monitor and clicked.

She had promised Chief Ballesteros a page-turner, but this one wasn't up to her usual standard. Not long after she had started writing, two more messages hit her phone from the same number. They pulled her thoughts back to the original text—the poem. When she first read it, since it carried no specific timeline or threat to any person, she had parked it as the ramblings of a frantic mind. Not so with these two new texts.

Her instinct said that whatever this DK planned to do, he had already done it. So, if she had reported the messages as soon as they came in, when she finished in Booking, she could have gone home to Chrissie and a hot shower. The beer still sticking to her back from the unchanged uniform shirt and the stench of vomit rising from her boot required no further incentive for a deep cleansing of this shift's filth.

But he had made it personal. *He knows my name.* As she walked to the garage elevator, she brought the messages up on her phone's display and found the first of the two most recent. The address on the screen was only a short ten-minute detour from her route home.

As the elevator descended the shaft to the first-level parking, she scrolled to the second message— an invitation: "door's open." Despite what Chief Ballesteros had said about her potential a couple hours before, even as an off-duty officer, investigating without reporting in could mean career suicide—or at least disciplinary action. Being a patrol officer, assigned to protect the streets from jaywalkers, illegal U-turns, and the drunk and disorderly, she had no authority to investigate a hangnail, let alone a violent crime. But with two generations of cop in her DNA, the tug was too powerful to resist.

When the elevator door opened, she stepped into the garage and retrieved her keys from a clip on her belt. As she located the transponder for her cruiser, a thought that had been nagging at the back of her mind returned. *DK could have found my name anywhere, but my phone number?* He had chosen her SPD-issued phone to be the communication link, yet department cell phone numbers were unlisted. Does DK have a connection inside the department?

A few minutes later as she merged onto Interstate 5 South, she knew she shouldn't proceed without laying some ground work. She needed help with the phone number that had sent the texts. To do that, she needed to take someone into her confidence—someone she probably didn't know. Risky, but she picked up her phone and dialed the number.

"Crime lab, Bimal," a perky fresh-from-college-on-his-first-real-job male voice said with more than a hint of a Hindi accent.

"This is Officer Kel Nyte, Bimal. I'm wondering if you might do me a small favor."

"Off the record?"

"With your resources it should only take five minutes. Would you mind?"

"Well, it's been a slow night. Sure, why not? Anything for the SPD, right?"

Minutes later, Kel stood aside her cruiser and stared up at the converted warehouse. Nestled under Interstate 5, the three-storey building stood a few hundred yards from the runway of Boeing Field, between the old Burlington Northern railroad tracks on the east and Airport Way South on the west. A developer during the inflated dotcom bubble at the end of the last century—despite the surround sound of trains, planes, and automobiles—had transformed this abandoned edifice into a trendy condo project.

She looked across the parking lot to the red brick structure. Sourness rose to the back of her tongue. She swallowed hard but was unable to cleanse the uneasy bitterness on her palate. Kel pulled her weapon from its holster and released the magazine. The weight in her hand gave witness to its lethal contents, and the click as she slapped it back in place gave her confidence. She moved forward. The weathered asphalt crunched under her boot heels as she crossed to what appeared to be the main entrance.

With a forceful jerk, the glass door opened wide enough for her to slip into the small sterile lobby. She followed the arrow though a short white-tiled hall to the elevator and pushed the call button. The door parted immediately as if it had anticipated her arrival. Once inside the cab, she pressed the "3" button and stood facing the door. She kept the gun angled toward the floor with her knees flexed and feet shoulder-width apart. When the lighted display flickered from "2" to "3," she took a deep breath. An anxious chill crested over her as the door slid left. The hallway stood empty.

Kel peered around the exit in both directions, blew her lungs empty and stepped into the corridor. Its sole personality was a brushed-steel table by the elevator with a colorful silk plant. With the suggestion of death in the air, the flowers seemed a proper, but permanent, funeral arrangement.

The door nearest her read 301. She took slow, cautious steps as she slunk toward the door marked 304. Every few feet she stole a glance behind her to ensure no one followed. No one did.

At the door, she slipped black leather gloves over her hands and reached for the handle. With no surprise, she found it unlocked—door's open. The anxiousness she had tried to swallow in the parking lot now manifested as fear. Not the paralyzing terror of an acrophobic on the brink of a precipice, but enough to heighten her senses—sight, sound, scent— to keep her at ready. To keep me alive.

She knew she wasn't bulletproof, but she believed that she had been summoned to this address not to take her last breath. DK hadn't sent the incoherent text just to execute her—at least not yet. One thing she did understand from that message suggested he had a plan—"mine to teach the lesson well." The most likely conclusion was that he had invited her here to expand her understanding of his mission.

Armed with the belief that if anyone was to die behind that door, they were already dead, she raised her pistol and thrust the door with her foot. With the light of a single table lamp in the corner on the opposite wall, she peered into the living room and searched for an indication that someone expected her.

No one stirred. The Glock in her right hand and her finger on the trigger, she pulled a flashlight from her belt with her left.

After she entered the apartment, she swung the front door closed behind her. A recliner sat, extended, next to the wall, and she skirted around it. As the approached the other end of the small living room, she stole a glance at a photo that took center stage on the lamp table. Her chest grew heavy as she looked at the two women. They leaned against the trunk of a palm tree, captured in a loving embrace. Victims? she wondered.

Behind the living room, the kitchen opened on the backside of a bar. Except for the clock on the microwave and the light streaming from the living room, it was dark. She slipped through the opening at the end of the bar and flashed her beam into the shadows. Other than a woman's purse and a set of keys on the counter, the room offered no other sign of human life.

In the hallway, she made her way to the bathroom. On the bathtub, a solitary glass of white wine stood next to an uncorked bottle. The sweat from the two glass containers had created puddles that had merged into one. The tub stood full yet unattended. She gripped the flashlight between her teeth and slipped one glove off. The water was clean and tepid. A eucalyptus scent rose to greet her. With the lack of soap residue on the surface and the towels dry and hung in place, she sensed the bath had been, ... interrupted.

She dried her fingers on her pant leg and pulled her glove over her hand again. Embracing the flashlight with the gun, Kel moved back into the hallway. From a room on the left, she saw a dim glow pouring out of the darkness. She peered around the doorframe and found nothing but the light of a computer monitor. With the flashlight, she swept the otherwise darkened room. Clear.

One room remained. As she confronted the opening, she felt the hairs on her arms stand erect. The knowledge of the killer's deeds emanated from the room beyond like the chilled wind of a cloudless winter's night—unseen but palpable. The beam from her flashlight, trained toward the doorway, was absorbed by the darkness beyond. A dense gloom spilled out of the chasm. It eclipsed her despair over the expected victim with the evil of the unknown assassin. Yet it drew her from the void.

Behind her, from somewhere she had already cleared, a sound resonated off the walls—a distinct metallic click. A surge of panic filled her ears with the sudden hammer of blood. She sensed the muzzle of a cocked pistol pointed at her back. He had a clean shot; he could drop her before she took her next breath.

It's said that in unexpected life-threatening moments, a disjointed newsreel of memory flashes through the mind. The good, bad, and ugly fly by in a fast-forward display of pride, disappointment, and regret. Joy over accomplishments, sadness over loved ones left behind, remorse over unfulfilled dreams, guilt over fractured relationships.

But none of that distracted Kel from her duty—not this time. Her only thought? "How'd I miss him?"

As quick as the sound touched her ears, she twisted with a jerk to face down DK and dropped to one knee to make a smaller target. She swept the hallway with her handgun and was surprised to find no one there. Nothing threatened.

Then a second click from the living room brought with it the familiar Big Ben chime. The carillon from an old clock rang the three-quarter hour. She recognized the clicks now as the clock's works as they slipped into action. She caught her breath, stood, and turned back.

With only three steps, she reached the doorway to the master bedroom. She thrust her hands inside and followed the swath of light as it severed the murk from right to left. When the shaft swept over the bed, it fell on the form of a woman.

Kel stood frozen for several seconds and waited for signs of life—a breath, a twitch, a sigh—but the woman didn't stir. The position of the figure suggested that she had lain on top of the bedspread, perhaps waiting for the tub to fill, and fell asleep.

Kel shook her head and swept the room until she was certain that she was the only other soul in the bedroom. Next to the bed, the only things out of place—a bedside lamp and a telephone—had tumbled to the floor. Adjacent to them laid a Browning nine-millimeter pistol. Its magazine rested a foot away.

She turned her beacon back toward the motionless body and found the mid-fortyish face of one of the two women in the photo on the living room table. She bent over to the body and, for the second time tonight, felt for a pulse. Though the skin warmed to the touch, unlike Marcel's, this time no throb greeted her fingertips.

She holstered her weapon and walked back to the second bedroom. As she passed through the hall, she pulled her phone from its sheath, called dispatch, and reported the suspicious death. With officers now on the way, and the medical examiner alerted, she turned to the glowing monitor and sat before the desk.

A four-line verse, the same rhyme and iambic meter as the one she had received earlier, was on the screen. But where the original poem had been vague, this one confirmed with the first line that what she discovered in the bedroom was the beginning of a planned series of murders. She pulled a notepad from under the dark blue flap of her shirt pocket and copied down the couplets.

"First the one who owes so much

Final payment by my touch
Breath of life fails to draw in
Pillow talk, my lethal sin"

As she slipped the pad back into her pocket, her phone rang.

"Officer Nyte? Bimal, from the crime lab. I think you'll want to hear this."

"Go."

"As you suspected, the number's untraceable. You can buy these prepaid phones just about anywhere."

"So there's no lead?"

"I didn't say that, but it took me more than the five minutes allowed."

"Okay. I owe you, but you're on the clock now."

"No longer off the record? Cool. Well, I've found some interesting things about it. It was bought online and drop-shipped to Seattle from Taipei, Taiwan."

"Taipei? How was it paid for?"

"Still working on that."

"Do you know where it was shipped?"

"Of course, but the trail gets cold at this point. The address is a shop in the Roxbury neighborhood that's been closed for a while. The tracking shows that the package didn't require a signature. It was left at the rear door, so there's no record of who received it."

"What about activity?"

"The last activity was almost an hour ago. It came from the same tower that's pinging your call right now."

"That's no surprise. The perp sent a text directing me to this address. What about GPS?"

"Well, it gets even more interesting there."

"Why? Where's the phone now?" Her mind flew into a sudden whirl of angst.

"Give or take... within three hundred feet of you."

Chapter Five

"BIMAL!" KEL SCREAMED as she yanked her Glock from its holster. She bolted toward the bedroom doorway. "You think that might have been the first thing you told me? Call dispatch. Get back up, and then come back on the line." She switched the phone to speaker and slipped it into the holster on her belt.

At the doorway, she pushed the pistol out in front of her and peered around the opening. Alone in the hallway, she turned toward the master bedroom. Minutes before, distracted by finding the victim's body, she had not cleared the whole room, a neglect which sometimes proved a mortal failure to rookies. But she was no rookie, and now she had to confront the bedroom again with the knowledge that DK likely lurked in the shadows beyond.

She again pierced the darkness with the flashlight beam. As she neared the entrance, something stirred below the shaft of light, so transient that she doubted she had seen anything at all. In her heightened sentience, it could just as well have been a shifting shadow caused by the nervous tremble of her hand as she focused the light into the gulf of uncertainty. Then, with a will of its own, her hand drew downward and the beacon fell on the glow of a pair of eyes. A cat, whose coat was as black as the murk in which it had hidden, whisked past her.

Her heart had been pounding before, but now it rattled her rib cage. She paused, took a couple of deep, silent breaths, and held the last one. Get to the living room and wait for backup, her mind cautioned. There she'd have the advantage of light and space. But she exhaled with slow purpose and pressed on, unwilling to give the murderer another moment's freedom.

She followed the light into the bedroom and swept, as before, from right to left. With her back to the wall, she skirted the armoire toward the only space left in the bedroom to hide. As she walked, her eyes continued to scan the periphery of the room for movement. When she reached the back side of the bed, she flicked the light momentarily into the void between the queen-sized bed with its lifeless burden and the wall. Clear.

Her eyes followed the beam as it rose toward the closet, and she crept to the opening. Before she entered, she paused and listened for the breath or the stir of someone beyond. If they had taken refuge inside, she envied their capacity for calm. She struggled for it now.

The light, married with her Glock, sliced the darkness. She left the last bastion of safety behind and entered the closet. She found herself in a narrow hallway. On the left, double-mirrored sliding doors concealed the wardrobe of the woman on the bed. The next time she's dressed it'll be by a mortician with clothes from behind that door. On the right, a bathroom door stood ajar.

The master bath made more sense as a hiding place—it was larger and gave the perp more room to maneuver—but the closed doors of the closet stole her attention first. She reached with her left hand to the nearest of the two doors and, with a quick thrust, pushed it open. The wheels sent it sideways until a thump indicated it had come to rest at the end of the track. She diverted her flashlight to the nook and peered into the space behind the double doors. An upright vacuum stood on the carpet below boxes on the shelf, garments on the pole, and shoes in a rack. Clear.

She turned the beam away and aimed it at the bathroom door, the last recess where DK could hide. She stepped to the side and raised her gun.

"Hands behind your head," she shouted, "and step out slowly."

She waited for the door to swing, the rustle of clothes or gunfire, but heard nothing. She raised her voice: "Now!"

Still nothing stirred within. She pushed the door open and entered the bathroom. It, too, was clear.

She retrieved her phone. "Bimal?"

"Yes, Officer Nyte. Dispatch is sending a squad your way."

"Well, there doesn't seem to be a rush. Except for me and a cat, there's nothing alive in this apartment. I'm hanging up now."

As she walked back into the master bedroom, a sudden electronic snap hit her ears just a gnat's breath before her muscles lost control to another force. Her hands gave an involuntary jerk. The pistol and flashlight tumbled away. Still conscious, she saw the floor coming up fast to meet her. Once prone, unable to move, she lay sprawled, her face in the carpet.

"Face to face, Kel," a male voice with tobacco breath behind whispered to her. "Are you listening?"

Kel, paralyzed in body from the two electrodes grabbing her back, was still able to think. A stun gun? He could have killed me instead. That meant she had been right earlier when she had reasoned that DK wanted her to learn more about his purpose. She pushed the embarrassment of being captured and the pain to the back of her consciousness—damn it, I didn't clear the second bedroom closet—and focused her attention on the voice above her.

"I've only lost one quest in my life, Kel," he murmured, "and that one bound me for years. Now, I invite you to the pursuit of your life. Only one of us may survive. If you're the fortunate one, it's because you've learned from the teacher and passed my test.

Failure is to your peril. I look forward to the final revelation."

In her mind, words formed without the ability to take voice. The cop bravado in her exclaimed, I'll nail you bastard, but if she could have asked just one question, it would have been, "Why me?" To her knowledge, she didn't have enemies—at least none who'd stoop to murder as a source of revenge, and certainly none who'd be willing to die to prove their point. And then a slit of clarity dawned. Is his demented lesson mine to learn, or mine to convey?

When the faint whisper of a siren in the distance seeped into the bedroom, DK kicked Kel's pistol under the dead woman's bed.

"This isn't our last meeting. Be careful, though; just like tonight, you'll never know what rock I'll slither out from under, and next time I may not be so nice."

He gave her a parting jolt and chuckled. "Good hunting, Kel."

The stun gun fell next to Kel's head. The vibration of the floor beneath her gave her indication that DK had run toward the living room door, and the subtle click as it closed verified it. It took over a minute for her mind to regain control of her body. Even still a little tipsy, once her muscles responded to her commands, she reached for the flashlight and then crawled toward the bed. She lifted the dust ruffle. The gun was not visible.

After circling behind the bed, she found the .357 next to the wall and picked it up. With DK getting away, she sprinted through the condo to the common hallway. The electric hum of the elevator at the far end caught her ear. She knew he wouldn't leave that way and had probably engaged it as a diversion. Next to it, the green glow of an exit sign hung from the ceiling over a door. She raced for it.

Once inside the concrete stairwell, a door slammed several floors below. She reached for her phone and started to run the three flights, taking two steps at a time. As she ran, she pressed and held the shortcut key for Dispatch.

"Where's my backup?" she screamed when they answered.

"Identify, please."

"Badge five-zero-niner, unit three-zero-four. Perp has left the building, officer in ground pursuit."

"Five-zero-niner, officers are on the way. Do you have a visual?"

"Negative."

She reached the ground floor, exited the building, and found herself in the parking lot. She ran away from the structure to the center of the lot and searched for movement. With the condos behind her, she turned toward the street. In her peripheral vision, she saw a tall man revealed under a streetlight. He ran on the sidewalk a hundred yards away on the far side of the street.

"Got him," she shouted into the phone. She had recovered from the Taser, and now, with all five senses in her body converged into the solitary pursuit, she put action to the words she couldn't utter moments before: "Nail the bastard." She turned and tore out in his direction. "Send units to South Lucile and Airport Way."

"Copy," the woman's voice acknowledged.

"Going silent," Kel said and slid the phone into its sheath.

She saw the man turn west on South Lucile and disappear behind a building. Kel continued her charge toward the intersection. As she reached the curb and leapt into the street, an air horn blasted to her left. She turned toward the sound. Rubber screeching against pavement robbed her thoughts of the task at hand. She stared, frozen, into a pair of headlights just yards away.

Chapter Six

"WHAT THE HELL do you think you're doing, Officer Nyte?" Lieutenant Louis Martinez shouted. The black hair slicked back on his head like John Travolta's in Grease wasn't as thick, but the full mustache covering his upper lip made up for the lack.

It had taken over two hours before the first crime scene investigators made their way to the scene. Martinez, her boss, and Chief of Detectives Nathanial Ballesteros followed close on their heels. They entered the building together.

After releasing the crime scene to a South Precinct officer, she had stayed out of the way in her cruiser, as ordered. While she waited, the paramedics on the scene cleansed the superficial scrapes ground into the heels of her hands. She had used them to break her fall after jumping out the path of the eighteen-wheeler. They also offered two—she insisted on three—aspirin, which had helped to dissipate the ache in her knees. But they had nothing to offer for the earful she knew was imminent.

She had rehearsed the conversation. She hoped it'd be after a morning double shot espresso or two. With the stern look on Martinez's face when he exited the building after fifteen minutes, she knew that no amount of caffeine could prepare her for what was about to explode. Judging from the deep furrows on his brow and the glowing embers that glared at her through the window, a civil conversation wasn't likely. To make matters worse, the scowl on Chief Ballesteros's face gave no confidence that the next few minutes would be anything other than grueling.

The way Lieutenant Martinez had called her by her title rather than his usual address, "Kel," brought back memories of her dad when she had done something stupid as a teenager—a frequent occurrence. Then, she'd expect the immediate outcome of being sent to her room. But now, there was no room to go to, and Lou seemed in no mood to send her away—yet.

"Without backup?" he continued.

She stepped out of the cruiser. Martinez, a man short in stature but broad in girth, stood about the same height as Kel. Now facing him, her eyes to his, she hoped to subdue his wrath. As in the squad room, she addressed him by name. "I'm sorry, Lou."

"'Lou' my ass. It's Lieutenant Martinez."

"Yes, sir."

"It's just after six in the goddamn morning. My captain woke me from a dead sleep to tell me to get my ass over here because one of my reports is wandering around a crime scene alone. Do you have any idea how pissed I am?"

"I think I'm beginning to understand, Lieutenant Martinez. But I—"

"But what, Officer Nyte?" Chief Ballesteros asked and his distinctive eyebrows closed the gap between them. "What compelled you to walk into this crime scene?"

Kel was surprised at the disparity between the kindness the chief had shown her after the bar scuffle only hours before and his agitation now. He didn't seem as full of rage as Lou, but there was nevertheless a succinct quality in his tone. She sensed something was wrong with the situation—more than just her discovery of a murder.

"I didn't know it was a crime scene, sir."

"So what brought you here?"

"I received a message on my phone with this address," she said. She was willing to let them in on the latest two texts, but she needed to quiet their ire before she revealed the mysterious poem she had received earlier. "So I came to see why."

"Let me see that," Martinez said and snapped his hand out, palm open.

Kel took her phone from its holster on her service belt and thumbed to the right message. She ignored Martinez's hand and held it up for both men to read.

"So whoever sent this," Ballesteros said, "told you to expect an open door. Did you think the suspect might have been waiting on the other side of that door?"

"I certainly gave it thought, sir, and I was prepared."

"But you entered without backup," Lieutenant Martinez said, and Kel saw anger's flames crawl up his stumpy neck. He crossed his arms and rested them on his protruding abdomen.

"Yes, sir. I didn't think I'd need backup."

"And yet he was lying in wait for you. Maybe he wanted to kill you."

"Perhaps, but not tonight. He had a chance but didn't take it. Somehow, in his mind, I'm connected to this. Sirs, he knows my name. He dared me to chase him."

"So what are you saying?" Ballesteros asked and reached to pull on his left earlobe.

"Sirs, I need to work this case."

"You're not a detective," Martinez shouted.

"I've passed the exam," she said and paused, considering whether this was the time to express her derision. She decided she might not get an opportunity like this again and, with Ballesteros already seeming to side with her earlier, she continued. "But you've been holding me back."

"If you're saying I've held you back for any reason other than the fact that there's no opening or you're not qualified, then this conversation is over."

"That I am qualified speaks for itself, Lieutenant," she said, and flicked a quick glance toward Chief Ballesteros. "But I'm not asking for a promotion, just a chance to work this case."

"For all I know, you did this."

"Me?" she said, and her eyelids pulled back in astonishment. "What motive would I have to kill her?"

"Let's try to turn the volume down here," Ballesteros said, and nodded toward the edge of the parking lot.

"You don't know, do you?" Lieutenant Martinez continued at the same intensity, as if the chief hadn't spoken.

"Know what?" Kel asked. She looked in the direction the chief indicated. A couple of news crews had their cameras pointed toward them. "What's going on?"

"The victim is Suzanne Lowen."

"Suzanne Lowen... from the crime lab? So that's why you're here, Chief. I've never met her. I had no idea."

"With Suzanne having single-handedly destroyed your dad's biggest case, would it surprise anyone if he wanted her dead?"

"So that's it? You think my dad put me up to this? That doesn't sound like the open mind I'd expect from an officer of the law. What's next— contrive evidence? While you're throwing around baseless theories, sir, why don't you ask yourself this: if I killed her, why would I call it in? Why would I hang around here and implicate myself? And why would I have these Taser burns on my back? Sir, this is only the beginning. You saw the poem he left up there. 'First—'"

"That's enough, and that's an order," Ballesteros said. His voice boomed over Kel's.

"Look, Chief, Lieutenant…" She calmed her tone and flipped through the messages on her phone. "He speaks in poems like the one he left Suzanne. He sent me one just a few hours ago. Listen to this. 'Recompense is yours to pay, mine to reap for Hell each day.'"

"Sounds like he is after you," the chief said.

"Maybe, but isn't it obvious that Suzanne's murder is the first of several he's planning? Why he's chosen to communicate to me, I don't know. But if I'm on his list, who better to investigate? I have motivation, and with this..." She shook the phone toward them. "It's a road map to his mind. I'm just asking for a chance. I'm due some vacation. Let me take a week and see where it takes me. I'll keep you informed."

"Forty-eight hours," Martinez interjected. "And you can't investigate a cop killer unless you're on the clock."

"Two days isn't much time to generate leads. How about four?"

"You're just a Temp-D, so two, and if you're making progress, we'll talk."

"You'll need a partner," Ballesteros said.

He turned toward a uniformed officer who was manning the crime scene-taped barricade a few yards away and said, "Go find Jake deLaurenti. He's probably with the body."

"Jake?" Kel said. "You've assigned Jake to investigate a cop killer?"

Chapter Seven

AFTER SHE LEFT Suzanne Lowen's crime scene, Kel stopped by her West Seattle townhome. As soon as she opened the front door, Saul's paws hit the hardwood floor at the base of the kitchen stairs. She couldn't help but smile when he slid across the floor, nails clattering for traction. It made his challenge, while he skidded into a four-footed protective stance, look like a clown at the rodeo trying to distract a bull. Once Saul recognized her, though, he dropped his guard, trotted over, and nuzzled his snout into her hand.

"Hey, boy. Let's find Chrissie."

As Saul ran up the stairs, Kel stopped in the kitchen. She dropped two slices of whole-wheat bread into the toaster, and set a couple of place settings on the bar with dishes from the white over-the-bar cupboard.

When she reached the top of the stairs, Kel stuck her head into Chrissie's room. Saul stood next to the bed and looked eagerly back and forth between the two women in his life. Chrissie rose to her elbows, blinked the sleep from her hazel eyes, and stared at her mother.

"What time is it?" Chrissie asked.

"Seven-twenty. Breakfast in, five minutes."

Kel walked across the hall to her own room to swap the beer-spattered uniform for something clean. She dropped the soiled clothes into the bathroom hamper and, with no time to shower, washed the stickiness off her back as best she could with a damp washcloth.

Standing at the closet, she stared inside. On any other day, dressing for work was no issue—a clean uniform and out the door. But today was different. It was the first day of her new career, albeit temporary for the moment. What does a detective wear to work on the first day?

Visions of female television detectives came to mind. They certainly didn't dress off the rack. With their garments always getting ripped and ruined on the job, she paused, with her hand stroking her chin, to wonder how they afforded the new clothes. Must be a hefty expense account or credit card limit—or the studio's budget and the actress' image.

She smiled at the thought as she flipped through her wardrobe and settled on a pair of black jeans and a white tee. Fitting attire for a Northwest detective. But after laying them on the bed, she decided that this wasn't the statement she wanted to make—at least not today. Back at the closet, the dark slacks and light blue uniform blouse spoke to her with thoughts of routine. There was something comfortable about predictability. Okay, no fashion statement today, she thought. Maybe tomorrow.

By the time she arrived back in the kitchen with a fresh pair of boots, since the others still stunk with Razor-Wire's retch, Chrissie had breakfast ready. Buttered toast, sliced in half, lay on a single plate, and cereal—Coco Puffs for herself and Wheaties for Kel—had been poured into bowls. They sat side by side with a carton of milk on the countertop.

"Morning, sweetie," Kel said and slipped her arm around her daughter's shoulders. Chrissie's hair, now chopped at her shoulder blades, was originally a couple shades darker than her father's hair. But in the last few months, with the exception of a purple strip on the left side, she had died it black. Even though she was maturing in body, the freckles on her cheeks still gave her an innocent, childlike look.

"You look tired, Mom."

"Been a long night, but I'm fine," Kel said and took her place at the outside end of three sea foam-colored barstools. Chrissie took the seat next to her.

"Hey, do I get my phone back on Sunday?"

So Kel could spend most of the day with Chrissie, she had volunteered to take swing shift during the summer months. Chrissie's job, over her summer vacation, was to keep up with the chores around the house in the evenings so they could spend the daytime hours together. But she had gotten distracted with texting her friends. After numerous reminders of the dirty dishes and laundry scattered around the house, and the bedroom that resembled the path of a Midwestern twister, she went on restriction.

"Do you think two weeks is enough to learn about privilege and responsibility?" Kel asked, with a spoonful of the last scrapings of flakes on the way to her mouth.

Chrissie swallowed a bite of toast and grunted, "Uh-huh. I learned my lesson."

Kel gave her a wary look. "Well ... you continue to keep up with your chores this week, and you'll have your phone on Sunday. By the way, I'll be working days this week. I got a reassignment I'll tell you about later. So, you need anything, give me a call, okay?"

"'Kay, Mom."

"Now give me a kiss. I've got to run."

Even though the thermometer read the low sixties, with an attitude born in the Northwest—the sun is for basking, no matter what the temperature—Kel decided the get acquainted cup of coffee with Jake deLaurenti should be best taken outside. She secured the last unoccupied sidewalk table at Starbucks—just around the corner from the Wishing Well—from a young woman dressed in a tan business suit. As Kel approached, the woman was packing her laptop into a satchel. She shot Kel a "don't rush me" glare and took her time gathering her things. Then, as if resigned to her fate, she joined the Monday morning pedestrian parade of frown-etched faces as they inched their way toward another work week.

Alone under the broad green canopy of maple trees lining the avenue, Kel unlatched the citadel which protected the painful yet pleasant memory that the shoulder-length auburn-haired man had evoked last night. It transported her to a summer vacation when Chrissie was six and Lance, her partner, had yet to leave for the Middle East the first time. Her mind filled with hoof-beats clomping on pavement as a draft horse drew a creaking street car on steel tracks. It took her to a safe place that the forces of circumstance could never breach.

Kel and Lance, exhausted after a long day, had stopped to rest for a few minutes inside the ice cream parlor on Main Street, Disneyland. Chrissie, who should have been whining and out of gas like normal six-year-olds, pranced around the table and pointed out the window, jabbering.

As Lance returned to the table, he held Chrissie's cone out and asked, "Ice cream?"

"Goofy, Daddy," she said and grabbed the treat. She pointed again out the window to the center of Main Street where, surrounded by kids and parents, the over-sized, floppy-eared character posed for pictures. "See Goofy?"

"You've got it, punkin," he said, and picked her up in his arms. "Goofy it is."

Kel took her own cone from Lance and, as the other two left the parlor, she pulled a camera from her purse. "This is what life's about," she thought as she watched Chrissie's arm slip around her daddy's neck and disappear under his shoulder-length auburn hair.

"Three simple rules," Jake said after he placed two recyclable cups on the table. He pulled out a chair and twisted into it.

Before this morning, Kel had never met Jake. His solid frame indicated that he spent time in the precinct's gym, but the dark circles under his eyes were either genetic markers or—more likely—signs of poor sleeping habits. He wore a dark gray blazer over an open-necked aqua button-down shirt and blue jeans.

With the word around the department, she wondered why he hadn't been forced to trade his unmarked Sedan for a three-wheeled Cushman—SPD parking enforcement's typical mode of transportation. He had a good closing ratio, but partnering with Jake wasn't for the risk-averse. Of his last two partners, one lay in the hospital hooked to feeding and oxygen tubes. The other, Willie Jenkins, ended up dead.

"Only three?" Kel slipped her hands around her cup. Steam from the latte floated up through the drinking hole like a wisp of white papal smoke.

"First, stay the hell out of my way," Jake said. His eyes twisted away from her with a jerk of his head. "My closing ratio's high, and I plan to keep it that way. No rookie slows me down, got it?"

Kel turned her eyes from the slender forty-five-year-old man and followed his gaze. Across the street, in Pioneer Park, a male guide led a group of two dozen tourists under the wrought iron Victorian Pergola between flanks of the homeless, who sat on benches for their morning social.

She lifted the beverage to her lips and slurped at the steamed-milk foam on the surface. Nodding an acknowledgement, she turned back toward him.

"Next, if you forget rule number one, I'll squash you like a cockroach no matter who your dad is or was."

"And number three?" she asked.

"Ah, yes, number three." He shifted his whole body toward her. "Rookies are a boil on my ass, and female rookies are the infected core. Any questions?"

"Just one."

"And what the hell is that, plebe?"

"Are you always this sweet on a first date?"

"I don't have first dates. Just conquests." He scanned her body from head to toe. "Interested?"

She recognized in Jake's eyes the same leer that she saw in so many men during a first encounter. It was hard enough being taken seriously as a woman in the SPD, but she piqued when she was seen as a desirable possession rather than a person. Other women might use their appearance as a tool, but for her, the natural olive-toned skin, gentle bone structure, and eyes the color of spring growth on fir trees were a curse.

"You're such a charmer. I hate to disappoint you, but ..." She paused and rubbed her chin. "I'll pass. However, now that we have the rules established, we have a serial killer with a tight timeline. We should swap notes."

"I'll go first so you see how this works."

"By your leave," she agreed, and shot him a sneer.

He turned his gaze back toward the park. "Well, for starters, my victim worked for the police department in the crime lab. That makes this personal. From the two sizes of women's clothes and shoes in the closet, and mail addressed to two different women, she likely has a live-in partner who is female. At the moment we don't know where she is, so she'll be a person of interest. I'll do some background on her today."

"I hate to disagree with you so soon, but—"

"Rule one!" he shouted. A couple at the next table broke off their conversation to stare at him.

While the two stood and left, he continued as if there had been no interruption. "See how this works? There was no forced entry, so either it was the partner or someone else with a key—or someone she knew and let in."

"Or someone jimmied the lock—" Kel added.

"No tool marks on the lock." He raised his voice over hers. "So if there's the remote possibility that's true, the perp has access to professional lock picking tools. Except for a few things out of place in the bedroom," he continued, "there didn't seem to be much of a struggle. That leads me to believe she either knew her assailant or was somehow incapacitated very quickly—"

"He did stun me—"

"We'll get to that," he interrupted and faced her again. "Are you following me? Am I going too fast?"

"Not at all," she said. "So far it sounds cliché, by the book … but when you're ready for facts and not assumptions, you'll let me know, right?"

He rolled his eyes, shook his head, and paused to take a swallow of his coffee. "The lab guys will go over the computer to see if any leads can be generated from the poem. Once they've finished, I may have other doors to knock on. And then there's you."

"I thought I covered that with Martinez and Ballesteros."

"Why do you think they want you to ride shotgun with me?"

"I had hoped it was so I might just learn something from a seasoned professional, but I see now it's so you can keep an eye on me."

"Right," he said, and nodded. "You've passed your first test in deductive reasoning. Stick around and you just might learn something yet. For now I have a short suspect list: a lesbian lover, and a green-eyed boil acting on behalf of her dad. What astute words of wisdom can you offer?"

"Well ... the ME's preliminary the time of death is between midnight and two this morning." She placed her cup on the table grate and turned to glare at him. "If that's accurate, you'll be able to corroborate my story, because I was waist-deep in drunks at the time. And then there's the gender of the perp. I have doubts that the killer's female."

"Based on what?"

"I did have a personal encounter and, as you already know, I have the Taser burns to prove it."

"So you say. Anybody could have put those there."

"My God. Are you just thick or brain dead?"

"Just doing my job. So this person who stunned you—"

"You mean the man who stunned me?"

"Okay, the man. You saw him and can give a description?"

"Not exactly. Being pinned to the floor with fifty-thousand volts hammering you kind of puts a person's observation skills at a disadvantage. He stayed out of my line of sight. But when I gave chase, he passed under a streetlight and I saw he was over six feet in height and wore a red baseball cap."

"Look around, plebe. See any suspects?"

Kel scanned the square. A man and a woman with the tour guide wore matching red ball caps. She shook her head.

"What you meant to say is that you saw someone running. You have no way of knowing it was him. It could just as easily have been some guy with a red hat out for a jog."

"At four o'clock in the morning?"

"There are hundreds of reasons why he was out running. Maybe he just got caught by his lover's husband. Point is, that may have been the perp, but you have no way of knowing for certain."

"I suppose you're right, but my gut says the coincidence of him running on that street at the very moment I gave chase—"

"Coincidence is usable, but not enough. That's called circumstantial. It can be used to build a case, but there has to be more. What else you got? Did he speak to you with a distinctive male tone?"

"No. He whispered, but it was a male whisper."

"Really?" Jake gave her a noncommittal shoulder shrug and tipped his cup for another draw of caffeine.

Kel's eyes drifted toward the tourists again. They had moved another half-block toward an alley entrance to Seattle's underground tour of the remnants of the great fire of 1889. Another block and a half away to the west, the sun glanced off the dark-tinted side window of a black Audi limo as it turned from Elliott Avenue, on the waterfront, and crawled up Yesler Way.

"The suspect is most likely not the victim's partner," she continued. "Suzanne is an unfortunate part of a much larger plan, but not the endgame. This victim was probably not known to the suspect, but not a random choice, either."

"Humph."

"Chief Ballesteros told you about the text I received last night. It's a poem just like what we saw on Suzanne's computer." She held it up for him. "You can see there's a line that gives indication to motive: 'Mine to teach the lesson well.' He feels self-appointed to impart some knowledge to a specific pupil."

"And who's the pupil?"

"He hasn't given enough to know that yet, but it seems personal."

"As in … you're the pupil?"

"Maybe, but I'm not sure. You see that line, 'Recompense is yours to pay'? I don't know if 'yours' is in reference to me, or if the pupil is something even bigger, like the SPD or the city. As I said, I don't know enough yet, but there are other clues."

"Like?"

"For example, he uses the singular form of 'lesson,' so it appears there's only one lesson, but he goes on to say, 'Witnesses their stories tell.' 'Witnesses' and 'stories' being plural. I believe he intends to bring multiple witnesses, each telling some story about the pupil to confirm the evidence of whatever truth he intends to reveal. Suzanne's investigation, then, must center on finding the intersection between her and the pupil. So, yes, we should dig into her past. Let's look for old lovers, snubbed girlfriends … and since she was SPD, closed cases. But let's also keep an open mind. She may have been coincidental to her own death, not the subject of it. The deeper we dig into her history, we might begin to understand who the pupil is, and when we know that, there's a good chance he or she'll lead us to DK."

"DK? You're so convinced it's a serial you've already named him. Just like dear old Dad. Let's see, what did he call his serial, the one Suzanne set free? Oh, yeah, the Rat City Exterminator."

Kel glared at him. The mention of Rat City, a local colloquial reference to a part of southern West Seattle and the district where the Exterminator disposed of his victims, stirred a thought. The Roxbury neighborhood, where DK had had his phone delivered, sat in the middle of Rat City.

"What, no sharp retort?" Jake asked.

"The press dubbed him with that moniker," Kel snapped. "Dad hated it. Now, may I go on?"

"Of course. I'm so enjoying your spin on this."

"'DK' is the tag on the texts, so until we know more, for me, it's 'DK,' rather than perp or UNSUB. I don't think we have much time," she continued. "The opening word of the poem on Suzanne's monitor is 'First.' Suzanne is the first witness and was the first victim, but more will soon follow. The final line of the poem right here," she said and shook her phone, "is 'Mine to reap for Hell each day.' There's urgency here. If he's literal, then tomorrow there'll be another murder. That may give us more clues about the pupil, but the murders continue until either he teaches his lesson or we stop him."

Jake started clapping his hands. The sound echoed off the storefront behind them. "Daughter of the Chief of Police, aspiring Nancy Drew, and pop psychologist all rolled into one slick chick. You need to leave the psychoanalysis to the pros. Take your phone to the lab and then stay the hell out of my way. I'll start with Suzanne's partner."

As Kel took another swallow from the cup, she noticed the black Sedan she had seen a couple of minutes before had now pulled to a stop. It sat double-parked in the street opposite their table. In her peripheral vision, she noticed Jake sit erect. She turned. His facial muscles twitched as his jaw clenched. He released his cup, slipped his hands below the table, and pushed his gray blazer aside. His hand fell on the butt of his service weapon.

Kel slowly reached to release the strap of her Glock.

She turned back to the Audi. The tint on the rear window was too dark to reveal anyone inside. After a few seconds, though, the window powered down, and the face of an Asian man peered out. Kel thought his age deceptive—perhaps early thirties?—due to the leathery texture of the skin on his face. He nodded towards her with a polite gesture, and then turned to Jake and forced a half-smile, like one side of his face had been stricken with Bell's Palsy. One hand appeared above the window frame. He formed a pistol with his finger and thumb, and aimed it at Jake. He dropped his thumb and, as if the hammer had just fallen on the chamber, jerked his hand back. With a quick puff, he pretended to blow the smoke away from the barrel. Then, his smile dissolved into a scowl and, after a long glare, he turned toward the driver and powered the window closed.

Kel looked back at Jake. She noticed that he had released his pistol and wrapped his hands around the cup again. Although she felt the man's gesture a threat, it was as if Jake, seeing who was behind the window, knew it wasn't. She stood, walked to the curb, and watched the car amble up the street toward the next signal.

"Who the hell was that?" she asked as she returned to the table.

"Nothing for your pretty little head to worry about. He's my concern."

"You reached for your gun," she said as she found her chair again. "Like you were expecting trouble."

"Trouble is something there's always plenty of, plebe. You best stick to the case and out of my business, or ..."

She leaned forward with her elbows on the table. "That sounds like a warning, Jake."

"It is what it is. You just keep rule one in your head, and you'll be fine."

"Did Willie forget rule one?"

"Damn it," he said. Every muscle in this face tightened. "Willie got himself killed."

"And the case is still unsolved, even though the department has spared no expense or resource."

Without a response, he got up from the table and stepped to the curb to jaywalk to his car. "We're done here," he shouted.

"And what should I do, partner?"

From the middle of the street, he barked without losing stride or looking back, "Go to Hell for all I care. Just stop trying so hard to be a boil on my ass."

"Just the infected core," she yelled. "The most painful part."

Chapter Eight

WHEN LAST SHE had seen him, he had been strapped to a gurney, unconscious. Now, as Kel approached the side of his bed at Harborview Medical Center, his eyes, from behind a raccoon's mask of bruises, followed her. Since he generally carried a red-tipped cane, she thought him blind, but with his eyes on her face, now it seemed more of a prop.

"Marcel?" she asked, and glanced around at the three other occupied beds in the ward. The other men were either asleep or watching television. Marcel's set was off. He stared back at her. She patted the hand not connected to an IV tube. "May I call you Marcel?"

He nodded.

"I'm glad to see you're awake. I'm Officer Kel Nyte. I broke up the fight last night that put you here."

Again he nodded.

"I need to ask you some questions. Would that be alright?"

He started to grin but winced instead. It was enough, though, to reveal that one of his front teeth had been broken, leaving a jagged hole in his smile.

She squeezed his hand. "I'm sorry you hurt so much. Did you know the man who hit you?"

He shook his head.

"Can you identify him? I have a picture." She pulled out her phone and scrolled to a booking photo of Razor-Wire, the man she had witnessed punching Marcel. "Is this him?"

Marcel reached for the phone and brought it close to his face, as if his nearsighted vision was off the chart. After a few seconds, in an exaggerated motion, he shrugged his shoulders and pouted his lower lip.

"I'm sure it happened so fast. That's okay for now. We can talk about it later."

Behind her, a woman's voice drew Kel's attention away from Marcel.

"Officer?"

Kel turned to see a middle-aged doughty woman in green scrubs at the foot of the bed.

"Yes, Officer Nyte. Can we speak?"

The nurse tucked shoulder-length blonde hair behind one ear and then flipped through Marcel's chart. "Certainly."

"I'll be right back, Marcel," Kel said with a smile. She squeezed and released his hand, and then followed the nurse out the door.

"I know you can't divulge much about his condition, but we arrested the man on the scene who did this. He's in jail now. He's due to be arraigned later today, which means bail will likely be set. I just need to know if Marcel, besides a broken nose and tooth, is going to suffer any long-term affects from this beating. Any reason that might affect bail?"

"The damage to his face is superficial, and except what you've observed, he isn't busted up any other way. We've done X-rays and taken an MRI which showed some brain swelling, but that's to be expected. Your assailant was probably too stoned to do any real harm. I wouldn't be surprised to see Marcel ... is that his real name?"

"As far as I know, no one around here knows his real name."

"Well, I'd be surprised if he didn't walk out of here after another day or two. He doesn't talk much—"

"'Much'? Has he spoken to you?"

"No, just a few moans and groans. He was unconscious until a couple hours ago, but he seems alert now."

"That puts me more at ease."

Kel reached into her wallet and pulled out two SPD business cards. She held one out to the nurse. "I don't know if he has any next of kin, so if anything changes, or he's ready to check out, please see that I'm called."

The nurse nodded and clipped the card to the chart.

"Thanks," Kel said, and stepped back into the ward. She held out the second card to Marcel.

"The nurse says you're doing fine and should be able to get out of here in a day or so. SPD impounded your bike, so when you're ready, you call me, and I'll deliver it to you."

Besides the mime paint, one of Marcel's idiosyncrasies was to peddle his bike along the downtown streets with his cane for the sight-impaired extended. He'd rap it against the cars parked along the street as if using it to find his way.

Marcel took the card and pointed at the phone number. He started to smile again but gave up when a painful look passed over his face. He held up the card, shook his head, and wagged his finger back and forth over the card.

"I don't get it. What are you trying to tell me?"

He extended his thumb and pinkie finger. An imaginary telephone receiver formed and he lifted it to his ear. With his other hand, he dialed an invisible rotary phone and mouthed, "Hello." Then, like he was telling someone to be silent, he put one finger to his lips and looked at Kel.

"Got it. You could call but couldn't speak."

Marcel nodded his head and began to act like he was typing on a computer keyboard. When finished, he circled his index finger in the air and then dropped it to press a fictional "enter" key. Then, pointing to Kel, he pretended to have a cell phone and receive a message.

"I see. You can send a message to my phone from a computer."

He tried to smile again, but a grimace caught it short.

She took the business card from him and wrote her smartphone number in the back in large figures. "Okay, I'll wait for your text," she said as she handed it back.

Chapter Nine

KEL PARKED IN the underground garage of West Precinct on Virginia Street and pressed the elevator call button. She made her way to the third floor. As she entered the detective's bullpen, the clock on the far mint green wall showed the time at three minutes after nine a.m. Even at this hour, the gurgle of fresh coffee dripping into the pot, and the scents of testosterone, cologne, and sweat permeated this place that she dreamed of serving. An honor still to be earned, the room went silent as she passed through the doors, and she realized she wasn't alone in that opinion.

She felt the weight of eight pairs of eyes glare at her, and said, "Good morning."

Her voice expressed enthusiasm and willingness to be part of the team, but when their heads turned away to find some way to look busy, she reminded herself that the gap between her experience and their trust might take a while to close. Besides, she had two strikes against her—boss' kid, and she had to sit when she peed.

The office of the precinct's captain of detectives was on the wall to the left and, through the open blinds, she recognized a crew cut from around the department. She made her way to the door of the small space and, even though it stood ajar, she knocked and waited in the doorway.

"Nyte." Captain Marcos Silva looked up from the clutter of papers on his desk and stood to his five-nine height. He wore a white shirt and two-toned blue striped tie, tied loose at the neck. "I heard you'd be joining us. Chief Ballesteros gave me a call and told me to expect you."

Silva stepped out from behind his desk and walked to the doorway. Kel, who still stood in the opening, backed out of the way and let him pass.

"Okay, guys, back to work. Show's over."

He turned to Kel and continued. "They're a curious bunch, you know—boss' kid and all-but curiosity is a good thing for a detective. I've read some of your arrest reports. You have a probing quality to your work. That should serve you and the department well. This'll be a big case, Kel. Cop killings always are. I can't pretend to understand why the chief assigned you to it, but I'm sure he has good reason, so I'm here to assist any way I can."

"Thank you, Captain. Since you mention it, it may be temporary, but I could use a place to work."

"Of course. The desk opposite Jake's is presently unoccupied."

The desk belonged to Jake's current partner—the last to fall victim to his curse. The official story read that Eddy had gone rogue on a case without Jake's or his superior's knowledge, and that one night he had taken three bullets. One of those, to his head, put him in a coma. But the gossip within the department spun a different story. Jake knew what Eddy had been up to on the night in question. However, he was too busy flashing Franklins around a Belltown pub, looking to get laid, and had turned his phone off.

As Silva led her to Eddy's desk, he said, "You can sit here for now. As you've said, it's not permanent. Just until this case is solved or Eddy walks back into the bullpen on his own steam."

"Of course, sir," she said with a smile.

"You look pretty rough, if you don't mind me saying."

"It's been a long night, sir, and not much sleep before it started."

"There's a shower in the back where you can freshen up."

"Thanks, but I'm not going to be long. Just want to lay out the case and do some research. Then I'll get a few hours' sleep."

"Suit yourself. You can log into the computer with your own credentials. I think you'll find everything you need." He reached out his hand and concluded, "Good to have you aboard."

She took the offered hand. "Thank you, sir. This'll be perfect."

After the captain sauntered back toward his office, Kel pulled the chair out from the kneehole in the desk and sat. She hit the switch on the computer monitor and the screen came to life. The cursor blinked, awaiting her command. She savored the moment like a first kiss. Her next action would begin the first chapter in her new life. Her username and password flowed from her fingers and she pressed the "enter" key. Pride swept over her like a wisp of warm breeze as the Seattle Police Department's intranet painted the monitor in front of her. The dream of serving her community by solving crime, rather than busting speeders, was reality.

She guided the mouse with a few clicks until she navigated to a photo of Suzanne Lowen and printed the full-color representation of her in life. A whiteboard on wheels stood unused in the corner, so she pulled it over near the desk. With a blue marker, she wrote "DK" at the top, and six inches below the title, she drew the spine and first two ribs of a fishbone chart. At the left end, she wrote, "Sunday night—first text," and filled in the rest of the known events in a similar manner. Under "Monday morning—first victim killed," she taped the printed image and wrote Suzanne's name below it.

Satisfied that she had documented the facts in chronological order, she slipped behind the desk again and steered the web browser to the Department of Licensing.

Chapter Ten

"DAMNI IT," KEL shouted. Her voice echoed off the dark-veined white granite floor of the King County Courthouse. "He shouldn't be out on bail, ADA Johnson."

After catching three hours sleep in the SPD quiet room—out so dead that she didn't notice the mattress lumps pressed against her ribs—Kel had made her way to the courthouse. Razor-Wire's arraignment over Marcel Marceau's beating Sunday night was scheduled for two p.m. After the hearing, she confronted the assistant district attorney, a man in his mid-thirties who was about her age. He wore a suit jacket two sizes too small to cover his corpulent belly. They stood in the hallway just outside the courtroom.

Kel glared into Johnson's eyes. "Marcel's going to spend more time in the hospital and recovery than that piece of shit will behind bars."

"You testified yourself, under oath, Officer Nyte," Johnson said, holding his brief case in front of his groin like an ancient Roman shield, "that Mr. Marceau's injuries weren't life-threatening."

"Well, a broken nose and tooth may not be life-threatening, but they deserve more than a slap on the wrist."

"Remember, I'm on your side, officer. That 'piece of shit,' as you describe him, will get his day in court, and—"

"I'm not only the arresting officer. I'm an eyewitness. You remember that and make sure I'm on your witness list."

Twenty minutes after leaving the ADA behind, Kel had been directed through a maze of shoulder-height, translucent walls in the crime lab. Within the cubicles, she noticed that at each opening, busy crime analysts were sifting with meticulous care through evidence. Her first time in the lab, she was awed by the state-of-the-art forensic equipment and wondered just how much of the evidence had come from the CSI's at Suzanne Lowen's.

With a couple of false turns, she finally stood behind a tall skinny man wearing a white, thigh-length lab coat. He hovered over a steel worktable and faced an eighty-inch wall-mounted monitor.

"Excuse me," Kel said.

The young man turned toward her. His tangled black hair, dark circles under even darker eyes, and wrinkled clothes gave the appearance that five minutes earlier, he had been comatose.

"Yes … uh, officer?"

Kel understood that his last word came as an acknowledgement of the uniform she had decided to wear. She recognized his Indian accent. "Bimal?" she asked. As she had suspected from his voice on the phone last night, he was so fresh that he probably hadn't had enough time with the department to find a wall to hang his diploma.

"Yes, and you are ...?"

"Kel Nyte."

"Officer Nyte," he said and thrust his hand out.

She took his hand. "It's 'Detective' now, at least temporarily, but Kel will do fine. You look exhausted."

"I haven't been home since my shift started at midnight last night, but cop killings mean all-hands. I don't suppose most of us here'll get much sleep until we nail this perp."

He turned back to his table and sliced the tip off a cotton swab. It dropped into a small tube.

"Bimal, what do you know about Suzanne's personal life?"

"Nothing. I just started with the SPD last month. We worked different shifts. Her friend Georgia, though—she said that she liked cats and lived with a partner."

"I met the cat, but we'll need to clear the partner."

"I think Georgia said she's out of town this weekend."

"I saw a photo in Suzanne's condo. She was with a woman. You can't always tell from a picture, but they looked happy together."

Bimal pointed across the room to another photo of Suzanne Lowen. The notes fixed to the wall around it expressed people's prayers and memories. Even though it was the same picture she had hung on the crime board in the bullpen just a few hours ago, this one spoke of her life, not her death.

"It seems her coworkers want to remember her that way," Bimal said. "Not as a body on a slab."

An inscription painted on the wall above the photo pulled Kel's attention upward. A quote from the New Testament Book of Hebrews read: "Though he is dead, he still speaks."

"That's our calling," Bimal said. "It's taken out of context, of course, but it says what we feel about our mission. We try to let our unwilling guests tell the story of their life ... and death."

"Is Suzanne speaking?"

"We know a few things that might help build your profile, but nothing definitive. The CSI's swept Suzanne's home with all the forensic gear and tricks in their kit, but so far there's no trace the perp had ever been inside the condo—no prints, no hairs, no skin, no fluids, not even the lingering scent of bad breath. He's a ghost, Kel."

"Well, that phantom left Taser burns on my back. He had to buy it somewhere."

"To be honest, trying to track its origin may not give us any more help than the phone he used to text you. We have the stun gun and we're tracing the serial number, but don't expect it to lead anywhere."

"There was a pistol at the scene on the floor."

"Yes, a nine-mill. Registered to Suzanne. Only her prints on it. No bullets or spent rounds."

"I saw the magazine on the floor. She tried to hold him off with an empty gun."

"Our theory is he had removed the bullets before she got home," Bimal said. "Let her think she had a chance."

"Playing with her just as an old tomcat does a mouse. Bastard. You said you found something, though."

"It's not much. Toxicology found succinylcholine in Suzanne's blood." He clicked the computer mouse and a folder opened on the screen with a series of photos overlaid in a stack. He selected two and dragged them out of the folder. Each focused on separate small flesh wounds. "It was probably delivered by one or both of these needle sticks we found on her body."

"This guy has access to drugs and medical supplies? Might be some kind of medical professional."

"Possibly, but not necessarily. We all have access if we know where to look."

"How's that?"

"The Internet, Kel. Everything's there: where to buy it, dosage, even how to use a syringe. It's probably where he got the Taser, and we already know that the phone came from there."

"He's not making this easy."

"His point, you think?" He winked at Kel. "You know what's sad? Succinylcholine is generally used to immobilize patients during surgical procedures, but it can also be used as a fast-acting paralytic. You see that wound here at the base of the neck?" He moved the pointer of the mouse until it rested on the wound. "It presents with a lot of bruising around it."

"So you think it was the first blow, to stop her from fighting. Was she awake after that?"

"Probably. Our theory is that he immobilized her for some reason. Then, when he was ready, he gave her a second dose. That one was a more skillful penetration of the median cubital vein right here in the elbow joint." He tapped the vein of his left arm with his right forefinger.

"Did that kill her?"

"It could have induced death, but in her case, the dosage was enough to put her to sleep, but not stop her heart."

"There were no signs of rape or trauma at the scene. What was he doing with her?"

"Convincing her why she had to die? Terrorizing her? We may never know, Detective. What we do know is that he kept her powerless and awake until he was ready to finish her."

"When I found her she was lying on her bed with a pillow under her head. Maybe that's why he used the phrase 'pillow talk' in the poem he left on her computer. I suppose he might have been trying to absolve his guilt or something like that. So, if the drug didn't kill her, what did?"

Bimal pulled another photo from the folder onto the monitor's desktop. Suzanne's face appeared. "Asphyxiation. Do you see the tiny specks in her eyes? That's petechial hemorrhaging. When the airway is obstructed through manual strangulation, it puts a lot of pressure on the tiny blood vessels in the eyes. They'll burst, leaving this bruising."

"That's consistent with the poem also. 'Breath of life fails to draw in.' He smothered her with a pillow, didn't he?"

"We believe so. There's trace of her saliva and mucus on a pillow. That's not uncommon for a bed pillow, but the placement puts the stains in the exact location of her mouth and nose. What's interesting is that the fluids were on the underside of the pillow—against the bed, not her head. We believe he held it over her face, and once she expired, he slipped it under her head as if she was asleep. Almost as if he cared about her."

"So you're saying he put her to sleep with the drug so she wouldn't have to endure the further panic of suffocation?"

"It looks that way."

"Who intentionally kills someone but doesn't want them to suffer?"

"Someone very sick, Detective, but he doesn't get off on their struggle or pain."

"Wait, what if killing her was not the point? Obviously it wasn't random. She was intentionally selected. He could have put her to sleep permanently with the drug, but he chose to suffocate her instead. Cause of death might be a piece of the puzzle."

"Isn't COD always a part of the killer's signature?"

"Of course, but he's made a point of reaching out to me. He knows who I am. He waited for me at Suzanne's to lure me into the chase. The poem on her computer was specific, and he left it where I was sure to see it. No, in this case I'm not convinced COD is as much a signature as it is part of the message. Part of his ... lesson plan."

"Interesting theory."

"Speaking of his lesson plan, you should download the messages DK texted me so we can get them into evidence. They need to be analyzed."

"Of course. Just need your phone," Bimal said.

Kel watched as Bimal located a cable to fit her Blackberry and plugged it in. He clicked the mouse on a pop-up bubble that appeared at the bottom of the large monitor.

"Haven't learned anything new yet about the perp's phone," he said as he clicked a folder inside her smartphone's hard drive. "We have inquiries out to the manufacturer. Should hear back soon ... there they are. This'll only take a few seconds."

She watched the green progress bar speed across the screen.

"Has anyone been working on Suzanne's computer?" Kel asked.

Bimal disconnected the cable on the phone and handed it back to Kel.

"Yeah, I've taken a peek. Just like everything else—no leads. Maybe he typed the poem while he sat in front of the monitor, or delivered it via some kind of portable media like a memory stick. There's no external metadata to lead us anywhere. I'm still digging, but it looks like another dead end."

She slipped the phone into the holster on her belt. "I want you to keep me informed of any developments, got it?"

"Got it."

With confirmation that Suzanne lived with a same-sex partner, and that she was probably out of town, as she walked away from Bimal, she called Jake.

"Spoke to Trisha this afternoon, plebe," he said, and even with the poor connection, his condescension came through clear. "She was in Denver at the time, and is on her way back now. I said stay the hell out of my investigation."

She felt the warm flush of outrage crawl up the back of her slender neck. "I'm supposed to ride shotgun. If you don't let me in, I'll solve this solo."

"Like hell," he said, laughing.

"What do you know about Tribune Investments?"

Before she left her new desk, she searched the Department of Licensing database for the plate number of the Audi that had stopped on the street next to her and Jake at Starbucks. The record showed that the vehicle was registered to Tribune Investments.

"Stay out of it or suffer the consequences," he said.

"Now that sounds like a threat."

"It can sound like whatever you want it to. Just remember rule one."

"Stay the hell out of your way," Kel said, and then realized that she was speaking to dead air.

Chapter Eleven

BUILT AFTER WORLD War II, except for fresh coats of white paint, the three-dormer Cape Cod home that Dirk and Clarissa Nyte had owned on Queen Anne Hill for thirty-seven years hadn't changed. They had struggled in the early days. The combined income of a rookie cop and third-grade teacher weren't enough to afford the spacious home. So, five years after they recited their marriage vows, Dirk took a second job as a security guard, and they moved in. Only when the family began to come along did the house transform into a haven, and the Nytes knew they'd spend the remainder of their days under this roof.

The evening had been perfect for a barbecue, but as the day's shadows grew long, clouds draped the sky with dappled gray sheets and threatened rain before morning. When the wind shifted and a cool breeze from the Puget Sound crept across the yard, everyone retreated into the family home to continue Danny's, Dirk's four-year-old grandson, birthday party.

Exhausted from the day, Dirk had settled his six-foot-two frame into his favorite place—an overstuffed brown leather armchair. His short-sleeved gold shirt pulled at his neck so he yanked the tail from the waistband of his jeans. For sixty-four years he had kept his body in shape, an example his oldest daughter, Kel, now followed, but in recent months the urgency of the discipline had waned. He had lost so much of his muscle tone and weight that in short order the skin of his arms were beginning to sag like a Shar-Pei's.

As he gazed around the study, echoes of laughter and tears leeched from the hidden recesses in the lath and plaster. They lived in reserve behind the dark oak paneling to form memories on demand as vivid as the Kodachrome prints in his family photo albums.

Some of the tales were happy, like when Clarissa sat on the raised red-brick hearth and announced that Dirk was soon to be a first-time daddy. Or the day he told her he had quit his extra job, since he had been promoted to sergeant with the Seattle Police Department. Others weren't so kind. He had been seated in this very chair when he got the phone call from his now-deceased dad, also a retired cop, telling him that his mother had been diagnosed with Alzheimer's disease. And Clarissa had sat next to him in her chair when she broke the news of her inoperable brain tumor.

The familiar moan of a loose board from the hallway's hardwood floor brought his mind back to the present. His two daughters had finished cleaning the kitchen and from the sound, one of them was about ten feet from the doorway. He looked up as Shelia, his youngest daughter and Danny's mother, entered and walked across the room. She sat next to him on the hearth, took his hand, and caressed it. A ruthless litigator with an unquenchable desire to win, she was still daddy's little girl. Her tender smile always warmed him.

She generally didn't appear in public without her business suit, but tonight she had worn a pair of white thigh-length shorts which showed off her long legs. Her chestnut hair fell in loose curls around her pretty oval face onto her shoulders and bounced when she walked.

"You look awfully comfortable there, Dad. You feeling okay?"

He massaged his left humerus. From time to time an old battle wound ached when the weather suddenly turned cool and damp. "I was getting kind of tired, but I'm better now. Can't believe Jackson would miss Danny's party."

Jackson Savell was Shelia's husband. Long before they had exchanged vows, however, he had worked his way into the fabric of the Nyte family. Even more than Kel's Lance, for Dirk Jackson filled a void—his first son. The vice president of a local pharmaceutical research company, frequent travel was part of the job.

"He's in the other Washington this week. Meetings with the FDA. Couldn't be avoided."

Kel, who had been a few steps behind Shelia, entered the room and stopped inside the doorway. She took a heart-shaped, framed picture of her mother from a shelf in the walnut bookcase and studied the image taken the year before her mom's health began to fail.

"You know, I still miss her," she said, and caught a tear with the back of her hand before it left a tiny rivulet on her cheek. "It's been over a year and a half, and I miss her like it was yesterday."

Dirk looked between the photo and Kel, and saw Clarissa's reincarnation in the doorway. Her skin tone and deep brown hair, even when pulled back into a bristly ponytail as it was today, were genetic gifts from Clarissa's Sicilian heritage. Like her mother, when she walked into a room, Kel brought the radiance reserved for a solitary crimson rose. Without any pretense or knowledge of her effect, everything else diminished by comparison.

"I know, girls," Dirk said and nodded his head. "I still feel her, too." He looked beyond the room and through the years like he was reaching for a favorite comforter. Then, without warning, as if the blanket had become a leaden cloak, his eyesight blurred, his shoulders bowed and his head became too heavy to hold up. He forced his eyes closed and shook his head to clear the despair. "I know you'll think I'm losing it, but ... I talk to her."

"About?" Shelia asked.

"Mostly you two."

Kel placed the picture back on the shelf and turned toward him. "What else, Daddy? You said 'mostly.' What else do you talk about?"

He turned his eyes to the floor.

"Judging from that pained look a moment ago, there's something else." Kel paused and smiled. "It's okay, Daddy. We're big girls. We can take it."

"Well, it's not that I'm depressed or morose. I know you won't get this, but I'm okay with it. So I talk to your mom about what it's like ... afterwards. You know."

Kel's tone turned serious. "After death. Of course that's got to be on your mind. But there's more; I sense it. Something in the living is eating you."

He turned to look each of his daughters in the eye. "Six months isn't enough time to say all the goodbyes, give all the hugs, and put everything right. I have a death sentence, and I'm okay with it now. I've had a good life—not as long as I would've liked, mind you—but I promised your mother I'd keep an eye on you and hopefully keep you out of trouble." He looked Kel in the eye, raised his eyebrows, and winked. "Not that you've made that easy."

Everyone laughed, and Dirk absorbed the airy lightness it offered for the moment. He didn't want his final days to be shrouded with grief. The family's reprieve had been short after Clarissa's death when, three months ago, the doctor had given him a six-month life expectancy.

Kel walked across the room and took her mom's matching leather armchair next to Dirk. She reached for his hand.

"The truth is," he continued, "I miss your mom every day. God knows I tried to move on, but I just can't do it. So, on the plus side …" His cop instinct surfaced as he slipped into making a list like the pros and cons of a suspect. "Being terminal means I know the loneliness of missing my best friend will soon be over. But on the other hand, knowing the day doesn't mean you stop thinking about the others you love or wondering if your life had purpose."

"You have purpose, Dad," Shelia said, "and right now the important thing is that you know people care. Look at what the mayor's done to show appreciation."

A month ago, no longer able to give full vigor to the office, Dirk gave in to the pancreatic cancer ravaging his body and stepped down as Police Chief. The mayor held him in such high regard, he had declared Dirk the Grand Marshall in the Torchlight Parade, Seattle's annual celebration of the return of summer, on the following Friday.

"I know, but there are regrets. Things your mother and I worked through. But …" He turned his eyes back to the floor. "Dying with the knowledge that someday these things may come to light is an unbearable weight. I can't go in peace wondering if someday you'll return to my grave for the last time and ask, 'Who was this man, anyway?'"

Shelia leaned forward and slipped her arm around his shoulder. "Dad, as scary and as utterly absurd as that sounds, we all have secrets."

"I know, angel," Dirk said and met her gaze. "But every day they seem to invade my present more and more. I so fear you'll be hurt. It's keeping me awake these days."

"I understand, Dad," Shelia said. "Kel?"

"Got it, but unless you want to open the confessional now, how 'bout we keep the lid on Pandora's Box for another week? Maybe longer. Then"—she crinkled the corners of her mouth and winked—"when you're ready, you can tell us where the bodies are buried, okay?"

Dirk shook his head at the daughter who always tried to joke her way through even the heaviest matters. His years and position had given him insight into human nature. He knew Kel's sarcastic wit put off an "I don't take myself too seriously" attitude. But he feared it was really defensive posturing to camouflage her secret torments.

"This week, though," she continued, "as the mayor declared, it's 'Dirk Nyte Week,' and Friday you're the guest of honor. Can you live with that?"

"Probably, but I still worry that when the day comes—"

"Don't even say it, Daddy. One thing you and Mom always taught us, despite the seriousness of our actions or the embarrassment we caused the family, forgiveness always followed. Consequences, yes— but always forgiveness. Whatever's haunting you, when you're ready for the exorcist, we'll be here, and we'll still love you. Don't lose another minute's sleep over it."

"Mom," Chrissie interrupted, her subtle contempt indicated an urgency only known to fourteen-year-old girls.

Seeing his only granddaughter, a smile returned to Dirk's face. "There's my sweet cherry pie, and where's that Danny boy?"

"He thinks it's time for birthday cake, but I got him busy watching Steamboat Willie again," she said and cocked her reddish-blond eyebrows, "for the first time."

"Ah, yes. Mickey Mouse. One of our favorites."

"What is it, Chrissie?" Kel asked, and shot a grin toward her daughter.

Chrissie, with her jet black hair tucked behind her ears, held up a newspaper and pointed to a front page headline. "You're in the paper."

Chapter Twelve

"THE NEWS SAID you were an off-duty officer who happened on Suzanne Lowen's crime scene," Dirk said. "But there's more to it, isn't there? Why were you there?"

"This can't leave the room," Kel said, and caught Chrissie's eye. "This wasn't released to the press yet, so it's important."

Chrissie sat on a leather hassock in front of Dirk and nodded in agreement.

Kel pulled her cellular from its belt holster and searched her messages. She stood. "I got a text, a poem, on my phone last night. The first part seems like a blathering rant and is hard to make sense of, but the last four lines seem pretty clear."

"Read it all," Dirk said.

She read.

"DK: Hear the wail from the cage
Lifting its clamor in a rage
From the grave forever sealed
Secret things will be revealed
Witnesses their stories tell
Mine to teach the lesson well
Recompense is yours to pay
Mine to reap for Hell each day."

When she finished, except for the distinguishable falsetto of Mickey Mouse's voice drifting in from the television in the living room and the innocent laughter of a four-year-old, the study was silent.

After a few moments, Dirk spoke. "May I see that?"

He read it again to himself. "Rant or not, this is a manifesto. The first couple of lines give clues to his identity. A cage could mean many things. It might be literal, like a prison cell, or perhaps something intangible—a psychological cage. Whatever it is, he's angered by it. 'Clamor in rage' seems to indicate the cage is unfair. The grave is interesting, but I can't tell from this if the secret it holds is from the past or future. Whatever it is, it's the key to his main purpose—to teach someone a lesson—and obviously, he's going to keep killing until his target learns it."

"He wants me to pursue him. He made that clear while he pinned me to the floor."

"Mom?" Chrissie shouted. She jumped up from the hassock and threw her arms around Kel's waist. "Are you okay?"

"I'm fine, sweetie," she said and stroked Chrissie's hair. "He just wanted my attention."

"I can pull some strings," Dirk said, "and get you assigned to Captain Silva."

"No need. Chief Ballesteros already saw to it."

"Really? Fill me in."

"Not much to tell. I convinced Chief Ballesteros and Lou Martinez that since DK choose to communicate through me, I should be part of the investigation."

"And they agreed?"

"Martinez not so much, but the chief seemed convinced. Anyway, they put me on a short leash—two days."

"That's not much time."

"No, but Martinez has a theory," she said, and sat in her mother's chair again. "Your name has been thrown into the suspect pool."

"Pops?" Chrissie asked, and looked toward Dirk. "They think you killed that woman?"

"I'm not surprised," Dirk said. "If there's a chance Lou can smear my name, he'll take it without blinking twice."

"Why, Dad?" Shelia asked.

"I'm not going there, Angel. Maybe someday, but not now. You were saying, Princess?"

"His motive's as weak as you've been lately, Daddy. Just because Suzanne did her job with your Exterminator case doesn't turn you into a murderer."

"Vince Buckley's guilty," Dirk said. "He may have gotten released from prison, but it's where he belongs."

"Careful, Dad," Shelia cut in. "The court freed him. Besides, he works at my firm."

"Neither of which makes him innocent. He slaughtered nineteen women before we nailed him in ninety-two. How many victims have there been since I locked him up? None. Taking him off the street stopped the slaughter."

"Dad, I know how you feel, but to make accusations with nothing to back them is no different than what got him kicked a few months ago. I don't mean to be cruel, but he's free today because the only physical evidence you produced is the same evidence that overturned his conviction."

"What was that?" Chrissie asked.

"The Rat City Exterminator," Dirk said to his granddaughter, "whether it was Buckley or not, was ruthless. The victims were prosti ..." He stopped short and shot a glance between Chrissie and Kel.

"Pops, I know what a hooker is."

Dirk looked back at her, sighed, and shook his head.

"Well, after he finished with the ... hooker business, he took each of the victims to an alley near where he had picked them up. Ligature marks on the victims' necks pointed to strangulation, but we never found the garrote. But from the smoke in their lungs, we determined that once they lost consciousness, he poured gas on them and then lit them on fire."

"They were still alive?" Chrissie asked.

"I told you he was ruthless. At one of the scenes, we found a cigarette underneath the girl. It was the same brand found in the ashtray of Buckley's truck. Our theory had been that he used a lit cigarette to ignite the gasoline. If that was true, in all but one case the cigarettes were completely consumed in the fire. But in this one, it appeared she rolled on top of the cigarette and smothered whatever flames might have burned it up."

"So, Chrissie," Kel interjected, "the woman who was murdered this morning was ordered by the court on a motion from Buckley's court-appointed attorney to retest the butt. She found that the only DNA came from the victim herself. She had smoked the cigarette."

"It didn't prove Buckley's innocence," Dirk added, as if defending his own actions. "He could have offered the girl a smoke before he killed her. But that was enough to convince the judge that there was reasonable doubt, and rather than declare a new trial, he threw the case out. After serving a decade and a half, he just walked right out of prison. Tainted evidence!"

While Chrissie returned to the hassock, Kel laid her hand on Dirk's arm.

"That was The Seattle Globe's headline," he continued. "Suzanne's report never used those words, but once the story broke, the public never heard anything else. There was nothing manufactured about the evidence, but the Globe editor used the column to launch an attack on me. He fixated on how a detective on a slow rise through the ranks was suddenly lifted on the wings of the Exterminator's conviction, ultimately becoming police chief, and how Suzanne's report threatened to undermine my credibility."

"But the district attorney exonerated you, Dad," Shelia said. "Martinez's theory doesn't make sense. If you were going to kill Suzanne, why now and not then?"

"I didn't kill her, but if this is Buckley's work, it wasn't because she set him free."

"Why then, Pops? Why would he murder her when she got him out?"

"Because her testimony put him away in the first place."

Chapter Thirteen

DK HAD TURNED east off Interstate 5. His commander, the sterile voice of a GPS tracking device, guided him to the country road he now drove along. As if he willed it, the moon had taken cover behind a heavy blanket of clouds which left the landscape cloaked in darkness. As he passed through a rural neighborhood, an occasional stake-mounted mailbox and random security light gave evidence of the sparse population. That suited his purpose—the fewer prying eyes, the better the likelihood of success.

After another three quarters of a mile, he drove under a covering of tall fir trees. Just as the voice intoned, "Turn right in fifty feet on Balados Road," his headlights caught a green street marker. He made the turn, and as he pressed the accelerator to the floor, his eyes drifted toward the dashboard clock's amber digital display. It recorded 2:37.

Before the voice announced his arrival, a hundred feet ahead on the right he saw what had to be his destination. Like a beacon to an approaching airplane, three red reflectors attached to a post caught his high beams.

"Destination on your right," the simulated female voice commanded.

DK responded by steering his Acura to the edge of the road. He read the numbers on the mailbox that were caught in his headlamps, and confirmed that this was his target. He powered down the GPS and drove ahead until he found the wide spot he had scouted last week. He looked into the distance—both to the front and in the rearview mirror. His nerves settled a degree when he saw no headlights in either direction. He made a U-turn, switched his headlamps off, and pulled his car under an evergreen tree.

A shoulder bag with everything he needed lay on the passenger seat. He grabbed the strap, eased the driver's door open, and stepped out onto the soil dampened by an earlier Pacific Northwest rain shower. With a nudge of his hip, the door clicked shut. He glanced up and down the road again for signs of life. When none appeared, he threw the bag's strap over his shoulder and started the seventy-five-yard jog back to the mailbox.

Distant gunfire and exploding mines had been familiar companions on his last night mission. It had been hotter then—much hotter than this cool night—and rather than fir trees, the surrounding flora had been jungle.

As each second passed, the blue glow on the horizon grew brighter. Even though darkness still prevailed, Lone Wolf knew that in moments Charlie, on the other side of the clearing, would swarm like the Biblical plague of locusts from their cover. Despite the human costs, they wouldn't relent until every GI was dead.

"Hell, you're a long ways over here," O'Leary said as he rolled in behind the Khasi pine where Wolf had made cover for the last twenty-five minutes. "Nearly got my ass shot off."

"Why'd you bother?" Wolf asked with a shout over the sound of bullets tearing into the trunk providing them cover. "We're all dead, anyway."

Wolf looked around the left side of the tree, took aim at an automatic muzzle flash, and pulled off one round. To his satisfaction, the rifle on the other side of the clearing went silent.

"Sarge ordered the Scorpion. One klick," O'Leary said, and pointed to the rear of their position. "I've got to get back to Lefty. He took a hit to the gut and can't get out without help."

"Scorpion, huh?" Wolf dared to hope he might yet get out of this one alive. But to see his wife and son again was more than hope could afford. "You stay here. I'll get Lefty. We'll see you at the LZ."

Wolf rolled to his back and exposed a shoulder wound caked with blood and dirt.

"You're hit."

"It's just a damn nick. I still got one good shoulder for Lefty."

"You hold here. I've got him," O'Leary said and, before Wolf could object, rolled to his stomach and crawled away to the right under the jungle vegetation.

Wolf drew to his knees and rested his body snug against the tree trunk in preparation to run on the signal. He kept his eyes on O'Leary. The gloom of dawn's slow approach hadn't yet covered him when he crawled through a clearing. His body jerked and then went limp. Damn it, he thought. So close to surviving this massacre. Must have been caught in a night-vision scope. With no fear, Wolf slung his M-16 over his back and, as fast as his limbs carried him, even with the wounded shoulder, low-crawled to O'Leary's side. On his stomach beside the downed man, he listened for breath. None came.

Logic said he should go back to the relative safety behind the tree trunk until the signal, but he couldn't rely on logic alone. The gunfire had stopped on his side of the field, and he knew that in just moments the enemy should ceasefire, too, thinking the Americans either dead or retreated.

He couldn't wait for the lead to stop flying, though. Not knowing how far away Lefty lay wounded, he stooped low and ran into the thicket. In the relative darkness, he thought himself invisible, but after he took a half a dozen steps, like he had been hit in the side with an anti-tank rocket, he fell hard. Consciousness dissolved.

Now, as DK crossed the distance in a crouched trot, he welcomed the throb in his chest pounding harder with each step and the dry, gritty taste on his tongue. He had not only lived through that operation but the years of isolation following it. And now he had a lesson to teach One that will outlive us all.

His ears, alert to any sound disrupting the silence, picked up the frantic yelp of a pack of coyotes in an adjacent field as they closed in on a kill. They'll be busy feeding for a while. He pressed on and found the opening to the driveway.

Paved with gravel, it headed off the road through a stand of trees. He stepped to the side of the rock bed to silence his footsteps on the moist, weed-choked earth, careful not to alert his target.

Fifty feet from the road, a clearing opened before him. A dim porch light marked the front door of a double-wide manufactured home another hundred feet away, and gave off enough light to expose the silhouette of his objective. At the edge of the lawn next to the tree line, the black Kenworth tractor stood stalwart.

He moved to the driver's side of the rig, the side facing away from the home. Stooped behind it, he ran his hand along the cool steel until he passed the cab. He dropped to his knees and felt along the chassis until his hand bumped into the one hundred-and-twenty-gallon diesel fuel tank in front of the rear tires.

As he slid underneath the truck, the ground felt cool to his back, and although the moisture from the grass seeped through his windbreaker, he didn't shiver. His mission took precedence. He sat the bag next to him and reached into the outside pocket for a flashlight.

With the switch flipped on, he clamped the light between his teeth and began his inspection. Before he finished, nothing more than blades of grass parting under a gentle force caused him to freeze. He turned his ears back to the night sounds. The coyotes had gone silent. If one tore into his flesh, his blood scent would draw the others, and his entire operation, not just tonight's mission, would fail. Fear of pain or death, however, was an emotion he had long ago expelled from his mind. His plan was on a tight clock and could not be scuttled by something so tangential.

From the opposite side of the rig, a low growl rolled across the lawn. He doused the flashlight and twisted his head to look behind him toward the house. The porch light revealed the shadowed figure of a single four-legged beast creeping up on him, near the other side of the truck.

In a silent but swift movement, he slipped his hand into the satchel and searched by feel until he located a sealed baggie. He unzipped the top, removed a T-bone steak, and tossed it to the rear of the truck near the animal. Then, he lay still and waited.

When the creature's jaw chomped into the meat, he switched the flashlight back on and pointed the beam in the direction of the sound. Relieved, he found a black and white Border-Collie. The dog turned its head toward the source of the light but, more interested in the unexpected meal than alarmed by the intruder, it lay down and continued to gnaw.

Chapter Fourteen

THE BEDSIDE CLOCK buzzed at 3:02 a.m. on Tuesday morning, and Kel rolled toward it.

While she had studied psychology at the University of Washington sixteen years earlier, one night without sleep was exhausting. Now she felt like she had pulled two back-to-back all-nighters cramming for college midterms. Her mind threatened to congeal into a gelatinous pool of incoherence. Five hours just won't do.

She opened her eyes, and a smile crept onto her dimpled cheeks. From the street lamp's shaft of light streaming through a gap in her mini-blinds, Saul, Chrissie's Rottweiler, laid snout to nose inches away.

Over her ardent objections, Kel had sent Chrissie to spend the night with Shelia. Since Kel believed she had unwittingly become the epicenter of DK's plot, she felt Chrissie safer with family. If DK did act on his "each day" threat, she wouldn't have to leave her daughter at home alone again as she did last night.

Saul snorted.

Kel reached to slap the snooze button on the clock and then realized the annoyance had come from her SPD smartphone vibrating against the white-birch nightstand.

"Okay, let's see who it is, Saul," she said, and brushed a cascade of thick brunette hair from her face. She glanced at the phone's display, engaged the call, and then thrust the fingers and thumb of her free hand into her swollen eyes.

"This better be good." She flopped to her back and stared toward the ceiling.

"Better than good."

She recognized the voice of the fresh-from-college lab tech. "Why are you calling at this God-awful hour, Bimal?"

"It wasn't God-awful when you called me about this time last night."

"Touché," she said, raised her torso to one elbow, and yawned. "So, what's up?"

"You remember the phone number you gave me last night?"

"Yeah, it's a burner. We've been over that."

"You asked me to track the shipment."

"I asked you to track the payment."

"Right," Bimal said, and paused. "Okay, we spoke to the manufacturer today. They said the payment arrived by mail in a money order."

"So another dead end?"

"Yeah, but we can track the pings. Your text buddy didn't just buy one disposable phone. He bought four."

"Four?" she shouted and sat up on the edge of the king-sized bed. "Could he really be serial?"

"Possibly, but I have great news. I just found an email from the manufacturer's warehouse as a result of our query, and I have the subscriber identity module num—"

"Subscriber what?" She shook her head and stroked Saul under his chin.

"The SIM card numbers. I know the four phone numbers. I'm about to put a trace on the other three."

"Has there been any activity on the first one?"

"Not since after we talked last, but—"

"You mean not since you almost got me killed."

"Yeah, well, I'm real sorry about that. Anyway, with this new data I can follow his movements and maybe get a step ahead of him."

"But only when the phone is on, right?"

"Yeah, but with a trace on the phones, the moment any one hits the BTS—"

"Hey, stop showing off. I may still be sleepy, but I do carry a gun and know where you are right now."

"Point taken. Enough techno speak. BTS. Base transceiver station. You'd know it better as a cell tower or cell site."

"See, that wasn't so hard. So what you're saying is that when the cellular is turned on, it'll ping a cell site, and then you'll have a location. What's the range?"

"That's the tricky part. It depends on a lot of factors. It could be anywhere from a quarter mile to fifty miles. Quarter mile if the phone is downtown, fifty miles if it's out in some—"

"Got it. Density and terrain. So, is anything pinging?"

"I just got the SIM's, and I'm setting up the tracking as we speak, so how 'bout I keep you informed?"

"Do that, Bimal, but I need more than pings on towers. I need activity. I need to know what numbers he's calling and texting."

"That means a warrant."

"Of course, do it legally. Whose side you on, anyway?"

"Yours, Detective. You said before that I'm on the clock, so let's do it right. Don't leave him a crack to slip through."

Kel knew he was right, but it meant she might have to play nice with someone she had possibly burned a bridge with twelve hours before.

"Did you check out that address?" Bimal asked.

Kel paused for a moment, working through what he meant by "that address." Exhaustion had already taken its toll, and she had just started the investigation. She looked to Saul for inspiration, but with his head still resting on the edge of the bed, his sleepy eyes gave nothing away. She stroked his snout.

"Ah, you mean the Roxbury address where the phones where shipped? I dropped by yesterday after I left you and spoke to the neighboring shop owners. No one remembers a delivery truck on that day or anyone snooping about the deserted shop. It wouldn't take much for DK to see that the store had been closed for a while. There's another thing I want to check out about that address."

"What's that? Can I help?"

"Let's just call it a hunch. I'll let you know if it leads somewhere. You keep working on the phones."

She disengaged the call, placed the phone back on the nightstand, and switched on the table lamp. On her back, she stared at Saul. He now sat on his haunches panting. He wasn't just a dog or even a welcomed companion. Like a war memorial, he represented a connection to the past—her past. She patted the edge of her lonely bed and he moved next to it. Her hand felt at home as she stroked the curvatures of his head, and she turned her attention to the oscillating ceiling fan.

The townhome had been stuffy when she arrived home last night, so she had opened the upstairs windows for ventilation, despite the patter of rain on the porch roof below. Before hitting the bed, she had switched on the fan. Now, the click of the gold pull chain tapped a constant rhythm on the clear bell-shaped glass shade, and the breaths of warm air wafting over her body drew her thoughts back in time.

It had been too long since she had felt Lance's breath on her neck. She took her personal cell phone from the lamp table. The closest she could come to him now was the digital photo she used as the background for her phone. Taken the morning he boarded that 747 to fly to the Middle East, he sat in the kitchen in his army uniform and looked up from a bowl of dry cereal like it was any other day.

She flipped to the photo gallery app. Until the day he went missing, there were few days he didn't text or email. Often he sent photos, and without realizing their significance, she stored every one—another connection. As she scrolled through them now, she paused as each image resolved on the screen. The painful fusion of desire and dread she suffered each day weighted her heart until, with Saul's head still in her hand, it ruptured and tears flowed.

Kel met Lance Thorson at a fraternity party at the end of her junior year at the University of Washington. He had joined the U.S. Army and served a tour of duty which included a role in the ground force that freed Kuwait in the first Gulf War, so Lance was four years ahead of Kel in age, but just one year ahead of her in college. After he graduated, he started a career in the field of business intelligence while Kel finished her BA in psychology. A brief courtship found them in love. They moved in together then, and before two years had passed, Chrissie came along. Life for Kel had felt perfect.

A few months after Chrissie's fifth birthday, the World Trade Center towers fell. The recession that followed cost Lance his job in the spring of 2002. He had been among the many patriots who felt that after freeing Kuwait in 1991, the coalition forces should have turned north and marched on Iraq. So, despite his young family, just after their trip to Disneyland, he reenlisted in the Army and within months, headed for his first mission to the Middle East.

Saul jerked his head away from Kel's hand and turned toward the nightstand. The phone vibrated again. "Easy, boy," she said, and swallowed her tears. She reached for the phone.

Kel scrolled to the text icon on the screen, but before she punched it, a phone call came in. She pressed the "answer" button on the touch screen.

"Got a ping. Well, two pings," Bimal said, and was so excited that he gasped for air like he had just finished running a hundred-yard dash.

"One was to me, right? I just got a text."

"One is the phone he texted you from last night, but the other is from one of the other phones."

"Where are they?"

"One is pinging a tower north of Bellingham, near Lynden."

"Lynden? That's a couple hours north of here, near the Canadian border."

"Right. The first one's still pinging, but the one he's been using to communicate with you came in just a couple minutes ago."

"Just long enough to send me another text."

"Right. What does it say?"

Kel scrolled to the message and read it aloud. "'Boom.'"

Chapter Fifteen

"I'VE GOT TO go," Kel said. She rose from the bed and swung her legs over the edge.

Saul, at the word "go," trotted to the doorway and then looked back.

"Not you, Saul," she said. "Come here, boy."

Saul hesitated and looked from her to the hallway. When Kel dropped to her knees with her arms outstretched, he made his way to her.

"That's a good boy." She put her arms around him and stroked his short black coat. "We both have our jobs to do. You keep the house safe, and I make the streets safe."

Saul whined.

"I know you want to go, but not this time, okay?"

As if he realized this was an argument he wasn't going to win, Saul lay on the floor next to her.

"Good boy. Now I've got to get dressed."

With the belief that DK might strike at any minute, she had tossed the clothes she had worn to Danny's birthday party across the back of her grandmother's antique wooden rocker. Now, she slipped into the black jeans and white tee she had almost worn on her first day as detective. Five minutes later—after settling Saul and binding her hair in a ponytail—she had strapped her Glock to her waist and then backed her silver metallic Jeep Liberty out of the garage.

As she made her way over the residential street lined with vacant vehicles awaiting the morning light to rise and engage the commute, her headlights illumined the trees in adjacent yards. The shifting shadows on both sides crept like silent ninja warriors silhouetted against the facades of the house fronts. The still gloom brought with it the inky foreboding that she had felt last night before she discovered Suzanne's body. It sank into her bones like a damp chill, yet forced her to move toward the event to which she had become unwillingly conscripted.

The aroma of fresh drip coffee drifted into Terry Graham's bedroom and nudged him from sleep like the gentle caress of a woman snuggled to his back. He rose and disregarded the sweatpants in a heap on the floor by the edge of the bed. His sixty-two-year-old belly bulge rode over the waistband of his boxers just enough to be noticed. Many years ago he had kept himself in top shape. Over the last decade, though, he didn't think he had let himself go, but the treadmill in the bedroom had not been plugged into the wall for at least the last seven years.

His bare feet slapped the vinyl floor on the way to the kitchen. "Smoky?" he called as he reached for a cup. After he filled a mug with the steaming brew and a bowl with dry cereal, he slipped a cigarette behind his ear and stepped onto the cedar-planked front porch. It needed a pressure wash. He shook his head. Maybe next spring.

The sun had not yet made an appearance and the air was cool on his bare skin. He let the shiver ride up his back and sat on the porch step. Before resting the coffee next to him, he took a swallow.

"Smoky, where are you, boy? Chasin' rabbits? Come here, boy."

Terry spooned a bite of cereal into his mouth and scanned the front yard, looking for signs of movement. There were none.

Over the last decade, Terry had exiled himself to the obscurity of a small town and the hard life of an independent short haul trucker. His only consistent companion had been his Border Collie, Smoky. Raised from a pup on his spread, with few fences to dampen his spirit, he knew the freedom of exploration and thrived on a brisk romp through the fields looking for sport. He also knew Terry's voice and never failed to respond.

The cereal finished, Terry lit the cigarette, picked up the mug, and walked toward his rig. His eyes scanned the yard for his companion. Worried because of the coyotes in the area, he did not feel the wet grass slide in and out between his toes. As he approached the tractor, he saw Smoky lying on the ground under the truck, just inside the rear tires.

"Hey, boy," he said as he stooped. He placed his right hand on the dog's long black and white coat. "You okay?"

Smoky lifted his head and whined, and then dropped it back to the ground again.

"Come here, boy. Let's go into the house."

Terry tossed the rest of the coffee out of the cup, slid his arms under the dog, and carried him to the kitchen. Sprawled on the floor, he ran his hands over Smoky's coat to see if he had been injured in a fight. When his fingers found nothing obvious, he poured fresh water into his dish and then placed it next to him.

"Here, boy. Drink."

Smoky looked at Terry again and then rolled to his belly. He dropped his face into the bowl and began to lap at the water like he was parched.

"I think you'll stay in today, buddy, but Daddy's got to go to work."

Smoky looked up from the bowl and whined.

"Be a good boy. Don't fuss. You rest today, and tomorrow we'll go to work together."

Smoky cocked his head, as if he understood but still had a question.

"No arguments, okay? While I get ready for work, you eat your breakfast, and if you do that, I'll give you a treat before I head out."

More than an hour passed as Kel travelled northbound on Interstate 5. She turned her eyes to the east of the highway. Minutes before, Arlington had passed by, and now the valley floor rose toward Whitehorse Mountain. Across the sky, she saw that the sun, not yet above the horizon, had painted the scattered clouds with the striking hues of a school of koi.

Her phone rang, and she pulled her attention back to the road ahead. She lifted her hand to the Bluetooth device in her ear and engaged the call.

"Nyte."

"Bimal here. About five minutes ago my tracker showed that we have movement."

"What direction?"

"It's heading west. No, wait," he said and paused. "It just hit another tower. Looks like it's heading south now."

"Can you ID the tower enough to know what road it's on?"

"Of course. It's on State Highway 539. If it keeps heading in that direction, in a few minutes it'll be in Bellingham. It should be easier to pin an actual location there."

"Keep tracking. I'm still an hour out. Let me know if the other phone goes live."

"Refill?" The high school-aged girl with a half dozen silver studs piercing the helix of each ear slid a breakfast platter in front of DK. She hovered over his mug with a glass carafe.

Her interruption pulled his thoughts back to the clatter of silverware on ceramic plates and the low conversational din of the nondescript twenty-four-hour café. He sucked in the fragrance of bacon-fried crisp, smiled, and nodded toward the cup.

"Sun'll be peeking through that window in a few minutes," she said when she finished pouring. "Want me to close the blinds?"

"No thanks, dear. I'm enjoying the view."

"Looks like it's going to be a nice day."

"Yep, a real scorcher."

As she turned back to the kitchen, the throb of a powerful diesel engine drifted into his left ear. He lifted his eyes to the window. The black Kenworth passed by.

Another twenty-five minutes passed, and Kel's phone rang again.

"It stopped moving just north of Bellingham," Bimal said. "The signal hasn't changed in over ten minutes. I gave it a few before calling, to make sure it wasn't just a traffic signal or bagel stop, but it's been still now for a while."

"Is he still on five-three-nine?"

"Or somewhere real close."

"Have any of the perp's other phones powered on?"

"No, all's quiet there."

"Keep an eye on it. I'm still a ways out, but there's no traffic, so I'm making good time. And Bimal?"

"Yes, ma'am?"

"You're doing good work today, but I need you to do one more thing."

Chapter Sixteen

DK KNEW THE truck driver's routine. He had cased him for several days and was a patient man. A damn cage will teach you the meaning of "wait for it."

Wolf never felt the bullet enter his body. When he regained consciousness, his gut felt like someone had dug into it with a dull pocket knife and used splintery chopsticks to extract a foreign object. The last thing he remembered, O'Leary told him Sarge had ordered a retreat. As he was lying on his stomach, he knew it could only have been seconds since he had been hit.

He listened for battle sounds and found it quiet. Not even a bird dared peep. The lull before the storm—a storm Charlie couldn't survive. Since the shooting had stopped, he pictured, along their line, that what remained of his squad was waiting for the Vietcong to creep from their cover to investigate. O'Leary was dead, and he needed to get to Lefty to help him to the chopper. One klick.

If Wolf had a buddy in this godforsaken place, it was Lefty. He was due to rotate home in two weeks. Can't let that goddamn short-timer die out here.

He opened his eyes and tried to blink away the delirium that closed in like a sudden dense fog. Yet, even though darkness surrounded him, he was hot. The last he remembered, it was just the break of day, the cool before the dawn, and he realized that the sweltering jungle hadn't caused the sensation. The burning radiated from inside his body. This disorientation blurred his vision further, and he was unable to bring his surroundings into focus.

Yet he knew Lefty couldn't be far away. He had to stand. As he struggled to his hands and knees, something above him arrested his movement. Whether a tree limb, extending just above the ground, pressed against his back, or the hand of God held him in place, he couldn't tell. He paused. That simple movement took every ounce of strength from his reserve. He gasped for air and the burning retch in his stomach felt like a witch's caldron filled with a boiling, acrid brew. He couldn't move forward. His eyes slid closed and he tried to gather his essence. Lefty waited not far away and he needed to save him. But with his mind swirling on the verge of catalepsy, he came to a new realization. He, too, needed to be rescued. Someone'll come for me.

An overpowering urge to lie back down swept through him, like the torrent of a swollen river. He eased to his right side and reached to his belly to find comfort for the unrelenting fire tormenting him. He expected to find his olive green blouse soaked with blood. Rather, he discovered his shirt missing. The cloth wrapped around him felt like soiled rags from a kitchen spill. It was stiff and crusted with something dried. Blood? My blood!

"Nurse," he yelled, thinking he was in a MASH unit, "my dressing needs changed."

"There's no nurse here."

The shock of the unfamiliar voice from somewhere behind him disoriented him further. Another wounded soldier in the next bed? He began a painful roll in the direction of the voice and found that his back, again, encountered restriction. When he reached with his left hand to free himself from the constraint, it fell on a piece of steel pipe. Panic set in, and he grabbed the vertical bar. It had the rough surface and narrow diameter of rebar. He shook it. When it didn't budge, he slid his hand a few inches and confirmed another pipe, and another, and another.

He rolled back to his side and extended his arm in every direction. A cage! He stretched his legs only inches and, with sudden clarity, knew that the only way he'd fit in his new home was to stay in a fetal position. He was a long way from a medic unit.

The voice behind him groaned again. "You'll just find gooks here, GI."

Always punctual—the atomic clock is probably set to his comings and goings. That served DK, a man of order and control, well. With that knowledge, he didn't need to sit and observe. He could have pulled the trigger from his lounge chair while he watched the morning news. But this was too big and too personal to view in reruns on television or read about in the newspaper. He needed to see it firsthand.

He waved to the server, who was chatting with a customer at the counter. When she approached, he said, "Dear, I'm ready for my bill, and I'll take the rest of the coffee to go."

As he waited for her return, he checked his watch again. Time is running short for witness two.

Chapter Seventeen

KEL PASSED THROUGH Bellingham and from the freeway exit took a right on State Highway 539. She headed northbound and dialed the crime lab.

"Where are the locals?" she asked as soon as Bimal picked up the call.

"I couldn't tell them exactly where to go, and besides, they weren't inclined to go anywhere on my word."

"Has the signal moved yet?"

"No."

"Am I close?"

"You're pinging off the same tower. What do you see?"

"Just normal stuff," she said as she scanned the buildings on either side of the highway. "When did I hit this tower?

"Just a few seconds ago. Maybe I should call the number. Then I could triangulate and get an exact position."

"But only if he answers, and then he'll know we're onto him."

"Good point."

"I'll keep driving north. You tell me when I hit another tower."

"That's good. Then we'll have an idea of its north and south boundaries."

"Wait," she said, and paused. "I may have some—"

"Kel? The other phone just powered up."

DK checked the digital clock on the dashboard as he drove south on Highway 539. It was time. He found the speed dial button on the keyboard and paused while his soul fed on the rush of retribution. It cascaded over the spillway.

Chapter Eighteen

WITH BIMAL STILL on the line, Kel pulled across the street from a petroleum distribution terminal. Behind the twelve-foot chain link fence, with a coil of barbed wire running along the top, she saw numerous cylindrical storage tanks. Parked in front of one of them, fifty yards behind the galvanized barrier, stood a black truck connected to two chrome tanker trailers. The sun reflected shafts of light off the containers, and a man crouched on top of the rear trailer. His hand rested on a large hose that disappeared into an opening.

She turned off the engine, stepped from her car, and waited by the hood for the last car on the four-lane to pass. A security shack stood outside of the gate, several dozen yards off the highway. A guard seated inside glanced through the open door in her direction. He appeared to be a young man in his late teens or early twenties.

As he stood, behind him the gates of Hell burst wide open.

The powerful blowback from the blast pushed Kel backward over the hood of her SUV. She landed face down in the dirt on the passenger side. Kel pushed herself up to her elbows. Disoriented, she shook her head from side to side until her hearing returned and her head cleared.

She scrabbled to her feet and crouched behind the front fender. On the other side of the highway the flames and black smoke belched upward and outward. It reminded her of everything she had imagined as an adolescent girl when her priest preached about the follies of sin and Hell's fire and brimstone. Engulfed behind an orange and black wall, she couldn't see to the center of the firestorm where the truck had stood, but it was obvious that the tanker had burst. Like molten lava racing in multiple tributaries down the sides of a volcano, flames spread across the concrete yard. They consumed everything in their path.

Seconds ago, a guard shack had stood twenty-five yards from the highway. The flames now had overtaken the structure. Their greedy orange fingers wrapped around it to feed its ravenous appetite.

Out of that inferno, like a scene from a horror movie, the guard ran into the sea of flames. His clothes aflame, a wretched scream escaped from within the staggering blaze, followed by a shriek that could only be emitted by someone realizing the futility of their struggle. It wasn't a cry for help but a plea for mercy. The guard fell, and the fire feasted on his flesh.

Terror wrapped icy tentacles around her chest. She realized that if she hadn't waited for the car on the highway to pass a few seconds earlier, she'd have walked into the direct path of the firestorm. And Chrissie might now be an orphan. She had sworn to protect, but now felt her utter uselessness as she watched from behind the Liberty's fender. Her heart ached with regret for the souls she couldn't save. What kind of maniacal rage could cause someone to do this to innocent people?

She remembered Bimal and reached to her ear for the Bluetooth. It was gone. She made a quick search on the ground around her and found it in pieces a few feet away. Kel grabbed the phone from her belt and disengaged the wireless connection. Bimal's familiar Hindi accent entered her ear.

"What the hell's going on, Kel?" Even over the roar of the flames, the hysteria was evident in his voice. "Are you alright? What's happening?"

"Call every emergency agency in Bellingham," she shouted, "and send them to my location. Armageddon just happened. Do it now!"

As she finished, she felt the telling vibration of another text message and remembered the last one—Boom.

DK pulled to a stop in the middle of the highway behind several morning commuters. He had seen the effects of napalm dropped on an enemy, but what he witnessed now as the plant erupted was far worse than the white heat of those attacks. He lit a cigarette and took the final swallow from the cup of coffee he had taken from the diner. Unlike witness two, it was lukewarm.

Chapter Nineteen

"QUITE A SIGHT
     Rain of flames.
     I deliver."

Kel looked up after reading the text and stared aghast at the raging hellhole across the street. The intense heat lashed against her face like a whip of flame.

Does he know I'm here? Is he tracking me?

"Kel, Kel," Bimal's voice exploded through the speaker phone.

"I thought you were getting help."

"Did that, but he's pinging the same tower as you."

"Is he moving?" She looked up from the phone. In the distance, to the left, she heard the blare of sirens, and saw a pulsating stream of emergency lights snake their way toward the scene.

"Hard to tell."

The phone vibrated again. She tore her eyes away from the devastation. On the screen appeared an address and a curious instruction: "Take care of the mutt."

She lifted her eyes to the southbound lanes. A vehicle was stopped in the center of both lanes. The driver stood on the pavement next to the car's open door. Even with the distance between them, she could see that he was taking pictures with his cell phone. Curious—or collecting trophies, she thought.

Despite the searing heat, she slipped the phone back into its holster, rested her right hand on the butt of her Glock, and ran toward him. She had been unable to save anyone at the plant. If this was a bystander and not DK, maybe she could save his life.

When she was within fifty feet of the man, another blast came from inside the plant. She turned in the direction of the sound. Out of the whirling, snarling firestorm, a flaming missile had launched on an arc toward the highway. She stopped running and glanced toward the man who continued to snap photos. If he didn't move, he might be hit by the small tank, but she was too far away to help him.

"Watch out!" she screamed.

Above the roar of the fire she was certain he didn't hear her call. When he looked up away from the camera, though, the jerk of his body indicated that he had recognized the imminent threat. The tank plummeted to the ground a few feet in front of his car. He dove back into the driver's seat.

On impact, flames, sparks, and shards of steel sprayed out. A large section of the cylinder bounced onto the hood of the car and slammed into the windshield. Without breaking it, the projectile continued on its trajectory and slid over the roof of the Sedan. It fell to the asphalt next to the driver's door and skittered to a stop on the far side of the road.

Anxious, Kel had been prepared to dart any way she needed to avoid the same fate as the man's car. Yet, when none of the fragments flew in her direction, she sprinted again toward the vehicle.

She grabbed the open door and shouted, "Police." She flashed her badge fast enough for him to see it but not long enough to notice she wasn't the Bellingham Police. "Are you alright?"

"Damn it, that thing almost got me."

She reached her right hand again to the Glock. "Please stay in the car. Give me your phone and then place both your hands on the steering wheel."

"Phone? What are you talking about? That thing almost killed me!"

"This was no accident, sir. Please do as I ask."

"You shitting me? You think I did this? I almost pissed myself when that thing hit."

"Your phone, now, and your hands on the wheel."

"Okay, okay—here," he said, and handed it to Kel.

Kel kept her eye on his hands until he placed them at the ten and two position on the steering wheel. She located the call log and scrolled through the last few calls. Her number didn't appear. She retrieved her phone and dialed DK's number.

When the driver's phone didn't ring, Kel gave it back to him. Not convinced that the phone she sought wasn't somewhere silenced in the car, but with nothing on which to hold him, she said, "It's not safe here. Turn around and find another way to your destination."

She stepped back from the door and closed it. The driver shot her a final glare through the windshield and powered his car into a U-turn. As she stepped out of his path, she noticed several cars up the line. Further back, a black Sedan had already turned around and was moving away. She called Bimal.

"What's his location?" she asked as she jogged back toward her car. She stayed as far to the left of the highway, away from the heat, as possible.

"He turned his cell off, but before that, he was stationary."

She turned her head back to glance over her shoulder, and realized that by the time she'd reach her Jeep, she'd have no hope of finding him. "Damn," she said with her teeth clenched together. "He was right here."

Kel looked back to the direction she was running and passed her SUV. Several fire and police vehicles had taken position, and one police cruiser headed toward her. As she reached the Jeep, the officer came to a halt next to her.

"Kel Nyte, Seattle PD," she said through the passenger window and held her shield up. "Badge five-zero-nine."

"You need to get to safety, Officer Nyte."

From the tag on his chest, she saw that his last name was Monroe. As she spoke, she also noticed the chevron on his shirt sleeve. "Just clearing some spectators, Sergeant Monroe."

"And we appreciate your assistance, officer, but you're in danger here."

"Sergeant, you're right, this thing could blow again. I'll move my car and help clear citizens, but this was no accident. This is the perp's second lethal act in the last two days. By the way," she lifted her phone to show him the text display, "will you be able to direct me to this address?"

Chapter Twenty

KEL TURNED INTO the driveway at a few minutes after 8:00 a.m. Parked nose in, a Whatcom County Sheriff's SUV sat idle on the gravel drive. She stopped behind the vehicle and stepped out.

The tan uniform on the young female deputy standing on the front porch of the manufactured home looked like it had just come from the cleaners—heavy on starch. Next to the slim woman, a long-haired black and white Border Collie pranced, his tongue hanging from his mouth.

"Officer Nyte?" asked the woman with a twist of blond hair pinned at the crown of her head.

"Yes," Kel said, her badge clipped to her belt for confirmation. As she walked toward the porch, gray with mildew, the decomposed granite crunched under her boots.

"Deputy Carter," she said. "Sondra, if you please. Why are we here?"

"You heard about the fuel plant?" Kel asked, and took a quick glance around the front yard.

"Yes. How awful. I understand you were there?"

"When it blew. First on scene."

For the second time in so many days she could make that claim. She had been drawn to Suzanne

Lowen's. But this time the suspect couldn't have known she was tracking him—or could he? Yet, as if timed to perfection, she found herself outside the fuel terminal, almost caught in the blast.

"Do you know how many victims?" Sondra asked.

"At least two fatalities. We're at the home of who I suspect was the main target. Who's your friend?"

Kel took the two steps to the covered porch, crouched, and let the dog greet her. Saul's scent must have lingered on her as the collie became excited. He jumped up and lapped at her face.

"Don't know," Sondra said with a stroke of his coat. "Came from around the house when I arrived."

Kel remembered the last text. "Take care of the mutt."

"He looks friendly enough," Kel said. She rose to her full five foot five height. "Do you know who lives here?"

"The property's registered to a Terrance Graham."

"Terrance Graham." Kel repeated the name and rubbed the back of her neck in search of the memory.

"Do you know him?"

"Sounds familiar, but distant. Anyone home?"

"I rang the bell, but the only response was our new friend."

"Let's knock this time." Kel pounded on the front door.

When the dog growled, she crouched again. She wrapped her arms around his neck, and dug her fingers into his coat, giving him a firm rub.

"It's okay. We're here to help," she said, and wondered what would happen to the dog now that his owner was gone.

The collie responded with a bark of approval.

"Good boy," she said and patted his side.

Sondra smiled. "Looks like we both passed the sniff test."

Kel stood and reached for the knob. The door swung open. The collie sauntered inside and then turned as if to welcome the two officers into his home. Kel turned her face to the deputy and gave her a puzzled look.

"People don't lock their doors so much around here."

"I see," Kel said.

The living room opened before her. DK's invitation yesterday—door's open—still resonated. With the Taser burns still a dull sting on her back, and even with the dog being so friendly, she was unprepared to accept the deputy's explanation. She drew her weapon and entered.

"Do you think that's necessary?" Sondra asked. She stepped through the doorway behind Kel.

"Precaution," Kel replied, and scanned the room. "You take the left. I'll take the right." With the memory of DK's hiding place in Suzanne's condo, she added, "Don't forget closets."

"Closets?"

"Long story. Just do it," she said and then realized her tone was sharp, making it sound like an order in a county where she had no jurisdiction. "Please," she added.

Minutes later when they finished clearing the small home, they met in the kitchen. Kel glanced at the counter. Next to the coffee pot, yesterday's newspaper lay with a stack of mail piled on top. She picked up one of the envelopes and read the name: Terry Graham. That brought it back. But there must be hundreds of Terry Grahams. She needed confirmation.

Back in the living room, on a table next to the large plasma television, a picture drew her attention. She lifted the frame and recognized the face of one of the three men holding sockeye salmons by the gills. His features were older, and the hair thinner, than her recollection.

"Witnesses their stories tell." She knew this witness' tale. Her stomach clenched as she placed the picture back on the table and tucked the memory, and the conversation soon to come, away.

"Did you find a computer?" she asked the deputy.

"No, didn't see one. Why?"

"Look, Sondra, I'm on the trail of a murderer. I believe Terry's his second victim. At the first vic's house, he left a message on her computer."

"If Graham had one, it must be a laptop, and he took it with him."

"You okay with your friend there? I'm going to have a look around outside."

"I'll freshen his water. We'll be fine."

Kel nodded and left them. From the porch she noticed the tire tracks of Terry's rig in the grass. She marched over to the depressions. At the rear of the indentations, the remains of a T-bone steak lay on the lawn. The grass next to it was matted as if the collie had lain there. She moved around the tracks and stooped to examine the remnants. Little meat remained on the bone, but from what she could see, canine teeth had ripped and gnawed at it.

She left the bone lie, stood, and surveyed the rest of the area where the truck had been parked. In the middle of the tracks on the driver's side, a much larger depression, about the size of man's torso, matted the damp grass in front of where the other set of rear tires had rested.

"What you got?" Sondra asked. She came up next to Kel with the dog at her heel.

"That bone is evidence, deputy. You should collect it before he has a chance at it again. Could be the perp spiked it to put the dog to sleep."

"Bastard," Sondra said and shook her head. She pulled gloves from her pocket and picked up the bone.

"I think our suspect," Kel continued, pointing to the larger depression in the lawn, "lay over there in the night to place a bomb under Terry's truck. There might be other evidence here, Sondra. You need to get your investigators on the scene."

"I'll make the call now." She turned toward her SUV.

Awakened by Bimal with only five hours sleep, Kel rubbed her tired eyes. Something had been nagging at her about DK's last text. As she watched Sondra and the Border Collie cross the lawn, the annoyance returned. Like trying to focus on eye floaters exposed against the blue afternoon sky, she hadn't been able to get an absolute fix on the object. The closer she got, the further it drifted, never quite lining up.

She pulled her phone from the belt holster and thumbed through the messages. There she found the source of the harassment and read it again.

"Quite a sight
Rain of flames.
I deliver."

She had read the first two lines to mean the massive explosion and interpreted the last to mean that he had delivered on his earlier promise: "Boom." But now the last phrase didn't fit as well. The first two were like lines of the same verse. They had rhyme and rhythm, and their context was obvious. But the last line didn't mesh and, unlike any of his other poems, it was separated by a period. It was more like "door's open" or "boom," meant specifically for her.

But what did he deliver? The bomb, obviously, but if he stayed true to his MO, there had to be something else. With no computer, was he telling her where the victim's poem waited with the explanation of the lesson?

"I deliver."

Who delivers? Truckers, like Terry, deliver. Fed Ex delivers, speeches are delivered, but what would a poet deliver? A poem, of course, but where?

Then, as if a whisper echoed off a canyon wall, she remembered a slogan she had often repeated as a child while she waited for the mail on a snow day. Neither snow nor rain nor heat nor gloom of night stays these couriers from the swift completion of their appointed rounds.

The U.S. Post Office delivers ... mail.

She had seen Terry's mail on the kitchen counter, but nothing had seemed out of place there. Then, remembering the address on the mailbox as she turned into the driveway, she darted across the lawn. As she hurried through the gavel, her phone vibrated. She checked the number and recognized it as her partner's. Jake deLaurenti's. Not now! She let it go to voicemail.

"What is it, Officer Nyte?" Sondra said when she caught up to Kel at the mailbox.

"I think I know where the message is," Kel said, and opened the door to the box.

"But tampering with mail is a federal crime."

"Well, murdering a truck driver may not be a federal crime, but if I'm right, there's a letter waiting for me, which means our suspect tampered first."

Chapter Twenty-One

DIRK NYTE STOOD in the kitchen where he had been measuring coffee grounds into the drip basket. Due to a slight tremor in his hand from his weakness, a few grounds got away and fell onto the yellow tiled counter. Clarissa, his wife, had been meticulous in keeping the kitchen spotless, but with his illness, he hadn't been able to keep it up as well. He went after the stragglers, though, even the ones in the grout, with the dishcloth.

The ring of the turquoise wall phone pulled him away from his routine. A familiar voice spoke in his ear. Jared Collins, a newspaper columnist of national merit, had called when the story broke about the Rat City Exterminator's release. He wanted an interview.

"One of the victims," Jared said, "was Terry Graham, your former partner ..."

Despair's swift fist knocked the air from Dirk's lungs. He almost dropped the phone when he grabbed for the counter with his free hand to fight the illusion that he had been pushed from the brink into an abyss.

"... And according to your daughter, this may be related to the death of Suzanne Lowen last night ... Chief Nyte?"

The concerned voice in his ear centered his thoughts, and he found breath. "Terry is one of the victims?"

"Yes. I thought you would know by now."

"No ... my God, Terry ..."

"Yes, I'm sorry. It sounds like you were close."

"At one time we were like brothers, but still ..." Dirk didn't finish the thought.

"So, as I was saying—"

"Yes, as you were saying. You think Terry Graham was killed by the same person who killed Suzanne Lowen?"

"No, your daughter stated that."

"And you're calling me because you want an exclusive, due to my connection with both victims?"

"That, and you're an expert in solving serial cases. I'm particularly interested in the minds of mass murderers."

"Look, Mr. Collins, with all due respect, there are two detectives assigned to the case. One of them happens to be my daughter, and I'm only saying this because you already know it. The SPD doesn't comment on ongoing investigations and even though I'm retired, I still honor the code. Until your call, I didn't know about Terry's death, so with no offense intended, I just can't talk about this right now."

"No offense taken, Chief, and I understand completely. If and when you're ready to talk, you'll give me a call?"

"I have your number," Dirk said, and then placed the receiver in the telephone on the hook.

Chapter Twenty-Two

PETER MCCABE FOUND a parking stall near the back entrance of the store. He looked to the envelope on the passenger seat. The instructions had arrived Sunday.

"Sir." The hostess had approached the table and swept her long black hair away from her face as she leaned over his shoulder with the envelope.

The tall, stunning Malaysian woman always called him "sir"—in public. She was one of the lucky ones—and smart. McCabe recognized it in her eyes the moment he first saw her. And for that, he rescued her from a life destined for drugs, prostitution, and likely an early, unmarked grave. She still prostituted herself, but that was what made her smart. She only had one client, the one who arranged the day job at the Highlands Country Club and the one who paid for the downtown Seattle waterfront condo where she lived.

"This just came for you by courier," she whispered in his ear and placed an envelope in his hand. The scent of her perfume drifted past his nose, and he took a greedy drink.

"Thank you, honey," he said and slipped a twenty-dollar bill into the same hand she used in the evenings to massage him in just the right places.

He looked back to the three men around the table who had made up the rest of the foursome for this morning's golf round. He smiled, folded the envelope, and tucked it into this hip pocket. With a wave of his hand, he said, "This'll wait, I'm sure."

Now he looked at the envelope again. Since Sunday he had personally tested it for any trace of the sender. The courier company stated that the job had been sent to them via the Internet, and that they kept no records of IP addresses transmitting orders. Only the accounts of individuals or companies paying the bill interested them, but in this case, along with the envelope, there had been cash.

The envelope itself had been left on the front porch of a house in the Blue Ridge community, an exclusive neighborhood not far from the Highlands Golf Course. The owner and his family had been out of town for the entire weekend and had no idea how the note had ended up on their porch. Even a telephone canvass of the neighbors didn't yield a clue. No one noticed any strangers on the sidewalks or suspicious vehicles on the street.

The note disturbed him, but what made it worse was that someone knew his routine. During the summer, he golfed every Sunday, even in the rain, and finished the round with a martini lunch with his associates. That explained why he had waited nearly forty-eight hours before following the instructions. If anyone had been tracking him, he wanted to be sure they wearied of the wait.

He looked at the note again. Its message shook him.

"Open if you dare."

He removed the key stamped "37" that rested in the bottom, and looked around the parking lot. Alone, he stepped from his Lexus.

Inside the back door of the unfamiliar private mailbox and shipping store, he found himself in a narrow hallway lined on one wall with dozens of mailboxes. Thirty-seven was set on the third row from the top among similar-sized little doors. He slid the key into the slot, and when the door opened, he reached in. One letter-sized parcel awaited his eyes. It was addressed to "The Don."

Locally, a mythical mobster known in the press as "the Don of the Docks" had risen to the level of legend. No one knew who he was or if he really existed, but whoever had sent him this message was making a statement.

"Ludicrous," he mumbled under his breath, and then looked to see if anyone had heard.

At the desk twenty-five feet away, a lone male clerk in his mid-forties wrestled a large box from the counter to a cart. His long scraggly hair covered his face, but it looked as if he didn't even know Peter was in the shop.

McCabe took out a pocket knife and slid the blade along the fold to open the nondescript, number ten white envelope. A single sheet of paper inside waited for his eyes. He removed it and unfolded the two creases. The brief note had been printed on recycled copy paper, common in any office supply store by an inkjet printer—impossible to trace. As he read the short message, his heart skipped a beat and then pounded against his ribs.

Above a Hotmail email account name, the words screamed from the page. "My blood's on your hands."

Twenty-five minutes after had she left Deputy Carter in charge of the investigation at Terry Graham's home, Kel turned her car into a Bellingham parking lot. As she passed through town on the way to Interstate 5, two shops at the mini-mall beckoned her like a compass dial drawn to magnetic north: Starbucks and Radio Shack. Now with a triple-shot latte resting in the Jeep's cup holder, a raspberry scone on the console beside her, and a new Bluetooth earpiece, she was ready to face the rest of the morning.

As she reached the parking lot's driveway, she remembered letting her temporary partner's call go to voicemail. She listened just long enough to hear his

"Where the hell are you?" message, and placed the call.

"Plebe," he said as he picked up. "Been lookin' for you."

"I've been busy, and so has our perp."

"What are you talking about?"

"Have you seen the news?"

"Been busy."

"With who?"

"That's between me and the sheets. What's your DK up to?"

Kel brought him abreast of the suspect's activity over the last several hours.

"Damn it, why didn't you call me before you headed north?" Jake said.

From his tone, Kel knew he was angry. He couldn't let a rookie get ahead of him, or worse, solve the case without him. He'd get credit for it on his closing record, but the word would get out that he hadn't done much, if anything, to crack the case.

"Rule number one, remember?" she said, and felt justified as the sarcasm spirited through the wireless connection straight into his ear.

"We've got to work together. I'm the primary here, so if you have a lead, I'm your next call. Got it?"

"That cuts both ways, so why don't you tell me about your leads?"

"My leads?"

"Yeah, you called me. Do you mean to say you've got nothing?"

"Well ..." He paused. "Do you know who Terry Graham is?"

"That's all you've got? Something I told you? Of course I know who he is, and that's one of my next calls."

Peter McCabe approached the counter where the clerk had finished with the large box.

"I wish to close my account," he said.

"Certainly, sir. What's the number?"

McCabe handed him the key.

The clerk reached under the counter for a file box. While he thumbed through three-by-five cards, McCabe waited and quelled the urge to drum his fingers on the countertop.

When the clerk pulled a card from the wooden box, he said, "Here it is, Mr. Jenkins. Are you sure you want to close this? You just opened it two weeks ago."

McCabe took the card and searched for the owner's name on the mailbox. Again, his heart shook his rib cage, and he felt the blood drain from his face.

"Are you alright?" the clerk asked.

"Fine. Yes, fine, young man. I know I just opened it, but I got the parcel I was expecting."

He studied the name. Someone was toying with him. They had set a dangerous game in motion, one they couldn't possibly win with his resources. This pile of shit's just showing off. Before he slid the index card back across the counter, he studied the box owner's name again. It read "Willie Jenkins."

Kel tapped the Bluetooth and navigated her way through the telephone tree until an actual live human voice entered her ear.

"ADA Johnson."

Shit. Of all the lawyers in the DA's office, why did I draw him?

"Detective Kel Nyte," she said. "I need to pull a warrant to trap several cell phone numbers."

"Is this the same Nyte who tried to rip me a new one just yesterday?"

She remembered standing in the hallway outside the courtroom where Razor-Wire had just been released on a small bond. ADA Johnson had thrown his briefcase up between them as if she was about to knee him in the crotch.

She smiled at that thought and said, "'Fraid so, and I apologize. I was coming off an all-nighter with just three hours of sleep."

"I told you then we're on the same side, Detective. So build me a case. Why do you need a warrant on the riot?"

"It's not for the riot," she said. After she explained how DK was using cell phones to communicate his messages to her, she concluded by saying, "Bimal at the crime lab has the numbers. I'll have him call you."

"I'll get your warrant, Detective."

"Thanks, Johnson. Now there's just one more thing I'd like to ask …"

Dirk leaned over to the gas stove, the same stove that had cooked every hot meal eaten in this house for thirty-seven years. The Nytes could have bought a new one with more burners, a center grill, and a self-cleaning oven, but Clarissa had never wanted one. She preferred things traditional, and surrounded herself with simple, comfortable effects, like the white porcelain stove with black cast-iron burner grates.

Routine had always been Dirk's way to ward off emotional distractions. An act as simple as scrambling an egg gave his mind the room needed to distill information. With his cancer, routine had kept him grounded. The daily rhythm seemed a stay of execution. But this week, instead of feeling his life ebb away one heartbeat at a time, his mind was absorbed by the others whose lives were being sacrificed in a demented plan to posit a message. But to whom, and why?

He took an egg from the carton. Mundane habits seemed pointless when Terry and Suzanne would never eat another breakfast, but he held the oval in the palm of his hand. The rough, protective exterior gave the impression of durability but, just like the illusion of immortality, its fate would render to the will of the one who held it.

He was about to crack the egg on the edge of the skillet when the phone rang.

"Daddy, DK struck again." Kel said before he said hello.

"I know. I saw it on the news."

"I was there when it happened."

"Are you okay?"

"I may need to pencil in eyebrows for a while, but otherwise I'm fine. Mad as hell, but fine. I think Terry was one of the victims."

"I just got off the phone with The Globe. I know about Terry."

"How'd they find out?"

"They must have released his name."

"I suppose that's possible, but it seems premature. I always liked Terry, Daddy. I still remember him and his wife coming to the house for barbecues. "

"I know, Princess. I can't believe it myself."

"This is the second victim in two days."

"He's making good on his promise, isn't he?" He remembered the line read in his study last night— Mine to reap for Hell each day. "Who would do this? What's behind it?"

"I've got some thoughts," she said. "I'll stop by this afternoon. We can talk then."

Chapter Twenty-Three

AT NOON, KEL entered into the lobby of The Seattle Globe, the Puget Sound's regional newspaper. A young man with a dark blue uniform stood guard behind a gray, chest-high marble counter and greeted her.

"May I help you, ma'am?" he said as the glass entrance door closed behind her.

"Detective Kel Nyte," she said, and approached the man with her shield raised in the palm of her hand. Even though she wasn't officially a detective—as her boss Lou Martinez said, "A Temp-D"—in the eyes of the man behind the counter, she was more than a plebe. With confidence, she continued, "I'm in the middle of an investigation, and I'd like to use The Globe's archives."

Five minutes passed while the guard made a call, and then a woman in her early fifties with stringy, shoulder-length gray hair appeared and walked across the marble floor.

"May I help you, Detective?" The woman removed her half-frame glasses and let them dangle to her chest on a black-beaded chain.

"Yes. May I use the newspaper's electronic archive to do some research?"

"You can get most of the same information online these days."

"I'm sure I can, but I thought I might be able to focus my search if I used your archives. Then I can weed out the other hits a web search will return."

"Hmm ... very well, then. If you'll follow me."

The woman made an abrupt turn toward the glass door by which she had entered the lobby. Kel followed and made one final glance toward the guard to thank him. Already absorbed in the newspaper, he didn't notice. They entered a hive of frantic activity behind the transparent wall. After passing half a dozen waist-high cubicles, she followed the woman to a darkened office.

"I believe this is available," the woman said as she entered the windowless room. She walked around the desk, found the knob on the solitary lamp, and turned it on. "I'll sign you in to the computer with a guest login and then point you to the archive."

"Thank you." Kel looked around at the sterile furnishings—a dark green steel desk and a matching pair of ladder-backed chairs were the most formidable pieces in the office. Obviously The Globe felt no need to tempt the current occupant with plush surroundings. In direct contrast to the stale setting, several writing awards, represented in polished wooden plaques of mahogany and walnut, donned the back wall.

"Jared Collins," she read aloud. "Why do I know that name?"

"New York Times bestselling author," the woman said as she tore her eyes from the keyboard and searched for Kel's. "He's a nationally syndicated columnist."

Kel looked toward the voice and found a look of contempt. Behind it, though, her eyes revealed something else—scorn—but it wasn't aimed at Kel. The woman had been rejected. She sensed they were in Mr. Collins's office because she had been smitten with him, and even though presently away, the office put her in his proximity. Either he had outright rejected her or had just ignored her like the rest of the plain furnishings in his world.

"Of course. I'm sorry. I wasn't aware he lived in Seattle."

"Just the last year or so. Moved here to start winding down his career. I think that's about got it," she continued, the disdain having crawled back into the dark recess from which it crept. "If you'll step over here."

A few minutes later, Kel found her way around The Globe's intranet. She had a vague recollection of when her dad's and Terry's partnership had collapsed, but at the time, her own life was taking such a dramatic twist. Reading it now was like digesting fresh copy. The article on the screen, dated February 23, 2000, outlined the details.

Terry Graham, a detective with the Seattle Police Department, was suspended from duty today pending investigation into allegations of driving while intoxicated and battery.

A neighbor, who asked not to be identified, stated that Graham arrived home just after two a.m. He and his wife were awakened when Graham's car crashed into a metal garbage can and ran up onto the Graham's front lawn.

"That's when the shouting started," the neighbor said. "It's become such a common thing over the last several months that we hardly pay attention anymore. But this time it was different. Mrs. Graham was screaming for him to stop."

The neighbor went on to report that the noise died down after a second car pulled up and another man—reported to be Detective Dirk Nyte, Graham's partner—went inside.

The SPD has refused comment other than a written statement. "Terry Graham is a highly decorated member of the Settle Police Department. No charges have been filed at this time, but Graham has been placed on paid administrative leave until the internal investigation is concluded."

Kel looked away from the monitor and rubbed her eyes. She had been staring at it for over an hour, and her mind had grown weary.

The breakup had been bad, that much she knew, but she had never considered her dad to be a whistle blower. Now here it was. A domestic dispute between two of Mom and Dad's friends had become the catalyst for Terry's dismissal. But whether he felt mandated or duty-bound, she couldn't see him intentionally ruining his partner's career.

She turned her thoughts to Tribune Investments. Jake had warned her to stay clear, but she typed the company name into The Globe's internal search engine anyway. Not many hits resulted. One reporter had posted his research notes. From what she read, Tribune was a shell company that had never filed a federal tax return and had no substantial assets. The reporter hadn't been able to link Tribune to a parent company, but he located the names of the principals of the company: Toshio Aoki, Yoshi Kobayashi, and Peter McCabe. Not only was Yoshi Kobayashi associated with Tribune, he was also listed as CFO for Saito Global, a shipping company doing overseas transport out of the Port of Seattle.

She opened a new tab on the web browser and searched for information on the names. Peter McCabe seemed out of place with the other two of Japanese origin, so she investigated him first. When no useful results were found, she looked for the other two. Only one of the names yielded anything helpful: Toshio Aoki's. A picture appeared on the screen. She recognized the man being led from a courtroom as the same leathery face who had peered out the rear window of the black Audi yesterday in Pioneer Square. According to the newspaper archives, Aoki had done time for racketeering, and until three months ago had been in prison. The arresting officer was Willie Jenkins.

Kel looked up from the monitor and drove her knuckles into her eyes. Too little sleep and too much adrenaline were on a collision course with the caffeine withdrawal in her head. She leaned back in the chair, laced her fingers behind her head, and closed her eyes for a few seconds to relieve the burn.

"May I help you?"

Tipping the chair forward, Kel forced her eyes open and jumped to her feet. The familiar face of a man she had seen in photos took shape on the opposite side of the desk. She rarely read his weekly column, which was why she hadn't immediately recognized the name earlier on the wall plaques. But it came together now. Aged by at least ten years since the last time he updated the photo running next to his byline, the man before her, without doubt, was Jared Collins.

"No. I mean, yes … well, I mean ... sorry, I'm Kel Nyte, SPD, and someone out there"—she waved toward the fortress of cubicles beyond the office—"said you'd be out the rest of the afternoon. Half-frame glasses on a neck chain?"

"That's Millicent the Magnificent," he said. A smile broke the stern look of a high school principal from this face. He ran his fingers through the bristling hair of his more-salt-than-pepper-shaded beard.

"Mid-fifties, shoulder-length gray hair?"

"By your careful observation, I'd say you're a detective."

"Yes, Detective. Plebe grade, according to my partner."

"That's our Millie. She's one of our better proofreaders."

"It's none of my business, sir, but I think she has a thing for you."

"Comes with the territory," Jared said, and waved his hand at the trophies of his success hanging on the back wall. "Happens so often I just ignore it."

"As I said, it's none of my business. I'll leave you to your desk."

"Don't leave on my account. If Millie said you could use my desk, you can use my desk."

"I do need to get going." She glanced at the Minnie Mouse watch she always kept strapped to her arm with a leather band. The animated face reminded her not to take life too seriously. "Oh my God, I had no idea it was so late. I just closed my eyes for a few seconds ... at least I thought. I must have napped for over an hour. I have to go. Thank you for the use of your computer."

She stepped out from behind the desk, and picked up her notepad and a couple of news reports she had printed.

"Plebe grade, huh? Who's your partner?"

"Jake deLaurenti. My first week on the job."

"I see. Doesn't he have trouble keeping a partner around?

"Shouldn't comment on that."

"It's public knowledge, Detective. Seems he has one in the hospital and one in the grave."

"You've been tracking him?"

"It's my business to keep an ear to the ground. Mr. deLaurenti has the makings of a good story."

"You won't learn much from me. We just met yesterday."

"I see. Well, you best be careful. I'd hate to see you meet the same fate as your predecessors."

"I'll keep that in mind," she said. She stepped toward the door.

"You said your name was Nyte, didn't you?" Jared asked as she walked by him.

"Yes. Kelsey Nyte." She stopped and placed her hand on the door jamb.

Few people used her birth name, and then it was generally people who didn't know her well. When she had started high school, she decided to shorten her name to Kel, as Kelsey was too girly. Even though her mother never quite accepted it, as Kel had been named for a favorite aunt, high school—and eventually college—branded her for life.

"You've been in the news today."

"I suppose I have."

"Talked to your father this morning."

"So that was you. Dad said a reporter called, but why? You're a columnist, not a staff writer."

"Even a columnist is interested in the plight of the human condition. If I didn't care about humanity, I wouldn't have many readers."

"I suppose that's true. So, on the heels of this tragedy, why's my dad suddenly a human interest story?"

"He and I share something. Your father Dirk and I both have an interest in depraved minds. He's become somewhat of a local celebrity, what with his success in catching the Rat City Exterminator, and then the recent overturn of the convict's verdict. I thought he might have an opinion on the series of murders you're investigating."

"What series is that, sir?"

"Don't be cagey. You said so yourself."

"I said there was a series of murders?"

"You said that to a sergeant on the scene from the Bellingham police just this morning. He let it slip to a reporter."

"Of course," she said, and turned her eyes away from his. She had thought the information was safe behind the blue veil, but apparently Sergeant Monroe felt otherwise. "I didn't realize the press had that information yet."

"Oh, we're pretty good at ferreting."

"Like Terry Graham's name?"

"Okay, that was an educated guess."

"Go on."

"The officer also said that you asked about an address, and shortly thereafter the local sheriff was called to it. Apparently, you showed up. It doesn't take too much digging to find out that Terry Graham lived there and drove fuel for the terminal that exploded."

"Alright, you've demonstrated that you're perhaps a superior detective and that I need to keep my mouth shut. Lesson learned. Now I need to get moving."

"Wouldn't dare stand in your way, Detective Nyte."

Chapter Twenty-Four

DIRK HAD TAKEN a carafe of coffee with him when he retired to the study after breakfast. From the built-in dark walnut bookshelf he pulled Ken Follett's Pillars of the Earth. Even though he had read the novel several times, it always took him to a place where his own trials didn't bear as much weight. Over the next several hours, he lost himself in the vivid characters and hoped to push Terry Graham's death out of his consciousness.

Reading had always been something he took pleasure in, even as a kid. When he was in grade school his parents had subscribed to "My Weekly Reader," and as soon as it arrived, Dirk tore into it. Before the first day passed, he was ready for the next issue. As an adult, he drifted towards books, and always had one or two in process stashed in different places where he might steal a few minutes. Once Kel and Shelia came along, though, that slowed to an almost complete halt until they were old enough not be underfoot at every turn. He and Clarissa had spent many hours reading in this very room. But in the last six years, the demands on the office of police chief made pleasure reading a luxury for which he had little time and even less energy. Now, it brought a comforting means of escape from the pain of his disease, and whenever he picked up a hardbound edition, it seemed to invite his wife's spirit to join him.

As midafternoon crept in and the sun continued to heat the house, he found it difficult to concentrate, despite the intriguing plot developing on the page. Something more evil than Follett's antagonist wove a spider's web of brutality on his city, and Dirk saw no end in sight.

The news of Susan Lowen's murder had been as difficult to take as any cop's death. But she was more than just a cop. Although they hadn't worked together side by side, she had analyzed in her lab the evidence that he uncovered on the street. Together they had brought a number of criminals to justice.

But nothing compared to a good partner, and Terry Graham had been a great one. To say they had each other's backs was cliché. Even when they fought like brothers, that being a frequent disruption in the bullpen, their passion for the victims and commitment to closing the cases gave them an unstoppable edge.

From the moment Jared Collins told him about Terry, Dirk felt like he'd been hit with a doubling punch to the gut and an upper cut to the jaw. Not only was the sudden loss of his old friend shattering, but it came with a hostile reminder that the breech between them had never been restored. Time, distance, and a decade of life had dulled the ache, but with all the fences he could have mended in his last days, Terry's was one that mattered most. Now it's too late.

He stood from the chair where he had sat for several hours, stretched, and then made his way to the refrigerator. Pillars always put him in the mood for courser fare, so he pulled out some summer sausage and a block of sharp cheddar to slice a snack.

His thoughts drifted back over the more than twenty years of their association. Terry had been closer to Dirk than his own brother for more than ten of those years. Although the friendship failed in 2000, during the decade of the nineties, Dirk and Terry had been inseparable. They had closed more cases leading to conviction than any other two detectives in the city.

Their streak started when they became the primaries on the Exterminator case in 1990. While every spare resource worked the case, two seasoned detectives managed the taskforce. When they both retired the same year, Dirk and Terry took the lead and saw it through, from suspect to conviction. On the day Vince Buckley had stepped off the bus for what they thought was his last breath of free air, they waited outside the gate of the Washington State Penitentiary in Walla Walla. It wasn't until that gate slammed behind him that they knew it was for keeps.

Finished with the knife, Dirk piled the snack on a small plate, refilled his carafe, and grabbed a box of crackers on his way back to the study. He eased himself back into his leather chair and balanced the plate in his lap. He lifted his cup, which was resting on the table, and took a deep swallow. Like the bitterness of his and Terry's war, the aftertaste of the cold coffee lingered on his palate.

A ten-minute drive from The Globe put Kel on her dad's narrow street. She pulled her Liberty from under the tree-lined awning into the driveway and walked up the concrete steps to the covered porch. She let herself into the living room through the front door. The handmade Turkish rug under her feet, and the familiar scents of furniture polish and hardwood floors, welcomed her.

No matter how many years she had been on her own, this was always home. What would happen to it after Dirk's passing hadn't been a topic of discussion in the last few months, but she knew he would have it covered in his will. Without Dad and Mom, though, the home would lose its comforting significance. Even if she or her sister moved in, the nostalgic memories wouldn't replay without their parents' presence. But then, the thought of putting it on the market and seeing strangers move in left an awful void.

"Daddy?" she called.

"In the study, Princess. Bring a couple of cups."

Moments later, Kel entered the study and went straight to Dirk. She wrapped her arms around him and rested her cheek against his. "I love you, Daddy. I'm so sorry about Terry."

"We both are, Princess," he said, and turned his face to kiss her cheek.

She spied the carafe on the lamp table, released her hug, and began to fill the two mugs.

"How are you and Jake getting on?" Dirk asked.

"He calls me 'plebe,'" she replied, and handed him one of the cups. A few strands of her dark brunette hair had slipped from her ponytail and fell forward when she leaned toward her dad.

"Plebe, huh? Guess you've got to start somewhere."

"May as well be at the bottom, right?" she asked after settling into her mom's chair and brushed the straggling hair behind her ear.

"So he's working you?"

"No, we're stuck on rule one." The cheese and sausage on the edge of the table and the rumble of her stomach reminded her that her last meal had been a raspberry scone this morning. "Hey, you eating those?"

Dirk offered her the plate with a wave of his hand. "Rule one? What's that?"

"'Stay the hell out of my way,'" she said and placed her cup on the table to take the plate.

"He's a bit of a loner, but he does have a good closing ratio."

"So I've been told."

"And a little ego."

"Now there I must disagree categorically." A grin passed over her lips. "He has enough ego for the entire department. So I'm running my investigation, and he's running his. He's going to be by shortly."

"I'm still on the list?"

"As far as I know, Daddy, from his perspective, you are the list. It's still early, but the only thing we can find in common between Suzanne Lowen and Terry Graham is you. So Jake's coming by to ask some questions."

"I'd rather hear them from you."

"I'd rather ask them, but due to the circumstances ... well, you understand."

Dirk nodded his head and shifted to face her.

"It seems," she continued as she picked up a bite of sausage and cracker, "like Jake works one lead at a time. Not so much a multitasker as far as I've seen. I can't figure out how he closes so many cases. But right now, since you're the main attraction, I think he just needs to get it out of his system."

"Do you think I'm guilty?"

The leather grunted against her jeans as she shifted and leaned forward to look straight into his eyes.

"Everything inside me screams no, but the evidence says maybe. Daddy, I have this recurring thought. If the daughter of a serial killer was asked before her father was arrested if he might senselessly take someone's life, she'd say, 'No damn way.' And now I'm that girl."

"Kel, you wouldn't be doing your job if you didn't look to me as a suspect, especially now with the second death so close to me, even closer than Suzanne."

"It's not right, though."

"Be that as it may, search in every nook and cluttered closet. Just keep an open mind." He tilted his head, forced a smirk to his lips, and continued, "I could have hired a hitman, you know."

"Daddy!" she shouted.

"Think like a detective, not a daughter. There is a murderer out there. You keep following the evidence, and you'll bust this perp. Have you thought any more about Vince Buckley?"

"I put a BOLO out last night, but he's off the grid. Once I find him, we'll have a little chat about his whereabouts the last few days. Then I can escalate or eliminate him."

"No telling if Buckley's taking out everyone who was a part of his conviction and, through you, giving me a firsthand view of his master plan."

"It's possible," she said, "but until I find him, I can't ask the questions." She placed the plate on the table, picked up the cup, and leaned back into the leather. She crossed her legs. "Daddy, there's something about the case I haven't told you."

"If I'm a suspect, you shouldn't tell me anything else."

"If you're the doer, you already know what I'm about to tell you. If you're not, you might be able to help."

When he didn't object further, she continued. "You know about the poem DK sent me, but there're more. To date, he's left a poem at every scene. Each one is in a very structured seven beat, iambic style. Did you ever study or write poetry?"

"Never even tried. Does that take me off the list?"

"Not necessarily. They're pretty simple, but that's good to know. There are some things in each poem that give an indication of his point. The first line in each one, for example, seems to show a relationship between the victim and DK's target."

Kel opened her notebook and continued, "Last night you said Suzanne worked in the lab in the nineties. That made me wonder who the first line was written about. Listen: 'First the one who owes so much.' Can you make sense of it?"

Dirk leaned back into the chair and sipped from his cup. He looked straight ahead, toward the bookcase, but Kel could see that he wasn't focusing on anything animate.

He nodded his head. "Me. Maybe I'm his student."

"Why? What did Suzanne owe you?" Kel asked.

Dirk met her eyes. "After Buckley's arrest, Terry and I gained a lot of notoriety—not just departmental, but in the press. We had brought an end to a crime spree that had the whole town on edge. Even though we were a long way from conviction, the press painted us as heroes. This naturally found its way to the police chief who was always eager to shine a positive spotlight on the department, so commendations were handed out.

"At the time, I had a friend who was a detective in South Precinct. His friend's niece had recently graduated with a double major in biology and criminology and was looking for work in the public sector. I knew of her, and since I had the ear of the police chief, I put her name in front of him. Suzanne owed her career to me. What does Terry's poem say?"

She placed the mug back on the table without taking a drink and pulled gloves from her hip pocket. She slipped them over her hands. From her notebook she withdrew a white envelope with her name hand-printed in block letters on the outside. A single piece of white paper was inside. She extracted and unfolded it, and then read.

"Two is he who joined your cause
Now must suffer from my laws

Tissues scorched, torn asunder
Victim of my hurled thunder."

"What do your make of the first couple of lines, Daddy?" she asked, and stood. "The phrase 'joined your cause' …" she continued, without waiting for an answer. "If Suzanne's poem is directed to you, then knowing this was written with Terry in mind, could it also be a reference to you?"

"My partner. Makes sense."

"So if that's true, then," she said, pacing the floor, "and you're the target, you need to look past Buckley. Make a list of people with the means, motive, and mindset to commit these acts."

"Pretty long list, I'd think."

"Regardless, it's the place to start. Look for any reference to someone with the initials DK. Now …" she continued, and looked back at the paper. "He uses the word 'laws.' I think that might be a play on words."

"Possibly. Terry and I both being cops at the time of Buckley's arrest."

"You're still fixated on him," she said, and glanced up from the paper into Dirk's eyes. "Broaden the pool, Daddy."

"Of course. You just said that."

"Are you feeling okay?"

It wasn't like her dad to lose focus. He had always been the first to put things together, but over the last several weeks, she had noticed that his mind didn't process as fast as it used to. She felt pressure behind her eyes and walked away to the window where he wouldn't notice if she cried. She hated what was happening to him, and in moments where it became obvious he was failing, her heart grieved.

"I'm fine. Just get tired in the afternoon, even when I haven't done anything all day. Damn this disease."

"Why don't you rest? We can continue this later."

"No, please go on. I want to hear your thoughts."

She turned her head toward him. "Okay, if you're sure."

"Please. In some ways this is cathartic. I spend most of the day killing time, just waiting to die. This is at least a break in that dreadful deathwatch."

She turned to face the window again. "It seems to me that DK has his own set of laws. He calls them 'my laws.' I think he believes something in his life gave him the authority to throw out one of our most basic human rights, the right to life. He's replaced it with something he feels trumps it, and I fear that until we figure out what's driving him, we're going to be powerless to stop him."

Dirk lifted his cup to his lips and took a swallow. "But if I'm the object, why doesn't he just come after me? Why do others have to be hurt?"

She stared blankly out the window. "Because he claims to be a teacher. Remember he said, 'Mine to teach the lesson well.' If my theory's true and you're the object, you have to learn the lesson. He's giving you hints, but it's up to you to search for the answer. Ultimately, since whatever it is you need to learn revolves around him, I think he plans to reveal himself once you figure it out. He wants to he caught, but not before you know at what crossroads you two intersected." She turned back to him and continued, "And I hate to say it, but so far he's been punctual. Remember his first message to me, 'Mine to reap for Hell each day'? There's no time to waste, Daddy. I need your help."

"I kept personal journals. I'll read through them. Maybe there's a DK lurking in there, if those are his real initials."

"I think they are. Probably another clue."

"What I don't understand," he said, placing his cup on the table, "is why you? Why is he communicating with you and not me?"

"Maybe it's through me, rather than with me. Obviously he knows I'm your daughter. So, in essence, he might be using me as your tutor. It seems like he feeds me just enough information so I get up close and personal. What if he knows you're ill and is using me to pass on to you what I see?

"But," she said as she folded the letter back into the envelope, "we've found a way to track him."

"How's that?"

She walked across the room toward he mom's chair, placed her hands on the leather back and told him about the four burner phones DK had purchased.

"That's how I knew something was about to happen up north. A second of the four phones became active."

"Do you think he knows you're tracking him?"

"It's because we're tracking him, I knew he was at the fuel terminal when it exploded. He could have seen me then but even if not, if he watches the evening news, it's obvious I knew enough to be on scene. So … yeah, if he doesn't know yet, he will soon enough." She paused while she walked around the chair, and then took a seat on the edge, facing him. "But Daddy, if I can track him, he might be able to track me. He does know my phone number, so it's possible he knows my every move. He might even know I'm here with you right now."

"Which means you're in danger."

"We might both be in danger," she said, leaning back into the soft leather, "but you've taught me to face threats head on, not run from them."

"That sounded a lot better when I was talking about me."

"Comes with the territory, Daddy. You know that."

"I've stared down the barrel of a lot of guns before and survived them all. As if it weren't enough, I sit here day after day with an unseen enemy killing me from the inside. If I'm the true target, now I have to worry about what this damned DK has planned for those I care about."

"I'm going to catch him, Daddy. You can count on that."

"I know you will, Princess. I have no doubt."

"Now, before Jake gets here, there's something else I want to ask." She picked up a slice of cheese and poked into her mouth. "Do you know the name Toshio Aoki?"

"Aoki? Of course. What does he have to do with DK?"

"Probably nothing, but he seems to know Jake, and I'm trying to run down how."

"That's interesting. How'd you make that connection?"

"Yesterday, Jake and I had a meet 'n greet over coffee, and Aoki drove by. He had his driver stop long enough to make eye contact with Jake. Something definitely passed between them, but Jake denies it and as much as told me to stay out of it."

"But of course you couldn't do that."

"I'm just naturally inquisitive, Daddy," she said, and grinned. "Comes with the Nyte blood in my veins. Anyway, I ran across his name when I searched for the owner of the Audi. It led me to Tribune Investments."

"That's a shell."

"I know, but for who or what? I did some research this afternoon. I found that one of the principles of Tribune, Yoshi Kobayashi, is also the CFO of Saito Global, which seems to be a legitimate shipping company."

"We've never been able to nail Aoki for much, but we're pretty sure he's part of a crime syndicate. As for Kobayashi, he's like Teflon."

"There's a third name associated with Tribune, Peter McCabe. I can't find anything on him."

"And you won't. I'm sure you've heard of the Don of the Docks."

"Is McCabe the Don?"

"No one knows. We can't even confirm that the Don exists. What we do know is that the syndicate Aoki is part of has a very long and very tight-lipped reach into the longshoreman's local at the Port. We've suspected that it goes all the way up to my counterpart at the Port Police."

"The Port Police Chief?"

"Possibly. Even though the docks are within the Seattle city limits, they have jurisdiction. We've tried forging cooperation between the SPD and the Port Police, but it's been difficult. Jake and your friend Willie Jenkins were the first."

"And then Willie ended up dead in a shipping container nearly halfway around the world, just about the time Aoki went to prison."

"Coincidence or retribution?" Dirk asked. "No one's talking."

"Code of silence?"

"Within the police community, that's more sacrosanct than a novice monk's vow."

Chapter Twenty-Five

DK WEPT.

DEEP in the bowels of the Emerald City, the muted bustle of the burgeoning evening commute drifted into his sanctuary. The whine of a hybrid articulated-bus, the hollow rumble of an SUV passing over a steel grate, and the thunder of a motorcycle's glass-pack exhaust pipe echoed between the concrete walls. Submerged so deep in his subterranean refuge, he could only imagine the shuffle of feet on sidewalks on every course to their daily escape from making a living to having a life. Office managers transformed into soccer moms, Harvard grads turned into homework dads—each one exploiting God's ultimate gift: freedom of choice.

The beam of the battery-powered flashlight, resting next to him on the floor, rose like a beacon to the low ceiling and radiated off the exposed pipes and rafters overhead. The small abandoned room had escaped the eyes of everyone, despite the frantic activity of the courts and the contractors.

On his knees in this condemned hovel, he looked to the shrine he had erected rising above a wooden altar made of short lengths of wall studs. Over the collage of photos and artwork, a paper banner with a

Biblical quote from the Book of Deuteronomy stretched across the wall before him.

"The secret things belong to God, but the things revealed belong to us."

Displayed in a montage of faded photos of people he had estranged, the only life DK truly lived spread before him on the memorial wall. In the center was the purest, immortalized in a white wedding gown.

His hands drew instinctively to the invisible scars of the facial reconstruction surgery he had self-imposed so many years ago. It had been necessary to save those he loved, and now it was even more important as he walked near his nemesis. They had become a silent testimony to the man he unwillingly had had to become.

He looked to the altar on which he had placed photos of five victims, each face concealed by a two-inch white pillar candle. Suzanne Lowen's likeness was on his far left. The candle had burned once, but now rested cold, extinguished like her breath. He turned his thoughts to the next, leaned forward and blew on the flame dancing on Terry Graham's wick. It sputtered into darkness and sent a thin white ribbon of smoke in a spiraling ascent like Terry's soul. It mingled in the confined space with the dust particles floating in the stagnant air. Except for the waxy scent, its distinction dissipated.

Before him the third victim's photo rested on the altar. He removed the candle from her face for one final look. As he did, tears flowed again and he sobbed without embarrassment in deep remorse. He didn't mourn for the victim who soon would die. She didn't matter to him. He'd grant her a gift, though—something she could not attain on her own. For those who loved her, she would reach omnipresent immortality every time they memorialized her. It was the very least he could bequeath, as her death was necessary, a payment on a long-owed debt—deserted, imprisoned, hunted like a beast, and then forced to forsake everything.

The scent of cold rice roused Wolf from sleep. Like the gentle brush of his wife when she rolled over in bed, it brought a welcomed comfort. The bowl arrived every morning before dawn and had become his only luxury. Like breathing in and out, the rice tethered him by a fragile thread to life, to sanity. It embodied his daily quest.

When the imprisonment began, he had used his fingernail to memorialize each sunrise with a hash-mark on the wooden floor of his prison, but after two years ticked by, it just didn't matter. He had become like a circus animal. Chained by day and caged by night, he performed his mindless tasks from daylight to nightfall.

Nine years of exposure in the sweltering jungle had baked his mind to an anesthetized numbness. The macabre screams of the innocent lives he had slaughtered and the thrashing visions of his buddies' last breathes vanished from his nightmares. The image of the three-year-old son he had left crying on the front porch had long faded like an echo in a secret crevasse. Yet there remained a child-sized breach in his memory that yearned to be filled.

Although his own name retreated so far into the past, it seemed of no importance to his daily existence—not worth the effort to recall—that a phantom stalked day and night. The questions he asked in the beginning—intentionality, cowardice, misinformation, dereliction—had faded with the other bits of his life. But in the void, the face of the sergeant symbolized his loss and gave sustenance to his present reality.

Sold and resold, stolen and re-stolen, beaten only to revive to be beaten again, if he had ever been a prisoner of war, those days were long passed. He was now MIA, yet even more true, a slave who gave willing assent to whoever held the key to his coop—the faceless men who delivered the rice.

So why eat?

Reduced to the most basic human precedence, even pain by whip no longer gave witness to life. It would have been easier to acquiesce to the evidence. Release, rescue, or escape would never be attained.

He should have forsaken the hope that the next marauding gang might be someone sent from home to rescue him, and not another warring tribe to seize his servitude. Death offered an almost uncontrollable appeal, yet he fought the longing with each breath. He purposed to stall its final onset because there remained one thing, one leash, one faith—the end of the cage.

He sat up, leaned his back against the familiar bars of his home, and caressed the bowl. Around him, the familiar sounds of the jungle waking for a new day—chattering vernal hanging parrots and a couple of black-crested gibbons singing their morning breeding song—filled his ears.

In his hand the only meal he'd see today writhed like a bucket of snakes. He reached in with two fingers, scooped the white rice and maggots into his mouth, and savored the insipid pleasure.

The bride in the collection earned DK's long-suffering lament—his wife, the mother of his children, who to this day thought he was dead. Such joy she had given to him before the end. When he shipped over, he had pledged that if his life ran its course before he returned, her love would be enough. But then the single action of one man caused him to lose it all to a living death. That act might have been forgiven as the residue of war, but when his recklessness reared again, the only means of atonement required the ultimate price.

DK returned the candle to cover the smiling image of the middle victim and reached to his breast pocket. He tore a paper match from the book, slid the head across the striker, and listened as it crackled into its transitory existence. Then, holding the match to the center candle, he watched as the flame passed its life to the candle wick resting over the face of his next sacrifice.

Chapter Twenty-Six

VOICES AND THE clanking of dishes in the kitchen drifted into his study. Dirk wasn't worried about the meeting to take place there, but he didn't look forward to it, either. Bad blood, rather than anything resembling rational police work, had driven Lou Martinez to throw his name into the suspect pool. But now, with it there, and two dead cops both connected to him, the only way out was for the lack of evidence to eliminate him.

"Daddy!" Kel, who had left the study when the doorbell rang, reentered the room. "You know Jake deLaurenti."

"Of course," Dirk said, and pushed himself to his feet using the arms of the leather chair for support. He offered his hand in greeting. "Good to see you again."

"Not the best circumstances," Jake said as he took Dirk's hand. He shook it with a single jerk. Over a pale green shirt, Jake wore the same gray blazer he wore for his coffee meeting with Kel yesterday.

"No, I think not. Please sit." Dirk waved to a rocker opposite his chair on the other end of the red-brick hearth.

While Dirk eased himself back into the soft leather, Kel poured coffee from the carafe into a fresh cup she had brought from the kitchen and handed it to Jake. Then, as she repeated the action, warming her father's and her brew, she said, "Jake has some questions we need to ask." After handing him his mug, she patted his leg and then sat on the edge of her mom's old chair.

"Do you have much pain these days?" Jake rested the cup on the arm of the rocker.

"It's my body's way of talking back to the disease. Pancreatic cancer is no picnic, son."

"I can't imagine. Not only the pain, but the knowledge there's no cure. My God, Chief, it's awful. I'm so sorry."

"Thank you Jake. Now, I don't mean to be rude, but today's been a difficult day, and I'm already beat. Before I fade further, you better go for it."

"Of course." Jake placed the mug on the hearth and unzipped a three-ring-binder-sized portfolio. From an inside pocket, he pulled a pen, and raised it, poised to take notes. "You knew Suzanne Lowen, correct?"

"Yes."

"How did you first meet?"

"We had an opening in the crime lab, and I put her name in front of the police chief."

"And?"

"She was hired." Dirk crossed his legs and placed the steaming cup on the lamp table. "She helped me solve any number of cases. Her lab skills are legendary. It's such a tremendous loss."

"I agree." Jake leaned forward. "Then … fast forward. She undermined the Vince Buckley serial murder case."

"It's true, but not her fault. The evidence was weak. The whole case was a house of circumstantial cards, but we knew that going in. When his lawyer petitioned for a new trial, Suzanne pulled on the right one and the whole thing crumbled. I bear her no ill. She was doing what we paid her to do: process and analyze evidence. With the proper technology in the early nineties, he might have never been convicted. At least we got him off the street for a while."

"You said 'we.' Who helped you build that case?"

"You already know it was Terry."

"Terry Graham." Jake leaned back in the rocker, and took the cup from the hearth. "And you know he was killed this morning?"

"Ye—"

Before Dirk could finish his answer, Jake continued, "So how long was Terry your partner?"

"More than a decade."

"Were you close outside of work?"

"Extremely. We did family things together. Back then, the Grahams and the Nytes were inseparable."

Jake raised the mug to his lips, looked over the edge, and asked, "Then you know why he left the SPD?"

"Of course. It's in the record. He and his wife were having personal issues."

Jake lowered the cup and swallowed. "Personal issues? Can you elaborate?"

"What does this have to do with his murder? That's ancient history."

"Background."

"Background?" Dirk paused. He recognized the tactic. Jake was on a fishing expedition. Toss in the bait, feel for a nibble, and then set the hook. With a sigh, he continued, "Something had been gnawing at Terry for a long time. He had lost most of their life's savings on an investment."

Jake's questions were taking the conversation in a direction that made Kel wince. She didn't want her dad to shade any answers, so she stood and walked to the front window.

While she peered out toward the neighbor across the street mowing his lawn, she loosened the band that bound her ponytail to the crown of her head. With her fingers, she combed the loose hair that kept falling in her face back into it.

In the final years of the nineties, she had used her psychology degree to help an up-and-coming dotcom find a market. They were in the IPO process and one of her benefits was pre-IPO stock. In the days of overnight millionaires, confident of its success, she had boasted about it to her parents. They chose to buy in with a small amount, but Terry, when he heard about it from Dirk, poured in everything. Then, when it failed, and the Graham's divorce came on its heels, she had felt responsible.

She finished her hair by twisting the band around the plait but kept her back to the men while they continued the conversation.

"He always liked to stop for a drink before heading home," Dirk continued. "Trying to wash the day's debris out of his mind. You can understand that, son, I'm sure."

"Comes with the territory."

"About the time he lost his investment, the drinking became heavier. He didn't try to hide the tension building between him and his wife. We trusted each other and kept each other's confidences, so he told me that she had been complaining about the late nights. At the same time, a captain's position came open in the detective's squad at West Precinct. When he didn't make the cut, it was like pissing gasoline on a fire. Oh my God, how inappropriate." Dirk planted both feet on the floor, leaned forward, and threw his head into his hands. A vision of Terry being consumed in the flames at the fuel terminal played through his mind.

"It's alright, Daddy," Kel said. Dirk felt her hand massage his shoulders. "You meant no disrespect."

"Damn it. None of this is right. While we're sitting here drinking coffee, Terry and Suzanne's murderer is plotting his next move."

"We're going to get him, Daddy," Kel said.

"But this is such a waste of time. I have no motive now, and didn't then. Besides, I'm too sick to have committed these atrocities. "

"I know these questions seem pointless, Chief," Jake said, "but you know it's necessary. If you're alright, can we go on?"

"Of course." Dirk leaned back into the chair and lifted his legs one at a time to rest them on the hassock. "I'm sorry." He reached his hands up and took hold of Kel's.

"No apology needed. So, when Terry didn't make the cut, it angered him and made matters worse?"

"Yes, and it didn't help that I was on the short list."

"Did he confront you?"

"Yes. One night we were on our way to arrest a man we suspected of heading a car heist ring, and he brought the subject up. 'Hell,' he shouted, 'this is bullshit. We've both worked our balls to a nub and have damn good records.'"

"I see. Then what happened?"

"Well, it was the evening of Valentine's Day. Terry should have been home with his wife, but he was at the bar again. He was in terrible shape. I tried to get him to let me drive him home. But there was no convincing him. Clarissa—Kel's mom—and I had plans, so I made arrangements with the barkeep that if Terry got out of control he was to call me.

"After several hours, I got the call. By the time I arrived, Terry's vocabulary had disintegrated into halting phrases with one-syllable words. He wasn't making much sense and wouldn't listen to reason. I tried again to get him to let me take him home, but he was livid, spewing out trash about his marriage. He was embarrassing himself but he had no intention of leaving until they kicked him out on the street. So this time I left enough cash with the proprietor for a cab and headed home.

"It was about 2:30 a.m. when I got the next call. Clarissa answered and immediately handed me the receiver. It was Terry's wife. He had driven himself home, and once there, his words turned into fists, and she became the target. After quite a beating, she managed to lock herself in the bathroom and called me."

"Why not call 9-1-1?"

"Cops code, you know. She didn't want it on the record."

"Yet it did get on the record, didn't it? How'd that go down?"

Dirk glared at him released Kel's hands and shook his head. "A couple days later, her neighbor spoke to her. All the makeup and sunglasses in the world couldn't cover up the bruising. The neighbor called it in."

"So, then, you had attempted a cover-up?"

"We were off-duty at the time, so yes, I wanted to protect my partner—my friend—and the SPD from unnecessary embarrassment. In retrospect, that wasn't the best decision, because truth has a way of bubbling to the surface. As I said, we spent a lot of time together. The neighbor recognized my car at the curb."

"And somehow you came out of it without a stink."

"I was told to file an official report, Jake. 'Get it in his jacket,' they said."

"And how did that go?"

"Now that the truth was out, my first duty was to the people I served and the department. Even though I knew it might damage Terry's career, I had no option but to tell the truth."

"And there is no other reason you hung him out to dry?"

Dirk dropped his legs from the hassock and used his hands on the chair arms to pull his torso forward. He focused his eyes on Jake's with an intense glare. To control the building vehemence, he kept his next words clipped and terse. "First of all, son, I didn't hang him out to dry. I followed orders. Second, are you implying something?"

"Not implying anything, Chief, just getting background. If there's something else, just tell me the whole truth, as you said, before it bubbles to the surface."

Dirk shot Kel, who had stepped behind her mother's chair, an apprehensive glance. Last night she had joked about Pandora's Box, but he wasn't ready to take the lid off. Not like this. Not in front of Jake.

"Jake, maybe you should give him a break," Kel said. "He's exhausted."

"Like Hell!" Dirk said, and gave full voice to the rage he had checked. "If you think there's something else, spill it out."

Dirk paused to give Jake time to speak. When Jake lifted his cup and smiled, Dirk relaxed back into the chair. "Just as I thought: innuendo, nothing else. Once it came out, the department had no choice. They couldn't tolerate the bad press, and he was dismissed."

"And who did the dismissing?"

"That's a matter of public record, too. You know already, or you wouldn't ask."

"Just to tickle my ears, tell me anyway."

"Damn it, Jake, I feel bad enough that we never patched things up. Why are you dredging this up now?" Dirk sighed and shook his head. "By the time

Terry came clean, I had been promoted to captain and was now Terry's boss. So, since Terry had pled guilty to physically abusing his wife and then refused to see the department psychiatrist, I had no choice. I had to let him go. Hardest thing I ever did, but by the book."

"How did he feel about that?"

"How do you think he felt? He had just lost his career, and his marriage was in shambles. He lost his life savings, which included as much of his 401k he could borrow. And if that wasn't bad enough, his best friend sent him packing to the unemployment line at a time when unemployment was skyrocketing. So he probably wasn't very happy about it, or with me."

Jake placed his cup back on the hearth and then stood. "Do you mind if I use the restroom? That coffee seems to have gone right through me."

"Of course not," Dirk said, surprised by the abrupt shift. He nodded towards the door. "There's one just off the kitchen by the back door."

Jake took his notepad and left the room.

"What do you think, Daddy?" Kel turned her eyes to him as she stepped around and took a seat.

"I know he's just collecting background, but I thought he'd be more interested in my whereabouts this week."

"Maybe he's just getting warmed up. You still okay? This might go on a while longer."

"I'll be fine."

While they sat in silence, Kel took hold of Dirk's arm and gave it gentle squeeze. Dirk felt her hand and sensed she passed him a smile but couldn't look her way. Jake had stirred a monster that he thought had been buried a decade ago.

When Jake reappeared he didn't move to the rocker but stopped in the study's doorway. "Well, Chief Nyte, I think I have enough for now."

"What? You're not going to ask me where I was at the times in question?"

"Not right now. Besides, I'm not sure you have the strength to overpower someone like Suzanne Lowen. By the way, do you own a cell phone?"

"Don't use it much now, but yes."

"When was the last time?"

"I don't know. Maybe a couple of weeks ago. I take it with me when I go out."

"Do you mind if I pull your records?"

"Whatever you need—my landline, cell phone, computer … I have nothing to hide. And I just want to make one last statement, Jake. I've built my career on prosecuting criminals. With three months to live, do you really think I'm going to suddenly become one?"

"Ever hear of going out in a blaze of glory, Chief?"

Chapter Twenty-Seven

KEL PRESSED THE button on the remote to engage the automatic door opener to her single-car garage. She was relieved to finally be home. The day had started without enough sleep at three a.m., and with the clock on the dashboard now registering 7:58 p.m., she let her eyelids slide shut as the garage door slid open. The scent of pizza from the box on Chrissie's lap reminded her stomach that, except for the small snack she ate at her dad's, it had been neglected. Not since ten hours earlier when she devoured a raspberry scone in Bellingham had she eaten anything resembling a meal, and that hadn't been enough.

Once the door ground to a halt, she opened her eyes and guided the Jeep into the dimly lit cavern. Things too painful to encounter around the house on a daily basis, but too sentimental to donate, created a narrow passage. Stacked in boxes, Lance's things left just enough room on each side for slender bodies to squeeze through the SUV's open doors.

As Chrissie stepped from the car, Kel's phone rang. She tapped the Bluetooth. "Nyte."

"Detective Nyte?" The voice of the desk sergeant filled her ear. "We picked up Vince Buckley."

Inquiries with Buckley's neighbors and at his place of employment, her sister Shelia's law firm, had yielded no clues to his location. His supervisor stated that he had requested a couple days off but gave no indication as to his plans. With the malicious gossip mill circulating stories about his past, he made no friends in the time he had worked there, so no one could account for him. "He keeps to himself," his supervisor concluded when Kel interviewed him yesterday. With the knowledge that he was due to report to work on Wednesday morning, the SPD doubled the stakeout at his home.

Before she stepped from the SUV, she called Jake. "Got Buckley in the box?"

"Why?" he asked. "Your dad put you onto him?"

"He has motive, Jake, for both Terry's and Suzanne's murders. More than my dad has. If you'd get your head out of your ass, you'd see that."

"Where I put my head is my business, plebe. And I'll interview people I have a feel for when I have a feel for them. He's on my list, but he hasn't warmed up to me yet, so if you're going to interview him, it'll be without me."

"Hot date, huh?"

"Again, that's my damn business. Tonight, I'm otherwise engaged."

Otherwise engaged. Jake deLaurenti was an enigma. Around the precinct, people talked about Jake's company of women as if he were a Greek god. Some of them so exotic, reconciling his plain face and stunted personality with their stunning bodies was as likely as tanning to a golden brown in a Siberian blizzard. He relished being seen in public with them on his arm. How he met these beauties, or why they clung to him so attentively, he wasn't talking about—gloating by their mere presence, yes, but not talking. That they were escorts was the most obvious answer, but on a detective's pay he should have only been able to afford sidewalk skanks.

Although just in its second day, to say that he and Kel had formed a partnership would stretch even the most liberal definition of the word. No bridge had begun to take shape. In fact, to Kel, it felt more like the Great Wall of China had been dropped between them. He didn't take her seriously, and his track record proved that if things got rough, he wouldn't have her back.

She squeezed between the storage boxes and the Liberty, following the scent of the pizza, and eased through the door into the passageway between the detached garage and townhome. At the back door, which Chrissie had left ajar, an eager snout greeted her.

"Hey, Saul," she said as she squeezed through the door opening. She reached and petted his head. "What's up, boy? Want some dinner?"

More than a watchdog and family friend, Saul had been Lance's dog. Lance had left him in Chrissie's charge when he mustered out for Afghanistan on that final mission. When he didn't return, Saul became a welcomed ray of light on an otherwise dark and dismal path.

"How many slices?" Chrissie asked as she pulled two plates from the white particle-board cabinet above the Formica counter.

"Make it two." Kel took two napkins from the holder on the counter and placed them on the bar.

"Jessica invited me over to spend the night Friday. Would that be okay?"

"I don't know. Friday night's the Torchlight Parade. Pops is going to be in it, remember?"

"Yeah, and Jessica's family is planning to go. I'll be there to see Pops." She slid two pieces on a plate and handed it to Kel.

"Thanks, hon," Kel said, and placed the plate on the countertop. "We're going to sit together, to be his cheerleaders."

"Me and Jessica'll find you. Please?"

"Well, so long as you promise." She sat on the vinyl barstool and leaned into the padded back. "Aunt Shelia and Danny will be there. We should sit together. This'll probably be Pops' last special night."

"That makes me so sad, Mom," Chrissie said as she came around the counter and sat next to Kel. "I promise I won't miss it."

"This smells so good. Say, I have to go back to work in a few minutes."

"Mom," Chrissie said with her familiar sing-song whine.

"I know, sorry. How 'bout you ride along?"

"I don't know. Sounds pretty boring." She picked up the first slice and aimed it for her mouth.

"I'm going to interview Vince Buckley."

"The Rat City Exterminator? Cool."

"You've been doing your Internet research?"

"Yeah, since you and Pops were talking about him last night."

"We've been looking for him, and he just turned up. I need to ask him a few questions. You're welcome to come with. You probably won't see him, and it might be late, but I'd love to know you're just in the next room."

"I don't know," she said, her mouth full of pizza.

"You can see my new desk."

"Oh," she said with an exaggerated eye roll, "now that's real cool, Mom."

"So that's a no?"

"No," she said, and paused. "That's a yes." And then she took another bite.

Chapter Twenty-Eight

KEL LOGGED INTO her computer and turned the mouse over to Chrissie. She looked toward the DK crime board and noticed a lot of empty space. The last thing she had written was the timeline leading up to Suzanne's death. More than a day had passed since then, and three more victims had given their lives for DK's cause—whatever the hell that is. Not only Terry, but a man who assisted him as he filled his tankers at the fuel terminal, and the young guard she watched burn to death, had become collateral damage.

Beyond the board, a beige cinderblock wall separated her from the main suspect in her investigation. She placed her hand on Chrissie's shoulder, bent forward, and kissed her on the cheek. Then she began a deliberate walk that would lead her into the presence of the once-convicted serial killer.

Kel had seen photos of Vince Buckley, newspaper clippings at the time of his arrest and trial. She remembered one in particular, shot as he was leaving the courtroom moments after his conviction.

In the photo, he struggled against the shackles on his hands, throwing one of his shoulders back to thwart the deputy's grip. His eyes, the lids pulled back and his tiny pupils protruding from their sclera, looked like Charlie Manson's on a bad day. The veins popping in his neck gave life to the rage gripping his face, and on his lips formed a silent shout captured under the photo: "I'm innocent."

The years in Walla Walla had changed him. A maximum security prison in eastern Washington, there he kept company with the Green River Killer; Gary Ridgway; and one of the Hillside Stranglers, Kenneth Bianchi. The man Kel found sitting at the table in Interview 1, "The Box," bore no resemblance to the convicted murderer she had anticipated meeting. He had lost the majority of his hair, and what remained formed a gray fringe trimmed close to the scalp. The wild eyes she had expected to see were now covered with dark-rimmed glasses, giving him a surprising look of normalcy. Except for several days' beard growth, he could have passed for an accountant.

"Vince Buckley?" she asked as she pushed the door to the small eight-by-eight room closed behind her. She locked on his eyes and watched intently for something she knew might only have a second or two of life before it expired. If Buckley had been the man who attacked her with the Taser in Suzanne's condo, she might see it on his face, but a stoic stare met her eyes. They revealed nothing.

"What am I doing here, Detective?" Buckley said.

Kel could tell from his tone that he fought to hold back his wrath. He flicked his eyes to the tabletop.

"You've kept me here behind a guarded door for what must have been a couple hours. No one has offered me so much as a glass of cold water or told me anything. Am I being charged with something?"

Kel walked across the room, pulled a steel-framed chair from the table, and sat. "You're here so we can have a talk. Might I get you some water?"

"No, and I've already invoked," he said. He turned his dark eyes up to hers and placed the palms of his hands on the white laminate table top. "My lawyer should be here any minute."

"That's your right, of course." She opened her notebook and rested it on the table. "But unnecessary, since you haven't been charged with anything. I just have a few questions."

"I'm not talking without my attorney."

"Then I'll start while we wait, if that's okay?"

"Fine, but expect it to be a one-sided conversation," he said, and looked at his hands. He interlaced his fingers.

"Perfect, and excuse my rudeness. I didn't introduce myself. I'm Detective Kel Nyte."

As she said her name, she paused and watched again for his reaction. His eyes rolled up again and connected with hers. She saw the flash of name recognition pass over them. When he didn't comment, she continued.

"The man who charged you and saw you through to conviction is my father, Dirk Nyte."

Again, she hesitated and waited to measure his reaction.

A smirk curved across his lips and he scratched the stubble under his chin with the backs of his fingers. "So now there's a new generation of Nytes to roust me? What is it about my overturned conviction you people don't understand? Without new evidence, you have no right to hold me."

"That's true, Mr. Buckley, but you're not here as a direct result of evidence on the Rat City case. You're here so I can eliminate you as a suspect in another string of murders."

The door open behind Kel, and before she turned toward the new arrival, a familiar voice spoke.

"I do hope you're not questioning my client without counsel."

"Except to verify his name and to see if he needed some water, I haven't asked Mr. Buckley a single question. We're just getting acquainted."

Kel stood and followed the lawyer with her eyes as she walked around the end of the table to take a seat next to her client.

"I'm surprised to see you." Kel shook her head. "How'd you pull this case?"

"We'll talk later," Shelia Savell said. She moved the chair and sat a couple of feet from her client.

"You know each other?" Buckley asked.

"It's a small community, Mr. Buckley," Kel said, and returned to her chair, "and it gets even more convoluted. We're both Nytes. Your lawyer's my sister."

"Hell," he said, turning toward Shelia. "Is that the best our firm can do? Send the kid of the man who trumped up charges against me?"

"Snelling sent me to represent you," Shelia said, and pulled a yellow legal pad from her briefcase. "Not because of my dad, but because they knew I'd be unbiased and give you the best counsel." Then, to Kel, she continued, "Whatever questions you have for Mr. Buckley, I'm here to make sure he doesn't implicate or perjure himself."

"Of course." Kel turned to Buckley. "It's your call. Snelling, Hardcastle, and Purdin have plenty of other lawyers. We can wait until they send another, or we can proceed with the counsel at hand. I've known Shelia all her life, and she's always been above reproach."

"Why should I trust either one of you?"

"You have no reason to, but allow me to ask a few questions, and if at any time you want to stop, just say so."

He looked from Kel to Shelia, and then back at Kel. "Go ahead, but if I so much as hear the distant whistle of a goddamn train, I'm the hell out of here."

"Sounds fair. No railroad job. Now, if I may, according to the police report you live on Seventeenth Southwest. Is this true?"

"That's where your boys in blue picked me up?"

"So, that's a yes?"

"Yes. What about it?"

"According to your address, your house is only a couple blocks off Roxbury St. Is this also true?"

"What of it?"

"Well, maybe it's me, but it seems awfully coincidental that the trail I'm following begins about three blocks from your house."

"What trail's that?" he said, and leaned toward the table.

"Are you familiar with Suzanne Lowen?"

"Yeah, she's the lab rat that overturned my conviction."

"And the one who sent you up in the first place."

"True enough."

"What about Terry Graham?"

"Just another cum-filled cop trying to make his mark. Along with your daddy, he put me away."

"Would you be surprised to learn that both of these police officers were murdered?"

"You think I killed them?"

He jumped to his feet. His chair flew back and slammed hard into the wall with a loud metallic crash. Shelia twisted in her chair away from him and Kel rose to her feet, placing her hands, palms down, on the table.

He continued, "That's why I'm here? This trail just happens to start near my house and two people who had something to do with my imprisonment are dead? And now you accuse me?"

"Please sit back down, Mr. Buckley. I'm not making any accusations. But now that you bring it up, did you murder them?"

"Don't be ridiculous. I've never murdered anyone. "

"I'll ask you again to take your seat."

Buckley glared at Kel and then shot a glance at Shelia. Then he reached back for the chair and eased into it.

"So, can you account for yourself since yesterday morning?" Kel asked as she returned to her chair.

He looked at Shelia again. She leaned in toward him, and he turned to whisper into the ear facing away from Kel. After a few moments, Shelia nodded her head. "Go ahead and answer."

He bent forward toward Kel. "I've been in Yakima since Friday night with my kid sister and her family. You see, they never lost faith in me. They believed me innocent, and they still do." Kel noticed the tension receding from his face as he relaxed into the chair. "My nephew plays second base in the senior little league division, and this was the state playoffs. His team kept winning right up through this morning. Little shit struck out in the last inning of the final game. They lost."

"And your family can vouch for you twenty-four hours a day?"

"I had a separate hotel room, so not while I slept, but from breakfast through dinner, we were together."

"What time was breakfast yesterday?"

"The hotel served a continental breakfast, so we met in the dining room. Let's see, that might've been about ... eight."

"What about this morning?"

"'Bout the same time. No, wait, not this morning."

"Why not today?"

Shelia took hold of Buckley's arm and twisted toward his ear. After several exchanges of whispered secrets, Shelia sat back in the chair. "Against my advice, my client wishes to continue."

"Perfect," Kel said. She leaned forward and locked her green eyes on his. "So what time will your sister say you met up with her?"

"Uh ... 'round eleven this morning, before my nephew's final game."

Kel knew his timeline gave Buckley ample opportunity to commit both murders. With Yakima only two hours' driving time southeast of Seattle, he had opportunity to kill Suzanne Monday morning, wait around to attack her, and still return with time to spare for an eight o'clock breakfast. Bellingham was about five hours from Yakima, but since he had missed breakfast today, he had plenty of time to plant the bomb on Terry's truck and then set it off while still at the fuel terminal.

"What made you late this morning?"

"It's kind of personal." He rotated his head back and forth from Kel to Shelia. "But since you need an alibi. I split up from my sister's family after dinner last night and made my way to an alcoholic beverage establishment."

"We'll just say a bar, right?"

"Let's call it a lounge. The hotel lounge. I met a woman there and … well, one thing led to another and ... ah, hell, let's just say that this morning we were kind of tied up in the sheets. I didn't make breakfast."

Damn it, Kel thought, but said, "And you have this woman's name, of course?"

"Damn if I know." He laughed. "All those years out of circulation in Walla Walla, who cares about names? I'll say this, though. If you find her, you'll be able to verify my story because my DNA will be inside her—several times."

Disappointment clouded Kel's mind. Day two had been brutally long, and only a few hours remained to find a suspect before the deadline her boss, Lou Martinez, had given her. She had hoped Buckley would escalate to a viable suspect, but with this alibi, though flimsy, he was beginning to look less attractive. She turned her notepad around and slid it toward his side of the table.

"I need a description of the woman," she said, her tone reflecting her irritation, "and, since you've included your sister and the hotel in your story, I need their names and numbers."

Buckley glared at Kel for several seconds. "I shouldn't have to provide a goddamn alibi. I'm not a felon any longer. This has the stink of profiling."

"Stink or not," Kel said and glanced at Shelia, "from my point of view, you've been unaccounted for during the time of both crimes and have motive. On that alone I could hold you, but if you wish to cooperate, you'll give me the information. The more detailed the better."

He looked at Shelia again. When she didn't object, he took the pen and began to write.

Kel knew he was right. The only reason he was sitting across the table from her was because of what he had been convicted of doing—a conviction that no longer stood. But until she verified his story, she planned to keep him in her sights.

After he finished writing, he pushed the pad toward Kel. "Can I go now?"

She scanned over what he had written, stood and then walked to the door. She opened it with a jerk. "The officer outside will see that you get a ride home."

Kel gave her sister a "stay put" stare as he walked around behind Shelia and exited the room. A single step brought her back to the table and she gripped the ladder-back chair until her knuckles turned white.

"What the hell, Shelia? You're defending him?"

"It's what they call the law, sis. The suspect provides an account, and the police try to shake it."

"I like him for this, Shelia, but going up against you isn't my idea of fun. What if I break his alibi?"

"Then do it right this time," she said, and stood. "He walked out of that prison because Dad didn't seal the deal. You want him, work for it."

As she finished speaking, Chrissie's voice erupted from outside the door. "Don't touch me."

Kel turned and ran for the room's exit. She tore through the opening. Chrissie stood with her butt against the edge of the desk. Buckley leaned in toward her.

As a male officer grabbed Buckley's left arm, he said without moving his eyes from the teenager, "Lovely girl, Detective. You should be cautious about bringing her into a place like this. There are unsavory types lurking."

"Get him the hell out of here," Kel shouted to the officer, "before I find reason to hold him overnight."

"Sorry, Kel," the officer said, and tugged Buckley's arm toward the door. "Come on."

"Okay, okay." Buckley threw his palms up toward Chrissie. "I meant her no harm, Kel—just admiring your beautiful handwork. Takes some after you, don't you think? But that purple streak of hair, I'm not so sure about."

Chapter Twenty-Nine

MARILYN WINSTON ROLLED over in the bed she shared with her husband and looked at the clock. She hadn't slept well through the night. Now the clock's white digital beacon warned her that in five minutes what little rest she had taken would have to be sufficient today for her fifty-nine-year-old body.

While she tossed and turned in the night, she had cried silent tears, unable to shake the image of her ex-husband, Terry Graham, burning to death. Logic told her that he had never felt a thing. Likely the explosion itself had produced such a concussion that he probably was unconscious before he knew what happened. But the image of someone running out of a burning building with hair and clothes ablaze kept playing in her mind on an endless loop.

Though they hadn't spoken in years and their marriage had ended in a terrible disaster, she could imagine no reason he should fall victim to such an absurd overkill. She didn't still love him—not like before—but at one time she had committed her whole life to him. They had enjoyed such pleasurable intimacy that the thought of him being destroyed by such violence made her angry.

Even in divorce, Terry had been honorable. He took more blame than he should have for the failure. Shamed by the way he had treated her in the last few months of the marriage, he signed over the house they shared and what little remained of his 401k. She objected, but he could be obstinate. In the end she couldn't convince him otherwise. As he drove away for the last time in his little beater Sedan, she forced her eyes closed to dam her tears. Many were the days she wanted to call him to put things back together. She knew if she did, however, she'd have to keep one thing from him—a secret she planned to take to the grave, a betrayal he never knew.

The chorus of Rick Springfield's 1980's classic "Jesse's Girl" started low on the radio alarm, and Marilyn reached over to shut it off before it stirred her husband, Paul.

Paul had landed a telecommuting job a few years back, and since his clients were in Europe, he often worked through the night and spent much of the day asleep. She knew her boss would understand if she took a mental day due to Terry's death. Staying home with Paul asleep, though, meant she'd be alone with her thoughts, unable to detach the ugly vision of Terry's death from her mind. Her rescue from this idleness was work, at least for today. Work might distract her, give her solace, and if nothing else, fill the haunted void.

She slipped from between the linens and sat on the edge of the bed. The light of the morning sun brightened a glow behind the pale aqua drapes. A sudden breath of wind filled the curtain's folds like a hot air balloon, and then they exhaled, flattening against the window screen as the breeze shifted. Beyond the window a bird cried, chick-a-dee-dee-dee, and the painful images evaporated like a bad dream. She took her robe from the floor and strode across the carpet to the bathroom.

Marilyn stopped at the door and turned back to Paul. He had given her a second chance at love, and although he wasn't as attentive to her physical needs as Terry, he loved her, and she knew it. He inhaled a deep breath and then let it out like a sigh. If the clock had disturbed him, he had no knowledge of it now. She closed the bathroom door behind her and prepared for work.

Twenty-five minutes later, Marilyn reopened the bathroom door wearing a pastel blue cotton dress and saw that Paul, her husband, hadn't stirred. Caressed by a single blanket, she kissed two of her fingers, placed them to his cheek, and then turned toward the stairs.

In the kitchen, she reached for the door of her stainless steel freezer and selected a frozen Weight Watchers. With lunch in hand, she moved to the counter near the double sink and saw that Paul had done one of his thoughtful things. Before he turned in, he'd snipped a solitary red rose from her garden and placed it in a crystal bud vase. She didn't recognize the container, but that was like Paul—"Just to say 'I love you.'" A computer printout beside the rose read, "There are more like these in the garden."

She lifted the flower to her nose, breathed deep its fragrant perfume, and smiled at Paul's thoughtfulness. With lunch in her bag, she went out the back door and locked it behind her.

As she crossed the lawn to the garage, she saw the rose bed. As Paul had said, the garden had a colorful palette of fresh blooms. She drifted over to them. Overcome by the emotions of the last day, the brutal explosion that brought an end to Terry and the thoughtfulness of a lovely flower from Paul introduced fresh tears.

The clouds threatened rain and brought with them a cool morning breeze. It brushed against her bare arms and ruffled the tiny blond hairs. She shivered. At the garden, she bent at the waist and lifted a fresh bud. She sensed it'd burst into full aperture when the sun peaked over the roof top. The velvety-satin texture between her fingers and the palm of her hand as she stroked it ripped from her core a latent memory which arose with such power she trembled, yet she felt no shame. Terry, a passionate lover, blossomed just so before their bodies became one, and her mind, emotions, and will united in an all-consuming arousal. She released the rose, stood, and dabbed the tears from her cheeks with the back of her hand.

Movement behind her, as sudden and silent as a dandelion's parachute adrift on a gust of summer breeze, caught her breath in a gasp. She sensed the presence and warmth of a man's body close to her. Ready to fall into Paul's arms, she started to turn, but stopped short when, from behind, a hand clasped over her mouth. It pulled her head into a shoulder as if it were an intimate caress.

Her mind froze in terror when in front of her, her own fear-filled eyes reflected back in a chrome blade extended before her. Before she could react, the knife sliced deep into the tissues of her neck. It felt more like a razor nick on her leg than the fatal wound she knew she had been given. She reached to find the unseen face, but the cool morning air again caressed her body. This time it also whispered against the warm blood flowing from her throat. Her mind slipped fast toward emptiness. Her hands dropped, and no awareness remained.

Chapter Thirty

KEL PULLED AT the fabric of her blue jeans to
relieve the tightness surrounding her calves and
crouched next to a woman she hadn't seen in years.
More than a decade had passed since this same
woman stood in her daddy's backyard with a plate of
potato salad in one hand and a hamburger in the
other. Chrissie, who had always thought of her as
another aunt, had thrown her arms around Marilyn's
neck. She hugged her so tight that Marilyn had lost
her balance and fell backwards on the grass laughing
as she spilled her plate.

Now she was on the lawn again, but what had
spilled didn't bring laughter this time, and there was
no way to clean up this mess. Her blanched face set
in stark contrast to the scarlet stain on her dress, and
the red of the rose on Marilyn's breast. Her fingers
were wrapped around it like a funeral pose. Although
the blood had stopped flowing, it was clear Marilyn's
life had poured from the wound and soaked into the
soil.

When Kel received the text, she had just risen for
the day, glad to have slept through the night. She had
thought she'd find sleep evasive, that her mind may
well replay the interview with Buckley or the last two

days of murder and suspicion, but as soon as her head caressed the pillow, she drifted to sleep.

When the address had appeared on her phone, she knew without checking what phone number sent the text. She called her partner, Jake. When he didn't answer, she left a message. Then, not wanting to make the same error in judgment she had made Monday morning at Suzanne Lowen's condo, she called dispatch.

By the time she arrived at the address, a patrol officer had awakened the husband and discovered the body. Minutes later a full complement of uniformed officers and crime scene investigators were dispatched to the scene.

"COD is exsanguination due to a severed carotid artery," the medical examiner said, and turned his ruddy face toward Kel. "As if that's not obvious." He pointed to a ceramic-handled kitchen knife with a six-inch blade, bloody and lying next to the victim. "This looks to be the smoking gun. It appears that the perp killed her and then snipped the rose with it." He pointed to the rose bush. "If you look close at the stem, you'll see traces of blood."

Kel placed her hand on the victim's hands and looked to her face. "I'm so sorry, Marilyn," she said and, without turning away from her, asked the ME, "Where's the husband?"

"You knew her?" he asked.

"Old family friend."

"I'm sorry. You'll find the husband at the house." He raised his thin gray eyebrows as if pointing her in the right direction.

She paused a moment and thought of her dad. This was going to hit him hard—first Terry and then Marilyn. But as she started to stand, a sudden sense of relief washed over her with such power it startled her. And, just as fast as it came, shame followed like a flashflood.

Before leaving Marilyn, Kel reached to the breast pocket of her ecru blouse and dug out a pad and pen. She shook her head to push the emotions aside, and stood.

After drawing a quick diagram of the scene, she stepped to the backdoor of the house where a man in his early sixties with short cropped hair stood. His eyes, a few inches above hers, were trained on his wife's body. He wore a tattered blue bathrobe and filled more than half the doorway. On his face, a pained look of disbelief, anger, and sorrow mixed together.

"Mr. Winston?" she asked as she reached the patio.

"Yes," he said. The strain of grief made his voice crack.

"My name is Detective Kel Nyte." She showed him her shield. "May I ask you a few questions?"

"I already gave a statement."

"I know you did, but if you could tolerate just a little more … why don't we step inside?"

"Does he have to …?" he started to say to Kel. Then, raising his voice, he looked past her and shouted, "Do you have to do that? My God!"

She turned toward the crime scene and realized he had reacted to a tall, slender man who stooped over his wife's body with a digital camera.

"Mr. Winston," Kel said with a calm tone, "he's just doing his job. We have to document the scene and those photos may help to find her killer. Why don't we go inside? You don't have to watch this."

Paul rotated his face to hers and stared for a few seconds, and then made an abrupt turn. He led the way through the kitchen to the living room.

"I can't believe this." He lowered his head and shook it back and forth. "Yesterday it's her ex and today her. What's happening?"

"I'm sorry for your loss, Mr. Winston. I wish—"

"Paul, please."

"Of course. Paul, I wish I had answers, but at this time we don't know. Please, let's sit. Might I get you a glass of water or something?"

"Glasses are in the cupboard to the right of the sink."

Kel placed her hand on his forearm and squeezed it. "I'll only be a moment."

In the kitchen she found the glasses behind the cherry finished cupboard door and noticed the note lying next to a cut rose in a crystal vase.

She read it to herself: "There's more like these in the garden."

After she filled the tumbler with ice and water at the refrigerator, she stepped back into the living room. On the other side, Paul sat on the full-sized leather couch with his head dropped into his hands.

"Here, Paul." Kel extended the glass.

Paul raised his head and took it. He only drank a sip.

She slipped around a mahogany coffee table and sat beside him. "I noticed a rose in a vase in the kitchen. Did you leave that for Marilyn?"

"No, it must have been her killer. He was in my house—oh God, and I was just sleeping without a care."

"Is it your habit to sleep in?"

"I work from home. My clients are abroad, so I'm usually up all night. Generally, I'm still up when she leaves for the office, but last night I finished early and was tired, so I went to bed. I didn't hear her get up. It wasn't until your officer rang the doorbell that I saw she was gone. You never know when you've spoken your last word or given the last kiss, do you?"

"I know what you're feeling, Paul. I lost my closest friend and my daughter's dad in Afghanistan. As painful as that was—and truthfully, it still aches today … even though your every nerve feels raw right now, it'll get easier. The important thing is to find your wife's killer."

"But how did one of your officers know she might have been hurt?"

"We didn't know who was hurt. I can't discuss how, but I can say that I had reason to believe something bad happened, so I sent a squad to investigate. Earlier you mentioned Marilyn's ex-husband's murder. There was another victim earlier his week. Evidence indicates it's the same person who took all three lives. I'm sorry I have to ask this, but did you know Suzanne Lowen or Terry Graham?"

"You think I did this?" Paul shouted, and slammed the water glass hard on the table in front of him.

"What I think is not the issue," Kel said, keeping an even tone, "and you didn't answer my question."

"No, I've never heard of this Suzanne woman and I never met Terry. And before you ask, no, I did not kill either of them or my wife."

"I'm sorry, but I have to ask."

"My God, this is unbelievable!" He rested his forehead on his hands and shook his head. "One minute you're taking each other for granted, and before you can start planning their funeral, you have to mount a defense."

"To be honest, Paul," Kel said, placing her hand on his shoulder, "I have no reason at this time to believe you had anything to do with this. But it's my job to eliminate those with proximity so I can focus on the real suspects. I do need to ask some other questions, though, if you're up to it."

"Look, I already told you I was asleep. I didn't hear or see anything, so I'm not sure I'm going to be much help."

"You must have a computer."

"Yes, of course. That's how I communicate with Europe. Why?"

"The killer always leaves a specific message for me somewhere near his victim. Have you checked your computer since you were awakened?"

"No," he said as he stood. He gathered his bathrobe around his waist and cinched the belt tight. Without speaking further, he stepped around the coffee table and led the way to the downstairs office not far from the living room.

"What are we looking for?" he asked as he took a seat in a black executive chair. He swiveled to face the keyboard.

"Please don't touch anything."

"What ...? Oh ... of course. Fingerprints." He stood and gave a wave of his hand toward the chair.

Kel pulled a pair of latex gloves over her hands and sat before the laptop. Except for what appeared to be a company logo floating on the monitor, the screen was black. She slid the mouse back and forth until it came to life. Like on Suzanne's computer, four lines rose from the backlit screen. Kel read them aloud.

"Three's indulgence now plain view

No escape the sickle's hew

River red that will not heal

My death blade the soul to steal."

"What does it mean?" Paul asked.

"I don't know, Paul. For now it's another piece of evidence. I'm going to need to take the computer to our lab for analysis."

"You can't take my computer. That's my bread and butter."

"It'll only be for the day," Kel said with hesitation. She wondered if what he had said wasn't a tell. "You already claimed you sleep during the day."

The first people to be cleared were the people closest to the victim, the spouse and other family members. She didn't know the Winstons or anything about their marital relationship. It was possible there was discord in the home. Paul could have set up his wife's murder from the beginning. After all, every victim to date had at one time been in the news, as had she. Research wouldn't have been too difficult, especially for someone who appeared to be as computer-savvy as Paul. He could have easily gathered enough information to connect the victims to her dad and somehow located her phone number.

"But I ... I have people I need to contact," he said, and a tear began to course across his unshaven face. "My contacts are in there."

"I'm sorry, but we need to take it. There might be other clues to your wife's killer's identity. If you want, however, you can come with me to the station. Then, as soon as we're done with our investigation, you can take it with you."

"No ... No, I'm sorry." He stared at the floor, shaking his head. "That won't be necessary. Of course you need to take it. It's just that I'm closing on a big deal in Belgium at the moment, but my boss will understand. I'll give him a call."

An hour later, after canvassing a few neighbors, Kel walked back to her SUV parked in the Winstons' driveway, and left the scene for the investigators to process. As an officer herded the onlookers back by moving a barricade to open the way for her Jeep to pass, the euphoric feeling she had experienced as she stood over Marilyn's body returned. This time the guilt restrained itself. With Jake's logic, since her dad had no reason to kill Marilyn, she was sure this would take him off the short list.

Chapter Thirty-One

THE CLOCK READ 3:12 p.m. when Kel pushed the bullpen door open. Jake sat on the edge of his desk with his back to her. He turned away from the crime board toward her as she entered the room. The sleeves of his blue dress shirt were rolled up carefully to mid-forearm.

"Afternoon, plebe," he said. "Sent a squad to pick up your dad."

A flush of heat rushed to her cheeks, and there was no disguising her irritation. "Why? He's too sick to be rustled from his house on such short notice. If you have more questions, we should have done it there where he's more comfortable."

She looked beyond Jake's desk to the crime board she had started. Jake had made some changes since she saw it last night before Vince Buckley's interview. On the right edge, he wrote DK in quotes and below it taped a copy of the "manifesto" as her dad had called it—the first poem he sent to her. On the other side, under a handwritten "#1," the picture she had printed of Suzanne Lowen in her a white lab coat draped over pink scrubs, smiled at the room. Her eyes followed Kel as she stepped closer. The poem she had discovered at the scene was printed and taped beneath the picture. Below the "#2," Terry Graham's picture—the way she remembered him from more than a decade ago—grimaced from the newspaper photo of him pointing his gun at a suspect on the ground. Below it, the faces of the two men who died with Terry mocked her. She could still hear the young man's helpless shriek as the fire consumed him in the terminals driveway. A photocopy of the poem she had found in Terry's mailbox was secured to the board below the pictures. Next, "#3" was written above a picture of Marilyn Winston lying lifeless on the grass.

She took the printout of the poem taken from Paul Winston's computer, walked past Jake's desk toward the crime board, and taped it below Marilyn's picture.

Jake stood and said, "Because the three main victims have one thing in common …"

He removed another photo from a manila folder, and taped the image of the former Police Chief Dirk Nyte to the center of the board. With a black marker, he drew a connecting line from each victim to Kel's dad.

She took a step back and stared at the black lines. "My dad has nothing to do with this. What motive could he possibly have to kill Marilyn? In my worst nightmares I can't believe he'd do any of this."

"Which makes you prejudicial," Lieutenant Martinez said from behind her.

A shudder coursed its way up Kel's spine. She had known since this morning that this meeting was imminent, as Martinez had called her phone when she left the Winston's home. She let it go to voicemail and hoped a new lead might surface while she stalled the confrontation as long as possible. She believed the breadcrumbs DK had dropped might lead her to him. But she needed more time.

From the beginning, her service in the detective squad was bound by a tenuous thread Martinez could sever without hesitation. He had given her forty-eight hours to generate a suspect from the evidence. Now, just short of fifty-seven had elapsed since the countdown started in the parking lot of Suzanne Lowen's condo. Then, the Chief of D's, Nathaniel Ballesteros, had been her advocate, but she hadn't seen or heard from him since. He couldn't protect her now.

The man taking pictures of the explosion at the fuel terminal with his cell phone was the only real lead she produced. But she had run his vehicle plate through the Department of Licensing and pulled his phone history. Both brought her up empty. Other than Vince Buckley and his incomplete alibi, she had nothing solid. She looked at the crime board again and saw the black lines pointing to the man she loved more than life and shook her head.

"I'm still objective," she said, and made a determined twist of her body toward Lou's voice.

"Easy to say now," Martinez said, as he walked up to face Kel and stared at the white board, "but when you see the evidence piling up against him, your instinct will be to defend him despite the facts."

"He's not guilty."

"Of course he's not in the eyes of the law—until proven otherwise. But somehow, evidence implicating him is coming out, and you, with more than two days, haven't given us anything but hindsight."

"What evidence?" She swallowed hard to mollify the queasy churn in her stomach. "If I'm working this case, why am I not being informed of developments?"

"You're not going to like it," Jake said. He now stood beside her, wearing a smirk of defiance. "You'll just have to watch and lea—"

"Where have you been since this morning, following leads?" Martinez asked, and stroked his bushy mustache with is thumb and forefinger. "I've been trying to reach you."

Not long after she left Marilyn's crime scene, another text hit her phone following Lou's unanswered call.

"Where is my bike?" it read.

That reminded her of the promise she had made to the mime, Marcel, while he was in the hospital.

She turned back toward Martinez. "I was running an errand."

"And when was the last time you met with your partner?"

"Don't even go there."

"I assigned you to work with Jake."

She glanced toward her partner. His face curled with crooked sneer. "And he told me in so many words to piss off. Rule one—right, Jake?"

Jake's smile faded, and he picked up the now empty manila folder from his desk.

Kel shot a quick glance from him to the room and realized their confrontation was drawing an audience. Other detectives in the bullpen had stopped their work and chatter to observe the sparring match in the center of the room. Even Captain Silva had stepped from his office, and now stood at Martinez's right side with his arms folded across his chest.

"Rule one? What does that mean?" Martinez asked. His dark eyes bore holes into Kel's now only inches away.

"You should ask him." She twisted her torso to Jake and lifted an accusatory finger. "They're his rules." When Jake made no indication he'd offer an explanation, she shouted, "Stay the hell out of my way."

She faced Martinez again and continued. "That's rule one. As soon as Marilyn's address came across my phone this morning, I called Jake. But when the call went to voicemail I left him the address and called dispatch. I was on the scene for nearly two hours, but Jake never called or made an appearance. One has to wonder if he's too busy with other commitments or if he's so convinced that my dad's the only suspect, he's looking nowhere else. Who's not being objective here? As much as I don't want it to be my dad, at least I'm working the case. Except for Monday at Suzanne's, I can't put Jake on scene one time. We're now five dead into this, two of them cops, and he's not even phoning it in. He's just an absentee."

"If you have a complaint against your partner, take it up with the chief of detectives—that's his problem. But I'm yours, and I say you can't be objective. I want your phone."

"What?" she roared and dropped forward, placing her hands on the top of Jake's desk to stem the feeling that she had stepped off the edge of a cliff. "That's how the perp's communicating. Without that you're crippling the investigation."

"You're being benched, Nyte, get it? Off the case. Give me your damn phone, or I'll take it from you myself."

She felt like a barracuda caught in a school of hungry sharks. She needed an ally, and made eye contact with Captain Silva. He unfolded his arms, ran the fingers of his right hand over his crew cut, and then, with a subtle shake of his head, drove both hands into the pockets of his dress slacks. Thanks for the support.

"How can you do this?" Kel asked as she turned back to Martinez.

"I gave you two days, and you've turned up nothing. Your phone!"

"What about Vince Buckley?"

"Buckley? Why don't you, Nytes, get off his case? He's got nothing to do with this."

She knew this was a long shot. Before Marilyn's death she could see a connection. But as far as she knew now, Buckley had never met her. Still, it was something that might buy her another day or two.

On her way to the impound lot to pick up Marcel's bicycle, she made several calls to verify Buckley's alibi. His sister stated that he had been with them the whole weekend, but she admitted that they parted company each evening. The hotel said they'd turn their security tapes over to the Yakima Police Department, but went on to say that if the woman in the hotel lounge wasn't a registered guest, they probably can't identify her. And then, after she met Marcel, her cellular rang with the Yakima Police.

"We're coming up empty," the detective had said. "A hotel clerk reported she may have seen a woman matching the description you gave eating the hotel's complimentary breakfast Tuesday morning, but she doesn't appear on any security tape. We're processing the room, but housekeeping has cleaned it twice since Monday. Any evidence has likely been destroyed."

"Is there a way for him to leave the hotel and return without being detected?" she asked.

"The only cameras running are in the lobby," the detective concluded, "so if he took the elevator to the garage or a side door, yes."

Now, with the knowledge that his story was uncorroborated, she still had hope.

"He has motive for the first four murders, and his alibi has holes big enough to drive suspicion."

"Like?"

"For starters, no verified witnesses to his whereabouts for the twelve-to-fifteen-hour periods when the first two crimes were committed. And then there's Paul Winston—"

"Winston?"

"What if he's copycatting?"

"You're stretching it now and trying my patience. Your phone—and that's an order."

Kel glared at Lou. She saw by the throbbing veins in his neck and his jaw—clenched so tight that his face looked like a wooden mask—that his rage was beyond consolation at the moment. Resigned to being officially sidelined, she reached to her belt and retrieved the smartphone.

As she did, motion in her peripheral vision caught her attention, and she looked past Lieutenant Martinez, toward the doorway. Two uniformed officers led her dad into the room. They stood on either side of their former chief and held his arms, not in restraint, but rather in respect for a frail man too weak to depend on his own strength.

A proud smile lit up Dirk's face as he looked toward her—not arrogance, but a special pride reserved for someone he loved. But the drawn gray flesh of his face and the tremors of his arms under his short-sleeved burgundy golf shirt told Kel that this week, combined with his illness, was taking a toll on his fragile body. He might not have three months.

"Go write more tickets," Martinez shouted as he ripped the phone from hand.

Her heart skipped the next beat, and she felt a heavy lump in her throat beginning to apply pressure to her tears. Without turning away from her dad, she said, "Respectfully, sir, may I observe Jake's interview?"

Lieutenant Martinez followed her gaze and met Dirk's eyes.

"Observation, not participation," he said, his tone flat.

"Agreed."

Next to her, Jake raised his voice and said, "Interview Two." She rotated toward him and noticed a satisfied smirk cross his lips. As her dad and the officers walked across the bullpen to the glassed holding room, she turned her eyes back toward her boss.

"After Dad's done here, I need to take some personal time."

Martinez stared into her light green eyes for several seconds before responding. "Perhaps that'll be best, Officer Nyte. And while you're taking a break, maybe you could focus on learning respect."

"I'll make it a priority, sir."

Chapter Thirty-Two

KELL STOOD IN the observation room and watched her dad from behind a one-way mirror.

It could have been worse. The look in Lieutenant Martinez's eyes told her that if the disagreement had continued much longer, she might have been suspended for insubordination. That would have resulted in more than the loss of her police-issued phone. She'd have to surrender her gun and badge. But by taking personal time, she could continue to keep DK in her sites without the constraints of the department or an absentee partner.

Before she walked to observation, she left the bullpen to collect her personal phone from the locker in the women's washroom. Now, while she waited, she sent DK a message. "New number."

Her dad had been in Interview Two for half an hour waiting for Jake to begin his inquisition. Through the glass, she saw him grimace and shift his position every few seconds as if searching for comfort. But the hard chair he was confined to wasn't the source of his distress. The discomfort and weakness of his cancer played havoc on every tissue in his body. While he waited, she watched his face grow more pallid, and the tremors that had affected his arms in the bullpen were now spreading to the rest of his body. She was certain that the sudden interruption in his daily routine, and the knowledge that another friend had fallen victim to DK's lesson plan, had exacerbated his pain. She wanted to be in the room with him, to hold his hand and tell him she believed in him, but with her proximity to the case, and their relationship, she knew this would look wrong. She heard Jake say, "You could have been making up an alibi." So she hadn't broached the subject. She hoped her father understood.

When the door opened to Interview Two, Kel's eyes moved toward it. Her sister entered the room and looked immediately to Dirk. Kel had called Shelia at her office from the desk phone as soon as Lou Martinez left the bullpen. Shelia had been in a deposition at the time, and when Kel put Jake on the phone, Shelia asked him to wait until she arrived before proceeding with any questions.

Kel watched as Shelia, wearing a dark blue business suit with her chestnut hair at rest on her shoulders, walked around to the back side of the table. She took the seat next to her dad, put her arm around his shoulders, and kissed him on the cheek. Jake, who followed Shelia into Interview Two, grabbed the chair on the opposite side of the table, turned it backwards, and sat with his arms folded across the ladder back for support.

"Now that your attorney's here, can we begin?" Jake asked, his voice amplified through the speaker on Kel's side of the wall. "Dirk or Chief—which would you prefer?"

"Suit yourself," Dirk said, and folded his arms in front of him, resting them on his stomach. With Kel's psychology training, she recognized the silent barrier this action formed between her dad and his accuser.

"Three victims of violent murder," Jake said. He placed his zippered notebook on the simulated Mediterranean oak tabletop. "And two collateral damage. Cleaning house?"

"We talked about this. Do I really look like I'm physically capable of these horrific acts? I can hardly sit here in this uncomfortable chair, let alone fight with someone."

"Well, our suspect, which for now is you, seems to be perfectly capable of disabling a person very quickly. Did you kill Suzanne Lowen?"

"Don't answer that, Dad," Shelia said.

"Over my counsel's advice," Dirk said, placing his hand on Shelia's thigh, "I will answer that absurd question. What you're accusing me of is lying in wait for Suzanne, subduing her in my weak state, holding a pillow over her face until she suffocated, and then waiting for my own daughter so I could attack her with a stun gun. I retract, that's not an absurd question. It's preposterous."

"Well, you did dose Suzanne first."

"But wouldn't that require me to subdue her enough to inject the paralytic?"

"Is that how you did it? You injected her?"

"Dad, stop. Don't answer."

"You seem to have forgotten," Dirk said, as if Shelia hadn't spoken, "that my other daughter has intimate knowledge of this case."

"Dad, shut up now."

"Hmm …" Jake rubbed his chin. "Knowledge she shouldn't have passed along to a civilian, someone not involved with the case."

"In my opinion, I am involved in this case. Not as the suspect, though. As the target."

"So you think the perp is really after you. Why doesn't he just kill you and get it over with?"

"Maybe I'm the endgame. He said he wants to teach a lesson. So maybe after he's done, I'm last on his list."

"I guess we'll just have to take your word on that. So you and Terry Graham were partners."

"Is that a question?" Shelia asked.

"Statement of fact, counselor. Matter of record." He faced Dirk, pushed the sleeves of his blue shirt up to his elbows and said, "Now, Chief, let's go back to the domestic incident that occurred in the early morning hours of February 15, 2000."

"We've been over this. I've nothing to add."

"We'll see about that."

"Dad, what's he driving at?" Shelia asked.

Kel watched as her dad looked first at Shelia and then to the one-way mirror. Pain registered on his face, but it wasn't physical any longer. The memory of something long ago, rising out of the secret place and into the knowing, clouded his eyes. She remembered sitting next to him Monday evening when he said, "There are regrets. Things your mother and I worked through." Was this that furtive event that he had sheltered away? Was this Pandora's Box?

Dirk turned back to Jake, uncrossed his arms, and leaned forward. He grabbed the table with both hands to shift his position in the chair.

"Marilyn called me at home at about 2:30 a.m. She said that Terry had come home drunk and was beating her. She locked herself in the bathroom, but Terry pounded on the door with something harder than his fist. She thought it was his gun."

"Why did she call you and not 9-1-1?"

"As I said yesterday, she was trying to protect him."

"Is that it? Is that the only reason she called you?"

"Yes. Why else?"

"Where are you going with this?" Shelia asked, and straightened the lapel on her blazer.

"If you'll permit me, Counselor?" he said to Shelia, and directed his eyes back to Dirk. "You have two daughters—isn't that correct, Chief?"

"You know the answer to that, and you're wandering way off course."

"Am I? I only ask because I'm trying to give you a point of reference."

"For what?"

"Would you say your daughters are close?"

Kel wanted to smash the window that separated her from the people she loved and throttle Jake. Shelia turned toward her and shrugged her shoulders with a look of confusion across her face.

"Yes, I believe they're very close."

"Do you think there are things they might tell each other that no one else knows?"

"I'll ask you again, Detective," Shelia said, glaring at Jake, "where are you going with this?"

"Patience, Shelia."

Kel understood that Jake was grinding a point into her sister. Shelia was no longer in Interview Two as her dad's lawyer. She had slipped into the protective daughter role.

Jake rotated toward Dirk and cocked his head to the side. "Chief, I'm waiting for an answer."

After a brief pause, Dirk said, "The bond existing between sisters, especially sisters as close as my two daughters, is something no two men will ever understand. So, yes, it's true, they might tell each other their secrets and seal the vault."

"Would it surprise you to learn that Marilyn Winston had a sister?"

"I don't know much about Marilyn's family. I think she may have mentioned a sister at some point. So yes, she has a sister."

"Had a sister, you mean. Marilyn's dead."

"Obviously," Shelia said, "you don't know sisters well, Detective deLaurenti. Sisters are forever, in this life or the next. Death doesn't break that bond."

"In any case, Chief, Marilyn has a sister." He glanced at Shelia and then to the mirror on the wall. "You're so fond of talking about our conversation yesterday, Dirk. Do you remember when you mentioned that truth has a way of bubbling to the surface?"

"Of course I do."

"I spoke to Marilyn's sister a couple of hours ago, and she told me something you already know but have tried to conceal from everyone for more than a decade."

"And you revealing it now only has one goal, doesn't it? It has no bearing on this case. Your only motives are to catch me in an omission if you can and embarrass me in front of two people I love. Not a great strategy, Detective."

Shelia stood, walked behind Dirk's chair, and hugged her arms around his shoulders. She bent to his ear. "What's this about, Dad?"

Kel bolted for the separating door and burst into the interrogation room. She grabbed the end of the table, and it shook under her rage. "What's going on, Jake? What are you talking about?"

Dirk patted Shelia's hand and looked into Kel's eyes. He leaned toward the table and said, "I told you the other day, girls, that there were secrets. Things Mom and I worked through. This is one of them, and it's a big one. I didn't want it to come out this way, but ..."

He turned his eyes toward Jake and continued, "It's true. Marilyn called me and not the police that night in part because she didn't want it on Terry's record, but there was another reason. I'm sorry, girls. For several months, Marilyn and I had been having an affair."

Kel released the table, took a step back, and threw her arms up in front of her as if she were fending off an attacker's blows. Her breath caught in her throat and only a whisper escaped her lips. "Daddy?" She looked away, unable to bear eye contact with him. Then, with her voice recovered, she rolled her eyes toward Jake. "My God, you bastard. I won't believe this."

Shelia slid her hand away from her dad's shoulders. Dirk doubled his fist, slammed it to the table and rotated his head to face Kel. "Terry had been suspicious and accused me that night at the bar. I denied it, of course, but realized that Marilyn and I had to call it off. I told Mom the next morning. To this day I don't know why she, a much better soul than I ever will be, forgave me."

Of all the secrets to come out, an affair had been the last thing on Kel's mind. She had always believed her dad a man of honor, infallible, and her mother the personification of truth. If there had ever been discord in their marriage, they had masterfully shielded it from her and the world. Now, her heart sagged heavy with bereavement as she saw the long years of innocence gasping for life—without hope. Tears began to form, but something more powerful held them back.

A new reaction emerged, unexpected, like of a bolt of lightning before the clap of thunder—betrayal. A traitorous collusion between her parents to hide this unspeakable fact now threatened to drive a breach too wide to ever heal. An understandable secret between them, but once revealed, trust so cherished was crushed by the utterance of that one ugly word: affair.

Kel was angry. She glared at Jake but saw DK. How dare he force this confession to the surface? How dare he expose such an embarrassing family secret? Her dad had indicated on Monday night that he intended to step into the confessional before his death, but then it would have been on his terms. Even though wretched and raw, it could have been worked through. Now DK, through Jake, had exposed the most intimate failure of her dad's life as a matter of public record.

Finally able to face him, Kel turned back to Dirk. Their eyes met. The sadness he expressed grasped for her heart and begged for understanding. She had to avert again before he could gauge the cauldron of anger seething inside her. Almost impossible to tell the difference between them, the revulsion was not toward him directly, but for the concealment of the act. And for the way it came to light—once exposed, there was no way to extinguish it.

Shelia shifted and drew Kel's attention. She had retreated as far away from her dad as possible— against the wall in the corner of the small room. Her eyes had become moist pools and the first trickle now overflowed onto her cheeks. By the stunned look on her face, Kel knew that she no longer wanted to be in the room. The burden of this new knowledge was too much for even this powerful litigator to bear, but she had a client, and had no choice but to remain there.

Dirk directed his eyes back to Jake and asked, "Are you satisfied? Is this the affect you wanted? You want my daughters to hate me in my last days? Why, a decade after it's over and everyone's moved on, would I start a killing spree? Is this the best you can do?"

Kel struggled against the loathsome news to change the subject in her mind. The first line of DK's poem on Marilyn's death drifted by, and she grabbed it. "Three's indulgence now plain view." It was clear that DK was referring to the affair, but Jake had had no prior knowledge of it, at least as she could tell. Yesterday at Dad's he had been on a fishing expedition, looking for some other reason for Marilyn not to call 9-1-1. But today, armed with her sister's statement, the connection to motive, on theory alone, became clear.

But how did DK know? It seemed to have been a closely guarded secret, known only, with the exception of Marilyn's sister, to the four people involved. Dad and Mom never spoke of it, so unless DK got to the sister, which is unlikely, Marilyn or Terry must have confided it to someone—someone who could be trusted. Someone with an ax to grind. So did Terry know DK?

Jake's voice interrupted her thoughts.

"Maybe adultery did lead to this. Maybe you're taking out old memories before your passing. I can't speak to motive at this point, only evidence."

"Kel." Jake focused on his newest ex-partner. "I'm not done yet. Get your ass back to observation, or I'll have you escorted from the building."

Chapter Thirty-Three

"WHAT EVIDENCE?" DIRK asked after Kel left Interview Two.

Kel reached for the volume switch in the dark room and increased it. She didn't want to miss anything Jake threw at her dad.

"Hard to hear, isn't it, Officer Nyte?"

The voice from the darkness behind her made her flinch. Her eyes had adjusted to the light while in Interview Two, so she didn't notice that Lieutenant Martinez had entered and now stood against the back wall in the shadows.

"Someday I'd want to understand what you have against my dad," Kel said without turning to the voice.

She kept her eyes on the three people in the room beyond. "He is a good man, was a good cop, and he's been good for Seattle. I don't know why you can't see it and why you hold me responsible for whatever it is. But right now, with all respect, sir, I want to hear what Jake is about to say."

She shoved her hands in her blue jeans' pockets and prepared for his terse response. She was surprised when, without retort, the side door opened and the swish of his suit jacket gave indication of his exit.

After standing to flip his chair round, Jake sat properly and leaned toward Dirk. He placed his elbows on the table and stared at the chief. "Physical evidence, Chief."

Dirk broke the stare and looked toward the opposite wall. Jake smiled and drew a photo from his zippered notebook and, laying it on the table, shoved it to where Shelia had been sitting.

Shelia wiped the residual moister from her eyes with the back of her hand and walked toward her dad. She picked up the paper and then took her chair again next to Dirk. She spoke with a matter-of-fact tone. "What's this? A picture of a keyboard?"

"Look close, counselor. We found a hair resting on the keyboard of Paul Winston's laptop computer."

"And?"

"We can't prove it until we have the DNA results, but the hair doesn't match the color of either of the Winstons."

"So you've concluded that the hair came from some other donor?"

"Of course, but look closely. Is it a coincidence that the hair is the same color and texture as the Chief's? How would your dad's hair come to be on Paul's computer?"

Kel's mouth dropped open and she leaned forward with her hands on the glass. If she hadn't insisted the computer be brought to the lab, it was likely the hair would have gone undiscovered. Her good detective skills were driving home the suspicion that her dad was involved in these crimes. Now there existed a possible connection she could not have anticipated. Without knowing it, she had moved her dad up another notch on Jake's suspect list. The euphoric feeling she had had when she left the Winston's house this morning, that Jake would be forced to take her dad off his list, was now beginning to syphon away.

"Just because that hair—at first glance—looks like my client's doesn't make it true."

Shelia faced Dirk. He continued to sit stoically staring across the room.

"Are you okay, Dad?" she asked.

"I'm fine, Angel. Just thinking." He focused on Jake again. "At the moment, if the hair is mine, and that's a stretch, I have no explanation for it. As you can see, I don't have much on my head to leave lying around. Though I do have reason to believe it might be mine, let's wait until all the evidence is on the table. What else do you have?"

Jake paused for a few seconds and then retrieved a second photograph from his notebook. He laid it on the table and spun it one hundred and eighty degrees so Dirk and Shelia could see it.

"Is this the murder weapon?" Shelia asked.

"It was collected right next to the victim's body. The wound track is consistent with the blade, and the blood has been found to be hers. So, yes, we're sure the killer left this knife after slashing her throat."

He pulled another photo from his folder and placed it in front of the couple on the opposite side of the table.

"This is the same knife after we got it back to the lab. As you can see, there is a clear print on the handle."

"And whose print is it?" Shelia asked.

"Whose do you think, Counselor?"

"It's mine, isn't it?" Dirk asked. He turned toward his daughter.

"I think you've said enough, Dad. This interview's over."

"No, I want to hear this."

"Yes," Jake said, "it's your print. Can you explain it?"

Dirk took a second look at the knife in the photo. "I'd like a private word with my lawyer."

Jake smiled and rose to his feet. Without speaking, he looked up to the camera suspended from the ceiling in the corner and motioned "cut" with his right hand, as if slashing his own throat with his fingertips. He walked to the adjoining door and passed through the opening to where Kel stood on the other side of the glass.

So he couldn't listen in on their privileged communication, she turned the volume switch hard to the left in one swift movement.

"Do you see what I'm saying?" Jake asked. He stared through the one-way mirror. "Evidence. That's how you build a case, plebe."

The wound Jake had caused by exposing her dad's affair still stung. Her eyes were unable to even glance in his direction, so she stood next to him and watched her dad and Shelia. "I'm sure there's a perfectly sound explanation for his prints being on the murder weapon."

"Sure. He did the deed."

"Or something else."

"Yeah, like the story they're fabricating right now."

Interview rooms at West Precinct weren't really for interviews at all. They were interrogation cells, and as such, they were bugged. There was no expectation of privacy in the room. Jake had made a public show of indicating the recording devices were to be shut off. Somewhere out of sight, however, an analyst had a pair of headphones over his ears while he watched a monitor, capturing the entire conversation, both audio and video. The ruse often worked, and lesser suspects revealed their guilt when they thought no one was listening. But behind the glass her dad and sister were making use of the only hope of privacy, whispered tones behind cupped hands.

"Do you really think he's stupid enough to leave his prints at a crime scene? Whoever the killer is planted those prints to implicate him."

"Could be," Jake said, and pivoted his body toward Kel. "But we'll have to see what angle they come up with."

"They're not making up anything, Jake. He's conferring with his counsel, just like the Miranda Rights state."

"He's not under arrest."

"Yet," she said and turned to face him, her light green eyes a shade darker as her anger peaked. "You had him brought in here like a common thug. You and Martinez have jumped to a conclusion that he must be guilty, even though he's physically incapable of doing the things you've accused him of. You've twisted a poor decision he made ten years ago to make it fit this case. Tell me, what evidence have you found on his phone or computer which ties him in any way to this?" She paused, but he didn't answer. "As I suspected, nothing. You don't care about the truth. Find a suspect, hook him up, and close the case. Guilty until proven innocent. You want the truth? Here it is."

When Kel had asked ADA Johnson about Jake yesterday, Johnson had been honest about Jake's record and courthouse reputation, saying, "Beyond my better judgment, I like you. I don't want to see you end up like either one of his last two partners."

Kel faced Jake. "I've done my research, and while it's true you have a high closing ratio, it's also true you have a low conviction rate. Talk around the courthouse is that defense attorneys love to take cases when you've been the primary. They know that more than fifty percent of the time, your evidence is contrived and easily kicked. You're just a dumpster diver. You look for the easy pickin's to build circumstantial cases."

"Pretty smug, aren't you? So damn self-righteous. What good could ever come from a police chief's daughter?"

There it is. Men only need women for three things: cooking, cleaning, and cumming. That made the hairs on Kel's neck bristle

"What I can't understand is why Chief Ballesteros hasn't kicked you to the curb long ago. No one wants to partner up with you 'cause of your curse. Let's talk about Toshio Aoki."

Even in the darkened room, Kel sensed Jake stiffen.

Jake turned back to face the window. "What about him? I locked him up, he served his time, and then he got out. Happens every day."

"So you were the arresting officer?"

"Willie Jenkins and I took him down."

"And right after that, Willie disappeared and ended up dead."

"Aoki's connected. If you'd have done your research you'd know that."

She ignored him and continued. "So if you both took him down, why didn't they come after you, too?"

"Maybe they did."

"If they did, there'd be a record somewhere, but there's no trace of it."

"I told you before to leave this alone. If you know what's good for your health, you'll get the hell out of my business and leave Aoki alone. This is way over your head."

"That sounds like another threat."

Jake suddenly stood taller and lifted his head. Kel shifted her eyes to the window as Shelia waved an invitation for Jake to reenter.

"Guess our little discussion's over," Jake said. "Looks like they're ready to confess. Make sure you turn the volume up. You won't want you to miss this."

While Kel advanced the volume knob, Jake tore the door open and whisked back to the lighted room to take his seat at the table.

"The reason my print is on that knife handle," Dirk said, with his finger on the photo, "is because it came from my kitchen."

"Is that a confession?" Jake asked as he settled back into his chair.

"Only that the knife belongs to me, not that I took it to the murder scene."

"Then who do you suppose took it to Marilyn Winston's?"

"Obviously, the murderer with the intent of framing me."

"When was the last time you saw the knife?"

"Yesterday, about an hour before you came to my house."

"So, now I'm the killer?"

"Is that a confession?"

"Hardly. I have no motive."

"Neither do I. Yet it seems the UNSUB has information about me that's not common knowledge."

"Are you implying that's me?"

"No! Unlike you and Lou Martinez, I don't jump to conclusions. I weigh the facts. And the fact is, that's my knife," he said, and tapped his finger on the photo.

From Kel's point of view through the one-way mirror, her dad's tremors had stopped. For the moment, he had forgotten his disease while he focused his emotions on the case.

"But there are more facts," he continued. "You see, after you abruptly left last night without finishing my rudimentary interview, I was too tired to clean up the kitchen, so I went straight to my bedroom. It wasn't until I went to fix breakfast this morning that I noticed the knife missing—another fact. When you left to use the bathroom last evening, you took your notebook, and it was unzipped. When you returned, it was zipped—more facts. You had to pass right through my kitchen, right by that knife. It could have easily fit inside your notebook.

"Not only that, the bathroom you used is the one I use every day, all day. So, it's likely a stray hair of mine might be lying around that room. You could have easily picked one up and then transferred it to the laptop. Since you're the primary detective on this case, no one would question you about checking out the laptop from the evidence locker.

"Do you see how facts work, son? If I was the conclusion-jumping type, I'd say it's just as likely you're the murderer as it is me."

"Are you accusing me of something?"

"Doesn't feel good, does it, son? Now, besides my hair, and the prints on my knife, is there any other evidence?"

Jake stared at him, expressionless, and didn't answer.

"Well, Detective?" Shelia asked. She tipped forward toward the table.

Jake looked at each of them and gave an almost imperceptible shake of his head. Then, without speaking, he gathered the photos and reports strewn across the table, dropped them in his notebook, and stood. As he opened the door, he said, "You're free to go," and then slammed it behind him.

Chapter Thirty-Four

AFTER SHELIA AND their dad left West Precinct, Kel stepped into Captain Marcos Silva's office. Since the knife and hair had come from her dad's house, it meant that if Jake hadn't taken them, DK had while her dad slept upstairs. She asked Silva if he'd send a team of investigators to the Nyte's Queen Anne home and set a protective patrol at the curb until the case closed.

Now, as she sat at her desk, she felt as violated as if an intruder had rummaged through her underwear drawer touching her personal things. To think of DK being inside the house in which she grew up brought a knot of anger to her chest. Their home had always been a shelter of safety, with nothing but fond memories. Now it had been desecrated by a man, a stranger, a murderer who might have killed her dad last night if not for his own restraint. Just as he waited for her at Suzanne Lowen's, rather than take her life, he had chosen to draw her into his game. Now he was doing the same thing with her dad, like he was saying, "I can get to you anytime I choose. But first, watch and learn."

She studied the crime board with the photos of the dead. The lines Jake had drawn to connect her dad to the three crime scenes had given her an idea. Her dad said that someone had information about him that wasn't common knowledge. So, as much as there was a common suspect, was there also a common source of this information? And if that were true, and she located the source, that might lead to the suspect.

She considered that DK and Terry Graham might have spoken. If that had happened, she was sure DK had initiated the dialog. And Terry, eager to vent years of frustration for the life he sacrificed, didn't foresee his own fate—tissues scorched, torn asunder—or Marilyn's—river red that will not heal. So DK had to come across to Terry as sympathetic. Someone Terry could entrust the troubled demons in his soul to, someone he'd pour out information about his own personal failures to without fear of judgment. If Terry saw this as a means to bring disgrace on her dad, he would have believed DK embodied the influence required to bring down someone as powerful and well-loved as Dirk Nyte.

But who?

Doubtless her father had enemies, but since he resigned his post, he had lost his power, so political opponents would have nothing to gain in pursuing him now. But convicted felons like Vince Buckley would. Yet as much as she wanted him to be DK, seeing Terry connected to that man as the source was flawed. First, she couldn't imagine Terry volunteering to him any sordid details of his life. And then, despite the reversal of Buckley's conviction, he wasn't a popular man, so he didn't have the influence.

But what if her dad's enemies were internal? If a conspiracy existed, it'd involve people within the SPD. This had first occurred to her when she realized that somehow DK had gotten her SPD-issued phone number. Now it seemed even more plausible.

Besides Terry, she let her thoughts drift to other sources. Lou Martinez was a possibility. He and her dad had gone through police academy together. With his longevity in the department, there'd be few doors restricted to him. Once the murders started, he went right after her dad. Was he so blinded by rage that, although he hadn't anticipated murder as the outcome, he twisted it into an opportunity to point a finger at an old adversary? Did he agree to her taking part in the investigation because he believed she'd fail? Was he relying on her insistence that DK was anyone other than her dad part of his plan to discredit her as well?

Jake, on the other hand, had been assigned to the DK case as the primary right after Suzanne Lowen's murder. She remembered that Martinez and Chief Ballesteros had arrived together at Suzanne's condo. They, too, went back a long ways in the department. Had Lou influenced the chief to put Jake on the case? That would have put him in the perfect position to manufacture and manage the evidence. A single focus to the exclusion of any other suspects had been on Lou's lips from the beginning of the investigation. Now it seemed to bind Jake and Lou together. Over the last two and a half days, they shared the same tunnel vision toward her dad.

But where's the proof? She needed help, someone to confide in, someone who knew the turf.

A voice interrupted Shelia's thoughts.

"Excuse me, Counselor."

"Yes?" She glanced at the time on the computer clock—6:17 p.m.—and looked up from the email she was writing, into Vince Buckley's dark eyes.

While incarcerated for his conviction as the Rat City Exterminator, Buckley filled his free hours studying computer technology. One of the named partners of Snelling, Hardcastle, and Purdin had turned the defense of Buckley's serial case over to a second-year associate who mismanaged the case. So, when his conviction had been overturned, the partners of Snelling decided that it was in the best interest of the firm to hire him for their Help Desk team. Shelia hadn't favored the move since her dad put him away nearly a decade and a half earlier, but being an associate attorney, she held no status.

"Just a verbal," he said. "Friday evening we'll be shutting down the systems for a global refresh. You'll get an email reminder Friday afternoon."

"Thank you, Vince," Shelia said, and turned back to the monitor.

"Since I've interrupted you, I also wanted to thank you for standing up for me yesterday during that interrogation. A complex situation, what with your dad and sister."

Shelia wanted to say, "Just doing my job," but said, "The firm fully supports you, Vince. The partnership believes in you and is ready to stand behind you."

"Well, I appreciate it. Hey, who's your friend?" he asked.

"My son Danny." She smiled at the towheaded boy sitting on the floor drawing a picture. "Say goodnight to Mr. Buckley."

"'Night, Mr. Buckley," Danny said.

"Goodnight, son."

She turned her attention back to the figure in her doorway. "Thanks."

She followed him with her eyes until he passed. Not until she heard his voice speak to the person in the next occupied office did she turn to Danny.

"Almost done," she said.

"McDonald's?"

"Then McDonald's."

Kel stepped through the elevator doorway into the secure parking garage at West Precinct. The light fell on Chief of Detectives, Nathaniel Ballesteros, dressed in a dark suit and green striped tie.

"Good evening, Chief," she said as he made way for her to pass.

"Detective," he said with a nod.

She rotated back and asked, "Do you have a moment?"

He took the last draw from his cigar and then snuffed it in the ashtray by the elevator door. The access was still open, so he entered the cab, turned, and held the door for Kel.

As the elevator motor engaged and she felt the first tug of the lift, apprehension tightened her stomach. Some of what she had to say had a direct bearing on his role as Chief, but the first thing to "clear up" didn't. And she was certain that that part of the conversation was destined not to go well.

"There're a few details I'd like to clear up, if you don't mind."

He didn't answer, but looked straight ahead at the door and slipped the remains of his smoke into the breast pocket of his jacket.

The throb of her increased heart rate pounded in her temples, but she pressed on. "First, Monday morning at the Wishing Well, you told me you'd just come from Benaroya Hall." She noticed a subtle upturn of his head. When he didn't respond, she continued. "You remember, of course, that I'm a patrol officer. I had passed by Benaroya just a few hours earlier, about nine-thirty, and it was dark. So I checked—"

"You're investigating me," he said, and kept his eyes focused on the door.

Kel knew that it wasn't a question, and that she was about to traverse a deep murky bog where one misstep could get her buried alive.

"Well, sir, I'm sure it's just a simple mistake," she said, although she couldn't see how he could have forgotten where he had been just an hour before meeting her. "The Summer Festival was on Saturday night and got over about ten-thirty."

"And your point is I couldn't have been there. Is that correct?"

"Begging your pardon, sir, but ... yes."

He turned his head slowly to face her. The tension in his brow was as taught has the skin on a snare drum. "Perhaps I misspoke. Being in Pioneer Square brought back memories of a quite pleasant evening. As you can imagine, the demands of my job are many. I'm sure I was just confused. But it goes without saying, Nyte. My comings and goings are police business, and not yours. You don't need you to be investigating me."

That wasn't a satisfactory answer. She knew that someone within the department had given her SPD-issued cell phone number to DK. For all she knew, the Chief was DK and he had hit her with the stun gun in Suzanne Lowen's condo. But he out-ranked her, and the rumors in the locker room had him in a dead heat with the acting police chief as the next top cop. It probably was nothing more than a mistake. So as a matter of preservation and respect, she decided to let it go.

"Of course, sir. I'll say no more about it."

"Now, then, you said there was something else?"

"Yes. Lou kicked me from the case you assigned me right in the middle of the bullpen."

"I see." He flicked his eyes back to the door. "And why do you think he did that?"

"He said it was because he gave me two days to find a suspect. I gave him several options, but he didn't like my list."

He pulled at one of his eyebrows and stood silent until the elevator came to a stop. When the door opened, he said, "Go on," and led the way into the hall.

"Well, sir, I've begun to have concerns about both Lou and Jake. First, in my opinion, they've focused all their attention toward my dad on the DK case. They don't talk about any other suspects. They've prejudiced themselves, and rather than look at the field, they're trying to build a case against the most convenient suspect. I concede to their theory, but I don't believe they welcome another. Jake shut me out from day one, and now being fired from the case makes it appear Jake and Lou are colluding."

"That's a serious accusation, Officer Nyte. It implies something illegal. We better take this in my office."

Kel followed the chief, and after he entered his office, she filed in behind him and pushed the door closed. As the motion sensor brought up the lights, through his window she glanced at the high rise across the street. The night crew was busy cleaning one of the offices. She wondered what it'd be like to work a job where the biggest issue was whether her wipe-down rag had enough moisture to clean up someone else's coffee rings. She turned her attention back to the chief. He had walked behind his desk but didn't sit. She took this as a sign that the meeting would be brief, and rested her hands on the back of a tan leather side chair.

"I didn't mean to imply they're doing anything illegal, but—"

"I sense," Ballesteros said, "there's more angst with Jake than just a rough start."

It surprised her that he had cut Lou out of the conversation and zeroed in on Jake. He had done something similar when she brought up Willie Jenkins' death after the bar brawl Monday morning. True, she had issues with Jake reaching far beyond DK, but she couldn't put her finger on what she might have said to indicate such.

"What's really bothering you about him?" Ballesteros asked.

"Sir, I don't know that I can trust him. I know he works for you, and that makes him your concern. I get that, but he's come up short in a couple of things, and then ..." She paused.

"What do you mean by 'come up short'?" he asked.

Kel noted that his tone had turned inquisitional. "Perhaps I've said too much, sir." She backed her way to the door. "I should leave you to your desk."

"You'll do no such thing. You're making an accusation about one of my men, and I'll hear it now."

She hesitated. "If I may be permitted to make a couple of observations, sir, then you can judge if they warrant further inquiry." She paused again until he acknowledged. When he nodded, she continued. "Jake stated that he and Willie Jenkins took Toshio Aoki down, and then right after Aoki went to prison, Willie was found dead. Yet I find it curious, sir, that there's no record of anyone ever coming after Jake, and he offers no evidence that anyone did. And then what makes my instincts flare even more is the fact that he reported being indisposed at the Belltown Pump the night his last partner, Eddy, was shot. Sir, the bar was closed that night and had been for a week while the health department identified the source of an outbreak of salmonella."

"I see," he said, again not registering any emotion under his black brows. "I believe you indicated there's something else, Detective. What else is on your mind? Let's get it all out into the open."

She exhaled like she was blowing out the thirty-six candles on her last birthday cake with a single breath. "I hesitate to bring this up, Chief, but an incident happened Monday morning that made me curious. I did some background, and when I asked him about it, he got very defensive."

"What kind of background?"

"Sir, he seems to have some connection to Toshio Aoki, more than just as his arresting officer. I'm just wondering if ..." She shook her head.

"Spell it out for me, Detective. Are you saying he has ties to organized crime? That's a serious charge."

"No, sir. I haven't any basis to make such an accusation, but as I said, something just doesn't add up. Tribune Investments, a company where Aoki is a principle, might be a shell for Saito Global. They owned the cargo container in which Willie was found. Is it possible Jake is involved with Tribune? Is that why no one ever came after him like they did Willie? Does Jake know who killed Willie and is covering?"

Ballesteros leaned forward. He placed his clenched fist knuckles down on the top of his desk and drew his eyebrows into one.

Kel saw an expression she didn't expect. Aggravation hovered on the surface but beneath, uneasiness threatened.

"Kel, I think I've heard quite enough. As you said, your assumptions are baseless, and that's all they are: assumptions. Rather than try to solve Willie's death—and I do remember you telling me that he was your friend—you should leave this to the seasoned detectives. As I told you the other day, we have resources dedicated to his murder. You flailing around with these kinds of allegations only muddies the water. Now, if there's nothing else, I'll bid you goodnight."

Chapter Thirty-Five

DK ARRIVED EARLY at his sanctuary long before the buses and the bustle of the Thursday-morning commuters interrupted his tranquility. On his knees before the two-by-four altar, he lifted his eyes and read again the words stretched above the photos and artwork of the memorial collage.

"The secret things belong to God, but the things revealed belong to us."

Yesterday's revelation had been the most fulfilling thus far and had brought atonement for his wife's abandonment into another man's arms. Today, another surreptitious journey into the past would bring expiation for a long-held debt. Among his collection, taped to the wall, a picture of his son on his third birthday ripping the wrapping paper off a Tonka dump truck took prominence.

He extinguished the flame on the candle resting on the photo of Marilyn Winston with a silent breath and watched the smoke rise like the bouquet of a Biblical sacrifice. It offered no redemption. God had forsaken him, and his offerings now would never appease the wrath of the One who'd punish him for his actions. Wounds too deep to be seen but mercilessly felt couldn't be absolved by the passage of time. He remembered a quote from Mark Twain. "Forgiveness is the fragrance that the violet sheds on the heel that has crushed it." Time, however, had transmuted the aroma into the stench of retribution. He could no more turn away from the path he had elected than a vulture might stop circling the dead. Vengeance was his lone reward.

Wolf didn't know what year it was, or how many he had passed stooped in this remedial task, but he straightened his aching back and took a brief respite from his labor. The shade from the scorching sun thrown on his back, and the relief of fourteen years of the spinal aches, was only temporary, but savored. With his feet shackled by a three-foot chain, he sidestepped to the left. He bent forward again and as he finished planting another hand full of rice seedlings into the ankle-deep paddy, two gunshots rumbled through the clearing and into the forest behind him.

Raiding bands of Asian paramilitary were common, and he had been stolen so many times that he no longer feared for his life. He stood erect again and, rather than turn toward the sound, looked in the direction of his guard. When last he had seen him, he had been sitting on a tree stump ten feet away, taking a toke from a hand-rolled marijuana joint. He wasn't surprised to see him lying crumpled on the ground. The smoke from the joint curled around his face. He then twisted his body toward the direction of the weapon fire and saw four men in camouflage uniforms stomping through the field about forty meters away.

He dropped the seedlings from his hands like discarded trash. It wasn't another troop of gooks vying to take him by force. Although an updated version, the uniforms had a familiar American appearance, and the M-16 rifles they carried across their bodies confirmed his hope. After all this time, someone back home had remembered and sent a rescue squad. It was over—finally over. No more nights in the cage. No more bowls of rice. No more blistering sun. Her face had blurred from recognition, but he could see his wife racing to him as he stepped off the airplane to wrap her arms around him again.

The soldiers split up. One walked toward him and the other three turned toward his buddies in the field. These few men—captured, left behind, forgotten—had shared a common threat and had bonded in a way people in comfort could never fathom. In disbelief he saw their salvation slogging through the field to embrace them. To take them home.

Then another shot echoed deep into the surrounding trees. It came from his left. He thought it must have been one of his other captor's rifles. He'd have heard the initial report and come running to protect their property. Wolf had too much at stake to watch the murderous bastards take his chance at freedom away. He rotated toward the sound.

Even in his world without hope, what he saw was worse than he could imagine. He often had visions of someday outliving his usefulness in the paddies. That image had him shot or knifed, and buried in an unmarked grave. But, as if in slow motion, one of his friends fell backward into the swamp. Then another shot exploded, and another, until, in just seconds, he was the only POW still standing.

He turned back to the soldier who approached him. He was now on a run crossing the paddy. His boots splashed through the water. Twenty meters away, he raised his weapon.

Without thought, Wolf's body acted on impulse, as if the infantry training he had drafted into at Fort Bragg had been yesterday, but with his feet chained, he was unable to run the ten feet to cover. A bullet from another explosion behind him buzzed past his ear, and he lunged toward the dead sentry. Wolf fell to the ground behind his lifeless captor and scooted until the stump stood between him and the oncoming soldier. He rolled the dead guard to his side to increase cover and seized the lookout's automatic rifle. On his stomach, he placed the gun across the deceased man's torso. On the other end of the barrel, the rogue combatant continued to fire random blasts. Ten meters out, Wolf squeezed off his first round.

The projectile made a direct hit to the soldier's chest, and a burst of blood blossomed on his shirt as he fell backwards.

With his mind clear, he realized this was no rescue. Rather these men meant to murder him. Why, he couldn't imagine, but, now in survival mode, he searched the field for the other armed men. The three had taken defensive positions on their knees in the paddy, and they took fire at their new target. Still prone behind the stump, he took aim at one of the men and fired a round. It went wild.

He needed to focus, breathe, and remember.

The bullets buzzing around him—striking the stump, tunneling into the ground, and ripping into the flesh of the dead guard—brought it back. Years before, more time than his broken mind could process, he had lain behind a downed tree and faced odds worse than this. The suddenness of the memory was like the surprise eruption of a long-dormant volcano. He had been a marksman. His eye had been trained to the point where an enemy soldier in his sites had no chance of survival. A single shot was all it took.

Even though he was unacquainted with the AK-47 in his hands, the embrace of the handgrips and the site on the barrel felt familiar. He brought the second man down. By the time he turned to the others, they had cut and run toward the opposite side of the swamp. With the sights now set on surrogates for those who had complete disregard for his right to life, his blood ran cold. They, too, fell.

DK lifted the fourth candle, lit its wick, and placed it over the photo of the next to die.

Chapter Thirty-Six

KEL'S BODY JERKED to a sitting position. She raised the cell phone she had been grasping in her sleep and saw that a new text announced itself. The clock on her personal phoner showed 6:08 a.m.

After being fired from the case and then finding Chief Ballesteros unsympathetic to her suspicions, she needed time to think. Lance had always been a good listener, without needing to interject his opinion or advice. But in the last couple of hours before she left West Precinct, she had witnessed all her support vanish. Her partner, her boss, the chief of detectives, and even Captain Silva had abandoned her like a bad idea. The perfidy of her dad's affair had sent Shelia scurrying back to her office, presumably to bury herself in work—Shelia's preferred coping mechanism. Unable to look at her dad without wanting to punch something or someone had left Kel exposed and alone. There was no one to turn to.

With police presence at his curb, she believed her dad's house safe, so she convinced Chrissie that Pops needed his only granddaughter to comfort him in the loss of his two close friends. Chrissie, unlike on Monday night, went willingly. Kel dropped her at the curb and then made her way to the townhome she had shared with Lance. Rather than find comfort in his lingering presence, though, she collapsed into a deep sleep on the couch.

Twenty-five minutes after being awakened, Kel looked again at the Rainier Valley address on the phone's display. She drove her Liberty south on Rainier Avenue, what the locals called "the valley of stray bullets." Strip clubs, seedy bars, abandoned store fronts, and mini-markets passed on either side of the road where drug deals and prostitution went down in the parking lots and shadows without fear of arrest.

She turned left on the street DK texted to her phone and made her way along a narrow street lined with seventy-year-old ramshackle homes featuring steel-barred windows and chain link fenced yards. In the morning light, they seemed disconnected to the polished, newer vehicles parked along the street. Apparently, pride in this neighborhood was best expressed in the car you drove, not in the house you slept in.

When she arrived at the address, she found herself in front of a fortress. Instead of chain link, an eight-foot cinderblock fence topped with a four-foot steel spike-tipped railing loomed like the curtain wall of a medieval castle. Its duty was clear: keep the riff-raff out and give the occupants a sense of security. To Kel it looked like a dare. Some enterprising youth on a gang initiation challenge would score big points by breaking into the house to steal the blue-ray DVD player or plasma TV.

A single SPD cruiser parked in the driveway waited for Kel. Two officers sat inside. As Kel pulled up behind them, the officer behind the wheel stepped from the blue cruiser and approached her silver Jeep.

Scott Nillson in uniform, a light blue shirt with dark blue pocket flaps that matched his slacks, bent at the waist and placed his hands on the window opening. "What do we have here, Kel?" her former mentor asked.

"Don't know for sure. Have you spoken with the occupants?"

"No, just arrived."

"Then let's do it."

Scott walked back to the car. Before he dropped inside, he pushed a speaker button on a post next to the ten-foot steel gate. Moments later, it swung open, and once the gap was large enough, Kel followed the cruiser through.

Behind the gate, Kel was confronted with an anomaly. The short driveway rose up a steep incline, and the house erected on top of it was a small, two-storey mansion. Overbuilt for the neighborhood, she deduced that the owner must be the drug lord of some of the dealers she had passed on the street. But why DK had brought her here she couldn't reconcile.

Kel took the three steps to the wooden porch, her boots thumping like a bass drum, and knocked on the front door. When an overweight Caucasian woman in her late forties answered, the contrast between the appearance of the figure before her and her assumptions moments before struck her dumb. With bed hair and a crumpled, ankle-length nightgown under an untied bathrobe, the woman didn't appear to be the girlfriend of a wealthy drug kingpin.

She looked first to Kel and then to the two uniformed officers behind Kel. She asked, "May I help you?"

"Tracy Kinnear?" Kel asked. She had gained the name of the home owners from dispatch. "I'm Detective Kel Nyte."

"Yes. What do the police want with me at this hour?"

"Do you live alone?"

"No, with my husband, but he left for work at about six. Why?"

"May we come in, please? I have a few questions."

"You're frightening me. Is Roger okay?"

"As far as we know, he's fine. If we might just speak for a few minutes …?"

Tracy moved aside, opening the door wider. Kel, followed by Scott and his trainee, Valerie, passed into the hardwood entry. Over the east-facing door, the arched windows allowed the ascending sun to penetrate its warming rays. As Tracy turned toward the living room, the swirl of her robe caused dust particles caught in the light to shimmer like the glitter of a snow globe.

Twin designer sofas tufted with forest green buttons across the back graced either side of a marble faced fireplace. Tracy walked between them and turned to face Kel.

"Mrs. Kinnear," Kel said, "where does your husband work?"

"Why? What's happening?" The tone of the questions and her arms folded tight across her bulging stomach revealed her irritation.

"We don't know for sure that anything's happening, ma'am, but your husband could be in danger. Where does he work?"

"Danger? Oh my God," she said, with a quick change to despair. "We own a home furnishings store in Ballard. He gets there early to do paperwork and tidy the store before it opens."

"Where's the store located?" Kel asked, unable to mask the urgency she felt.

Kel pulled a pad and pen from her back jean pocket, and took a note of the Market Street address. Then, she ripped the page out and sent Valerie outside to make the call to dispatch. She turned back to Mrs. Kinnear. Kel recognized the strained expression on her visage and the terror in her eyes. They both spoke of the fear that what she was about to be told would include the fate of having to face the rest of her life without the security of her husband.

"We have officers on the way," Kel said. With Tracy's countenance unchanged, the positive inflection in Kel's voice had done little to assure the woman that tragedy was certain to be averted. Kel had too much history with DK to believe it either.

"My God," Tracy pleaded, "what's happening?"

"I'll explain everything, but every second that passes increases his risk. Please help me."

"Oh my God, this can't be happening. What do you need?"

"Two things. First, do you have a computer in the house?"

"Of course. He keeps it in his office, through the hall and to the left." She pointed toward the doorway. "What else?"

As Scott left the room to locate the computer, Kel asked, "Can you reach Roger right now?"

"I can't believe this is happening." She dabbed at tears with the sleeve of her robe.

"Tracy, this is important."

"Sure. I'll try," she said through sobs, and went to a lamp table at the end of one of the couches. She picked up the telephone receiver. Her hand shook so that she had difficulty finding the right speed dial number to press, but the task completed, she held the receiver to her ear.

"Come on, Roger. Pick up, pick up. Please!"

She disconnected the call and looked up toward Kel.

"Voicemail," she said. Her eyes pleaded for mercy. She looked back toward the instrument in her hand and pressed another speed dial number, this time with more precision.

"He always carries his cell phone. He's sure to answer."

Kel heard in her tone an attempt to build confidence that all was well, but with five deaths to date in DK's lesson plan, she knew it wasn't.

"Roger," she shouted into the phone. "Ro ... Ro ... Where's Roger?"

Kel watched as the woman listened. She pressed the receiver against her ear as if the voice on the other end was almost inaudible. Then her expression changed as the blood drained from her face. Kel had seen hope, but now despair took Tracy captive. Her knees buckled, and she collapsed onto the couch.

"Oh my God," she said, and look up toward Kel. She held the phone out, and through anguished sobs asked, "Did you say ... name ... Kel?"

Chapter Thirty-Seven

THIRTY MINUTES EARLIER, DK had sat in his car parked on the street. From his place at the curb, he watched the alley behind the Kinnears' home furnishings store. While he waited, he smoked a stream of cigarettes and filled the ashtray.

Right on time, Roger Kinnear pulled into the alley and slipped his Mercedes into a parking space next to the rear entrance. After he stepped from the car, he entered the shop through a man-sized door next to the ground-level cargo rollup.

DK gave him five minutes alone, enough time to fill his lungs with the scent of fine furnishings and to relish for the last time the successful empire he had built over the past two decades. Then he drove his car into the alley and parked behind the Mercedes. He nudged the car's door closed with his hip and tucked his pistol into his belt at the small of his back. The alley door opened with a heavy tug, and he stepped inside to a small warehouse. He listened for sounds of life, and after two silent minutes, the squeak of a desk chair's dry spring gave him directionality. He moved toward the mournful squawk.

Between the racks of couches and chairs draped with clear plastic dust covers, he saw a light from a small interior office. Inside, his target—the one for whom the candle burned beneath the condemned façade of a previous era—sat bent over a desk filled with papers.

As quiet as a winged owl at midnight, DK moved between the cavernous rows of towering shelves toward his objective. Another secret to reveal. At the end of the row, he paused. Roger stood and then exited the office. The cup in Roger's plump hand led DK to believe the interruption to be temporary, so once Roger was out of sight, DK slipped into the office and took cover behind the door.

He waited.

Moments later, Roger reentered the room with coffee and a napkin-wrapped apple fritter. The phone on the desk rang and he let the automated attendant take the call while he took a bite of the pastry. A swallow from the cup followed, and he placed the cup and treat on the desk. He glanced at a stack of paperwork arranged in a neat pile, but then looked up and inhaled deep.

DK knew that Roger had picked up the scent of tobacco that lingered on his clothes, and within seconds would discover his hiding place. It didn't matter. Roger was out of time. DK stepped from behind the door and said, "Roger."

Roger turned quickly to the voice. His face flushed, his mouth gaped, and his eyelids drew back as he stared at the barrel of DK's pistol.

DK didn't want to prolong Roger's terror, but he knew that for the next few moments it would be unavoidable. Like Suzanne Lowen, powerless to stop what was about to happen, he could see Roger searching for his voice.

"Wh ... who are you?" he said. His voice strained to remain calm, as if talk might spare his life. "If it's cash, there's some in the safe. I'll open it for you."

"What I want you can't give. I must take it."

DK pulled the trigger and watched as Roger staggered backwards, falling over his chair and then onto the cement floor. He landed on his back. A trickle of red flowed from the black hole in Roger's forehead and pooled around the casters of the chair. Death had come mercifully quick.

DK placed the pistol on the desk and turned to leave before any employees arrived. As he reached the door, from Roger's hip, his cell phone began to ring. It's probably her.

He reached for the phone, saw a name on the display, and smiled. He pressed the button on the screen labeled "answer."

"Where's Roger!" a woman's voice screamed in his ear.

"He can't come to the phone, Mrs. Kinnear. Is Kel with you?"

Chapter Thirty-Eight

"DETECTIVE NYTE," KEL said into the mouthpiece after she took the phone from Mrs. Kinnear. She turned to face the entryway.

"Kel."

The woman's voice on the other end jarred her.

"DK?" she asked.

"Yes. You give me that name?"

The last time he had spoken to her, he had whispered. He wasn't whispering now. She realized that he was modulating his voice with a voice changer, which meant he knew she'd recognize him.

She ignored his last question and pressed her agenda forward. "Let me speak to Roger."

"I'm afraid he's taken his last call."

Since Tracy was still within earshot, she forced the words into a calm tone. "I see."

Valerie walked back into the carpeted living room and gave Kel a "follow me" wave.

Kel kept the wireless phone to her ear and fell in behind the officer as she led the way. They left Mrs. Kinnear alone in her uncertainty in the living room.

"What's this about?" Kel asked once out in the hallway.

"I'm sure your daddy will soon figure it out. I've left a gift."

"The best gift would be for you to stop this and give yourself up."

"Can't see that happening. Not until he understands what he did to me."

"There has to be another way."

Valerie led her to where Scott stood in a small office. On the desk, a computer monitor displayed four lines of type. Kel didn't need to read it to know what they contained.

"Why don't you tell me about it? Maybe I can help."

"You're doing enough already."

"We're going to find you."

"Of that I have no doubt, and I look forward to it. That's why I picked you. But I've not yet completed your daddy's curriculum, so for now it seems I must take my leave, since I hear the siren's wail of Seattle's finest. Keep up the hunt, Kel."

"Why Roger?" Kel shouted, but the question went unanswered as the call disconnected.

"What happened to Roger?"

The despair-filled voice behind Kel spoke with such passion that it was all she could do to keep her own emotions from pouring over the spillway. She looked from Scott to Valerie, who faced her on either side, and then turned to the woman with red, swollen eyes and tear stains still wet on her cheeks.

"Please." Kel motioned for Tracy to sit on a cabernet-colored wing-backed chair in the corner of the office. She glanced back at Scott and pointed to the monitor. "Print a copy of that."

Scott, who already had a glove on his hand, manipulated the mouse. Kel walked across the room and knelt in front of the recent widow.

"Officers will be on the scene in a few moments, and we'll know for certain—"

"That my Roger's dead?"

"—'If Roger's okay,' is what I was going to say."

"I still don't understand how you knew he might be in trouble."

Kel pulled her phone from the holster on her belt and searched for the latest message.

"A man sends me a text with an address." She held the phone so Tracy could see the screen. "At just after six this morning, your address appeared on my phone. Have you followed the news this week about the man the press is calling 'DK'?"

"Oh my God, and now he's killed Roger, too."

"As I said, we won't know for certain until our officers arrive at your store, but if this man follows the same pattern ..."

"Roger's dead, I can feel it."

"Believe me, I understand the horror of uncertainty you're going through at the moment. My best friend, the father of my daughter, left for the war a year and a half ago. I lived for months not knowing if he'd ever come home again."

The crackle of a garbled radio message broke the conversation, and Valerie shot a glance at Kel. As she walked for the door, she raised her hand to squeeze the trigger on the microphone attached to the shoulder of her blouse. Valarie said, "One moment," and then stepped into the hallway to take the call.

"Did he come home?" Tracy asked.

"He left three times but only returned twice. They say he was killed in action, but they never found him."

"And my future lies in the message that kind officer is taking right now."

"It's possible, but despite what you're feeling, I need to ask you a question. May I?"

When she answered with a slight nod, Kel continued. "DK's other victims have a common thread. They have a connection to Chief Dirk Nyte. What connection do you or Roger have with him?"

Kel felt what the woman's face said. The anguish between knowing the actual truth and praying for it to be a nightmare was a weight too heavy to bear. But Kel needed an answer before the death knell lost Tracy in grief.

"Tracy, stay with me. I need you to think."

"Uh, nothing."

"Neither you nor Roger have any relationship to Dirk Nyte, now or in the past? What about family history?"

"I only know the chief's name from the papers, but my family has no relationship with him. I don't think Roger's does either. Chief Nyte being such a public figure, Roger would have said something."

The rustle of Valerie's uniform as she reentered the room behind Kel drew Tracy's eyes to meet the officer's. Valarie walked over to the woman in the chair and squatted in front of her. She took her hand.

"I'm so sorry," she said.

Tracy stared at the messenger. The shock of certainty had cloaked whatever was left of her emotions in merciful numbness.

"Why would he want to kill Roger and Suzanne?" she asked and stared through Valerie as if she were a crystal figurine. "What did they do?"

Kel leaned forward and wrapped her arms around Tracy. She pressed her face against Tracy's cheek and felt hot tears flow again. Kel wept, too. When Tracy's chest convulsed into heaves, she held on until they slowed.

Once Tracy found control, Kel pushed back and asked, "Did you know Suzanne Lowen?"

While she had held her, Kel wondered why Tracy mentioned Suzanne and none of the other victims. There had been more press coverage over Terry's death due to the spectacular explosion, and then, with the connection to Terry's ex-wife, Marilyn, the local news media hadn't been able to put the story down.

"Yes, we were very close. Her memorial's today. Roger was going to the shop to get things ready for the day, and then we were taking the rest of the day with his family."

"Family? Are you somehow related to Suzanne?"

"Suzanne? Yes, she's Roger's younger sister."

Chapter Thirty-Nine

ON THE WAY to the Kinnear residence forty-five minutes earlier, Kel had placed a call to Jake deLaurenti. Though Lieutenant Martinez had taken her off the case yesterday, she had reason to keep Jake abreast of new developments in the case. He was the lead detective, and each victim, at least until Roger, seemed to draw closer to her dad. With the order to surrender her phone, it might have come as a surprise to Jake that she was still in contact with DK, but that didn't worry her. *What can they do, order me to turn over my own phone?*

As expected, her call had gone to voicemail. She hadn't given him her new number, so it was a number he wouldn't recognize. He had been known to turn his cell off when not on duty. Under normal conditions, that would be puzzling, if not insubordination, for a detective—but in his case, it wasn't out of character at all.

Now, on the Kinnear's front porch, she leaned against the polished oak railing and punched his number into the phone's keypad again. When she reached voicemail, she said, "Get your ass out of the sheets, Jake. We have another victim."

Kel disconnected the call and looked over the top of the security fence surrounding the Kinnear home. Across the street, behind a steel-barred window, backlit silhouettes stood and peered through the open blinds. She knew their thoughts as they stared toward the fortress they had come to know and probably despise. If their neighbors could fall victim behind a twelve-foot fence, what possible salvation was there from the certainty of their own demise? The irony was that even with the stronghold Roger had built to keep predators out, his armor was not without flaw. A secret marauder plundered the most priceless possession Roger had: his own life.

The thump of footsteps behind her on the wood planking pulled Kel from her reverie. Officer Scott Nillson stepped onto the front porch and joined her at the railing.

"Thought you'd want this," he said, and gave her the printout from Roger's computer.

She took it and read each line as if the meaning were hidden in code between the letters. Despite the wrench ratcheting her heart, she tried to distance her feelings from the words. Only then might she find clarity.

"Four the sowing of wild fruit
Guilty now there's no dispute
Armor cracks, it cannot shield
My jacket's load, death will wield."

The last two lines were clear. She had confirmed with the first responder at the crime scene that a single gunshot wound to the head was the most likely cause of death. "Armor cracks"—his skull, the helmet. "jacket's load"—a reference to a lead-filled bullet known as a full metal jacket. The second line—"Guilty now"—contained the obvious verdict. But what's Daddy guilty of?

She read the poem again and hoped, like the optical illusion of the old hag and beautiful young woman she had been introduced to in Psych 101, the first line's riddle would snap into focus. Each of the previous verse's coded lines hadn't been difficult to decipher. They pointed to the relationship between the murdered victim and her dad. Without knowing who Roger was, however, and if being Suzanne Lowen's brother held any significance, this new addition to the demented collection gave no obvious clue. It set off a mental itch, though, that she couldn't quite scratch.

"I need to get to the scene, Scott," Kel said, "but we can't leave Tracy alone."

Scott opened his mouth to answer but a voice behind them interrupted.

"I'm going with you," Tracy said.

By the tone of her voice, Kel recognized she wasn't making a request. She turned to look into the face that a few minutes before had been ravaged with horror. Only the dark gray skin sagging around her eyes and her whites, now webbed with red, gave indication of her grief. Her resolute expression indicated that "no" wasn't an option.

"I tried to tell her that's not a good idea," Valerie said, having followed Tracy out to the door.

"I insist," Tracy said. "I want to see my husband."

"You don't want to see him like this, Mrs. Kinnear." Kel put her hands on Tracy's shoulders. "If you do, it's an image you may never forget. There'll be time for viewing later, but right now is the time for grieving. Is there someone we should call? Children, your mother, your pastor?"

"I just won't believe it until I see him."

"Tracy, you know I understand how hard this is for you right now. You've been so brave this morning. But we're closing in on the man who did this, and we'll be able to work much faster, and maybe even stop him before he hurts someone else, if you let us do our job."

Jake deLaurenti disconnected from voicemail. "Get your ass out of the sheets," he said out loud to the two men facing him in the back of the limousine. "Who does that goddamn bitch think she is?"

"Maybe she's just doing her job better than you're doing yours," Peter McCabe said, and starred out the window as a reach stacker dropped an intermodal container onto a flatbed trailer. "That one ours, Tosh?"

Toshio Aoki trained a pair of binoculars on the end of the blue Saito Global cargo box.

"Her job? Hell, she's got her nose right up our ass," Jake said. "She may be smarter than I've been crediting,"

"What does she know?" McCabe asked.

"She saw me and Tosh together on Monday when we first met. Now she's like a horny dog chasing heat. I want to think she's got shit, but she knows about you, Toshio, and Tribune. I think she's close to making the connection."

"You may be right, but no one else has found the missing pieces. Even if she did, what can she prove?"

"That's ours," Toshio said. He placed the binoculars on the unoccupied seat between himself and Peter. "The container number matches." He turned his gaze across the passenger compartment to Jake. "Shit or not, you're in it to your waist and sinking like quicksand. You keep giving her no respect and she's going to get stink all over you. So lighten up, asshole, or you're a loose end."

"'Loose end'? Now I'm expendable?"

"Maybe expendable's a little extreme, but before she ties the knot between us, we've got to take her out."

"Is that always your solution?" Peter asked. He withdrew a cigar from his thin lips and sent a smoke ring floating toward Jake. "Think about it, shithead. Two dead cops?"

"Do you always have to pollute the air with those foul-smelling things?" Jake asked.

Peter cocked his head, furrowed his dark eyebrows, and blew the rest of the smoke in his lungs across to Jake. He laughed.

Toshio looked first at Jake and then back at Peter. "People die. Cost of doing business, and like Willie, if she's getting too close ... anyway, how many shallow graves you got out in that goddamn desert from cargo that didn't survive the crossing?"

"That's different. They paid us to bring them here."

"For jobs and a better life. We make promises and then herd them into an untenable container under subhuman conditions that we wouldn't expose a stray dog to."

"Exotic Malaysian pussy fetches a far better price than stray dogs. I don't see you complaining on the way to the bank. You having regrets, Tosh?"

"Hell no. We're providing a service. I'm just reminding you that whether it's a cop or a cunt, dead is dead. Their voice is silent."

"We could make it look like DK pulled the trigger," Jake said, "whoever the hell he is."

"Whoever he is?" Peter asked. "If you were doing your job, that bastard would be in the tank by now. But implicating DK in Kel's murder, as easy as that would be, may not be enough."

"Why? What do you mean?" Jake asked.

"Someone besides Nyte thinks he knows."

Jake glared at Peter and tried to mask the fear he felt building in his chest. "Who?"

"Damned if I know, but someone left me a note. It claimed to have been written by him and said, 'My blood's on your hands.'"

"Willie!" Jake shouted. He leaned forward in the bench seat. The new leather talked back to his chinos with a grunt. "The note came from Willie?"

"Of course not, asshole. He's dead, but someone put it together."

"And not Nyte?" Jake asked.

"No. I was tipped off about the note on Sunday. You said it wasn't until Monday that Kel started to make the connection. No, it has to be someone else. Someone with either deep resources or a very long fishing pole."

"Katana rattling," Toshio said.

Jake missed the samurai sword reference and ignored Toshio with a glare. To Peter he said, "Hell, I'm not going down for this. It was your damn call. You set it up."

"Piss off," Peter said and took another draw from the cigar. He looked back toward the window. "We've been able to contain this up to now. Nothing's changed."

"Up to now, it's been our little secret," Jake said, "but if we've got an unknown shooting off his goddamn mouth, I'd say something's changed."

"Look, he gave a Hotmail address. I'll set up a meet."

"That's validation," Toshio said, his tone a warning.

"Validation or not," Jake said, "we've got to find out what, if anything, he knows."

"You don't get it. Just showing up confirms guilt."

"And what do you suggest?" Jake asked. "Ignore him? If we do nothing, what's his next move? The cops? Face it, he's got us by the balls."

"Leave me out of 'us,'" Toshio said. "Remember putting me in prison, shithead? He must think it's one or the both of you, and we all know who pulled the rug out from under Willie. Set up the meet in a public place. He'll demand it. I'll have my men stake it out, and once we know who it is, we'll discretely show him the gates of Hell."

"There it is again," Peter said. "Kill the bastard. And what if he's wired and his last words utter my name into some cop's ear?"

"Then you're in even deeper shit than your protégé here. I thought you said you could contain it."

Chapter Forty

KEL PULLED INTO the single-row, street-front parking lot just before 7:30 a.m. Three SPD cruisers had beaten her to the scene, and their red and blue strobe lights danced a syncopated rhythm in the Kinnear's store window. She approached the front glass door and a uniformed officer reached to open it for her.

"Good morning, Zek," Kel said as she paused and waited for the opening to appear.

"Morning, Kel," he said, and let her pass through. "Body's in the back office."

Damn shame, she thought. An hour ago Roger was a living soul. Now he's just a body, a piece of a puzzle.

Once inside, she took a moment to scan the showroom. At a glance she saw that the Kinnear's had good taste. The high-quality furniture looked more fitting of a Ballard or Blue Ridge home than the Rainier Valley neighborhood where Roger and Tracy lived. The pungent reek of death hadn't spilled out from the back room yet, so she teased her sense with the fragrance of fine leather and hand-polished walnut.

Despite the fact that the showroom had more uniformed officers in it than it probably did customers at any one time, the scene demanded the respect of silence. They stood in three scattered groups. Two officers with their arms folded across their chests took their station just inside the front door, grounded like Roman sentries to protect the scene from unauthorized entry. Three others gathered around a bar-height counter. One rested his elbows on it and drank coffee from a biodegradable cup with the others. Another lone figure stood with her hand on the facing of a door in the back of the showroom. She peered through the opening.

Kel walked to the backdoor and drew next to the officer.

"Hey, Nancy."

"The ME's with the vic now," Nancy said, and didn't look away from the view behind the door. She pulled it open and Kel slipped past her.

Kel entered the warehouse, and as she walked by a small kitchen on her left, she glanced in. The coffee in the glass pot had nearly been drained—I could certainly use a barista right now—but the lid was still secure on a distinctive aqua-colored box with the name "Flaky's" printed in white letters on the side. Despite his grief over his sister's death, Roger had bought pastries for his staff. It might have been the one thing grounding him to the constant ebb and flow of life—birth, donuts, death—and as long as there were donuts, death could be forestalled.

She peered through the open doorway to a small office.

"One shot, dead center."

The medical examiner kneeled next to a man in his late forties or early fifties. The guest of honor, Roger Kinnear, lay on his back. Gravity had drawn what blood hadn't spilled onto the cool concrete floor toward the corpse's backside. The void left his face a pallid mask. Despite this, there was something familiar about him. She had seen him before, perhaps at a fundraiser. Her dad, since her mom's death, had dragged her to a few. Even though socializing wasn't her strength, as she was more comfortable in blue jeans than an evening gown, to support him as the Chief of Police she had tagged along to make polite talk.

A slender man who stood six foot, three inches, pointed a digital camera toward the victim, shooting frames with a rapid click, click, click. He was the same man Paul Winston had yelled at the morning before while he photographed Marilyn's lifeless body.

"Detective Nyte," Kel said.

As if the man with the camera felt a sudden panic of claustrophobia in the tight office, he began to back out and said, "I'll wait outside." On his exit he brushed against Kel's hip and jerked to his right as if to avoid further physical contact with a woman. "Excuse me, ma'am. Damn small space. I'm ... I'm done for now."

Kel thought, The world is a pathetic place when a man thinks he'll be accused of sexual harassment if he accidentally bumps into a female coworker. She said, 'Thanks," and followed his exit with her green eyes and a smile. Once the way was clear, she moved inside to fill the space he vacated.

"Forty-five caliber to the forehead," the medical examiner said, looking up only high enough to see Kel's boots. "Probably came from that Remington on the desk. We'll test it to make sure. Your doer military?"

"Might be. Why?" Kel bent at the waist to examine the gun. I've left a gift, she remembered DK saying less than an hour before. This scene was no different than the others. With each victim, in addition to their poem, he left the instrument of their demise behind—a pillow, fragments of the bomb's detonator, and her dad's kitchen knife.

"Standard issue sidearm for U.S. military from before World War I until after Vietnam," the ME said. "But he could have bought it at a secondhand gun store."

Kel turned from the desk and squatted next to the body, eye level with the medical examiner. She looked into the eyes of the ME on the other side of the lifeless form. "I have no doubt that he left it.

That's been his MO. He likes leaving clues, so it probably has significance. Anything else seem out of place?"

"What about that?" He pointed to a cigarette butt lying on the floor next to him. "No ashtray in here."

"That's got to be it."

"Be what?" he asked. The ME reached into his kit for a plastic evidence bag.

Before she answered, a voice behind her said, "Hey, plebe. Thanks for the wakeup call, but what the Hell are you doing in my crime scene?"

Kel chose not to turn toward the voice as she examined the cigarette the ME dropped into the bag. "You only know about this crime scene 'cause I called you ... twice."

"And you knew about it how?"

"DK texted me the Kinnear's home address."

"Lieutenant Martinez threw you off the case and confiscated your phone." His tone was terse.

"More than one phone receives text messages, and a good cop is never really off-duty. Do you think I'm going to sit by if I have a chance to stop a murder?"

"Point taken," Jake said with his hands raised in surrender. He squeezed his way into the already crowded office and leaned over the body. "So what's up with the butt?"

"It seems out of place." She turned her faced to his. The circles under his eyes had not improved since last she noticed them at their first meeting at Starbucks on Monday. Today the gray saddlebags were almost black and overstuffed. "There's no ashtray in the office, and I was in his home. There was no trace of tobacco there, either. Take a deep breath, Jake. What does your nose tell you?"

Jake crinkled his brow. "Okay, I'll play along." He took a deep exaggerated breath through his nose and then exhaled. "Let's see. Leather, stale coffee, and the glaze of that apple fritter on the desk."

"Exactly. No burnt tobacco, right? DK left it. I spoke to him on the phone and—"

"You spoke to him?"

"I asked Mrs. Kinnear to call Roger so I could warn him, but DK answered and asked for me—by name—and said he was going to leave a gift. I've felt all along that he wants me to figure out who he is, and when we process this, we'll find a clue to his identity."

Kel turned to the ME and held up the evidence bag. "This is top priority. We need to get this to the lab for processing immediately. I'm going to send it with one of the uniforms. Any objections?"

"None from me."

She stood and looked at Jake.

"I agree. Good idea."

She turned back to the ME and asked, "We good here?"

"Yep. The investigators are waiting outside to process the room when you're finished."

"Good. Now," she said to Jake, "let's step outside."

As they left the office, Jake took the lead. They made their way toward the back door between two rows of high shelving stacked with furniture.

Once they were outside and away from the emergency vehicles blocking the alley, Kel said, "Look, I think we got off on the wrong foot."

"I know what you're going to say, and it's not necessary," Jake said. "I tried my damn level best to get you kicked from this case and out of my way. As far as I was concerned, I wanted a chasm between us big enough to float a fully-loaded aircraft carrier. But you've done alright. Despite my efforts, you've not only kept up, but in some ways you're ahead of me.

"So here's the deal. Until we've solved the case, you're my speed dial number one. No more voicemail. I'm still not going to appreciate the finer things, like getting my ass out of the sheets, especially when someone else's ass is keeping me company. But we've got to figure this out. We need to start fresh now."

"You kidding me?" She felt as if he had poured ice water on her fury. "Why the sudden conversion?"

"Do you want to work together or not?"

"No more rule one?"

"Of course."

"No more plebe?"

"Granted."

"Okay, then, on a trial basis. And …" she said, averting her eyes. "What I said the other day about your conviction ratio was below the belt."

"No apologies. It's true, and I know it. Besides, with two partners either dead or disabled, I have this constant reminder that my rule one may be the problem."

"Well, on the record, I don't want to be signing up to be another casualty in the line of duty, but if we could work together to bust this UNSUB ..."

"Okay, then. Who's the victim, and what does he have to do with your dad?"

"According to his wife, nothing—but there's another twist. Roger Kinnear and Suzanne Lowen are siblings."

"So all the victims are connected in some way. This has to be more than coincidence."

"I know, and even though we don't know if Mr. Kinnear's connection to my dad, until we unravel that knot, we've still got nothing but a ticking clock."

"That leaves us only one person who can fill in this piece," Jake said.

"And even though you and I have this new bond of collaboration, I'll take this interview without you."

Chapter Forty-One

SHELIA SAVELL PUSHED her chair back from the desk, stood, and walked to the window. From the fifteenth floor of the Mangorn Building, her eyes drifted across the cityscape. Despite the recession of the last couple of years, newly built and renovated office towers cast their shadows across the city. The vistas of the Puget Sound and the Olympic Mountain Range now hid behind the high-rise veil. That left the shriek of a gull or the occasional Washington State Ferry's air horn drifting through the skyline to serve as evidence that Seattle still thrived on the waterfront.

Directly across the street, a seventeen-storey terra cotta-style tower—built in 1922 and damaged by the Nisqually Earthquake nine years earlier—stood stripped of its former dignity. With Shelia's near-flawless court record, the structure had become a reminder of one of her only failures.

Shelia, with the backing of the firm, had taken on the city and the developers who wanted to level the building to make way for a fifty-two-storey cracker-box style steel-and-glass atrocity. The architect, from the looks of the elevation drawings, was a third-grader with a small set of broken crayons. In the end, she lost her bid to have it declared an historic landmark.

Now, the former edifice gaped like a bombed-out Baghdad shell. Most of the window glass had been removed in preparation for the demolition soon to commence. By the end of August, an implosion would reduce the artifact to a pile of rubble. She could already imagine its last whimper—the rumble of heavy equipment hauling away its broken remains.

One case she wouldn't have minded losing worked at the Snelling Help Desk three floors below her office. The criminal practice group chair, knowing of her dad's relationship to the Rat City Exterminator case, had said, "The full circle of justice will be served if you're assigned as Vince Buckley's lawyer. Besides, if it comes to trial and you win, your partnership's a lock." She had argued that she was a corporate litigator, not a defense lawyer, but she lost that argument, too.

To complicate her emotions, she wanted to buy her dad's and Kel's theory that Buckley was DK. She had little doubt that he was in fact the Exterminator, so seeing him sentenced to death for the DK murders would also restore justice for the nineteen known Exterminator victims. But now, being his lawyer, if Kel busted his alibi, she had an ethical obligation to provide him a proper defense.

A light knock on the open door turned Shelia from the window.

"Hey, sis," Kel said as she walked into the office. "Interrupting something?"

"No, come on in. How'd you get to this floor? It's passkey only."

"Isn't it obvious?"

Off Kel's left pocket, a shaft of light reflected from her gold shield. Covered in her dress blue uniform, Shelia realized her sister had come prepared to go directly to Suzanne Lowen's funeral. She had never quite understood what drove Kel to follow after her dad's and grandpa's career. However, seeing her decorated so reminded her of the pride she felt when, in a similar uniform, Kel had graduated from the police academy nine years earlier.

"Opens all kinds of doors," Kel said, and a smile lit her face. The twin dimples on her cheeks deepened.

"Apparently." Shelia walked to the desk.

"Brought you a little something, Sis." Kel held up a grande cappuccino in a disposable cup. In her other hand, she held her own latte.

"You're such a cop cliché, Kel. Always with the coffee. You just need a donut to complete the picture. Here, give me that and take a seat." Shelia waved to a chair. "We still have a couple of minutes."

As Kel reached to swing the door closed with her foot, a medium-built man with black hair appeared in the doorway.

Kel noticed Shelia's eyes lock on his.

"I need that file," he said.

Shelia reached forward and lifted a thick manila folder from the top of a stack on her desk. He entered the office and slipped the file from Shelia's hand.

"Ryung, I don't think you've met my sister. Kel Nyte, Ryung Kim."

"Obviously, you're a police officer," Ryung said to Kel and extended his hand.

Kel stepped to Shelia's desk, placed the cappuccino on the nearest corner, and then took his warm hand.

"Ryung's an associate attorney here at SHP," Shelia said. "We're working a case together and have a motion due in court on Monday. Since I'll be out this afternoon, he's going to help me with some research on precedence."

"Nice to meet you, Ryung." Kel gave his hand a firm shake.

With a polite smile, he left the office, and closed the door behind him. Kel took a side chair across the desk from her sister. Shelia took her seat and spun it around to face Kel.

"He's really smart," Shelia said. She leaned forward and rested her elbows on the desktop. "And single."

"Here we go. Not with the matchmaker again."

"I'm just saying, you're alone, Chrissie needs a dad—"

JEARL RUGH

"Oh, and now it's the dad card. You know how I feel about this. It's too soon. I'm not ready to even think about dating."

Eighteen months earlier, Lance had left for Afghanistan for a twelve-month deployment. Four months in, the caravan of armored vehicles he rode with came under attack. In the fight, he disappeared, and his body was never recovered.

"I just worry about my big sister living like a nun without that special person in her life."

"Even nuns have someone special. They're married to Jesus Christ, for God's sake."

"You know what I mean."

"Shelia, you know I miss Lance every day." She reached for the cup on the desk and took a swallow. "There may come a point when I feel certain he's not coming home. But it's the not knowing that has my heart bound. Am I holding onto the memory of a dead man or just keeping the spark of hope alive that, at the very worst, he's in some prison thousands of miles away?"

"I'm sorry. I don't mean to press you."

"Then can we change the subject?"

"Sure. The news says DK struck again."

"Roger Kinnear. The name mean anything to you?"

"Nothing. Who's he?"

"When I first saw him at the scene, I had an odd feeling there was something familiar about him. Still haven't put it together, but I have a hunch. Curiously, he and the first victim, the one we're burying today, were brother and sister."

"That can't be a coincidence."

"Not likely. All DK's main targets up to now have been killed presumably because they had something in common—Daddy—but so far I can't put him and Kinnear together. At first, my theory on the murders centered on the victim's relationship to the Exterminator case, but unless Marilyn had some connection to it, and there doesn't seem to be one … her death yesterday turned that notion upside-down.

"Buckley's not off my list, though," Kel continued. "What if he paid that hooker for his alibi? Or, since the police have yet to locate the woman he was supposed to be with, maybe she doesn't even exist."

"I seem to recall a report that a confirming witness was found."

Kel had learned from the Yakima Police that although Buckley's hooker alibi hadn't been found, another jailed prostitute claimed she overheard the woman boasting that she spent Monday night with the man who had been accused of being the Rat City Exterminator. According to her, Buckley had bragged over drinks that he knew one of the Hillside Stranglers and the Green River Killer. She stated that she gave him enough mind-blowing sex to make up for his years of drought in prison—on the house.

"She could have been bought off too. Shelia, they're hookers. They do what they're paid to do."

"You do remember this is my client you're talking about."

"So? I'm discussing a new theory with my sister, and holes in Buckley's alibi with his lawyer. You can keep that straight, right? I'm not asking you to comment or divulge any privileged communications. Just drink your coffee and hear me talk this through."

Shelia nodded, took her drink and leaned back in her chair.

"If I'm correct," Kel continued, "and Buckley did this, he planned a little misdirection. Suzanne and Terry's murders were designed to confuse the investigation, Daddy and Buckley both being implicated. But Marilyn's murder should take him out of the pool because she had nothing to do with Buckley's conviction. It's brilliant. What better way to absolve yourself than by pointing the finger right at yourself?"

"If I may speak candidly as his lawyer, I think you're missing something. How'd he know about Dad and Marilyn?"

"I've been thinking about that. If DK is the Exterminator, he must have connections. For one, he must know someone in the SPD. Otherwise, how did he get my unlisted department cell phone number? And then … how did he learn about Daddy's affair? But he certainly wouldn't have any friends within the

SPD, and Terry wouldn't give him the time of day, let alone information about his suspicions about Marilyn. He has to have an accomplice."

"That may be true, Detective, but if it's not my client, and you're giving me lots of reasonable doubt here, then DK may not need an accomplice. I'd say your new theory is a stretch, and a long one at that."

"Well, either way, we may not have long to wait. Shelia, DK intentionally left a clue to his identity at Roger's crime scene. Once the lab finishes, we should know who he is."

"That should put a stop to him."

"I'm not so sure. I have this gut feeling that even if we have his name, we still may not know who he is, at least not 'til he's ready. He's still in control and he's making it personal."

"What do you mean?" Shelia tipped forward and rested her forearms on the desk.

"Sorry I have to be so clinical about Daddy, but right now it's the only way I can handle it. Daddy had sex with Marilyn. Not just once, but apparently several times. What if DK had wanted to kill Mom, but since she's already dead, he went for the next best? Someone Daddy had been intimate with?"

"Assuming Marilyn was killed because Dad slept with her."

"True, but why else? Certainly not just because she was Terry's wife. That just doesn't fit."

"It doesn't fit your theory, you mean. But if we make that assumption, then why Kinnear? What does he have to do with Dad?"

"I don't have that answer yet, but look at this." She rested her cup on the desk again and from her notebook pulled the printout of the poem found on Roger Kinnear's home computer.

Shelia read it over, and then her eyes drifted up to meet Kel's.

"It's a similar style to one he texted to you before."

"Yes. The same seven-beat rhythm and feet. We've not released the poetry angle to the press, so there's no doubt that it's DK. What do you make of the first line?"

"'Four the sowing of wild fruit'?" Shelia asked. "It's not clear."

"Not clear, or you don't want to accept it? Shelia, I've had some time to think about it, and I think I know what it means. If I'm right, there's only one person who can confirm it."

"Dad?" Shelia said. Her eyes drifted back to the poem.

"Yes. So far it's all about him, and if my instinct's right, we're not going to like this answer any more than we did learning that Daddy was unfaithful to Mom."

Chapter Forty-Two

UNTIL THE ORGANIST fingered a natural instead of a flat, Kel couldn't tell if the background music was recorded or live. The aroma of fresh-cut daisies, roses, and begonias filled the small chapel at Vincent's Funeral Home. Their natural fragrances lost distinction as they conflated to cover the scent of death skulking in the corners. Around the room lining the walls, uniformed police and fire personnel stood frozen like wooden soldier decorations. They stared at the floor, each other, and the closed pink and gray coffin bearing the remains of a colleague most didn't know. The stoic features on their faces intoned what Kel's heart prayed: "But for the grace of God go I."

To allow family and close friends to crowd forward near their loved one, Kel had stayed with Shelia at the back of the chapel near the exit. Her dad, weak from his disease and the stress of the last several days, had been taken to a seat near the front. On his left, the acting Chief of Police sat with his head bowed as if entreating his god for the safety of his people and the soul of the departed. On his right, his escort sat. Her body in a constant state of fidget,

Chrissie looked over her shoulder for a familiar face in a sea of identically dressed warriors of the street. Kel understood by her expression that she didn't want to be that close to Suzanne Lowen's casket and was desperate for it to be over soon.

"Even though I walk through the valley of the shadow of death," the priest read from Psalms twenty-three, the New American Bible version, "I will fear no evil, for you are with me."

Kel listened as the homily began. The well-meaning man of about forty-five with the clerical collar had designed the sermon to give comfort to those who suffered sudden loss. She knew from her mom's service that it would fall short. No one's grief would be eased in the next few minutes.

She couldn't see to the front pews, but with the sniffling and an occasional heaving sob, someone—perhaps Suzanne's partner or her parents—was deep in uncontrolled grief. Kel mourned with them, and for the families of the other victims of DK's recompense. They, too, were headed for morose gatherings of their own.

When the service ended, the two sisters were some of the first to exit the chapel. There were too many people to try to move to their dad, so they left Chrissie to help her Pops navigate the crowd. Out on the sidewalk, a warm sun had eluded the cumulus clouds and, dressed in her blues, Kel's skin began to break out in sweat. She led the way to a shade tree on the front lawn.

"Afternoon, Detective."

Kel turned to the voice and found that Bimal had separated from the crowd on the sidewalk. He walked toward her and Shelia. Today he appeared more put-together and a little less like an unmade bed than the first time Kel met him. His hair was combed back, the three-day-old beard shaved.

"Shelia, this is Bimal. He's the lab analyst I've been working with on this case. Bimal, my little sister here is a lawyer."

"Nice to meet you, Shelia," Bimal said, and took her hand. "But what she was too kind to add was that I almost got her killed twice this week." He smiled and released her hand.

"So that was you," Shelia said, pouting her lips and placing her hands on her hips.

"So, she did tell you."

"No, I read it in the newspaper. You best be careful with my sister. She's the only one I've got."

"I'll make it my purpose to work on that skill set, but you must know she threatened to shoot me. Isn't there a law about that, counselor?" His face brightened into a smile.

"I'm sure I could find one, but it sounds more like self-defense," Shelia winked.

Bimal grinned and then turned his face to Kel. "I had hoped to catch you. I was still on duty when word came in about the Kinnear murder. I processed the gun found at the scene, and there's something interesting. A match to a slug pulled from a DB two months ago."

"Let me guess, an unsolved?"

He nodded his head and continued, "The body was found in a house fire. At first it looked like he fell asleep smoking, but the autopsy found a bullet lodged in his frontal lobe, much like Mr. Kinnear. If there was any trace evidence, though, it went up in smoke, so the case is still open."

"I remember seeing the story on the evening news," Shelia said. "High school teacher and freelance writer, as I recall."

"DK's first victim?" Kel stroked her chin. "What does a freelance writer have to do with this?"

While Bimal spoke behind him and Shelia, Kel noticed the flow of blue uniforms leaving the building by the double oak door had dwindled. She watched for her dad and Chrissie, but they hadn't yet appeared.

About thirty feet away, in the center of the sidewalk, Lieutenant Lou Martinez and Chief of Detectives, Nathanial Ballesteros, were deep in conversation. Lou was doing the majority of the speaking, his eyes flitting between Ballesteros, the ground, and the crowd. Although Kel couldn't hear his words, his tortured expression gave her the impression that the source of his distress wasn't the victim whose memorial had just concluded. Ballesteros looked on, offering a hand on the shoulder and a nod of sympathetic acknowledgement. When the Chief leaned in and spoke a quiet word in Lou's ear, the lieutenant looked up and scanned the crowd. The conversation abruptly ended.

Martinez turned away from Ballesteros and toward the parking lot behind Kel. Their eyes locked. A flash of anger crossed his countenance, and then guilt took its place. He dropped his eyes to the concrete at his feet. Then, with an unexpected shift, he found another route from the chapel.

"... Kinnear's autopsy is still pending," Bimal was saying as Kel tuned her ears back to him, "and we're searching for the registered owner of the gun."

"What about the cigarette butt?" Kel asked.

"No prints."

"DNA?"

"We did find skin follicles, and we're running them, but that takes a while. Don't get your hopes up. Most people aren't in the database. I'll keep you posted, though, as soon as we learn anything."

Out of the corner of her eye, she saw her daddy exit the doors of the funeral chapel. With Chrissie's arm laced in his on one side and the acting chief on the other, they cut a swath like Moses parting the Red Sea through the crowd. Kel waved. Chrissie nodded, whispered in Dirk's ear, and steered him with a gentle tug toward the trio under the tree.

As Dirk and his entourage approached, Bimal nodded an acknowledgment, turned, and left.

"Good afternoon, Chief," Kel said to the acting Chief of Police. She shook her head. "Tough day."

"They get no worse," he responded, and then faced Dirk. "Looks like you found the best place to escape this hot sun. Just yesterday it was raining, and today it's a bake-off. Now, if you're okay, Dirk, I have to lead the motorcade to the cemetery."

"Got my best people," he said, and threw a wink to Chrissie. "I'll see you there."

As the chief walked away and Shelia moved close to take his place, supporting her dad by the arm, Dirk said, "That service will be for me soon, and the way I feel this week, it won't be long now. I want a service like that, girls."

"We don't have to do this now," Shelia said.

"I know. I'm just saying, I want to make arrangements while I still have strength."

"We will, Dad, but for now, we should get you to the car."

"As long as I've got you and Chrissie, I'll make it just fine."

Kel looked beyond them to the crowd on the sidewalk. A man she recognized made his way to the family circle under the tree.

"Good afternoon, Chief, ladies," he said. "Jared Collins of The Globe. How goes the hunt, Detective?"

"We have leads," Kel said, "but you know I can't discuss them."

"Of course not. I wouldn't insert myself in an ongoing investigation. My apologies for poor timing, but I wonder if I might have a word with the chief?"

"Is that okay, Dad?" Shelia asked.

"I'll only be a moment. Just a quick question."

"It's alright, Angel," Dirk said. He turned to Collins. "What is it?"

"You remember our conversation the other day?"

"Of course. You called just after Terry's death. I know you want a story, and I have no good reason to disappoint you. But can it wait until this is over? With what's happened this week—three people I knew and loved, dead, not to mention the others who were caught in the blast in Bellingham—"

"Four," Jared said. "A true serial killer."

"Four!" Dirk met Kel's eyes. "Who else, Princess? When did this happen?"

"You've had enough on your mind today with all this," Kel said, and waved her hand to the crowd walking to their vehicles.

"Who?"

"From what we can tell, you don't know him. Maybe we're wrong, Daddy. Maybe this isn't about you at all."

"Who is it, damn it?"

"It's all over the news," Jared said.

"I haven't seen the news today."

"His name is Roger Kinnear," Jared said.

"Roger? Roger! Oh my God. I should have seen this coming."

Dirk's knees buckled, and he began to collapse on the grass. Chrissie and Shelia grabbed his arms tighter to keep him on his feet.

"This way," Kel said.

Together, Shelia and Chrissie led Dirk to a bench at the edge of the sidewalk. An older woman wearing a powder blue pant suit sat on the bench with a metal cane wedged between her thighs. Next to her sat a young man whose upraised brows and expressive eyes suggested he was engrossed in telling the woman a story.

With no place to sit, Kel ran ahead. "My dad needs to sit. Could you make room?"

The man turned abruptly, and jumped to his feet. "Here, take my seat. I'll get some water."

"Thank you," Kel said to the back of the man as he ran toward chapel.

"I'm so sorry. I had no idea he'd react this way," Jared said as he followed the group to the bench.

"Perhaps it's best if you go now, Mr. Collins," Kel said. "There'll be no interview today."

"Of course. My apologies." He backed away.

Shelia and Chrissie settled Dirk on the bench next to the woman. With his elbows on his knees, he hunched forward and massaged his temples with his fingers.

"Everything okay, dear?" the woman asked.

"He'll be alright now," Kel said. "He's not well and has had a very stressful week."

"So that's why," Dirk said.

"What do you mean, Daddy?" Kel asked.

"I kept looking for Roger at the service. He's Suzanne's brother. Damn it! Who is this DK, anyway? Does he know all my secrets?"

Chapter Forty-Three

DIRK NYTE SAT under a green canvas awning in a plastic folding chair. Seated in the second row at Suzanne Lowen's graveside service behind Trisha, Suzanne's partner, and Suzanne's parents, he couldn't focus his attention on the priest's discourse. His heart had been racked by grief this week, as if some monster had reached into his chest and ripped at his pulsating heart with a dull blade. So many had died due to him—and now Roger.

Just yesterday in Interview Two, he had sensed both of his daughters distance themselves from him emotionally at the revelation of his affair with Marilyn. Since then, neither one of them had been able to voice their feelings. He looked around the cemetery. The dried and decaying flowers that once graced a headstone two rows away brought back the fear he had expressed only Monday night: "I can't go in peace wondering if someday you'll return to my grave for the last time and ask, 'Who was this man, anyway?'" Now as the week wore on and the lessons DK claimed he had to teach kept mounting, the confidences were out of "Pandora's Box," as Kel had put it. And with Roger's death, a secret buried almost fifty years ago would now be revealed.

A bond existed between them of which even Roger had been unaware. Until today he had thought it known to only a small number of people who, for the good of everyone connected, had chosen to keep it sealed. But whoever DK was, his reach and his resources had no end. The master teacher had forced him to be exposed, stark naked before the world and more importantly, those he loved, with all his furtive past.

The priest's closing words pulled Dirk's thoughts back to the service.

"Ashes to ashes, dust to dust," he said. With the Aspergillum in one hand, he sprinkled holy water over Suzanne's casket to consecrate her spirit back to God.

Dirk's eyes ached with grief. They followed the priest as he made his way toward the friends and family seated in the row in front of him. As he greeted each one, he gave them a blessing. He paused when he reached Trisha and wrapped both of his hands around hers. "God bless you, Trisha," he said, and then turned to the woman next to her. The priest took Suzanne's mother's hand and leaned forward, whispering into her ear. Dirk felt her heartache. On the same day she was destined to bury her only daughter, something she thought she'd never do, she had also learned that her son had fallen victim to the same murderer—a murderer who was taking these innocent lives to settle a score with him.

When the priest finished with the family, two uniformed pallbearers stepped forward and took the corners of the American flag draping the coffin. As they folded it military style, the discordant wheeze of a lone bagpipe broke the silence. In moments, its sonorous voice began to play "Amazing Grace."

Behind Dirk, a single voice began to sing the first line. "Amazing grace, how sweet the sound …" Then another joined in. "… That saved a wretch like me!" And then another. By the time the music reached the final line, the whole gathering sang in unison: "Was blind, but now I see."

As the last phrase passed his lips, a revelation struck Dirk, and DK's motive became clear. A lump he couldn't swallow seized his throat, and the more pressure it produced, the more unrestrained tears flowed.

Chapter Forty-Four

THE BLAST RIPPED Dirk from a pleasant dream about a family he'd yet to know in a future he hoped to live in. As the images dissolved with the sleep webs, his heart responded with an anxious cadence and an unwelcomed, but all-too-familiar, disquiet usurped his euphoria. Tucked in behind a broad-trunked Indian Devil tree on a small rise, he rolled to his stomach. The plastic grips on his rifle filled his hands but offered no guarantee of safety, no matter how much his mind grappled for it. With the sights pointed in the direction of the thundering peal on retreat into the distance, Sergeant Dirk Nyte stared through the barrel-mounted Starlight night-vision scope, and scanned the field. Not thirty meters out, six green heat signatures, warm from the life he'd stolen from them, lay victim to the tripwire of a single M18 Claymore mine.

It was the first day of Tet Nguyen Dan, the celebration of the Vietnamese New Year. With a two-day ceasefire in place, most of the allied troops had taken a reprieve from the fighting. Nyte's squad, though, had been assigned to keep ears to the ground.

Dirk's eyes drifted above the gun barrel. The fading stars against the black canopy marked the beginning of the second day of their three-day recon mission. Until this discharge, they had observed not one confirmed slither of enemy movement.

He raised the scope to scan the near proximity, anxious to find that, like his men, it was just a few scouts on patrol. But despair mingled with dread as he saw scores of men crouched and running for cover across the open field to a tree line fifty meters away. He drew several deep breaths of tepid jungle air. The scent of dirt, foliage decay, and his own sweat filled his nostrils, but there just wasn't enough oxygen to subdue the relentless fear for the lives of his men clawing at his now fully conscious mind.

During the next two unsettling minutes while he scanned the brush in front of him for each of his men, he hoped that his squad remembered the mission briefing he had given before they left base: "Don't fire unless you're absolutely sure they're shooting at you, and not to see if anyone's home. You return fire and it throws the door open wide enough to drive a battalion of tanks." With each one hunkered behind whatever cover they could find, he rolled to his left side, traced the Sign of the Cross over his chest, and flung a prayer to the creator of those stars that they'd be safe if the force on the other side of the clearing decided to ring the doorbell.

When Charlie's volley erupted, Nyte sat up. He pressed his back against the rough gray bark. It jabbed into his flesh as if it were a bed of rough-cut gravel. He waited with his finger on the trigger of his M16. After thirty seconds, when the rain of hot lead stopped tearing through the jungle, he pursed his lips and forced the breath he now realized he'd been holding from his lungs. He raised the scope again, peered around the trunk, and glanced over the enemy. Their green glow indicated they were waiting for a response. Just hold on now, boys, he thought. Wait 'til they collect their dead and move on.

No sooner had the thought passed through his mind when the silence was broken by the chatter of automatic weapon fire to his right. He jerked the scope around to see who had engaged. Hal stood with his rifle at his hip like Burt Lancaster in Gunfight at the O.K. Corral, spraying short bursts toward the opposite stand of trees.

Over the last day, Nyte had felt a gnawing unrest for Hal, who had landed in Southeast Asia three days ago. On his first mission, his bravado said, "I'm here to kill gooks." But after a day of playing duck and cover with every sound the jungle uttered, Nyte knew his nerves were as taut as the E string on Jimi Hendrix's Fender Stratocaster.

Proof of life was just what Charlie needed. After getting three bursts off, with a single shot from the opposite side of the clearing, and without a noticeable flinch, Hal tipped backward like a felled tree. The rest of his magazine sent a single stream into the air.

Twenty minutes and countless rounds later, the sulfuric trace of spent gunpowder came with Nyte's every breath. Behind the far trees, dawn painted the black horizon with a deep blue brushstroke. While the firefight had raged, Nyte kept vigil on the body-heat signatures in the tree line. Vietcong reinforcements had been gathering from adjoining sectors like spotted hyenas on the scent of a kill. Because the morning light threatened to expose just how few of Uncle Sam's GI's opposed them, at any moment Nyte expected to see a wall of pajama-clad AK-47-bearing guerillas swarm from the trees behind a frenzy of fire power.

One of Dirk's men started the nickname practice while cleaning his weapon after a grisly mission. Without looking up, he had said, "Clive doesn't live in this hellhole. He'd never do to another human the things Uncle Sam demands. From now on it's Black Hail out there raining death and destruction. And if Hail survives 'til that ride home, Clive will greet him at the airport." Since that day, even those making their final trip home in a box earned their moniker.

Nyte looked again to the position of each man who had trusted him with his life. The bitterness of bile rose to his tongue as he found at least five whose confidence he'd betrayed. Lone Wolf on the far left flank still returned fire, but favored his left shoulder. A good soldier, he kept a distance from the squad whether on a mission or back in the barracks. Lefty, known for his accurate southpaw grenade tosses, writhed with his hands clutched to his stomach as if his guts were spilling out. Beside Hal on the far right, Boomer, the explosives expert, lay still as stone. And in the center of the line, just ten meters below Nyte, DJ, the radioman, sprawled motionless.

Since no air cover had arrived once the shooting started, Nyte figured DJ must have been taken out at about the same time as Hal. With so many of his men already dead or wounded, holding their position for much longer gave no hope of anyone's survival, which meant that they wouldn't fulfill their mission—to report that Charlie was not on holiday.

I need that radio, he thought.

The thick brush on the grade between him and DJ offered visual obscurity in the dull morning light, but the broad leafs were no shield from the bullets strafing the ground around him. He placed his hand over his left breast pocket and drew strength from his fiancée's tear-stained letter. The hope birthed on that one page covered his heart like a cloak of chainmail.

With his rifle resting in the crooks of his arms, in a flurry of elbows and knees, he dug into the carpet of decaying leaves and grass, crawled down the slope, and wriggled to the right side of the remains of the twenty-year-old's days on Earth. He turned toward DJ. His helmet lay next to him upside down like a turtle on its back. Nyte picked up the headgear. A bullet had pierced it and then burrowed into DJ's brain. Left behind, a moist stream of blood crossed his forehead just above the "what the hell just happened?" stare in his eyes.

"Sorry, kid," he said as he reached across DJ's body to slip the radio from his lifeless left hand. Nyte rolled to his right side and triggered the switch. A hiss of static hit his ears and impulse shot his fingers to the knob to silence the volume. Once adjusted, as he lifted the instrument to speak, like a small tree branch under the thwack of a machete, his arm fell useless. He gapped at the flaccid limb twisted across his chest at an incongruous angle, and clenched his teeth. "Damn it," he muttered, as if that'd take the bite from the sharp ache already radiating from the bone-fragging wound.

He grabbed the device in his right hand and growled into the mouthpiece, "Taking heavy fire. At least five down. Request an airstrike now!"

"Negative, Sarge," the voice through the speaker crackled. "Pilots are on holiday."

"There is no holiday, soldier. Half the damn Cong army's on the move and at my doorstep."

"It'll be at least forty-five before I can find one who ain't hungover."

"We'll be dead by then. Find that pilot ... but get me a chopper, now!"

Since they were twenty klicks from base, Nyte knew the timing of the retreat was crucial. He looked to his left. The closest man, O'Leary, swapped magazines. Nicknamed after the infamous Catherine O'Leary of the 1871 Great Chicago Fire, if he had toted his flamethrower on this patrol, they might have faced a different outcome. Nyte yelled, "O'Leary, Scorpion Run. One klick. Five minutes." O'Leary nodded. Nyte knew he'd carry the order to the others to the left flank.

With Charlie's sleet of lead sounding like a swarm of angry hornets buzzing around Nyte's ears, and since DJ hadn't survived this position, Nyte felt exposed. He dragged himself to the right under the brush with his weapon slung over his back and his useless arm in tow. Tarzan, so named because during battle he lurched from tree to tree firing into oncoming bullets, was pinned down. He reloaded magazines. Over the fray, Nyte repeated the order.

"Five minutes," Tarzan called back.

Nyte crawled the two meters to Hal. He wanted to be angry with him for causing this disaster, but Hal was just a boy under extreme stress who, like most teenagers, had thought he was invincible and didn't consider consequences. I've seen it too many times.

From Hal's web belt Nyte pulled a roll of gauze and bound it around his own arm. The blood flowed with such a heavy surge that it took several layers of wrap to stop the injury from soaking through red. Once he tied it off, he moved forward and repeated the retreat order to two other men laying down fire. When he reached Boomer, the blood-drenched olive drab blouse should have been convincing enough, but Nyte placed a finger to the silent man's neck anyway. No throb greeted his fingertips. He shook his head in disgust and then looked around the ground near Boomer for the triggers.

"Scorpion Run," Nyte said as he looked past Boomer to Boa.

Boa, whose moniker derived from the night he had slid into the enemy's camp and put several soldiers into chokeholds, stopped shooting and turned toward Nyte, waiting.

While the rest of Nyte's squad ceased fire, he rolled toward Boa and scooted until he could see across the clearing between two thick tree trunks. In less than a minute, the enemy's bullets stopped.

In the bloom of morning light, he sensed movement. He raised his field glasses and watched a small troop of about two dozen—not the entire force—emerge from the tree line. They crouched low with their weapons ready as they crossed the open field. Each step came slow and watchful as if dead men's bones lay in their path.

When they were within twenty meters, Nyte squeezed the detonators to set off the remaining Claymores. The fire, smoke, and dust kicked up by the massive discharge hid the advancing guerillas. Yet the deafening explosion and the shrieks of the dying as the pellets tore through their flesh was the signal. Only seconds remained before the enemy waiting in the trees, disoriented by the blood and horror and thanking their god that it wasn't them, realized that the discharge wasn't another accidental blast, but a diversion.

Nyte jumped to his feet, but after two steps, realized that Boa hadn't followed. He turned and forced a whispered order. "Retreat, now." He stooped low and ran.

Over the last couple of minutes, behind him, the blast of an occasional hand grenade drowned for a few seconds the frequent automatic AK-47 bursts and the footsteps of Charlie tramping through the jungle like a panicked sounder of wild boar. He had lost sight of his men in the retreat. As Dirk broke through the trees with his fragged left arm swaying at his side without purpose, he was relieved to see two soldiers racing for the chopper. It hovered at ground level twenty exposed meters ahead.

When the two warriors reached the helicopter, they fell to the ground just below the door and aimed their weapons at the tree line. Seconds later, Nyte swung onto the deck of the Huey and flattened prone. He pulled his fractured arm around in front of him to rest the barrel. But before he was in position, the two men on the ground resumed fire, and the chatter from two M60 machineguns erupted over his head.

He looked up. Tarzan loped along with Lefty and one other man on his shoulders. Behind him, dozens of Vietcong swarmed out of the jungle like ants racing from a fast spreading ground fire. No sooner did they appear than they fell as they ran head on into the wall of hot lead. But behind them, more came. More than the GI's guns were able cut down. Nyte joined the fire fight but it still wasn't enough.

Tarzan, just a few meters ahead of the throng, took a hit to his leg and fell. Without hesitation the two men at the door bolted for him. Each one took one of his burdens. The one with Lefty pulled Tarzan to his feet, and together they started to limp back.

It only took seconds, but it seemed like an eternity before the rotors accelerated and their deafening sound hit Nyte's ears. As the bird took flight, the reduced frequency of thunks as rounds passed through the steel body of the chopper was a welcome resonance. Finally, out of range, Nyte found a place to sit on the deck to make an assessment. Not ten minutes before, he'd taken a mental roll call, and he knew which of his men were among the living and which would be left dead. As expected, Hal, Boomer, and DJ were not present. One of the two men Tarzan had carried back was DOA. And Lefty didn't look so good. Tarzan ignored his own wound and stuffed as much available gauze as he could into Lefty's belly.

Nyte leaned back against the bulkhead. The ache in his left arm paled compared to what had happened to his men and what he had inflicted on the enemy. He took his helmet off to wipe the sweat from his brow with his forearm. Sad, weary eyes met his.

"You did good today," he said. "But damn it, three unaccounteds."

Chapter Forty-Five

"ROGER? OUR BROTHER?" Kel asked. She had sensed this was the only plausible answer to DK's riddle—Four the sowing of wild fruit—but now that the word was in the air, it seemed unreal.

Kel had driven Dirk, Shelia, and Chrissie back to the Queen Anne hill family home after the graveside service. Since it was almost six o'clock in the evening and no one had eaten anything since breakfast, they left Chrissie in the kitchen to warm some canned soup and make grilled cheese sandwiches. The other three settled into the study to learn about Roger Kinnear.

"Half-brother, actually," Dirk said as he adjusted himself in his brown leather chair.

"Mom's? Or yours, Dad?" Shelia asked as she took her mom's chair, each syllable clicked off her tongue in staccato.

"Mine—and before you ask, Mom knew about him."

"And not us?" Shelia continued her inquisition as if her dad was a hostile witness. "Yesterday we learn that you had an affair with your partner's wife, one of Mom's friends, and today we hear for the first time that we have a brother. I didn't know we had family secrets, Dad. I thought we were above that."

"It was a delicate and discrete situation." He rested his hand on her leg and she jerked it away. "The girl was fourteen, and at the time, I was sixteen."

"Fourteen?" Kel shouted and leaned forward from her seat on the rocking chair. The contempt for his actions rose in her throat. Still angered from the concealment of his affair with Marilyn, this new knowledge threw added fuel on an already raging fire. She had left her dark blue uniform jacket in the car, but now she stripped her clip-on tie off and loosened the neck button. "That's Chrissie's age."

"When you put it that way, I'm so ashamed," he said, and shifted his eyes away from Kel to the cold fireplace. "I was a child rapist by law. We never saw it that way, of course. We were two kids with raging hormones. By the time she figured out something was happening inside her body, she was in her second trimester.

"You have to remember," he continued and looked first to Kel and then to Shelia, "that back in 1961, it was a different world. That was before the free love movement, the space race … hell, it was before the Beatles.

"Despite the voices calling her a slut, our parents felt it in the best interest of the baby that the child be allowed to come to term and be put up for adoption.

Even before Roger was born, a couple said they'd raise him as their own on two conditions. First, that the two families paid all the costs of the birth and adoption, and second, that Roger never knew anything about it.

"Then, it must have been about ten years ago, I heard his name on television. Mom and I were watching Leno in bed one night, and a commercial came on. There was Roger pitching his furniture store. I had never seen him, not even as a baby. Mom saw the resemblance immediately. He had my chin—same as yours, Shelia."

"When I saw him this morning," Kel said, having brought her ire momentarily under control, "something seemed familiar about him, but I thought maybe I'd bumped into him somewhere. So when you saw him, did you tell Mom who he was?"

"She knew before we were married that I had a son out there. It was at the time I was fixing to head to Vietnam. Your mom had agreed to marry me as soon as I returned. So, I took some leave, and a couple of nights before I left, I told her about Roger."

"How did she take it?"

"I lost her. She had thought we were both coming into our marriage as virgins, and I had let her believe it. But somehow I knew that if we started our life together with a lie, if the truth ever did come out, it'd ruin us. She was so wounded by my deception she couldn't speak to me. You have to remember we met at church. Were both good Catholics, and even though it had been several years since I had been with the girl and before I knew your mom, it stung her deeply. Ultimately, I had orders to report to Travis Air Force Base in the Bay Area for transport to Saigon. I had to ship out without saying goodbye.

"After I left, I tried to write every day, yet it was weeks before I heard back. When I got that letter it was sheer torture. I was so afraid she had written just to tell me to stop bothering her that I couldn't open it for days. Then, when I did, it gutted me like a fish, girls. Her handwriting had been blurred with tear stains. She had wept her heart out to find forgiveness. That letter brought me home alive. It never left my breast pocket until I made my way back to her. I admit I failed her again with Marilyn, but after I got home we agreed to never keep secrets from each other."

"I guess we didn't warrant the same promise," Shelia said and, with a quick jerk, stood. She glared at him.

Dirk turned his head up to her. "DK has done his damnedest to publically flog me. I know I can't un-ring any of these bells, and I know this is hurting you both. I can only apologize for the secrecy, but my actions hurt others, not you. Not telling you two was for your protection."

"Let's at least be honest now," Kel said. "It was to protect our name from public scrutiny. From the stories you and Grandpa told us growing up, he was rising in rank at SPD at the time. His reputation couldn't bear being sullied by a son who, pardon my crudeness, couldn't keep his dick in his pants. I'll be the first to admit that I wasn't all that virtuous, but at least I owned it. I remember distinctly you chastising me for my promiscuity as a teenager and you weren't exactly thrilled that I chose to live with Lance outside of marriage.

"But with a brother we're just hearing about for the first time after more than three decades of life under this roof, an affair that lead to your partner's dismissal, and possibly your own rise to chief on Terry's broken life ... and now all three of them dead ... there's a lot to think about."

"I know. I just hope I live to see the day when we can mend this."

"Dad," Shelia shouted, "that's not like you. You don't have to yank on the 'I'm dying' card. Give us some time. We'll get past it. Just understand that even though these things happened years ago, in our minds they just happened. We need time to work through these raw emotions."

With a case to solve and her dad the focal point, Kel had to put her fury aside. She needed more information from him, but she also needed a break from the emotional pressure in the room.

She stood and walked toward the doorway. "I'll see if Chrissie needs help."

Chapter Forty-Six

"THIS SMELLS AND looks ridiculous, Chrissie," Shelia said as she reached for a sandwich.

Chrissie had placed a plate full of hot cheddar and Swiss cheese sandwiches stuffed with slices of tomato and green chilies in the center of the table. Bowls of steaming tomato soup rested on royal blue placemats on each side of the oval dinette. While Dirk took his usual chair at the end of the table, the others filled the remaining seats.

"Ridiculous?" Dirk asked. "I think it's magnificent."

"Magnificent is ridiculous when you're fourteen, Dad."

"Oh, there's that generation gap," Dirk said, and lifted a spoon full of soup to his mouth. "When I was a teen, good was bad."

Chrissie laughed. "Good's still bad, Pops."

"Speaking of bad," Dirk said after swallowing the first bite, "I have a theory about our bad guy, DK. Look at his MO. It's all over the map. But what if this has to do with my tours in 'Nam? What if DK was one of my men? Think about how people die in war and then correlate that with the cause of death for each of the victims."

"Suffocation, explosion, exsanguination, gunshot," Kel said. "You know, right after Suzanne's death I thought that COD must be just as much a part of the puzzle as anything else. Now, if this is true, it all makes sense."

"But what does this have to do with this guy?" Chrissie asked.

"Well, sweetie," Dirk said, "the modus operandi—or MO, as we cops say—that a serial killer chooses is generally the same act again and again. He attempts to absolve some heinous malformation in his psyche by reenacting the retribution he'd pay if the architect of his psychosis were present."

"The architect?"

"The person he feels has caused his pain. Typical criminal investigative analysis might find it difficult to nail the MO since he chooses different forms of violence for each victim. The normal profile has to be tweaked to understand this guy. As I see it now, each death symbolizes a different means of killing in war."

"Daddy," Kel said, "two days ago I asked you for a list of suspects from your past. You never gave it to me. People are dying. I need to know who's capable of doing this and has a severe enough grudge to carry it out."

"And just as important," Shelia added, "if this goes back over forty years, why now? Why not then? People die in war—how can that be your fault?"

"I haven't forgotten your list, Princess. As I said then, there's a lot to go through. I was so busy checking past cases this morning that I didn't hear the news about Roger's ... murder. So far, nothing's popped. It was only at the graveside that the war connection came to me. I'll dig into that next.

"As to why now, though, that's a different story, Angel. There has to be a trigger. Something happened recently to push him over the edge of sanity. Look, culpability is the prerogative of the human mind. We blame who we want to blame whether truth or fiction. It doesn't have to be right or just. So, without understanding the trigger, it may make no sense to anyone else. But in the serial killer's mind, human rights have no bearing. Victims are only collateral damage. They just happened to fall in the path of the killer's endgame."

"So what's DK's endgame?" Chrissie asked.

"Me," he said, and then turned to Kel. "You've asked me for a list, but has your investigation turned up any clues to his identity?"

"Not yet," Kel said, and placed a half-eaten sandwich on the plate next to her soup bowl. "But he intentionally left a cigarette butt in Roger's office."

"That may have his DNA," Dirk said.

"The lab's working it, Daddy." Kel paused. She held a glass of water halfway to her mouth. "I believe he left me that clue because he wants me to know who he is. But after his big reveal, what then? Does he plan to kill you next?"

"Maybe, but I don't think so. I think he wants me to ... suffer ... loss. Yes, that must be it. These people in his mind may represent people he lost. Does he have children? A wife? A brother? Is he blaming me for losing them somehow? We already know each death this week strikes closer and closer to me. Just like family relationships vary in proximity. Cousins aren't as close as siblings, for example. It's like he's firing mortar rounds."

"What do you mean, Pops?"

He turned to Chrissie. "Mortars are a bit unpredictable. It's about angles and distances. So let's say you're trying to take out a machine gun. You make your best calculations and fire the first round. Once it explodes, you adjust, right, left, forward, back by changing the angle."

"So Suzanne," Shelia said, "was associated to you, we thought, only because of her relationship to the Rat City Exterminator case."

"But there was more to it, I knew—"

"Because of Roger," Kel interrupted. "That makes sense. Then Terry was closer to you, because you were partners."

"And then there was Marilyn. My relationship with her was unknown to almost everyone. How DK found out is still a mystery, but he knew I'd know the significance. And with Roger related by blood—"

"Daddy," Kel said, "something's been gnawing at me since this afternoon. Bimal, one of SPD's lab analysts, said that ballistics proved the gun that killed Roger also killed a high school teacher a couple of months ago. Do you remember that case?"

"Yes. Our theory was that the house fire was an attempt to cover the true COD."

"Right. Since the same gun killed both Roger and the teacher, this makes DK the suspect in both murders. But why kill the teacher? What does he have to do with DK's lesson plan?"

"He was also a freelance writer," Shelia said. "Adam Cozens. He billed himself as an investigative journalist and had a popular blog. I followed it for a while. His mission was to expose corruption."

"That might be the missing link," Kel said. "Shelia, just this morning I said that Buckley would have to have an accomplice, a common source of information. What if Cozens is the source?"

"Again, you're implicating my client."

"Okay," Kel said, and shook her head. "But even if it's not Buckley, follow me a sec. He was killed shortly after the Rat City case was overturned. What if DK—who already hates you, Daddy—knows Cozens's penchant for exposé, and approached him?

What if he fed him some tidbits of information, some people to contact? All DK has to do is point him to two people with an ax to grind: Terry, and someone within the SPD.

"You said the other day that Terry confronted you about his suspicion of your affair with Marilyn. What if Cozens approached Terry, and Terry told him about it? Then what if he found out about your relationship to Roger?"

Dirk shifted his weight on the dinette chair. "But those records were sealed nearly fifty years ago. Except for my mother—and with her Alzheimer's she doesn't remember any of that—and Roger's adopted parents, who would have no reason to say anything … who might he contact?"

"One of your enemies, Daddy. What if DK knew of one and steered Cozens toward him? And what if that man used his authority in the SPD to dig around? And what if he ran into a fifty-year-old sealed record with the family name of his nemesis?"

"That's a lot of 'what ifs,'" Shelia said. "Do you have anyone in mind?"

Kel looked at Shelia and nodded. "I think I do." She turned back to Dirk. "Daddy, what happened between you and Lou?"

"Martinez?" Dirk asked, and shook his head. "Do we really need to go into that? What could he have to do with this?"

"It's just a hunch, Daddy, but since it seems to be casting a shadow on my career, humor me, please, okay?"

"Well," he began with a deep sigh, "when I became captain of detectives at West Precinct, Lou's father came under my command. There was a lot of corruption in the squad at the time. I discovered that some of the detectives were skimming. After a drug bust, they'd confiscate the contraband and the cash, and before they turned in the evidence, they'd take a cut. Seeing as I was new and needed to strengthen my platform, I suspended them all. The DA brought them up on charges.

"Lou's dad wasn't a part of the gang, but I found out he knew about it and was being paid for his silence. So, I offered him a deal. No prosecution if he'd resign and give up his pension. Trouble was, he was two years from retirement. He took the deal but couldn't take the dishonor. He swallowed his pistol, and Lou never forgave me. But what does this have to do with DK?"

"It may be nothing," Kel said. "But this afternoon, while Bimal was telling Shelia and me about the ballistics match on the bullet, I saw Lou and Chief Ballesteros talking outside the funeral chapel. Lou seemed very agitated. I'll swear in court that Ballesteros shut him down as if the sidewalk was not the place to have that conversation. Then right after that, Lou started to leave, and when his eyes fell on me, the look on his face was not his usual disdain. It was guilt. He couldn't look me eye to eye, and then he made an abrupt turn as if he needed to avoid me."

"So you think Lou's been digging into my past? But for what reason?"

"After what you just said, is it too far a reach to think he might want to destroy your reputation before you die? Think about it. If a noted blogger who was committed to expose corruption came to him looking for some secret in your past, do you think Lou could pass on that chance? Especially if the writer swore to keep his source's confidence? So when a positive link between Roger and the journalist showed up, Lou realized he was contributory to a serial murderer, which makes him just as guilty as DK."

"If that's true, I'll have his badge."

"There'll be time for that, Daddy. If he's guilty, I'll see to it myself. By the way, how well do you know Chief Ballesteros?"

"I've known him for over twenty years. Why?"

"It's probably nothing, but he either lied to me or made a mistake."

"In what context?"

"Early last Monday morning he showed up at the scene of a small riot. After we packed the perps on the bus, he came over to talk to me. He told me he had been at Benaroya for a concert. But there was no concert. He was a day off. I just wondered if it was out of character for him to get things confused."

"I've seen it a couple of times over the last year or so, but nothing consequential. Do you think this has anything to do with the DK murders?"

"Oh, I doubt that. You know me—every 'I' dotted and 'T' crossed."

In fact, since speaking with Ballesteros last night, her suspicions had only intensified. Fabrications of fact gave her reasons to doubt. From the timeline of the first murder, Ballesteros could have killed Suzanne Lowen on Monday morning, dropped by the Wishing Well to have their conversation about her future, and then gotten back to Suzanne's condo in plenty of time to use a stun gun on her. She had hardly noticed it then, but she remembered now that both Ballesteros and DK had at least one thing in common. They both smoked. It was a long shot, and nothing she could mention to anyone at this point. She needed facts. She needed the DNA from the cigarette butt.

"Enough of that," Kel said. "We have to figure out who DK is before he hits his next target."

"Do you think he's coming for one of us next?"

"Shelia," Kel shouted. She nodded her head toward Chrissie.

"Sorry, but it's obvious, isn't it? Dad said a couple minutes ago that every victim is closer to him. It can't get much closer than his immediate family."

"It's okay, Aunt Shelia. I get it. We're in danger," Chrissie said, and her eyes began to well. "Mom, I'm really scared."

"We're all scared, sweetheart." Kel stood, walked behind Chrissie's chair, and put her arms around her daughter's neck. "But we'll be okay." She kissed her on the cheek. "We have the whole police department to protect us."

"What would you do, Dad," Shelia asked, "if the mortars were zeroing in on your position?"

"I'd give the 'Scorpion Run' order."

"What's that, Pops?" Chrissie asked and wiped a tear from her cheek.

"Scorpion Run means everyone who can grabs everyone who's wounded, and runs to the nearest chopper like winged scorpions were at their back."

"We seem to be short of choppers, Dad."

"I know, Shelia, but this may be exactly what he's thinking we'll do. A Scorpion Run is every man for himself. Everyone scatters with the predetermined point to regroup. In each case so far, DK's waited until he had his victims alone, right?"

"Correct."

"Then none of us can be alone until we catch him. Alone makes you vulnerable."

"What about you, Dad? You're alone most of the time."

"We already know he's been in the house. I was alone then, and he didn't come after me. No, he wants me to live with the pain, not end my suffering by killing me. Besides, tomorrow is the Torchlight Parade. I'll have people around me most of the day."

"You'll be awfully exposed on the parade route," Kel said. "Are you sure you want to do this?"

"It's a once in a lifetime, Princess," he said with a twisted smirk, "and I can say that with assurance."

"Pops, let's not start talking about you dying again."

"Sorry, Chrissie, but honestly, I think I'll be fine."

"I've already set up round-the-clock police protection for you until this is over. Chrissie, you'll be with me tonight, and then tomorrow I'll have someone at the house until you go to Jessica's. What about you and Danny, Shelia?"

"Danny's with his au pair and will be tomorrow as well. I'll be working right up to the parade, so except for my drive to town, I'll be around people. I'm covered."

Chapter Forty-Seven

"MY BLOOD'S ON," he had written to the Don of the Docks, and the plan had worked. He now sat concealed in darkness in a street-level parking lot opposite the meeting place. The email the Don had sent to his untraceable Hotmail account gave him a time and place. But thirty minutes before the meet, they changed the site. That didn't matter to him. He had no intention of keeping this appointment.

He had cased the three men related to Tribune Investments for months. He knew their habits, their haunts—and this bar wasn't on their list. Though they could have sent any one of the three, he suspected Willie's murderer would be the one to show up. He'd have the most to lose if the truth surfaced and the most to gain by silencing the unknown witness. In reality, he was just playing a hunch, an educated hunch, but when Jake deLaurenti walked up the sidewalk an hour ago and then disappeared through the front door, his suspicions were confirmed.

Certain that the Capital Hill tavern was crawling with the syndicate's henchmen, he waited. By now deLaurenti would be convinced his target was a no-show. He pictured him at a table alone, nursing his third scotch, despondent with the certainty that he now had become the mark.

But the bar wasn't the place to take him. Someplace quiet, someplace less public, someplace where Jake deLaurenti would see the last of this world and might never be found again.

Chapter Forty-Eight

CHRISSIE LAY ON her bed with her pods stuffed in her ear canals listening to the latest download of the newest release by her favorite local band, Dead Toads. With the volume set at 7.0 on the Richter scale, she twisted a strand of her black hair. Maybe I'll dye it green next week, she thought as she glanced around her room at the posters of the Toads, Taylor Swift, and the boys of Twilight.

Saul, who had been absent when she awoke, nudged her arm with his cool, wet nose and then started for the door. Once at the doorway, he looked back at her.

"What is it, boy?" Chrissie asked as she removed the ear pods.

Saul whined and turned back to the door.

Chrissie followed Saul across the hall into her mom's bedroom. The Rottweiler put his paws on the ledge of the second story window and pressed his nose against the glass. Chrissie came up behind him and peeked out into the front yard.

"It's okay, boy," she said. She kneeled on the floor and took Saul's face in her hands. "Just the police."

She figured the Seattle police cruiser parked at her curb had been there since her mom had left for the day, but Saul seemed anxious as he pranced around her, sniffing and panting.

Back in her bedroom she slipped from her pajamas and threw on a pair of pink cotton shorts and a bulky black Dead Toads T-shirt. Saul trotted at her heels as she ran the stairs to the first floor and into the kitchen. While a small pot of coffee brewed, she found a single-serving container of creamed cheese and sliced a bagel. Once the coffee finished dripping, she filled a disposable cup and took the breakfast snack to the front yard. As she approached the curb, the driver's door opened, and a tall, slender man exited the car.

Saul jumped in front of Chrissie, bared his teeth, and gave a low growl.

"It's okay, Saul. Heel. He's the police."

Saul held his position between Chrissie and the officer, riveted on the uniformed man.

"Heel, Saul!" Chrissie shouted. The Rottweiler then relaxed, turned about, and came up next to her.

"Is there a problem, miss?" the officer asked.

"No, everything's fine. For some reason Saul thinks men in uniform pose a threat. Mom thinks it has to do with my dad leaving for war and not coming home. Anyway, thought you might want a snack. Coffee and a bagel?"

Her path took her to the street in front of the police car, and she stepped off the curb.

"That'd be nice, thank you," he said, and walked to meet her at the front of the cruiser. "I'm sorry to hear about your dad."

"It makes me sad, but I'm getting over it. Not Mom, though. Say, Officer Kent," Chrissie read the last name off his badge as she handed him the paper plate and cup. "I'm just fine here. As you can see, Saul's not going to let anything happen to me. I think you probably have better things to do than sit here watching the grass grow."

"That may be true, but I have a direct order to watch your house and make sure you're safe."

"I have a few chores, but after that my friend is coming over, and we're going back to her house."

"I'll be right here. You keep your doors locked." He lifted the plate. "And thanks for this."

Back in the house, Chrissie locked and bolted the front door. Then, walking through the kitchen, she unlocked and opened the back door to let Saul out into the yard.

"Play ball?" She picked up a tennis ball lying on the patio and threw it.

Saul ran across the small yard and retrieved it. After a few minutes, he tired of the game and lay down on the grass to gnaw on a bone he found. Chrissie walked back to the kitchen. Saul could come and go as he pleased through the doggie door, so she closed and locked the back door behind her, and went upstairs to pack for her sleepover with Jessica.

Chapter Forty-Nine

WEEKS AGO, LIEUTENANT Martinez had assigned Kel to traffic and crowd control duties during the Torchlight Parade, but since she had taken a few personal days, she was relieved of her post. Police estimates put the expected crowd at three hundred thousand. Now, at half past five in the afternoon, as Kel pressed her Jeep through the crowd clogging the sidewalks and surface streets, she believed it.

A traffic officer with his palm stretched out toward her forced her to wait at an intersection until he waved her through. On the cross street in front of her, motorists anxious to escape the city for their Friday evening commute jostled into position for a freeway entrance a few blocks away. Despite police presence, the revelers meandered across the avenue and stopped the flow of traffic. The temperature in the eighties, the commuter's frustration mounted, and they took it out on their horns without effect.

She needed to make sure her dad was as comfortable as possible, and safe. In the advanced stage of his disease, he was prone to exhaustion anyway. Yet with the added tension and grief he had suffered this week, yesterday she had noticed such fatigue in his face that she feared he would be hospitalized before the end of the day. Dirk, a proud man even when things were wearing on him, would soldier on without complaint.

She had not spoken to him after leaving his kitchen with Chrissie last night. During dinner, she dammed her anger by tapping into her dad's theory. Through the day, though, when her mind wasn't otherwise occupied with following leads, she tried to find a way to rationalize her dad's secret life. It wasn't as bad as it could be. At least there were no bodies to unearth, as she had joked with him earlier in the week. In the end, she only came up with one solution. Despite the pedestal on which she had placed him—the biggest hurdle of them all—he was just as human as she was, prone to mistakes and errors in judgment.

Fifteen minutes later, she made her way to the Seattle Center where the parade would begin its annual pilgrimage along Fourth Avenue in about two hours. She left her Liberty at the curb and made slow progress on foot through the mob of spectators. People in groups hustled to reserve their piece of sidewalk while street vendors hawked their wares.

As she neared the parking lot where her dad waited, white-faced Marcel Marceau rode past on his bicycle, tapping cars with his red-tipped cane. With the chaos of the week and the dread of what was still to come, she smiled and shook her head with the knowledge that life went on anyway. Marcel's behavior was bizarre, but today, his idiosyncrasy made the world eccentrically normal.

She stuck to the sidewalk, walked through the shadows of the iconic Space Needle and Experience Music Project, and made her way toward the convertible in which Dirk was to ride. Near it, on the edge of the lot, he sat dressed in his summer uniform, a long-sleeved light blue dress shirt with a dark blue tie, shaded under a white plastic awning. Around him, several uniformed officers with short-sleeved shirts stood watching the crowd—the human shield she had demanded to be put in place.

"Scot-tay," she said as she approach her friend Scott Nillson, "have you seen Jake out here? He was supposed be part of Dad's protection."

"No. Just me, Valarie, and the cycle cops over there."

"I haven't been able to reach him all day," Kel said.

"Well, your dad's in good hands," he said with a wave toward the entourage of officers milling about.

"Princess," Dirk said.

"Daddy." She ducked under the awning and kissed him on the cheek.

Where it often took weeks, or even months, to get over disappointments like she had experienced in the last few days, she knew he didn't have that much time. Despite what she needed, he needed to know she didn't retain any bitterness. She spoke low into his ear. "Everything's alright now. I get it."

"We're okay?" Dirk asked, and held her cheek to his.

She felt the wetness of his tears against her face. "We're good. Everything's going to be fine. Now, how're you feeling?"

"Couldn't be better now," he said as he released her. "Stop worrying. Say, after you left last night, I thought about some of the men in my squad." He pulled a black and white photo from his breast pocket and extended it to her. "I had to go through some old photos to come up with it, but I found this picture from when I was stationed in Vietnam. Look at the one standing just to the right of the group. Everyone earned a handle in that squad. We called him Lone Wolf, but his given name was Darrell Klineman. Could that be DK?"

Kel examined the photo. Faded and scratched by age, the picture still captured several U.S. Army soldiers with hardened faces. Wolf, a cigarette hanging from his lips, held his rifle by the muzzle like a putter over a golf caddy's shoulder, and he looked weary. His expression wasn't mere physical exhaustion, though; he manifested the weight of death as if it shrouded each breath he took.

"Has to be, but how does this man, more than forty years later, justify taking innocent lives just to

prove some depraved point? Daddy, how did Darrell
Klineman become DK?"

She lifted her eyes from the photo and looked
back to her dad. He had drifted from the present into
an unspoken memory.

Sergeant Dirk Nyte squinted against the debris
kicked up by the chopper's decelerating blades, and
surveyed the morgue patrol as they swung the first
body bag from the deck to the dirt. He adjusted the
sling supporting his left arm, just two days in a cast.
The ache in his bicep dulled as a metallic bitterness
coated his tongue, and his stomach soured as he
watched their perfunctory ritual. It lacked the solemn
respect due those who had given up everything. But
then he knew they weren't to blame. His job was to
keep his men safe. He gave a remorseful sigh and
stared as they continued to mop up his mess.

As soon as the first body was in place, Tarzan
unzipped the black bag enough to reveal the face.
Nyte knew what to expect. He had been here before.
But some hope dared him to believe the exposed
countenance had to be one he didn't recognize,
someone for whom he didn't have to prepare the
"With your government's deepest regrets" letter. The
first bag held Boomer. When Tarzan opened the
second bag, O'Leary's empty expression glared back
as if an accusation were being hurled from his
silenced lips.

As the third bag opened, Tarzan gasped. Nyte stood beside him and peered at the lifeless man. Grief rammed his throat and tears moistened his eyes when he saw that Boa filled it.

"That one's a hero," said one of the men as he placed DJ's remains next to Boa. "The area around him was littered with grenade pins. Looks like he gave you boys a little insurance before they brought him down."

When the last man, Hal, came to rest at Nyte's feet, there were five bodies in the row.

"There's one more. You must've missed one," he shouted, and turned back toward the empty helicopter bay.

"Where's Wolf?" Dirk said aloud.

"Daddy?" Kel squatted in front of him and took his hands.

Dirk turned his eyes to Kel. "I left him behind, Princess. He was wounded and I left him."

"You said yesterday that a Scorpion Run means every man for himself."

"True, but as the team leader, it was my responsibility to make sure every man alive got out. When he didn't show up at the LZ, I thought he must have been killed during the run."

"And you haven't heard of him since that day?"

"No. After I returned to the States, I kept up on the reports of MIA's and POW's. I followed every action taken during the seventies and eighties to bring the boys home, alive or dead. From time to time his name came up on a list, but as far as I knew, he never returned. Except for him, every other man who served with me was accounted for. I have nightmares to this day about losing him."

"But he is alive, Daddy. The lab learned something new about him today. Vietnam may be part of the motive, but the trigger just might be Willie Jenkins."

"Willie! How do you figure?"

"The DNA found on the cigarette at Roger's crime scene. It's a familial match to Willie Jenkins. DK isn't just Darrell Klineman. He's Willie's biological father."

"Oh my God," Dirk said, and grabbed hold of his forehead. "Darrell's son worked for me and then became another casualty under my command. That must have been more than his psyche could withstand. That's got to be the trigger. No wonder he needs recompense."

"This may help us understand him," Kel said. She looked first to her dad and then to Scott. "But we can't excuse him just because he's had a psychotic break. Even though he didn't strike this morning, he's still out there—Mine to reap for Hell each day. We have no indication he's completed his lesson plan."

She still held the old photo and looked back to it, focusing on Klineman's eyes. They showed the horrors of the senseless slaughter he had both witnessed and committed. But something else reached out from that picture despite its age and the distance in years. Klineman looked directly at her through the camera lens, and she felt something in her chest seize as she realized she had seen those same eyes this week.

She turned her eyes back to her dad's. "I know who DK is."

"Who?"

While she spoke, Kel felt the vibration from her cell phone. Now it rang. "Just a minute," she said as she stood and turned away from her dad and Scott. She pulled the phone from her belt harness and connected the call.

"Detective Nyte, this is central dispatch. There may be a problem at your house."

Chapter Fifty

"WHAT DO YOU mean Kent didn't check in?!" Kel shouted into her phone.

As she had driven away from her townhome this morning, leaving Chrissie asleep, Kel pulled her Jeep up next to Officer Kent's cruiser. "She's my life, Kent. Don't let anything happen to her."

Now, she threaded her way through the parked cars in the lot, taking a shortcut to her Jeep. Anger had stopped her initial tears over panic for Chrissie's safety, and she mopped the remaining moisture from her face with the heel of her hand.

"It appears that Officer Kent was drugged after his last report," the dispatcher said. "The man claimed to be DK."

"Damn it! How'd this happen? DK was at my house? When?"

"The last time Kent checked in was eleven. With the parade, we're stretched. We didn't think to check on him until about a half hour ago when he was late for his next assignment. When Kent didn't respond after several tries, we sent another officer."

"Shit! Where's my daughter? Has anyone checked the house?"

"Carl Sanders is on the scene now, but no one's answering your door. Should he go inside?"

"Hell yes! There's a key to the back door hidden on the patio. Tell Carl to be careful of the dog. His name is Saul. If Carl calls him by name and lets him give him a sniff, he'll calm down and let him by."

The dispatcher let the phone go silent.

Winded from the anxiety and the short jog, Kel approached her Liberty. From ten feet away she hit the transponder button, unlocking the door, and ran around the front end of the SUV. The press of passing motorists was heavy, so she waved her badge toward a man behind the wheel of an Acura and jumped into her Jeep. By the time the ignition fired the engine, the man had held the traffic back enough for her to pull away from the curb.

"Officer Sanders," the dispatcher said, "reports that Saul is lethargic. Maybe he was drugged, too, but he seems okay. The back door is unlocked. Sanders went inside."

"Stay with me until he's cleared the house." Even with the hole opened by the Acura, the congested streets around the Seattle Center made forward progress almost impossible. She slipped the Bluetooth into her ear, dropped the phone on the seat next to her, and said, "Dispatch, get me an escort out of this traffic."

Once headed east on Denny Way, she stayed in the left lane, following the workweek evacuation toward the freeway. She kept one eye focused on the door mirror. At last she saw the flashing lights of a police cruiser traveling east in the westbound lane. The incoming traffic veered right, making way. With her badge held out the window, she got the officer's attention and pulled in behind him as he pressed forward.

Even with the cruiser acting like an icebreaker in a clogged harbor, progress crawled. Several minutes later, as the freeway entrance came into view a block ahead, the dispatcher came back on the phone.

"No one's inside, Kel, but there are signs of a struggle."

"Like what? I need his eyes."

"In your daughter's room several things seem to be upended, but there's nothing to indicate she was injured."

Panic grew so fast in her chest that she wanted to scream. This was exactly how she had found Suzanne Lowen's bedroom. At first glance an overturned table lamp and a dropped phone—and then her dead body.

"My God, he has her," she said, forcing the hysteria from her voice. "Have Carl take a look at the computer in the kitchen. I need to hang up, but call back as soon as Carl is at the computer. "

Kel picked up her phone from the seat and scrolled through the contacts until she found Chrissie's friend Jessica's listing. She dialed. Voicemail answered.

"Jessica, this is Chrissie's mom. Call me as soon as you get this."

"Damn it," she muttered under her breath. With Chrissie still two days from having her cell phone restriction lifted, her phone lay hidden in the glove box of the Jeep.

Kel waved thanks to her escort as she slipped into a line of cars queued in the Interstate 5 onramp. Finally merging into traffic, she tried to change lanes heading south toward her West Seattle townhome, but the drivers on the four-lane were less forgiving than on the surface streets.

After a fruitless two minutes, dispatch called and she tapped the earpiece.

"There's a poem on the monitor."

"What does it say?" Kel asked, her mind in a sudden whirl of dread.

"Fifth the child princess bore you

Now a part of my plan too

Hard and stiff will be as such

Hands will show my final touch."

"Chrissie's poem," she whispered. Unable to slam her eyelids closed in the rush of commuters around her, she grit her teeth against new tears that formed.

"I'm sorry, Officer Nyte. Why a poem?"

"I don't know why, but DK always leaves a poem on the vic's computer."

Kel slammed the heel of her hand against the steering wheel, realizing she had leapt to depersonalizing Chrissie's fate like Nancy had at Roger Kinnear's crime scene—The ME's with the vic now. She hadn't been at the cat and mouse game long enough to be insensitive to others' suffering, but the reflex action fit as natural as a foot in a sock. Tell a joke, make a wisecrack, refer to the person as a fatality—anything to strip them of their humanity, or else lose perspective and end up cynical and broken.

A chirp from her phone broke her thoughts. She picked it up from the seat again and thumbed to the message screen.

"Snoqualmie Falls Lumber Mill," she read to the dispatcher and struck the steering wheel again. "Damn it! He has my daughter. Where the hell is this mill?"

Chapter Fifty-One

IT HAD TAKEN Kel over forty-five minutes to make the thirty-mile drive southeast of Seattle. Once at the off ramp from Interstate 90, she fell in behind a King County Sherriff's SUV. Now at the crest of a small rise on a county road, the wall of evergreens on her left parted. The two-hundred-and-eleven-foot brick smokestack of the Snoqualmie Falls Lumber Mill loomed into view. With its birth at the beginning of the twentieth century, it became the second largest electric lumber mill in the world. Now, the abandoned plant seemed to kneel in silence like a humbled subject at the foot of Mount Si's jagged monolith erupting nearly four thousand feet out of the valley floor.

She brought her Jeep to a skidding stop in the gravel parking lot. That caused a dust cloud to float toward a small cluster of county deputies. She tore open her door and stepped out. A man with sergeant's stripes on his chocolate brown shirt broke away and walked toward her.

"Sergeant Villa," he said without pronouncing either "L." "Everything's secure, ma'am. We've torn the plant apart. No one's there."

"I need to see for myself." She started toward the bleached-brick building.

"I know it's your daughter. I understand. I have kids, too. So believe me when I say there's no sign of her or anyone else in the power plant. You might be better served, ma'am, to join the search over there."

Kel stopped and turned. She saw Sergeant Villa pointing to a building behind her, some hundred yards away. The remains of the log-storage house rose to a height of thirty or forty feet and stretched at least a football field in length. Across the roof, the faded outline of the Weyerhaeuser brand stood out from the rusted tin like the embossed letters she remembered from her dad's original copy of The Beatles' "White Album."

Her mother's protective instinct trumped her cautious cop's training, and she broke into a sprint. She crossed the clearing in seconds and approached the central doorway. DK's whispered warning while he had her pinned with a Taser to Suzanne Lowen's floor echoed in her mind: Next time I may not be so nice. She pulled her Glock from its holster, embraced it with her flashlight, and entered the structure.

Shafts of light from deputies already searching the empty building looked to her like a lightsaber battle from a Star Wars movie, something Lance had loved. Since the effort was concentrated to her left, she moved right to the yet-unexplored section. Sergeant Villa and two other deputies followed. The declining western sun penetrated through the breaches in the walls and made quick work of inspecting the dirt floor. So, she focused a search grid on each ceiling support and cross beam. Except for resident pigeons, nothing living or unexpected revealed itself.

As she approached the back of the building, a small enclosure built into the lumber warehouse took shape. Two right-angled walls, connected in the corner to the exterior siding, rose to a height of about ten feet. Unlike the outside of the building, they weathered the years with more dignity.

She trained her flashlight on a man-sized door at the end of what looked to have been a tool shed. The padlock hanging from the hasp seemed incongruous with the rest of the structure.

"This building's been abandoned for decades," she said to no one in particular. "Why a lock?"

Kel holstered her gun and pointed the flashlight beam on the padlock. She lifted it and saw that the size of the lock and the scuff-marked indentions on the wooden door beneath it didn't match.

"Chrissie," she screamed, and banged on the door. When there was no answer, she turned her head toward Villa, whom she heard race to her side. "I need to get in here now." She turned back to the door, pounded on it, and shouted again, "Chrissie! Chrissie!"

Sergeant Villa dispatched a man with the name "Tarza" inscribed above the right pocket of his shirt, and within two minutes he pulled up in his sheriff's SUV. Tarza jumped from the driver's seat with bolt cutters, slipped the blades over the lock's shaft, and with a quick thrust, severed it. He tossed the lock to the ground.

Kel withdrew her pistol again and grabbed the door, swinging it open. She stepped into the room and penetrated the darkness with her flashlight. The beam traced the seams between the walls, floor, and ceiling until it rested on a tarp-covered mound in the furthest corner. She didn't know whether to pray for some sign of life, or that the heap had been abandoned decades ago.

"Chrissie, I'm here." She raced across the floor and kept the stream of light fixed on the canvas. It didn't move.

She fell to her knees in front of a filthy oilcloth draped over a human-sized object. The fear of what she just could not fathom lay concealed before her. Tears began to build behind her eyes, but her heart, pounding hard enough to rip apart, held them in place. The words she hadn't been able to say to her daughter on Sunday night drew her mind to a place she never wanted to leave: "I love you most."

"Chrissie?" she said; barely a whisper passed over her lips. She took hold of a corner of the tarp resting on the dirt floor. But as she started to lift it, she saw the decreasing white circles of light on it. A different panic seized hold of her. She didn't know these deputies, and they were approaching her baby with guns at the ready. She slid her Glock into its holster and looked toward Sergeant Villa.

"No one shoot, please."

Villa's eyes softened with passion and he threw one hand up to halt his men. Kel faced the bundle again. As if worshipping at the Pieta, Michelangelo's statue of the crucified Christ in the Madonna's lap, she bowed her head in a silent prayer. "God, no." Raising her eyelids slowly, she pulled the tarp back.

When the lights behind her came to rest on the lifeless nude adolescent female propped up in the corner, she gasped and then gave way to the tears. Chrissie's fixed hazel eyes stared back.

Chapter Fifty-Two

DK KNELT AT the makeshift altar in his subterranean sanctuary. The sound of the construction workers had long silenced and been replaced by the cacophonous, muffled roar of the throng echoing through the discarded building above. The time drew near.

Leaving for the war, he knew the risks of not seeing his wife and family again. Too many boys were coming home in body bags. So, earning the moniker Lone Wolf by separating himself from his comrades wasn't a protection from the sorrow of losing friends to the enemy. Rather, it grew out of the expectation that each sunrise would be his last. He had never been able to blame Agie for moving on with her life. The government had led her to believe he was dead. But abandoned in the jungle, ripped from the heart of those he loved, Dirk Nyte's face had become the symbol of his tormentors during captivity. Once stateside, though, he had realized that Dirk was not the enemy. Dirk was under orders. But when DK's son died, the disrespect that ensued fueled that latent rage.

A year of plotting strengthened the bastion of emptiness he had harbored in his soul for decades.

The unrequited love of those pictured on the wall collage tormented him in captivity until he could no longer remember, but now they drove him to fill the void with forgiveness not granted. And finally, Dirk would pay.

The sun beat on Darrell Klineman's back as he sat in the cemetery. Compared to the jungle's humidity and temperature, he didn't feel the above-average ninety-seven-degree dry heat. The caretaker had pointed him to this row of headstones. "You'll find him there," he said, but before walking the row, he sat on a stone bench and thought about what had brought him to this serene place.

To get stateside, he had taken the identification of one of the men who tried to kill him and found a halfway decent passport forger in Cambodia. When his plane did touch down in Spokane, Washington, the homecoming he had dreamed of didn't materialize. Then, over the last few days, he learned that the life he knew before shipping over to Southeast Asia for his fourteen year odyssey had vanished.

He had stood on the wooden porch of the house he had owned in 1967 and knocked on the front door. The clapboard needed a coat of paint then, and even though the siding was a deeper shade of brown now, it needed the attention of another brush.

He remembered a loose plank on the decking, and stooped to see if it had been fixed. Willie had gotten a sliver in his finger playing with the board. While he cried, his young wife, Agie, sat on the porch cross-legged with a pair of tweezers and eased it out, kissing it "all better."

When the door opened, a young Mexican woman appeared with a little boy at her side. He was about the age of Willie the last time he had seen him.

"Senor, 1967 was a long time ago," she explained after Darrell asked if she knew about his family. "My husband and I bought this house six years ago. I don't remember the previous people's name or where they moved to. Sorry."

That brief conversation led him to the county clerk's office at the Whitman County Courthouse on North Main Street in Colfax, Washington.

The high school-aged girl on the opposite side of the counter extended a piece of paper and said, "There's a record of a Molly Klineman. She was born on February 21, 1968. Let me check on the other name for you."

He laid the birth certificate on the faded linoleum and rubbed his fingers over the name. Molly had been the name he and Agie had decided on if it was a girl. On the day he shipped over, he hadn't known his wife was pregnant, but after a couple months, she had written him with the news. He never received the letter confirming her birth, though, nor had he been able to pass out the cigars stored in his foot locker. Now he knew why. Molly, named for his mother, had been born eight months after his deployment to Vietnam, and three weeks after his confinement to the cage. She had fallen away from him as if he didn't exist.

"There's a record of a marriage," the girl said when she returned from the file room, "between Thomas and Agnes Jenkins in 1975. She listed her former name as Klineman. Do you think that might be her?"

"Has to be," he said. He took the proffered document and turned away so she wouldn't see him weep.

After he left the courthouse, he stopped at a phone booth. He scanned the white page listing and found nothing for Tom, Thomas, or T. Jenkins anywhere in the county. Agie had moved on, taking his past with her.

Before visiting the cemetery, he also scoured back newspaper issues at the Whitman County Gazette office. He discovered that the United States Congress had been frustrated with public sentiment over the unresolved Vietnam era POW/MIA "problem." Congressmen weren't being reelected, and a public outcry demanded resolution. Steps had been taken to open political discourse with Hanoi, but progress was slow and deniability high on both sides of the Pacific. A hometown boy, his name was among the missing.

Now, after sitting on the warm granite bench for a while, Darrell stood, lifted his head, and scanned the row of headstones. He had come to the conclusion that the uniformed men in the field that day in Cambodia were a CIA sanctioned black-ops hit team on a mission to end the rumors that American GI's were still being held. So, if Darrell Klineman suddenly reappeared on U.S. soil with a story about operatives ordered to kill POW's, he believed that he and his family would be in danger.

Darrell stepped onto the grass and began to read the names on the memorial stones. As he approached the last few in the row, he found the one he had expected.

"Born a beloved son, 1947. Died a hero, 1968."

With the grave to prove it, he turned to walk back to his rented car and left Darrell Klineman to rest in peace.

DK read his mantra aloud. "The secret things belong to God, but the things revealed belong to us."

He brought shame on Dirk with the secrets he had exposed—lust for power, lust for pleasure, lust for life, just to name a few. Now, one final lesson remained—one to teach him the full burden of abandonment.

He touched a picture on the wall of Molly as an adult, found a match, and lit the final candle. He placed it over the pretty smiling face representing his daughter on the altar. Then, he stood and picked up a rifle and duffel bag from where they rested on the floor.

Chapter Fifty-Three

AT A FEW minutes before 8:00 p.m., the computer monitor flashed, and the image dissolved to black as if someone had tripped over the power cord.

"No," Shelia Savell screamed. She looked up from the hard copy of the transcript she had been reviewing and shifted her feet from the top of the oak desk to the mocha-colored carpet beneath it.

Yesterday her coworker, Ryung Kim, had found some precedence that shed new light on the case they were trying. Despite her son's attempts to get her away from the office by telling his Columbian au pair to text her personal phone every fifteen minutes—the last one was cute, asking, "RU DUN"—she had spent Friday afternoon writing a brief due in Superior Court on Monday morning. She was just researching the final citation.

Now, she couldn't remember the last time she had saved the document. If she lost her work, she'd either have to cancel her trip tomorrow with Danny to the Woodland Park Zoo or return on Sunday, missing the barbecue at Dad's. Neither option had an acceptable outcome. She had little enough time with Danny as it was, and since Dad had only three months to live, missing one moment with him would be one moment too many.

She leaned forward, still seated in her desk chair, grabbed the mouse, and shook it, attempting to wake the machine. Nothing changed. She knew pounding the "enter" key was futile, but did it anyway several times, punctuating each stroke with "Please!" But when the monitor's black eye reflected the despair on her face, it also seemed to leer a sinister taunt.

She remembered being warned repeatedly that the IT department was to shut down the entire network this evening for some kind of refresh, so she punched the speaker button on the office phone. When the audible dial tone confirmed she was able to make a call, she jabbed the five-digit code for the firm's Help Desk into the keypad. While she waited for a voice, she turned toward the window and glanced out. The sun had yet to set, and from what she could see, a fringe of smoke-gray clouds threatened to cloak the otherwise pristine sky and shower the events on Fourth Avenue fifteen floors below.

Danny waited there. His impatience, doubtless seeded by an ample supply of sugared and caffeinated snacks, was only exceeded by the excitement of the sound she heard in the near distance. The cadence of snare drums and the blare of the brass from an unseen marching band playing "Louie, Louie" echoed between the cavernous walls of the high-rise structures lining the street. The music marked the beginning of the Torchlight Parade.

Before assistance came on the line, a familiar chirp indicated that another text had arrived on her cell phone. She turned back toward the desk. "Danny, sweetie, Mommy's almost done," she said aloud as if he was squirming just behind her, staring out the window, impatient to accost a street hawker for cotton candy or ice cream dots.

But when she realized that the display on her firm's smartphone had come to life, she disengaged the land line and reached for the Blackberry.

Her heart pounded heavy as she read the text: "Hows danny"

She grabbed the device from the desktop and swiveled her chair toward the window again, a step away. She stood to type a message on the small keyboard. "Who RU," it read. While she waited for the reply, she searched the street below to locate her son. She knew the au pair had come early to hold seats just outside the entrance to the Mangorn Building. From her office, though, it was impossible to distinguish in the mob below one towhead from another.

The chirp and vibration seconds later indicted a second message arrived.

"No matter"

Frantic, she dialed the number, but after several rings with no answer, she disengaged the phone and dropped it on the desk next to the computer. She picked up her personal cell phone and skirted around the end of the desk on a run toward the door. She hadn't taken two steps when the firm's smartphone vibrated against the desk.

With her hand on the door jamb, she stopped and looked back, stalled in indecision between running to Danny and wondering if this call provided more information. She needed to protect him. With DK still at large—still threatening to teach her dad a lesson—she had to stop him before Danny became his next causality.

She turned back, slipped her cell in to the pocket of her slacks, and grabbed the smartphone from the desk.

"You called?"

The female voice in her ear took her by surprise, but then she remembered Kel saying that she was sure DK disguised his voice with a voice changer. She jabbed her finger into the speakerphone button, ready to shout with the intensity warranted the interrogation an opposing whistle-blower, something common as a corporate litigator. What she felt surging through her body, though, wasn't courtroom demeanor. The instinct to protect her young, whatever the cost, seethed.

She held the phone in front of her. "What the hell do you want?"

"You didn't answer my question. How's Danny?"

"Who are you? What do you want?"

When there was no answer, she raised her voice and repeated, "What do you want?" but still no response came. The connection died, and she knew this phase of the conversation had been terminated. She redialed, but when there was no answer, she tossed the Blackberry on the desk next to the computer again.

As she stood behind the desk waiting for further contact, her desk phone rang. She grabbed the handset and screamed, "What do you want, you bastard?"

"I'm sorry, Ms. Savell? This is Vince at the Help Desk. Did you need something?"

Of all people to fix her computer, Vince Buckley was the last person she'd reach out to. He was her client, but with his alibi still not verified and with the threat now looming, she didn't know what to believe. Just yesterday in this same office she had told her sister, Kel, that her theory about Buckley was a long stretch. She still wanted to believe it was someone else, but now his voice on the line seemed too circumstantial, and her professional resolve waivered.

"Huh … oh, ah, sorry," she said. "I thought it was someone else."

As she spoke, another text arrived on the firm's Blackberry.

"I see. You called. Did you need some help, Counselor?"

She sat on the desk chair and stared at the message. It said, "IT'S YOUR CHOICE"

She lifted her fingers to her temples and massaged them with a circular motion. "Just leave us the hell alone."

"Excuse me, Mrs. Savell?" Vince asked.

"Not you, Vince. Please stay on the line." She waited for a response. When it didn't come, she called out again, "Vince? Vince!" and then realized that the desk phone line had gone dead.

Chapter Fifty-Four

ONLY TEN MINUTES had passed since Kel had found the lifeless body in the tool shed, but each tick of Minnie Mouse's secondhand felt like hours. Her mission to rescue or recover Chrissie at the abandoned lumber camp had been DK's effective ploy to pull her away from the real target. Just like Chrissie's poem had said, the paper mask—made from a photo on Chrissie's Facebook page—was wrapped around the head of a manikin—Hard and stiff—and the inscription on the note taped to the figure's plastic hand—Hands will show—confirmed it. She read the note again now.

"False the lead that brings you here
Unspoiled still your one so dear
The messenger's last appeal
Reveals wounds that will not heal."

While she paced in the field awaiting a faster ride back to Seattle than she could navigate in her SUV, she called her partner, Jake. "Where the hell are you?" she shouted into the Bluetooth when he didn't pick up the call. "I thought we were done with voicemail."

The thump of distant rotors of the King County Sheriff's Bell 407 helicopter pulled her attention to a dot in the western sky, and she punched the code for Shelia's cell phone. Before it rang through, the number for Chrissie's friend, Jessica, appeared across the screen.

She tapped the button on the ear piece. "Jessica?"

"Mom?"

"Chrissie, are you alright?" she asked. A weight like a wrecking ball lifted from her chest as she recognized her daughter's voice.

"Yeah. Me and Jessica are walking toward Aunt Shelia's building. Her phone was in her bag, and we just now realized you called."

"Chrissie, I want you to listen to me. Find some place you and Jessica can go inside where there are lots of people."

"We're just leaving Westlake Center."

"That's good. Go back inside, and stay there."

"Mom, you're scaring me. You said I'd be okay if I wasn't alone."

"And you will be if you do what I say. Go to the top-floor food court. I'll send someone to find you."

"What about Pops and the parade?"

"Pops is fine. Just go to the food court and watch for the police."

As she disengaged the call, the helicopter landed in the field thirty feet away. She charged for the closest door and climbed into the rear passenger compartment.

"How fast does—?"

The pilot pointed to a headset hanging next to the rear seat. She grabbed it as she found her seat and slipped it over her ears. "How fast does this thing go?"

"It's rated at two hundred and fifty-six kilometers per hour."

"Then Seattle and floor it," she said.

She took a seat in the back on the left side, the opposite side of the pilot, and reached for a seatbelt. Beside her she heard voices, and turned just as Sergeant Villa stepped into the compartment. He smiled and sat in the seat next to her. Behind him, Deputy Tarza tossed two shotguns and a case of shells on the floor. He jumped into the cabin and found a seat facing Villa.

"Sure you're up to this, guys?" she asked. "It might get messy."

"Sure," Deputy Tarza grinned. "Just another day at the office."

The drone of the blades filled her head as they pulled the aircraft into the evening sky. She took a deep breath and exhaled the mounting frustration in her chest. Her mind had been gnawing on any hidden message contained in the last poem that might reveal DK's next target. The word "messenger"—The messenger's last appeal—seemed to have a double meaning. This week DK had fashioned himself a type of messenger when he conveyed his lessons. "I deliver," he had texted her on Tuesday at Terry Graham's crime scene. But a messenger was also known as an angel—Shelia's family nickname.

She slipped the headset off her ears and let it hang around her neck. She dialed her Shelia again. "Come on. Pick up, pick up," she said in a low voice.

When every one of Shelia's numbers went directly to voicemail, she called Scott Nillson. "Shelia's got to be the target," she said when he answered.

As soon as she disengaged the call, she punched the code for dispatch, sent someone to find Chrissie, and then punched in Bimal's number.

"Crime lab, Bimal."

"It's Kel Nyte. DK texted me a while ago. I need you to get a fix on his location. And check my sister, Shelia Savell's, numbers."

Chapter Fifty-Five

SCOTT NILLSON AND Valarie, Scott's trainee, walked to either side of Dirk Nyte's Grand Marshal's Chrysler Sebring convertible. Ahead of them, a pair of motorcycle units led the procession, as if they were a planned part of the parade. Scott's plan had been to flank the vehicle and keep their eyes on the crowd for anything suspicious. With the cheering throng lining the sidewalks on both sides, the task was impossible at best, so over Dirk's objection, they forced him to wear a Kevlar vest under his dress shirt. In the evening heat, perspiration beaded his forehead.

"You doing alright?" Scott asked as he came along side of the vehicle. He slid his phone into his holster.

"Never better," Dirk replied, and looked to the other side of the street to wave at some children who stood swaying foot-long battery-powered torches over their heads. "Never better."

"I need to run ahead. You sure you're okay?" he asked.

Dirk stopped waving and stared back at him. "What's happening?"

"Don't know, but I've got to go."

Meanwhile, Shelia punched a text back. "What choice?"

The silence that followed was only seconds, but it felt like hours. She jumped when a ping came through the monitor-mounted speakers. A small dialog box glared out from the dark display and asked permission to take control. She had no choice but to surrender. She aimed the mouse pointer at the "yes" option and clicked.

A scene from the parade route resolved. A high-stepping marching band approached her building from a block away. The music from the street below matched the rhythm of the steps of the band. Then the view panned the crowd on the Fourth Avenue sidewalk and stopped in front of her building.

As she watched, the picture zoomed in on Danny eating cotton candy off a white paper cone. His lips were pink and looked sweet. She never wanted to kiss his mouth more. Across his cherubic face, a happy, innocent smile beamed as he dove in for another bite. He tore off a piece and used two fingers to poke the treat onto his tongue. He looked toward the au pair, said something, and then he turned his head past her. He glanced over his shoulder toward the entrance of her building. He's looking for me, she thought.

"You see him?" The woman's voice goaded from the computer speakers.

"Yes," Shelia answered, with her heart in her throat, the one syllable squeezed out with such effort that it sounded like a final appeal at the end of a hangman's noose.

"You see that twinkling trinket necklace? It was a gift from me not twenty minutes ago. He was very happy with it."

"Damn it," she said finding her voice. "Leave my son alone."

"That's up to you."

"What do you want?"

"Patience, Angel."

Angel, a nickname her dad had called her since she was a little girl, was known within the family circle, but few outside were privy to his pet name. Is DK someone I've met, or is this another case of him having an inside resource?

"You see, I gave him that bauble so I could pick him out from the crowd. Look close at his chest. The lights almost cover it up, but do you see it?"

She leaned close to the monitor and grabbed it with her hands as if she wanted to pull Danny to her breast. She made a frantic search and found what DK referred to. A small red laser dot hovered just above Danny's heart. She drew on a breath that refused to come.

"My God, yes!" she gasped. "Don't do this, please."

"Like I said, you have a choice. He doesn't have to die today."

She released her right hand from the monitor and forced herself to control the frantic shaking as she reached into her pants pocket for her personal phone.

"I must say, you do look lovely today, albeit a little frazzled. It's too bad." The lilt of the mechanically altered voice sounded like he was in jovial mood.

"You can see me?

"Through your webcam—and I wouldn't advise turning it off, either." The sudden change in his tone had a ring of finality. "You don't want to piss me off any more than I am already. You know I have a clear shot at Danny. Any inconvenience and I won't hesitate to take it."

She tore her eyes away from her son's image on the monitor and stood.

"Where you going, Angel? You can't hide from me."

Shelia stepped away from the webcam and silenced the tones on her phone. She faced the window with one hand at her side. While she keyed a message to Kel with her thumb, she scanned the building under demolition across the street. With his line of sight to Danny, he could be taking cover somewhere in that hollowed-out structure. From her elevation on the fifteenth floor, and with the sun dipping toward the western horizon, the side of the building facing her was obscured by shadow.

With her initial heart-wrenching, breath-gasping reaction under control, she kept her tone even, relieved that DK couldn't see her hands. She asked, "You said, 'It's too bad.' What do you mean?"

"Too bad that things have to end this way."

"What way is that?"

"With a life-or-death decision, especially on a day that had promised to be so much fun for you and your family."

She knew she didn't need to ask, but did anyway. "What are my options?"

"Your life or your son's. It's your choice."

Terror returned and cinched a choke hold around her chest. She didn't want her words to come out pleading, but she was powerless to stop them.

"But why? What's this about? Why are you after Dad?"

Without looking toward her hand, she pushed the "send" button on her cell.

"Asked and answered," he said.

"You're so angry with him, and I'm sure for good reason. Why not just tell him?"

"After tonight, he'll know and never forget ... Stupid girl, stupid, stupid, stupid girl. And they tell me how smart you are—the rising star. Haven't you learned anything? Don't you realize I've taken control of your life? Everything you do is redirected

PRESUMED DEAD   413

to me. Every action you take from now on I'll dictate."

"What are you talking about?"

"Your text to your princess. Kel's not coming to your rescue."

"My God! How'd you do that?"

"Let's just say I have connections. But is that really the question you want to ask? Sit back down, now!"

The tangled thoughts in her head needed time to unravel. If she and Danny were to survive, she had to separate her emotions from the facts. True, he controlled every form of communication at her disposal: the computer and the three phones in the office. She needed a low-tech solution, something he couldn't track—like two tin cans and a string, a carrier pigeon, or a signal fire—but none of those options were available. The only thing she could depend on was her mind—her litigation skills—but she had never sparred with a lunatic.

"Okay, you've made your point," she said. She turned back to the webcam. The words came out as matter-of-fact as if she was ordering a pizza without anchovies, but her mind raced in a frantic search for a way to change the direction of this inevitable train wreck.

"I concede. You have control and my attention," she said, taking a step toward the desk. "So if I choose to let my son live, what do I have to do?"

The last line felt more like a root canal without drugs than a concession. She couldn't say "If I choose to die?" because she hadn't yet conceded it was an option. She had to believe there was a way to save them both. She sat behind the desk on the edge of her chair.

"Good girl. That's more like it. You listening now?" he asked.

"Yes. Oh my God, I can't believe this."

"Just so you know how deadly serious I am, watch this."

She was relieved to see the laser dot vanish from Danny's chest. The video panned up the street, and a convertible car came into view a few blocks up the street.

"Recognize him?"

"My God, Dad. Don't do this, please. You've made your point. I'll do whatever you want. Don't shoot him."

"Him? No, not him. I want him to feel the pain his action caused. That's why you or Danny must die tonight."

"What pain did he cause you? I don't understand."

"And you never will, Angel."

"Only my family calls me Angel," she said. "You certainly aren't part of my family."

"This is all about family. Years before you were born, Dirk called me his brother and then abandoned me. So we're all part of one big dysfunctional family, aren't we? Stop trying to distract me. Watch the screen."

As the scope moved away from her dad, she felt a momentary release of the terror tightening inside her until the crosshairs came to rest on a woman sitting in the bleachers in Westlake Park.

"No!" Shelia screamed. "Enough innocent people died this week. You don't have to spill her blood."

He didn't respond.

"Damn it, don't do this!"

As she spoke, the sights jerked up and came to rest on a light fixture on the side of a building three blocks away. The light shattered, and the view on the screen dropped to the shards of glass spraying on the crowd below.

"My God," Shelia said, her voice faltering from terror.

"You see, even after all these years, I'm still an excellent sniper. So, yes, I can pick Danny out in that mob, but I'd rather not. Think about it, Shelia, you have the power of life and death in your hands. You can choose life for yourself and let Danny die. I'm not sure you'll ever escape the regret. Yet, over time, you'll heal enough to live your full life, even if you have to do it with a shrink on speed dial.

"But I can't see you doing that. You wouldn't be much of a mother, would you? If you choose to save your son, though, you'll never know what caused your end, just like the others this week. Trouble is you'll die, and it's doubtful that Danny will ever understand it, either. Even if he remembers you, what is he? Four? The last time I saw my son he was three—oh, the innocence. Still, he won't understand and may just grow up thinking he caused you to commit suicide."

Chapter Fifty-Six

KEL CUPPED HER hand over her eyes to shield them against the declining sun as the Seattle skyline came into view. The top edge still blazed but was quickly being swallowed by a bank of clouds which poured over the Olympic Mountains. From the rear window seat of the six-passenger Bell, she dialed the phone. Bimal's voice entered her ear.

"Anything?" she shouted.

"One phone's on. There have been a couple of calls in the last few minutes to one of your sister's phones, but no activity around the time you said he text you. He could be using the phone as wireless hotspot."

"What does that mean?"

"Like a modem."

"A modem ...?" The picture of Marcel, battered from the Sunday night brawl, interrupted her question. He had lay in the bed at Harborview Hospital on Monday typing with his mime fingers on an invisible keyboard and then pretended to send a text to a telephone.

"Damn it, he's switched to computer," she said. "I need his location now."

"He's pinging a tower in downtown Seattle. He's disengaged the GPS so I can only get you within a quarter mile."

After Bimal gave her the street boundaries, she disconnected the call. She put the aircraft's headset back to her ear, Kel turned to the men sitting on the opposite window. Deputy Tarza and Sergeant Villa were busy shoving twelve-gauge shells into the magazine tube of their SLP semi-automatic shotguns.

"It's got to be the Mangorn," she shouted into the microphone.

"That's on the parade route," the pilot bawled, and looked over his shoulder toward her. "It's in the no-fly zone."

"For civilians, maybe. Get me there now."

"Suicide?" Shelia screamed at the computer speaker.

"Of course. What better way?"

"No one who knows me will believe I killed myself."

"Happens every day, Angel. The news reports that someone offed themselves and no one saw it coming."

"I'm not your angel."

"Of course, how could I be so callous? That aside, I'm getting weary of the chatter. Make your choice: you or Danny."

"Every mother's instinct I have is to save him. What if you're bluffing?"

"Let's see. How many people died this week in my lesson plan? Does that sound like a bluff? What's it going to be? No more stalling."

"Isn't there another option?"

"No. Like your computer, it's binary—zeros and ones. You live or he lives, and you have thirty seconds left to decide."

"First, what assurance do I have that if I kill myself you won't shoot my son next?"

"You have to trust me."

"Do you think that's likely?"

"Negotiations have been concluded. Tick-tock, missy. If you don't decide, I do—and your son sleeps with the real angels tonight."

"If I agree to sacrifice myself for my son, how will you know I've done it? What am I supposed to do? Do you have a gun hidden in my desk? Is there a razor blade so I can slash my wrists? Are there pills I can swallow?"

"No, those are too easy."

"Then what?"

"You're going to the twelfth floor and jump into the crowd below from the terrace."

"Jump!" she screamed. "I could never do that."

"Then say goodbye to Danny now."

She looked back at the monitor and saw the camera centered over her son's innocent little heart.

The twinkling necklace almost disguised the red dot, but she saw it as if it were a lighthouse beacon on a clear night.

"No," she shouted.

"So, you've made your decision?"

"Yes."

"Good. Now take your phone with you so we can keep in touch, and no unnecessary stops at a coworker's office or the ladies' room. If I don't see you on the twelfth-floor balcony in two minutes, Danny's blood will be on the sidewalk. Move now!"

"I don't know if I can get there in time. That's three floors below me."

"One minute, fifty-five seconds."

"The phone doesn't work well in elevators or the stairwell. What happens if I lose you?"

"One minute, forty-seven seconds."

While they flew over the high-rises, Kel realized that Danny might also be a target. She called Scott.

"Do you have Shelia yet?"

"No," he said, breathing heavy in Kel's ear. "We're just coming up to her building now."

"Look, Shelia's son could also be in danger. Get him to safety."

"In this mob? Are you kidding? How could anyone find him?"

"He'll be near the Mangorn. His name is Danny, and the nanny's name is Drina. Hurry."

Chapter Fifty-Seven

AS KEL DISCONNECTED the call, they hovered over the helipad atop the Mangorn Building. The phone rang again. She tapped the button on the Bluetooth.

"He just turned another phone on," Bimal said. "And he forgot to turn off the GPS."

"He didn't forget anything."

She had believed, since she lay on the bedroom floor of Susanne's condo with a Taser to her back, that DK meant for them to have another meeting—next time we meet. Leaving the GPS on was his calling card, just like "doors open."

She asked, "Where is it?"

"Patience. I need a few seconds."

"I've no patience left. Give it to me now. Where is he?"

"He's ... in the middle of the block on ... Fourth Avenue? Yeah, that's it. Between University and Union."

"The Mangorn? That's where I am."

Kel leaned forward and shouted to the pilot, "Put this thing down."

"Wait, Kel," Bimal said. "He might be across the street."

"Across the street? Damn it, of course." She disconnected the call.

"No, not here," she said into the microphone.

The pilot nodded and gave a gentle tug on the control. The Bell rose a few feet and banked left over the parade route on Fourth Avenue more than four hundred feet below.

Kel peered out the window. In the lights of the Mangorn, she saw the outline of the condemned terra-cotta building Shelia had tried to save twenty-three floors below. With the sun having dropped behind Mount Olympus, and no lights coming from the inside of the shell, the final glow of twilight defined the ridge surrounding the roof. It gave the only indication of the speck they'd have to land on.

"Put it down there," she said with her finger extended toward the rooftop.

"Cannot do," the pilot said, following her gesture. "Not big enough for touchdown."

"Can you get me in close?"

"How 'bout close enough you won't stub a toe?"

Shelia took the stairs two at a time, with one hand clenching her phone and the other grasping the handrail for balance, and arrived on the twelfth floor. A small red light on the panel next to the door showed that it was secure. She swiped her pass key, but the light stayed red. She slid it again, with no better result. She looked at her phone's display. Only one bar showed, but yet DK came through clear. "You have ten seconds, Angel."

"I'm on the twelfth floor now, but I'm in the stairwell and can't get out. Even if I could, I don't know if I can get out to the balcony. I have to go back up. I need more time. Please."

"Damn it," he said.

"What's happening?" Shelia asked. She knew by his tone that something had changed. He suddenly seemed distracted, but whether it swayed in her favor she couldn't discern.

"Nothing to concern your pretty little angel wings with. You have two more minutes to get to the balcony before Danny meets Jesus face-to-face."

"That's not enough time. I have to climb to an unsecured floor and then hope the elevator will take me to twelve."

"Why aren't you moving?"

A few moments before, Scott had entered the lobby of the Mangorn Building and found a young man who couldn't have reached his twentieth birthday in a blue blazer, white shirt, and skinny dark tie behind the security desk. "I have to get to Shelia Savell's office now. This is a high priority police matter."

"Yes, sir, right away," said the young man. As he moved out from behind the counter, a blush made a sudden appearance against his otherwise pale cheeks.

Scott turned to follow him to the elevator but stopped when he heard another voice.

"What's happening?" said a young Latin-American woman. She held the hand of a little blond boy.

Behind them, Valarie, Scott's partner, stepped into the lobby through the revolving door.

"Are you Danny?" Scott asked. He walked toward the two civilians.

Danny fingered the twinkling trinket around his neck and looked to the au pair as if asking permission to speak.

"What's going on? Am I in trouble? We were just waiting for Mrs. Savell, Danny's mother."

"You're in no trouble, but I need you to wait inside." Scott saw that the lobby window was tinted, impossible to see in from the outside. He pointed to it. "Maybe you can watch the parade from over there. Why don't you stay with this officer?"

"Si," she said, "but I don't understand."

"The officer will explain," he said and nodded to Valarie.

"Sure, let's go over here," Valarie said. "Danny, how 'bout you sit on my shoulders? You can probably see real good then."

As he turned back to the security guard who was holding the elevator, the lobby door spun again. Scott turned and was relieved to see three patrolmen—one a motor officer who had accompanied Dirk—enter.

Scott affirmed their presence with a nod, and then said to the guard, "Shelia Savell's office."

The sound waves of a helicopter's blades echoed off the surrounding buildings with such intensity that DK felt them in his chest. He looked toward the reverberation and saw the aircraft swoop over the top of the building across the street. With Fourth Avenue bright with the lights of the Torchlight Parade, the white underbelly and the bold word "Sheriff" across the tail boom were easy to target.

Frustrated that his final lesson might fail—if Shelia knows Danny's safe—he raised the barrel of a Mauser Airsoft sniper rifle.

Kel, twisted in her seat to face the window and with her eyes fixed on the building across the street, couldn't see any movement. DK had to be there for his final act of terror, but even though the building was a dwarf among its towering neighbors, every floor would have to be searched, room by room.

As she scanned each level with the aircraft's headset pressed to her right ear for communication with the pilot, a white flash appeared in her peripheral vision, followed by the thunk of metal piercing metal.

"We're taking fire," she screamed into the microphone.

"No shit," said the pilot, and pulled the stick hard right away from the building. "We got to land somewhere else."

"Like hell! You put me down there."

The G-force of the sudden lurch pressed Kel against the passenger window. She continued to scan the condemned building in search of any indication of where the gunfire had erupted. As she probed the shadowed hulk, a second muzzle flash burst. Just inches from her face, the window imploded and a shower of glass shards sprayed into the compartment. The ping of a single bullet ricocheted through the cabin. She twisted to her right on instinct and dropped her head away from the airborne shrapnel.

"You hit?" Sergeant Villa yelled.

"No," Kel said, and then looked up to Villa.

He had unfastened his seat belt and reached across to Deputy Tarza on the seat opposite him. Tarza's left hand was wrapped around his arm just below the right shoulder. Blood ran between his fingers as the sleeve of his dark brown uniform shirt turned several shades darker.

"Must'a caught that rebound," he said. "Bastard got a lucky shot. Guess I'm not going to be much help down there, Sarge." He nodded toward the street.

"Harborview," Villa shouted to the pilot.

"No way in hell," Deputy Tarza said to the pilot through his microphone. "Drop these two first, and then I'll take a ride to the hospital."

Chapter Fifty-Eight

SCOTT, THE THREE patrolmen, and the security guard arrived on the fifteenth floor. With their guns drawn, Scott led the three officers through the elevator doorway, leaving the guard in the car until they cleared the lobby.

To his right, the electric hum of an elevator's door sliding closed at the far end of the lobby arrested his attention. He turned to the sound.

"Wait! SPD!" he shouted, and ran to try to stop it. He was one step too late when the double doors shut.

"Damn it. That could have been Shelia." He rotated back to the guard, who had stepped out of the elevator. "Any way of knowing what floor that lift is heading for?"

"Not from here. Could from the main lobby, but I'm the only guard on duty tonight."

"Okay, then. Where's Mrs. Savell's office?"

"According to our floor map," the guard said, looking up from a magenta-colored three-ring binder, "she'd be on the west side. This way."

Scott stationed two of the patrolmen in the elevator lobby, one to secure each end's point of entry, and with the motor officer, he followed the guard. After the rosy-cheeked security officer slid a pass card through an electronic reader, a click released the glass door, and he pushed it open.

"Which way?" Scott asked as he followed the teenager through the opening.

"About halfway down." He pointed to the left.

"Wait here," Scott ordered.

Shelia's elevator stopped on the twelfth floor. Thank God, she thought, and then realized thankful was the least thing she felt. She was delivering herself to the murderous whims of a madman, but she couldn't focus on the terror facing her, only Danny's salvation.

As the elevator doors slid open, she looked at the display on her phone. Three bars showed.

She lifted the device and held it in front of her mouth. "I'm heading for the balcony now," she shouted. "Please don't hurt Danny."

"You only have a few seconds left before I pull the trigger."

"Please. God, no, wait. I'm at the door. Damn it, it's locked."

"Ten, nine ..."

"Stop, please. Don't shoot, please."

"Seven."

She slid her access card through the reader. The light turned red.

Scott and the motorcycle patrolman ran through the hallway between the secretary cubicles on the left and the windowed lawyers' offices on the right. Outside each door, a name plate identified the occupant. After passing four doors, they came to the one marked "Shelia Savell." Without hesitation, Scott burst inside the lighted room and made a quick assessment. Shelia wasn't there. However, from the stacks of folders piled on the desk and the one opened in the center resting under a yellow legal pad, it looked as if she had plans to return. No signs of struggle indicated she was in any trouble, so if she actually was, she had been coerced by some other means to leave the room.

While Scott secured the office, the second officer entered behind him and walked to the window. He glanced toward the parade fifteen floors below.

Satisfied that there were no clues to Shelia's state, Scott turned to leave. "We're clear here."

The motor officer turned to join him, and stopped when he faced the desk. "Look at this," he said with his finger pointed to the computer monitor.

Scott turned back and stepped around behind the desk to look where the officer pointed. The letters were a simple black Arial font set against a white background, but the words had been penned by a demented mind.

"Damn it to Hell," he uttered and the read words aloud.

"Fifth the angel of the court
Recompense with no retort
Falls from grace, she cannot fly
Chooses death without goodbye."

Chapter Fifty- Nine

THE PILOT SWUNG a full clockwise circle and brought the aircraft over the towers on the west side of Fourth Avenue. They made slow, forward progress until he pulled the Bell over the building next to the terra cotta structure.

"Get ready," shouted the pilot's voice in Kel's ear.

"I don't see it."

"It'll be below you in seconds. You guys get one chance. If we're lucky, we'll surprise the bastard, but in case he's on the roof, we're going in dark. Open your doors, step out on the skids, and be ready to jump on my go."

"All in a day's work," Deputy Tarza said with a wink to Kel.

She glanced at him and tossed him a smile. "Something tells me this day can only get worse, You take care of yourself."

Tarza, with his left hand clutching his injured right arm, turned his right hand into a thumbs-up sign. With a wink, he said, "Thumbs airborne."

The cabin lights went out.

She felt for the door handle, and as she slid the door open, she recalled stories her daddy had told about jumping out of choppers into firefights in Vietnam. She never pictured herself in a similar setting, but now that she was about to make a leap that might cost her life, she felt no fear.

She removed her seatbelt, sat on the floor, and hung her legs outside until she found the skid with her feet. Kel stood, twisted to face the fuselage of the aircraft, and took hold of the handrail on the outside.

"Ready," she shouted into the microphone.

When the aircraft lunged forward, Kel slammed her eyes shut and caught her breath. The several-storey vertical drop reminded her of a free-fall amusement park ride, a thrill she never relished. She steadied herself, tore her right hand away from the handrail, and pulled her Glock from its holster.

The chopper came to a sudden stop, and the pilot's voice screamed in her ear. "Go, go, go!"

She tossed the headset into the cabin, let go of the handrail, and jumped into the darkness.

"One," said the woman's voice through Shelia's speakerphone.

She slid her pass card through the reader again. This time, the light went green. She shoved the door out of the way and burst onto the deck.

"I'm here! Don't shoot Danny."

There was no response.

Above the sound of the parade below, the throb of an engine and a loud whirring above her caught her ears. Her eyes followed the noise across the street. The only thing visible was the green and white position lights and the dark shadow of a helicopter against the lights of the high-rise a block to the west. It rose into the night sky.

"I'm here!" The hysteria trembled her voice to where she could hardly speak.

"Climb out on the edge," said a new voice through her speakerphone. No longer masked by the voice changer, it was a voice she had heard before.

"Who is this?"

"Not your worry. I still have Danny in my sights, and I'll take him down if I don't see you step over that rail right now."

Shelia looked back across the street. She knew that DK had to be there, but the dark shell facing her gave no indication of where.

"Okay, I'm stepping over the edge. Oh my God, is there no other way to save my son?"

Shelia raised her left leg over the rail and sat on it. One more to go, she thought, but it was as if her foot had been nailed to the deck.

"My God, I can't do this. Just shoot me. You'll still have your revenge."

"That's not the deal. Now we know how much you love yourself. Just like good ol' Dad. Too concerned about self-preservation to make the final sacrifice. Seems you've chosen with your cowardice."

"No, wait. Look, I'll swing my other foot over."

She held onto the handrail and felt for the edge of the deck with the heel of the foot already over the edge. God help me. She lifted her other leg over the safety barrier, twisted her body to put the rail behind her, and found footing.

"Good girl. Now, don't look down. The next step is the easy one. Just close your eyes, lean forward, and let go."

"Where's the closest place someone could jump?" Scott said as he ran back to the building security guard. He stood inside the glass door to the elevator bay.

"Jump?"

"Yeah, commit suicide."

"Uh, don't get asked that question every day."

"Damn it, this is life-or-death, son."

"Uh ... uh ... uh ... twelfth floor. There's a balcony there."

"Lead the way."

Scott had pulled the "stop" button on the elevator before searching the floor. Now the five men raced to the open door.

"Twelve," Scott shouted.

The motorcycle officer slammed the "stop" button with the heel of his hand and then hit the "12" button. Nothing happened.

"Let me," said the guard. He pulled his access card on the elastic tether which bound it to his belt and swiped it across the reader. He pressed the button again.

The elevator dropped.

As soon as Kel felt the roof under her feet, she squatted, prepared to meet DK. As the whump of the helicopter's blades faded into the distance, a voice called out, "This way."

Kel pulled her flashlight and pointed the beam. It fell on Villa. He had run across the roof to the opposite side and now knelt next to a door that provided access to the building. Under his left arm he embraced two shotguns, and in his right hand he held a box of shells. He looked away as her beacon hit his face, so she lowered the light and ran after him.

"This is your scene," he said. "How do you want to play it?"

"Slow and careful. We'll take the stairs, clear each floor, and then meet back at the stairs before descending to the next level. When I saw the muzzle flashes a few minutes ago, they looked to be mid-building, but I couldn't tell what floor."

"He could have repositioned, too."

Kel nodded and eased the access door open. She cast her flashlight beam through the opening and made a quick search of the stairway before her.

"Clear. Let's move."

"Want this?" Villa asked, and held out Deputy Tarza's shotgun.

She stepped into the doorway. "Thanks, but this'll do me just fine." With her Glock held out in front of her, she descended the concrete stairs. Villa's breath labored with tension right behind her.

The door had been removed from its hinges on the next level. It left a wide opening to the floor. She motioned for Villa to check right, and then they stepped from the stairwell into a large, open room. Except for floor-to-ceiling columns, there were no walls to obstruct their view. They quickly swept their beams around the room and found it to be clear.

As they made their way back to the stairwell, the crack of a rifle exploded somewhere below them and echoed through the building.

Meanwhile, Scott and his men arrived at the twelfth floor.

"Where's the balcony?" Scott asked the guard as the door opened to the elevator lobby.

"On the west side. Follow me."

"No! You wait here."

The building guard, a year out of high school and a short-distance track runner, said, "This is my building, my responsibility." He shot through the elevator doorway and sprinted across the open lobby.

"Wait! Damn it!" Scott shouted after him. "This is a police matter."

He didn't stop. Scott gave chase with the other officers at his heels. The gap between them opened further.

The guard slid his access card through the reader and then charged through the doorway onto the balcony. Shelia stood on the outside of the handrail. With a soft, but reassured voice, he said, "Ma'am, don't do it."

The voice surprised Shelia, and she turned with a jerk and jarred her left foot. It slid off the edge and threw her off balance. She grabbed for the rail and wrapped her arms around it. As she did, the phone slipped from her hand. Her lifeline to Danny fell out of reach.

A shot blasted behind her, and the young guard crumpled to the deck in front of her.

"Oh my God!" she screamed.

Scott reached the door before it closed and stepped over the guard. "Shelia, don't jump."

"I have to save Danny." Tears of terror choked the words back.

The other three officers crowded through the doorway. While two of them took a kneeling position with their service weapons pointed across the street, the motor officer knelt by the guard.

"Danny's safe. We have him. I spoke to him and the nanny on my way up." Scott looked at the officer next to the guard.

He lifted his fingers away from the teenager's carotid artery and shook his head.

"Are you sure?" Shelia said.

"Yes. Let me help you."

As Scott reached out to take her arm, another pop echoed between the buildings. A slug hit him in the chest and knocked him backwards into the doorway.

"Scott," Shelia screamed. With Danny safe, yet two men on the balcony hurt—or worse, dead—in front of her, the emotional upheaval proved more than she could take. She felt consciousness falter and her knees buckled.

The second shot ring out as Kel and Villa approached the turn in the stairwell between floors.

"That one's close." A volley of distant rounds echoed through the vacant building and ricocheted off the concrete. "Reinforcements," she added.

"That's good news," Villa said. "Maybe they can keep him busy until we find him."

As he spoke, the vibration of her cell phone startled her at first. She grabbed it off her belt.

"Bimal?" she said with an agitated whisper. "This better be good."

"Not so sure that it is. In the last few minutes, he powered up a third phone. You're right on top of it."

"Damn it," she said, and disengaged the call.

"What's that?" Villa asked.

"Whatever it is, it can't be good. Watch for something suspicious."

"Can you give me a hint?"

"This guy knows bombs. He may have rigged the place. My guess is stairwells."

"Shit. That's comforting."

"Sorry I got you into this, Villa. Not too late to turn back."

"Never ran from a good fight. Don't plan to now."

"Then let's finish it."

She trained her flashlight beam and scanned the next dozen steps. Once cleared, she took each riser at a slow, deliberate pace. When they reached the next level, just as the floor above, the door was missing. They stepped through the opening.

Chapter Sixty

SHELIA HUNG IN midair only by the fingers of one hand grasping the bottom of the railing. Wet from the sweat of terror, she felt her hand start to slip. Above her, gunfire erupted, aimed at the building across the street behind her. They think I've already fallen. She looked toward the street. Twelve floors below her dangling feet, she saw the heads of parade spectators who were unaware that they were about to be crushed to death by her fall. Why they hadn't heard the gunfire, she could only attribute to the raucous noise of the parade below. She opened her mouth to scream for them to move—to cry for help—but her voice clamped shut. She couldn't even cough a sound.

Then, she felt a firm hand grab her forearm. Shelia looked up.

"Can you reach my other hand?" the voice connected to the arm asked. Through the wrought iron bars a second arm extended. With her free hand she flailed toward it. Finally, she felt the warmth of his hand and clutched it like a lifeline. She began to rise.

When her eyes came above the floor level, her ascent stopped. Only then did she realize that she was far from safety. A few moments before, she had begged DK to shoot her so she wouldn't die in the fall. Now, in the safety of the officer's hands, terror that the next bullet would rip through her body gripped her anew. Her back was to DK, and he had already demonstrated his accuracy with a gun. The shattered street lamp, the security guard, and Scott were witnesses to his skill with a rifle. And with Danny safe, DK had to take her out to finish his lesson plan.

"Could use some help here," the motor officer said.

Shelia turned her head toward one of the other officers who kneeled on the deck and fired his pistol at the hulk across the street. He holstered his gun and moved to the rail by Shelia. While the third officer continued to lay down a shield of bullets, the second officer leaned over the edge and wrapped his arms around her waist. The motor officer, whose hands were under the rail, let go of Shelia's arms. While the police man with his arms around Shelia pulled her over the rail, the motor officer grabbed her legs. As she came over the top of the barrier, another shot rang from the window across the street. She toppled into the two men, but not before the warmth of blood and tissue sprayed into her face.

A third shot echoed through the building and Kel realized that DK was still below her. She ran to the stairwell. Villa met her at the doorway, and they descended the stairs, taking them two at a time.

When they reached the landing of the next floor, Kel's flashlight caught an object wedged between the wall and a water pipe.

"Sergeant," she said, anxiety and panic reducing her breath to a whisper. She pointed to the object on the wall.

"Is that what I think it is?" he asked.

Shelia tumbled to the deck with the motor officer and landed on the still body of the security guard. The officer's left arm was slick with blood.

"He's been shot," Shelia said as another bullet disintegrated the window behind her.

"You get inside," the officer who had taken her by the waist said. "We'll take care of him." He dropped to the floor several feet from the third officer, took aim at the window across the street, and squeezed off three rounds in rapid succession.

Shelia found her phone on the deck and scooped it up as she slid toward the door on her stomach. As she slithered past Scott's body, she fought the urge to flee for safety. On instinct and adrenaline, she grabbed his arms and pulled him through it.

"Can you get yourself inside?" the second officer said, with a quick glance toward the motor officer.

"I think so," he said, and groaned. He rolled off the guard's body and made his way through the shattered window opening.

"It's meant for us," Kel said, and took two rapid steps toward the bomb. She peeled the C4 from the wall.

"What the hell?" Villa whispered. "That could go off at any second."

"With all that gunfire out there, I'd say he's too busy right now. Besides, it has a cell phone detonator. If I pull this wire, this thing's harmless—I think."

Chapter Sixty-One

SHELIA DRAGGED SCOTT to a small lounge and put a concrete pillar between him and the bullets ripping through the building. As she slumped to the floor next to him, she threw her face into her hands and gave in to the terror that had gripped her in the last few minutes. She braced against the uncontrolled tremors that surged through her body, and lost the battle with tears.

Next to her, she sensed movement.

"Damn asshole," Scott groaned. He opened his eyes and lifted his hand to rub his chest. "Feels like a Mac truck slammed into me."

Shelia dropped her hands from her face and smiled. She placed her hand on his shoulder and said, "Glad you're still alive, Scott. Are you sure Danny's safe?"

"Talked to him myself."

"My God, thank you. If you hadn't come ... I ... I'd be dead right now."

He supported his torso with his elbows and slid up to a sitting position with his back against the post. "Kel sent me, Shelia. It's her you should thank."

"You think?" Villa said.

"Don't you remember basic bomb training from the academy?" Her best defense against uncertainty had always been a sense of humor. "What's the worst that can happen?"

"That we get blown to Hell."

"I suppose that wouldn't be so good." She held the explosive up and examined it. As she grasped the green wire, her heart pounded hard against her breast bone.

"Why the green one?" His throat was tight with tension.

"I like green. You prefer red?" She took the red lead, looked toward Villa and with a quick jerk, pulled the tip from the plastique. "Whew, looks like we're not going anywhere just yet."

While the two officers continued to fire toward the windows in the condemned terra cotta, the motor officer low-crawled on his stomach, using his right arm to pull himself toward Shelia and Scott. He drew up next to them.

"Thought you bought the big sleep," he said to Scott.

"Early rumors, thank God ... and Kevlar," Scott said with a chuckle. "Oh God, that hurts! I think he broke a rib."

"While I was grabbing her," the motor officer said with a nod toward Shelia, "I saw a couple of flashlights on a floor or two above the perp."

"That's got to be Kel over there. Look, you're hurt bad. You stay here. Shelia, call 9-1-1 and get medics rolling. I'm going to help with cover fire."

Kel and Villa stepped back to the concrete wall next to the door and took cover. She looked around the jamb. Her flashlight beam revealed that, unlike the other floors, this one had interior walls. Rich walnut paneling, not yet removed by the recyclers, formed a hallway.

Kel used the flashlight beam to scope a path though the passage. She found the floor clear of rubble. Thirty feet ahead, a gap in the paneling opened to the left. She turned the light out and moved into the hallway.

Since the guns had gone silent on both sides of the street, she tried to push aside the fear that something dreadful had happened to her sister. But it nagged at the back of her mind like a developing migraine. She leaned against the wall next to the opening and was about to charge into the room when shouts and shrieks of the confused spectators on the parade route drifted into the building. A loudspeaker from a police cruiser cut through the chaos below. "Everyone clear the area immediately."

With her pistol pointed to the ceiling, she wondered if they had taken her daddy to safety yet, or if he was even in the proximity of the gunfire. In the ambient light from the city pouring through the open doorway, Villa appeared. He squatted against the wall across from her and pointed the shotgun toward the opening.

"God damnit!" a man's voice shrieked from inside the room followed immediately by the discharge of several rounds from an automatic pistol. The chatter echoed through the empty space.

"It's over, Klineman," Kel shouted, and waved Villa's shotgun off.

"Not yet. I'll drop you, Princess, just as I did Angel. Beautiful sight, her arms flailing helplessly as she plunged to the street."

Kel wouldn't allow herself to believe it. She had sent Scott to protect Shelia, and she trusted him. "I don't buy it, Darrell."

"Darrell Klineman's dead. Has been for decades. And now it's time to finish the hunt."

Just a few hours before when she had seen the picture of Darrell Klineman, she put the eyes with the man, but she still needed confirmation. And now she had it. She recognized the voice as soon as he spoke, but the word "hunt" gave absolute validation. Three times in the last five days, DK had spoken that word directly to her. Once, while he pinned her to the floor of Suzanne Lowen's condo with a Taser, and once on the phone while he stood over Roger Kinnear's murdered body. The last time she had heard it was at Suzanne Lowen's memorial.

Before she could speak, a hail of bullets from across the street tore holes and splintered the antique paneling above her. Kel waved to Villa to head back to the stairwell. She hesitated for two seconds and then followed, stooping low.

Chapter Sixty-Two

THE STAIRWELL THRUST Kel into complete darkness.

"Hey, Princess. I told you we'd meet again."

The voice came from the hallway where seconds before she had crouched. The sound of bullets, as they tore through the walls, seemed amplified as they echoed off the stairwell's concrete walls, and then they went silent. Next to her, Sergeant Villa panted heavy. Until the last hour, she didn't know him, but Villa next to her on the first riser, armed with two shotguns, gave her comfort.

"Be ready to move," she whispered. "This could go to Hell in a hand basket real quick."

She turned her head toward the opening and shouted, "Give it up, Collins. There's no reason you have to die today."

"So you know who I am." Jared Collins stopped in the hallway three feet beyond the opening to the room he had used for his blind.

Kel filtered the anxiety from her voice. "Daddy remembers you as Lone Wolf—a good soldier, he told me. He thought you were killed in the retreat, but when your body wasn't returned, only then he realized that he had left you behind."

"Yet here I am in the flesh."

"He still has nightmares about that day."

"I lived those nightmares in real time, and when I did get home, they didn't stop. Because of him, I lost my family, including the only woman I ever loved."

Kel heard the hatred in his voice. The syllables clicked off his tongue as percussive as the distant snare drums she heard even now tapping a marching cadence from blocks away.

She said, "But that's the catastrophe of war. Governments throw away innocent lives in their greedy quests. Dirk can't be blamed for what happened to you, or to any of his men, for that matter. It was out of his control. People die, are physically or emotionally maimed for life, and sometimes go missing in war, but—"

"I knew you of all people would understand."

"I do. I sympathize with you. Our government says my Lance is dead, but they never brought him home for me to bury. Yet I don't feel the urge to bring his superiors to some self-designed justice. We can't act out the lesson plans we might want just because life dealt us a bad hand."

"Dirk let my son be taken away from me twice."

"Willie?" she asked. Her tone became reverent.

"So you figured that one, too?"

"You made it easy. You gave me your DNA. Jared, Willie was my friend. I miss him, too."

"At least you got to know him. He hardly knew me as Dad, let alone a war hero or best-selling author."

"You said Dirk took him twice. What did you mean? Why did you want to point me to Willie?"

"Because after he was killed, Dirk turned his back on him just like he did me."

"Jared, he hasn't forgotten Willie. There's an ongoing investigation."

"Which, without me, would never have been solved. His death is an SPD cover-up."

"What? Are you saying the department knows who killed him?"

"I'm saying your police department assassinated him."

"That's preposterous," she said, unable to mask her surprise. "Who, exactly? And how do you know this?"

"You know it, too. I checked the history on my computer at The Globe after you left my office on Tuesday. There's only one reason you would be checking into Tribune Investments. If you're the detective I believe you are, you've made his connection."

"Do you mean Jake deLaurenti?"

"So you say."

"Is that why I can't raise him? Where is he, Jared? Have you killed him, too?"

"Those, Princess, are questions you may never find the answer to. But I'll say this: polluted waters run deep."

"Is this another of your riddles?"

"That's enough talk."

Kel realized she wasn't going to get an answer, and that negotiating with a sociopath with a death wish was beyond her bachelor's degree in psychology. She shouted, "Put your down weapons. You're under arrest."

"Not likely," Jared said.

The snap of a fresh magazine sliding into Jared's automatic pistol broke off the conversation, and before she had time to run for cover, the stairwell became claustrophobic. Bullets ricocheted off the concrete walls. The sound deafening, Kel threw her hands over her ears as she stumbled behind Villa in the gloom up the stairs half a flight to the turn. As she came around the corner, grasping for the unseen railing, something hit her hard in the side, and her foot slid out from under her. She cracked her shin against the concrete riser and fell to her knees.

"Damn it," she said under her breath and grabbed her side.

Villa, above her on the step, groaned.

"You hurt?" she asked.

"Caught one in the leg."

Her left side began to burn. "Can you continue up?"

"Think so."

"You go," she said. She reached to the pain and felt the warm ooze of blood from a bullet hole. "I'll hold him off."

"You sure?" Villa turned on his flashlight.

She knew the moment that his eyes saw the blood on her shirt. "It's just a nick. Don't argue. This is my war. He chose me."

Villa hesitated and shook his head. Then, with one hand on his wound and the other holding one of the shotguns, he made his way up the stairs.

She shook her head. Two men she barely knew had taken a bullet meant for her. This had to end. She felt for the handrail and pulled herself to her feet. The burn turned to an ache and radiated into her abdomen. A half-flight of stairs below, the metallic snap as Jared slipped another new magazine into the pistol rang through the stairwell.

"Still with me, Kel?" he asked.

"Not going down that easy." She reached to the wall on the downward side of the stairwell. The scuff of Jared's foot against the floor gave her an indication that he was walking toward her. She leaned against the wall. Weakness crept uncontrolled over her body like unwelcomed barbiturates. She couldn't shake the lethargy, but pressed on anyway.

"It might be easier than you think, Princess."

"I know you won't believe this, but I have you surrounded. It's time to end this."

"I certainly don't see anyone, but you are right. Lesson's over."

From somewhere below her, the detonation of an explosive device ripped through the stairwell. The concussion knocked her back to the floor. Before she could stand to run further up the steps or slam her eyelids closed, a torrent of broken concrete debris rebounded off the walls and risers. It rained around her like heavy hail. She threw her hands up to cover her head and her Glock skittered away.

Once the thunderous reverberation stopped, Kel opened her eyes. Enveloped in a dense cloud of dust and smoke, her lungs filled with it on her first gasp, and she coughed to expel the contaminated air. She pulled a cloth handkerchief from her pocket and held it over mouth. The deafening sound had muted her ears, but within seconds they began to ring back to life. She shook her head to expedite the clearing.

"You alright?" shouted Villa from a flight above.

"Okay," Kel said. She gritted her teeth against the throbbing pain in her side. "Stay put."

She reached to the floor to search for her pistol.

The explosion knocked Jared to the ground. With two voices inside the stairwell, he stood. He withdrew the pistol from his belt and pointed it toward the cloud billowing out the doorway.

"You told me I was surrounded, Princess. Still don't buy it, but one thing you probably don't know about me is that this isn't the first time the government has sent a team to kill me. They called it black ops in '82. I was unarmed when they arrived that day, but I put them in their grave just the same. You haven't got a chance. That first blast? It was just a warning. Next bomb's for real, Kel. Final lesson for dear ol' Dad."

While Jared ranted, she located her Glock. She made her way back to the wall and pulled herself to her feet. With the cloth over her mouth, she felt her way with her feet on each step so as not to slip or clatter any of the rubble littering the treads. Each step increased the agony, but she continued toward the opening.

"I would strongly recommend you don't do that again," she said when she reached the doorway. "The next one could be lethal."

"My point exactly," Jared said.

He raised the automatic pistol and was about to fire when above him, a series of shotgun blasts began to tear jagged holes through the ceiling. Just short of hitting him, Jared backed quickly toward the room he had used to coax Shelia to the balcony. As he moved, he raised the automatic pistol toward the new unseen threat and fired several bursts in response. The room opened to his right and as he ducked inside, several rounds exploded from the stairwell doorway behind him.

Kel kneeled in the opening with her Glock pointed into the empty hall.

"Still time to disarm, Collins. Lessons over."

"As you wish," Jared said.

From the opening thirty feet away, he tossed two guns out, and they crashed heavy to the floor.

"You know what the irony is?"

"No. Why don't you fill me in?" Kel asked.

"If I had died in the jungle that day," he said, stepping into her view, "the world would be no different because of it."

"Except that several people you killed this week would still be with us."

"Quit trying to shrink me. You can't fix this. Too many years of what they'll call 'displaced anger.'"

He took slow steps toward her. As he walked, just before his body fell into the shadow, Kel saw the cellphone in his hand. That devise had been her link to him this week, and now it could signal the end. A second later, only his voice indicated his approach.

Why," he continued, "do we try so desperately to hold on to life, anyway? In the end, it's all a shit-filled abyss. I survived war wounds to end up in a cage. Every day for fourteen years I was torn between begging for a bullet to put me face down in some godforsaken rice paddy and plotting my survival. Then, on the day that should have been my release, I became a political inconvenience. And when I did make it home, my life had moved on without me. I was no longer needed or wanted by anyone, yet I lived on."

"You've made your point, Jared. You've succeeded. Dirk understands your grief. You can stop this now."

"Now you're just whining. Just like Angel and your dad, trying to save yourself. Give it up."

His voice drew closer to the stairwell and she moved out of the doorway. Tucked in behind the concrete wall, she waited. For a moment she had forgotten her wound, but now a wave of nausea swept over her. She leaned back against the cool cement barrier.

"No, Jared." She took a couple of deep breaths to continue. "I'm trying to save you. I have the advantage. You're in an exposed position."

"You're not going to shoot an unarmed man. Neither is your buddy on the next floor. That wouldn't be kosher, now would it?"

"Just lay down on the floor where you are, and it'll be over."

"I don't think so," he said. "You're the one sitting in the trap."

"I wish you'd reconsider."

"Can't do that, Kel." His voice had the finality of the last words from the trapdoor at the gallows.

Despite her wavering consciousness and the pain in her side, which seemed to intensify with each passing second, Kel felt his presence slip through the doorway. "I told you next time we met that I may not be so nice."

"Don't do this, Jared."

In the light from the phone display in his hand, Kel saw an unnatural smile form on his bearded face. Her instinct was to throw her hands up to protect her ears, but she stared back at the hardened image before her. In his face she saw that he had planned to kill himself all along, but with her dying with him, the recompense of his own death would be complete. What he did not know was that she had moved and rearmed the bomb in the hallway minutes before.

Now she wished she hadn't. She reached to pull him behind the wall next to her, but she was too late. The call engaged and detonated the C4. As the pellets ripped into his body and he catapulted into the opposite stairwell wall, the flash of the explosion revealed that with his last flicker of cognizance, he knew he had failed to complete his final lesson.

After he crumpled to the floor, and the debris cloud choked the air for the second time, Kel felt a darkness supplant her consciousness. She pressed hard against her wound and tried to stop her life from ebbing away. She threw her back to the wall for support. I have to hold on, she thought, but it was as if the voice came from another's mind. Then, out of the pain, the blackness, and the regret, her body surrendered. Weakness took her knees. She could no longer resist the savage force, strangling every ounce of will left in her being. Her body began a slow descent down the concrete. Then, just before her thoughts receded into the vapor, a face appeared. It was ethereal, nothing but smoke. Chrissie, I love you mo—

Chapter Sixty-Three

THE SUN CARESSED Shelia Savell's face. She didn't feel it. The American flag-draped oak casket in front of her held her attention. Flanked by Danny and her husband, Jackson, she sat on a plastic folding chair in the front of several rows of mourners under a green awning. She pulled her bloodshot eyes away from the speaker and let them drift past Danny to Chrissie. Sitting next to her son, she held a crimson rose her one hand, and dabbed at the tears on her cheek with a tissue in the other. Shelia turned her thoughts back to the speaker.

"I'll conclude by saying," Mayor Sudan said, "that Dirk Nyte was my friend, sometimes my conscience, sometimes my confidant, sometimes a thorn in my flesh, but always my friend, and foremost an honorable man. Not many in the public eye can make that claim—not that he would—but he was one of the few.

"Anyone who knew him knew a man without pretense or vice. He was a master at showing his cards and then winning anyway—not because he was a strong competitor, but because he was right. And not that he was a perfect man. No one passes from womb to tomb without wearing a few scars, and no one slips the veil of this existence without leaving a few in the passing. But it's not these wounds that live on after a man. It's his choices. Did he choose to ignore the pain he caused, blame someone else for it, or accept his own failure? This will be his legacy."

He continued while he pulled a sheet of paper from his inside coat pocket. "Just a few weeks ago before Dirk entered the hospital for the last time, he stood where no one should ever stand, over the casket of a child—his child. On that day, he said these words."

He unfolded the paper and laid it on the podium. His reading glasses were in the breast pocket of his charcoal suit jacket. With a purposed reach, he retrieved them and mounted them on the bridge of his nose. He read:

"'After what Collins did to people I knew, cared about and loved profoundly, I can't hate him. His acts, yes—but not the man. Hatred is the coward's way out of the hard work, a device we manipulate to explain and blame, to medicate terrible, unthinkable loss. But its bitterness robs us of something vital. To replace our heartache with animosity is to trivialize those we lost. We must celebrate their lives, we must mourn our sudden separation … but we must also search deep into our hearts to understand Collins' pain. To do less is to allow it to happen again.

"'No one knows what circumstance would drive us to similar acts. He was a soldier, a man under orders to commit unspeakable brutality on the innocent people who were conscripted to perform the same unspeakable atrocities on him. His life in that context alone had changed forever. But then, already out of his control, through graver circumstance, the unimaginable happened. His heart still beat and yearned to be home, even while life for others went on as if he no longer existed. He was forgotten by those who should have fought for him, should have sought for him, and should have loved him.

"'He had choices.'" The mayor paused and looked to the gathering. "'Or did he? What would you choose if your life was stolen from you? Can we sit here today and say with absolute assurance that we could never express ourselves through acts of violence? I suggest that until you understand the depths of his anguish, the cage to which he was confined from that day in 1968 until last Friday night, you don't know, and neither do I.

"'So, no, despite what has happened in your lives and mine, I cannot give an inch to hatred. I must rather seek to forgive, for when I forgive it holds me captive no longer. Only then can I truly mourn my loss, and you can, too.'"

The mayor looked up from the page and concluded, "Pity we can't all ascend to such an ideal as Dirk posits for us."

In his dress blues, Nathanial Ballesteros, the new Chief of Police, walked the freshly folded flag to where Shelia and her family sat.

"With the department's deepest sympathies and gratitude, Counselor," he said, and took her hand. "That we had such integrity."

He released her hand, turned, and stepped to where, with the other pallbearers, Kel stood like a sentry near the casket. She turned to Scott, squeezed his shoulder, and then took a few steps back to separate from the others.

"Detective," Ballesteros said, and extended his hand. "The words your father spoke at your brother Roger's memorial leaves me convicted. If mankind was filled with the kind of grace he demonstrated every day, we cops would be out of business."

"Now that's something to pray for."

He lifted his twin black eyebrows, and his eyes widened. "I'm glad to see you've recovered enough from your wounds to be here this afternoon."

"Nothing but a matching casket could have kept me away, sir," she said, and glanced toward the crowd as they formed a single line to file by Dirk for the last time. "But the doctor released me just yesterday. I am going to take a few days, but I'll be back next week."

"Has Captain Silva assigned you a partner?"

"No, but he wants to add me to Willie's taskforce. Fresh perspective and all."

"Right where you wanted," he said, and his face sketched a look of disquiet that faded quickly.

"If Collins was correct, Jake was a dirty cop. But he said something to me just before he died: 'polluted waters run deep.' I've had a lot of time to muse over his final riddle. I believe it has a double meaning. First, I'm sure we'll never find Jake's remains. With Seattle being surrounded by deep bodies of water, there are limitless places to make his body disappear forever."

"And second?"

"He was telling me that Jake didn't act alone. He wouldn't give me anything else, 'cause at the time he thought he was about to kill me, but I think there's more to it. Silva agrees. Truth is, I'd go after it on my own time even if Silva didn't agree."

"Of course you would. You're a Nyte. Wouldn't expect anything less."

Chrissie came to Kel's side and slipped her arm into her mother's. Ballesteros smiled at her and nodded.

"My condolences, again."

His uniformed driver waited off to the side, and as he walked away, Kel looked toward the crowd. The procession was near the end, and most had begun to make their way back to vehicles parked along the paved roads crisscrossing the cemetery. She wasn't surprised to see that Lieutenant Martinez was not among the attendees. While still in the hospital recovering from surgery, she read in The Globe that he had been placed on administrative leave for his part in the DK murders. Her daddy may have been a gracious man, but Dirk's limits were the abuse of power. Martinez had been the leak revealing Roger and Dirk's relationship.

"I love you, Chrissie."

"I love you more, Mom."

Kel remembered the last time they had played their game—the night Jared had summoned her with his manifesto. They hadn't been able to finish their ritual since.

"I love you most," Kel said, and wrapped her arm tight around her daughter's waist.

"I'm going to miss Pops so much."

"We all will. You ready?"

Chrissie held out a second rose she had picked up and handed it to her mom. Kel took it while, arm in arm, they walked over to Shelia and her family. They all stood facing the casket. Each one in turn laid their rose on the lid and said goodbye in their own way—some with a tear, some with a word, and some with a hand resting on the polished wood.

After everyone finished, Kel placed her rose on the floral casket spray and said, "Go now, Daddy. Mom's waiting for you."

Acknowledgements

AMY HARKE-MOORE saw something of merit and awarded this novel first place in the "Novel Beginnings 1st Chapter Contest." Then as my first editor, she taught me, among many other things, many lessons on point of view and head hopping. From this, many people and scenes ended up on the cutting room floor, so to speak, but the finished product is worth the bloodletting (most of it mine).

My first readers—David S. Moore, Thom Rowe, Gene Zurcher, Silvia Shelton, Linda Garcia, and Deb—their honest critique brought light in dark places, saved Kel from breaking the law and made her a better mother.

"Thank you" seems too trivial to give to my wife, Anita. A first, second and third reader, her insight helps pull the story out of me. She believes in me when I don't and encourages me when I want to give up. Even now she says, "Write the next in the Nyte series."

About Jearl Rugh

 FROM THE TIME Jearl was thirteen and completed his first school term paper, he knew he wanted to write. At first, journalism seemed a logical pursuit, but the path down newspaper and magazine publication wasn't broad enough. He needed a multi-lane highway; somewhere he could floorboard the throttle of his psyche into unsuspecting characters. When his reading tastes drifted toward suspense thrillers, he knew this was more than just a turnpike, though; this was the Indianapolis Motor Speedway. Better buckle up.

When Jearl isn't enjoying his wife and family, you'll find him hunched over his computer creating characters and settings for the stories brewing in his mind.

You can reach him at:

http://www.jearlrugh.com/contact.html.

9 781364 977313